The beast and its latest victim were quiet. Zarhan Fastfire held their position in his mind. Perhaps the beast would feed tonight, as it had not fed before. If it did, then it might be distracted, and Zarhan was not so confident that he scorned to take his enemy unawares. As he moved closer he heard smaller sounds: low growls, rasping breath, and the tread of something heavy across the decaying leaves on the forest floor.

A sphere of emotion loomed before Fastfire, challenging him to pass between the last trees. He hesitated, changing his grip on the spear and swallowing hard through a constricted throat. The beast hadn't killed; it held its victim at bay. One more step and he'd be within the duel. The beast's blood-lust, rage, and madness would squeeze around him; a challenge far more deadly than any the Wolfriders offered. Zarhan touched the place in his mind where magic rested and, confident that he could touch it again, took the last step.

D1304501

Look for Volume I of THE BLOOD OF TEN CHIEFS
from Tor

ELFQUEST®

Wolfsong

The Blood of Ten Chiefs

Vol. 2

Edited by
Richard
Pini,
Robert Asprin
and
Lynn
Abbey

A TOM DOHERTY ASSOCIATES BOOK

THE BLOOD OF TEN CHIEFS II

Copyright © 1988 by WaRP Graphics, Inc.

Elfquest ® is a registered trademark of WaRP Graphics, Inc.

First printing: February 1988

A TOR Book

Published by Tom Doherty Associates, Inc.
49 West 24th Street
New York, NY 10010

Cover art by Wendy Pini

ISBN: 0-812-53037-3
Can. No.: 0-812-53038-1

Printed in the United States of America

0 9 8 7 6 5 4 3 2 1

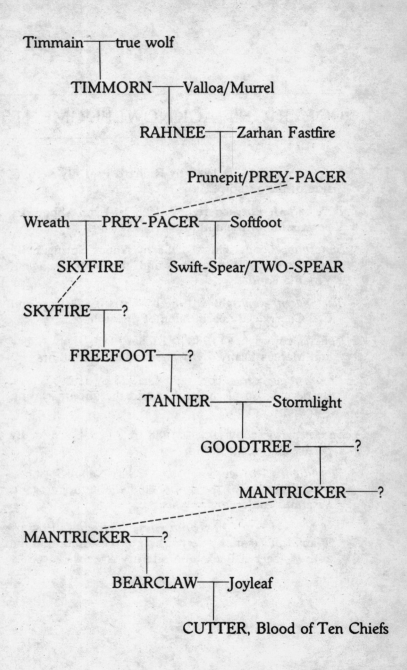

Timmain━━━true wolf

TIMMORN━━━Valloa/Murrel

RAHNEE━━━Zarhan Fastfire

Prunepit/PREY-PACER

Wreath━━━PREY-PACER━━━Softfoot

SKYFIRE   Swift-Spear/TWO-SPEAR

SKYFIRE━━━?

FREEFOOT━━━?

TANNER━━━━━━Stormlight

GOODTREE━━━?

MANTRICKER━━━?

MANTRICKER━━━?

BEARCLAW━━━Joyleaf

CUTTER, Blood of Ten Chiefs

Contents

Introduction

Life gets no sweeter than this, thought Longreach as he wandered aimlessly through the holt. The evening was as close to perfect as evenings got; the air was cool and dry, the sky was clear, the stars winked. Elfin voices came and went in the darkness, some youthful and bright, some murmuring in the midst of pleasure. The raven-haired elder still felt gently light-headed from the dreamberries he'd eaten and the talespinning he'd done earlier.

Earlier. Every howl lived in the memories of those who participated in it, and especially within the mind of the tribe's storyteller. But this night's jubilation outshone past ones as the full Mother moon outshines the smaller child. Tonight the Wolfriders raised their voices in wolfsong to the Recognition of Bearclaw and Joyleaf.

Longreach smiled to himself as he strolled. He knew that here and there, within the hollows of the great Father Tree or on mossy-soft forest resting places, other elves, young and old, were quietly celebrating their own life- or lovematings. Longreach was himself among the eldest of the woods-dwelling elves and he had seen many things in his many turns that had woven their way into the stories he spun for the tribe. But, he realized, even he had begun to wonder if the irresistible procreative urge of Recognition would ever snare the dark, blade-

1

featured chief of the Wolfriders and his golden-haired chosen lifemate.

For lifemates Bearclaw and Joyleaf were, and had been, together for as many turns of the seasons as even Longreach could remember. The two were indeed a pair, undeniable in the love that bound them, even if sometimes they seemed more like two flinty rocks, striking sharp-edged splinters off each other. Now, the storyteller mused, it would be another two turns before the cub was born, for he had no doubt—no one of the tribe did —that chief and chieftess had gladly given in to the mating urge the moment it hit. They would not have fought the inevitable, as some others had done in days and nights long past.

But all that was the stuff of stories, and this evening Longreach had outdone himself before the entire tribe, while the adult Wolfriders roared their delight and approval, and the cubs giggled and played their games. A fragment of memory plucked at the edge of his mind. No, not the entire tribe . . .

"Longreach!" a piping voice called.

For an instant, the elder was disoriented. Then he recognized the cub who bounded up to him. He pulled back the rust-colored hood he'd taken to wearing, shook his hair, and squatted down to come face to face with the violet-eyed, breathless six-turn-old.

"Skyfire and wind, Foxfur," Longreach said, smiling. "What's got you all up in a rush?"

The child pouted. "Oh, I was looking for Skywise. He was at the howl and then I couldn't find him after."

Longreach covered his mouth and pretended to stroke the black fringe of beard on his chin so the child wouldn't see his smile turn into a grin. It seemed that love—or at least an unmistakable infatuation—was in the air even here. And someone else had noticed that the silver-haired youth had slipped away early from the celebration.

"I saw that he was gone, too," the storyteller finally said. "I was looking for him myself."

Little Foxfur brightened. "Can I help you look?"

Longreach gambled. "Well, cubling, maybe he went off for some reason we don't know about yet, and maybe the two of us might be too much for him. I'll tell you what. You run on back to the others and when I find him I'll tell him to come looking for you. Is that all right?" The elder hoped that the counteroffer, lame as it must seem to the youngster, would have the desired, if begrudged, effect.

Foxfur pouted again, then sighed dramatically and shrugged her shoulders. "Oh, all right," she replied, almost whining. "Maybe Nightfall wants to go looking for moonpetal flowers."

The elf-child scrambled off to find her age-mate, and Longreach let go a small sigh of thanks. It had not been too difficult. The more he thought about Skywise, the more he truly wanted to talk to the youth alone.

After a while, it was clear that Skywise was not to be found anywhere near the holt. As unobtrusively as possible, Longreach had looked in and around the Father Tree, and then widened his search to the surrounding woods and paths. He'd considered sending for the missing elf, but discarded the thought. A mind-call might be disturbing, and Longreach's instinct was to go softly. For a moment he stood, nonplussed. Usually, Wolfriders simply weren't this difficult to find—unless they sought privacy, or just wanted not to be found. If that were Skywise's aim . . . Longreach thought he knew where the youth might be.

* * *

Introduction

The hill was part of the forest, rising in a gentle slope until its grassy crown overlooked the tops of the trees that surrounded it on all sides. Nothing larger than low, flowering bushes grew on it, and from it one could see to the horizon in all directions. It was a long walk from the holt and was a perfect place for stargazing.

At the moment, Longreach couldn't exactly remember who had told him, or how he had known, that Skywise was lately spending more and more time peering into the dark night skies. No other Wolfrider did it, or cared to. True, it was night that brought the elves to full life. But it was a life that concerned itself with the land and the woods, and with such things as hunting and tanning leathers and watching for humans. The stars were simply up there and did nothing.

Longreach found Skywise lying on his back at the top of the hill, stretched out on the ground, hands clasped comfortably behind the cloud of silver-white hair that was the young elf's most striking feature. Skywise did not stir as the elder came up, even though Longreach knew that the youth's keen hearing had noted the storyteller's approach an arrow's flight away. Longreach sat down beside Skywise and for a long moment neither spoke.

Finally Longreach broke the silence. "You left the howl before it was finished," he said quietly. Perhaps, he thought, this mood needs lightening. "Was my tale of the songshaper so badly told, then? Your leaving also disappointed one other. Little Foxfur was looking for you." Longreach hoped Skywise could hear the smile in his voice.

The silver-haired elf sat up and turned to face Longreach. Even in starlight, the elder could see that the youth's eyes were silver-gray, only a shade darker than his hair. The eyes, in a face whose wide cheeks and impish mouth were made for grinning, were very solemn. Such old eyes, Longreach thought, for one who is only half again as old as Foxfur. Such a troubled face. But then, Longreach reminded himself, perhaps the terrible thing that took his mother when he was newborn still lives in his mind and makes him seem old.

Skywise looked back into the sky. "There, Longreach," he said, pointing outward. "A great wolf walks among the stars. And over there is an arrow, and there is a stream like the one that flows by the Father Tree. Do you see them?"

For the second time that night, Longreach faltered. As many images of things and times gone by that he kept in his head, he, like everyone else, had not given a second thought to the points of light that twinkled every night over his head.

"You see—all those things?" he asked, then grunted thoughtfully. "I only see the stars."

"They sing to me, Longreach," Skywise said. "That's why I couldn't stay through your story. It made me feel—bad. The songshapers you were telling about —they heard things too that Wolfriders don't. Sometimes I think that's not a good thing. It's not the Way."

Skywise paused, as if he were wrestling with a great problem inside him. The storyteller started to say something, but Skywise jumped back in. "Why am I the only one who looks at the stars?" he asked miserably. "It's like they call to me, and send me the pictures I see. Did you know that the stars stay the same every night? No one else knows that, or cares. But I love them.

"And yet I do love the holt, and the woods, and the wolves too. When I ride Starjumper or play with him, I feel like I'm part of the world. The whole day goes by and I don't notice it. It's the best feeling there is." Skywise searched the elder's eyes. "They both sing to me, Longreach, world and sky. Which is the right one?"

The storyteller leaned back on his elbows and for a

moment just looked up into the starry sky, thinking. Then he said, "You're right. There have been others that have heard more than one song. Perhaps they felt this and perhaps they felt that, and perhaps I didn't tell just the right story, one *you* might like to hear. Maybe there's an answer to be found—"

Colors

by Richard Pini

The world was white. The sun was merely a brighter disk against the eye-hurting milkiness of the sky, which itself blended into the horizon of a land scarce less pale.

As they had done for many eights of winters since they had left—some might have said deserted—the still-embryonic tribe of the Wolfriders, the hunt roamed their wide territory, seeking food. This time, though, the white cold season was an odd one. The weather was quirky; days warm enough to begin to melt the surface snows were followed hard by bitterly cold nights that froze treacherous crusts onto the trails. Now and again sudden drizzles or sleets coated everything with a slick coat of ice, and made both moving and staying still an ordeal of tension and balance.

Game was scarce, though not threateningly so, and the skilled hunters usually had little trouble in locating prey. But finding the animals was less the problem than tracking them and bringing them down in the chase, for crusted snow, thick enough to support the weight of elves and wolves here might easily give way there, leaving pursuers foundering among sharp-edged icy fragments. A sudden run could end in comical and maddening disaster as hunters and hunted alike burst onto glare ice to lose all footing and slide, a tangle of scrabbling limbs, until momentum was gone. As a result, though no one starved, no one feasted.

7

In the milky light, shapes moved fitfully, groaning in the shadowless glare. One figure, huddled among the rest beneath glazed pelts, grunted and poked an elbow into the ribs of someone lying close by.

"Muck eater! Watch it!"

Threetoe, the son of Threetoe, had inherited a number of things from his father. There was much of the wolf in him, indeed more than there was of the elf, and though the dark fur which covered most of his body made him seem stockier than he actually was, still he was well muscled for all his leanness. The flaring temper was there too, quick to disgust or anger; the temper that, more than anything else, had been beneath his sire's decision to abandon the others long ago—the weak ones who looked to Timmorn's daughter for leadership and who had likely starved.

The elder Threetoe had gathered up the wolves one night and had taken all far from the Wolfrider camp. He had led the hunt for many turns of the seasons, and had led them well. In all that time he had often faced the direct stare of the challenger for his leadership, and he had not lost—until one of his own sons had turned upon him and forced him to show his throat in submission. He had quit the hunt then as he must, taking only his mate Rustruff, perhaps to find another wolf-pack to join, perhaps not, but he had left behind his name. The younger Threetoe had no idea what might have become of his father after that.

A yawn, breaking into a whine, played counterpoint to the creaking of ice-laden branches. A chorus of groans answered.

Timmorn Yellow-Eyes—now there was another matter entirely. The golden-furred son of a pure elf and a pure wolf, so much like a wolf who walked on two legs, Timmorn, even more than the weather, was beginning to irritate Threetoe. No one of the group was in good

8

spirits, nor had been for eights-of-days, but Threetoe was feeling the worst of the raw edge. And part of it was certainly because Timmorn had gone off again, and taken two of the wolves with him, thus lessening the numbers and skills available to the hunt for filling grumbling bellies. He'd been away longer this time as well, several days instead of the usual one or two. Then, too, Threetoe was once again feeling peevish because for as long as he could remember, and certainly for as long as he'd been leader, neither he nor anyone else of the hunt knew quite what to make of Timmorn.

The chill ivory-gray of the day gradually deepened to smoke and then to slate as the daystar, invisible behind the overcast, slid toward the horizon. As much as possible, the hunt rested during these times of unpredictable skies, and moved and hunted when it seemed safest; by day or by dusk, there should be something to catch. The ice storm had caught them early in this day's afternoon, and wolf and elf lay huddled in a mound for warmth and protection against the brief fury. Now, hunger was again a burr in empty bellies. Lean forms began to rise and stretch, furred hides crackling as bits of ice broke loose and were shaken free, revealing at last hints of frosted color.

Flinteye, who had once held a different name before losing in a challenge to Threetoe, stumped over to where his chief was worrying iceballs from his wolf's fur. "Anything?" he rumbled. Given the mood of the moment, he dared not ask more.

"No, nothing," was the curt reply, ill concealing Threetoe's resentment. The question was always in the air whenever Timmorn was gone, for while the half-elf neither fit into the tribe's rank order nor was quite an outsider, his contribution to the hunt's well-being was usually substantial—and was missed.

"I'm tired of 'nothing,'" complained one of the others, a temperamental youngster named Splinter. He thrust his way between Flinteye and Threetoe and faced his chief directly, locking eyes. "We can't count on him anymore. Why do you let him stay?"

Threetoe kept his anger at the implied challenge in check—the youth would have time to learn the real timing of such things—and simply glared back at him until the other turned away. This win had been easy, but the question still remained, and much as Threetoe hated it, it fell to the chief to answer questions.

"I heard this from my father," he began, as much to clarify things in his own mind as to answer Splinter's query. "Timmorn's mother was one of the weak ones, the ones with no wolf in them, even though she had enough magic to become a wolf. She was Timmain. The others called her kind high ones. His father was a true wolf. Timmorn was the first chief of the weak ones, though he wasn't weak. They needed him. There were a few others like him, with both bloods, but he was chief."

"He had pups. One of them, a daughter, he made chief after him—instead of my father, who was stronger! My father left that tribe then, for he couldn't challenge Timmorn but he couldn't stay. So he came here."

The others listened intently. All of them knew the tale in pieces, a bit here, a fragment there, but this was as long a speech as any of them had ever heard Threetoe make.

"Yellow-Eyes came a little later. He couldn't be chief here, because my father led the hunt then. But Timmorn was content to be with the pack, not leading it. He hunted well. He could talk to the wolves better than anyone. He knew tricks.

"But he's been strange for several turns," Threetoe finished. "He goes and comes, comes and goes. He helps less and less." Threetoe was relieved to have the long

speech be done. He gathered up his spear and, wordlessly, set out on this night's forage. The tribe followed.

Timmorn was there when they returned, as the sky
was just beginning to grow light. He was asleep on his
side, his head cradled in his arm, his face hidden. Of the
wolves that had gone with him there was no sign.

Threetoe noted disgustedly that the camp storehole
was as empty as it had been the dusk before—so
Timmorn had certainly not been successful at any
hunting, had he done any—and threw in his portion of
the night's meager catch: a few ravvits, a clutch of field
mice dug up from an ice-sealed nest of leaves.

Anger began to replace contempt inside Threetoe.
"Asleep!" he snarled to the hunt and no one in particular. "Asleep during the night like a weak one! No food
for the tribe, two wolves gone, maybe dead." The anger
began to grow, and Threetoe knew that Splinter's question was his own now, that no matter who or what
Timmorn had been before, he must make an accounting
of himself now or leave and take his all but useless
promise of tricks and skills with him. Enraged, Threetoe
took hold of Timmorn's shoulder, shouting, "Wake up,
useless sleeper!" and roughly threw Timmorn over onto
his back.

The hunt gasped as one. The figure stirring before
them was Timmorn, and was not. Timmain's son was
still covered head to toe with reddish-golden fur, even
though in places it was going to a bronzy gray. The wild
mane of hair still fell to his shoulders and framed his
face. But the face—had changed. It could never belong
to anyone but Timmorn, but the wildness had gone out
of it, the sharpness in eye and tooth of the wolf was gone.
Instead, it was a delicate face, with finer features more
like those of a weak one. The hands too seemed some-

11

how more frail, not quite suited to grasping a spear and driving it into fleeing prey. Timmorn opened his eyes to gaze at the circle of the hunt standing open-mouthed around him, and his eyes were calm. He looked slowly around and then fixed an almost languid stare on Threetoe.

I cannot stay with you, he sent into the minds of all, before anyone else could speak a word. Threetoe was thrown completely off balance. He had not heard the words-in-his-head almost since he was born; the hunt mostly used voice to speak, the language of the wolves. The mind language was difficult to do. Even Timmorn didn't like to use it.

Threetoe had expected anything—a challenge, an attack—but this. He started to object, wanting to recover his balance, to say that he was chief and that such decisions were his to make, and then he shut up. Things were happening too fast.

Timmorn stood up and continued, using voice now as if realizing that the others were unused to sending. "I have not brought my share to the hunt, and yet you have survived. I'm not needed here, and I need myself elsewhere. The wolves are well, but I will need them too."

Threetoe protested in earnest at this, coming face-to-face with Timmorn. "No! They are of the hunt. They belong with us." It was a deliberate move on Threetoe's part, born of the need to regain his balance, and challenge hung heavy in the air as eyes locked with eyes. For just a moment, Threetoe saw behind the placidity in Timmorn's eyes to a fiery hint of the wolf that was still there, and then the veil fell again. Timmorn smiled faintly and looked away.

"You are a good chief for the hunt," he said, "but you can't keep the wolves here if *they* wish to go. You know as well as any that they have their will too. You won't suffer for the pair that go with me."

Threetoe, still nonplussed, realized there was nothing he could say, no challenge he could bring.

Slowly, knowing that it would be for the last time, Timmorn made his way among the hunt, looking into each face, pausing to taste the air of the camp.

"It smells different this way," he said cryptically, then went on. "I dreamed. The dream started some turns ago, but last night was the strongest." He picked up his spear and felt the stone tip's sharpness with his finger. "In the dream I was a wolf running through the wood. It was dark. I was strong, and all the sounds and smells of the land were mine—there was nothing I couldn't know. I ran on and on, never tiring, a powerful song in my mind, the song of the wolf telling me that always was just like now."

Splinter whispered petulantly to Threetoe, "Dreams? What's he talking about?" Threetoe elbowed the youth into silence.

Timmorn paused and turned his gaze upward. A solitary patch of clearness had opened for a few moments in the pearly overcast, and a star or two sparkled in the darker night sky beyond. Timmorn was silent a bit longer, watching as the stars began to fade into the coming dawn light.

"As I ran," he went on, "I saw the ground beneath my feet. It glittered, the way a dry streambed does sometimes, with flecks of clearstone. Then the ground itself disappeared, and the glitters became the same as the stars overhead, and I knew I was running up there." He gestured with a nod of his head. "There was another song I heard, but I couldn't tell what it was. I—the wolf—never stopped running. The dream didn't tell me what I was running to, or from. But I think"—he paused again to look at his hands—"the dream has changed me somehow."

Timmorn walked to the edge of the camp. "There's a

thing I must find, somewhere. I think it's a place. I saw it in the dream. I tried to find it before, but I know now it will take longer than I have given it," he said, and then turned without ceremony and disappeared into the hazy half light.

Time passed; the world was brown. The summer season had, for reasons unknown at first, been a poor one for hunting, and now that the leaves and grasses were turning dry and brittle, prospects were even gloomier. Prey was still scarce. Things were worse than that. The Wolfriders were in trouble, and a pall lingered over the usually lively elves.

It had been fully two eights-of-days since the herd of great meat-eating lizards called allos first wandered into the wooded territory that Rahnee the She-Wolf had claimed for her tribe. Clumsier by far than the wolves and riders who harried them, they were still nearly unstoppable, and by sheer numbers they threatened to strip the land of prey beasts. Only the peculiar talent of Rahnee's son Prey-Pacer to link the minds of hunter and hunted had given the elves the slight edge they needed to stem the tide of the voracious creatures. The Wolfriders had not been able to kill all of the marauding reptiles, but over several days of concerted effort had slain enough so that the remaining allos were scattered. Someday they might again be a problem, but for now their threat was ended.

It had cost the tribe, though, and dear. Rahnee, chieftain, had taken a party of hunters and gone out after the allos when they first appeared. She had not returned. Prey-Pacer's lifemate, Softfoot, had brought him the news before she herself fell: two hunters dead, Rahnee's bond-wolf Silvertooth savaged, Rahnee's body nowhere to be found. There was much blood. The allos were carnivores. It could only mean one thing.

14

And so Prey-Pacer was made chief, and the Wolfriders were trying to put their lives back together. The high ones, those of pure blood and healing talent, helped as they could.

"Rellah, isn't there any more that you can do for her?" It was Wreath who spoke, and who glanced to where Softfoot now lay, a hide blanket covering her from the waist down. "Can't you mend the damage to her legs?" By now the entire tribe knew how Softfoot had thrown herself beneath a dying allo, pushing Wreath to safety by her action, but the chief's mate had suffered a terrible injury under the beast's crushing weight.

The high one looked down at the elfin huntress, a curious mix of emotions playing subtly across her delicate features. Rellah was taller by half than Wreath, or for that matter than any of the wolfriding elves. She had been with the tribe from before the beginning, from the time of the coming and the accident, the skyfall and the terror. She was as beautiful as milky ice, and had more of the healing power than anyone in the group, but she seemed distant, and did as little for the Wolfriders as she could.

She smiled tightly. "I'm sorry. I can undo some of the harm, but there were—problems—that the creature did not cause. Her legs were weak from birth, and the one problem has compounded the other. I will tend to her as I have done, but the power flows weakly." Then she turned and walked away.

Wreath stood a moment, her frosty mane tousling in a slight breeze. She was troubled. She did not entirely believe or trust Rellah, but asking for help was all she could think to do. She searched inside herself for some appropriate thanks and called them after the high one with as much grace as she could muster. Then she went off to do whatever needed doing.

Elsewhere, Prey-Pacer was coping, or trying to, with

15

the swarm of responsibilities that had descended upon him with his coming to chiefhood during a crisis.

"The allos are mostly gone," he said to Dampstar and Quill, two of the better hunters, "but rogues are still about. We won't be truly safe here until we get rid of all of them."

"And we can't move—not now—not with the injured, and especially your . . ." Dampstar's voice trailed off. He knew, as did all the Wolfriders, that something had passed among Prey-Pacer, Softfoot, and Wreath days ago during the allo hunt, something deep beyond words. None of the three had yet chosen to talk about it, but everyone had seen the changes.

Prey-Pacer smiled sadly. "You're right, of course. But then we still have the other problem. No treehorn will dare come back here as long as even one allo remains. We still can't hunt."

"And we can't even eat the meat of the dead ones," Quill piped in. "Either the allos feed on their own dead and leave nothing or else it goes to rot because the beasts won't let anything near. Either way we can't use it—and it probably tastes bad anyway."

Prey-Pacer sighed. "Our own numbers are small, smaller than they were just two eights ago, but the only thing I can think of is to send some of you out to find what game you can. Perhaps the treehorns are not so very far away that a hunting party can't bring back a fat buck or two. We can live like that until we clear out the last allos and the herds return on their own."

Quill and Dampstar knew that their chief had not finished, "If they ever do," even though the thought was there. For now, one problem at a time was enough.

Dampstar hesitated, then spoke. "There's another thing. The high ones, they're all acting funny. Especially Zarhan. He's always been more cheerful." The elf looked around the camp. "I can understand him, I guess—being Recognized to Rahnee and losing her that way. But the others too—I don't know. It's like watching animals dying. They're in shock—or something."

Prey-Pacer sighed again. "I'll talk to him. She was my mother, too."

Zarhan Fastfire was of the original pure blood, as were all the high ones, and his was the ability to bring fire to anything that would naturally burn. Though the Wolfriders tended to avoid cooking the lifeblood out of their kills over campfires, still the older elves liked the light and warmth. Zarhan's talent made that part of survival easy, at least.

Prey-Pacer found the red-haired high one sitting with his back against a tree, smiling dreamily. He had fashioned a simple figure—it looked to the Wolfrider like a crude allo—out of some twigs and creeping vines and set it on the ground beside him. Prey-Pacer watched as Zarhan stared at the figurine for a moment; suddenly a puff of smoke burst from the beast's mouth. Zarhan turned the model away from the breeze so that the allo seemed to breathe fire.

He grinned at the Wolfrider chief. "Now you can tell the story of the monsters' defeat and have something to show for it as well!"

Prey-Pacer smiled back, a little embarrassed. Even though the high ones had been part of the tribe since before his birth and had, for the most part, done their part for the survival of the group, still their ways were strange and sometimes downright incomprehensible. To watch one act as a child was disconcerting.

Abruptly Zarhan stared into Prey-Pacer's eyes for a long moment, as if he knew what Prey-Pacer was thinking. Neither elf spoke, neither elf sent, but the Wolfrider felt in his mind the way his senses did just before a skyfire storm, a fullness about to burst, a tension. Then Zarhan did send.

You live now. Of course you know future and past—you hope and you dream, but you live now. You have your stories, but not memories. The others and I, we remember the beginning, because we were there. We had barely arrived on this world when there was slaughter such as we had not known in more turns of the seasons than you can conceive. In Prey-Pacer's mind there formed a swirling image of blood and fire, of delicate bodies clubbed and crushed by hulking five-fingered beasts, of unreasoning flight. The mind-scent of blind fear and despair choked him. Zarhan went on. **We survived, a few of us, and we came through time and more time to here. It was difficult, but the world, though hard, seemed fair. We did not see slaughter again—blood and fire—until the allos came. We thought we had forgotten the feel and smell of it. We were wrong.**

For a time, neither Wolfrider nor high one moved. Then Zarhan spoke aloud again in a low voice. "No matter that none of my kind were even hurt this time. It appears the wound of that first memory has never healed in us. The battle with the lizard beasts, the blood and the deaths, ripped open the wound afresh. It will be a while numbing."

Suddenly the twig figure was engulfed in bright consuming flame, and Prey-Pacer jumped back in surprise. Zarhan grinned once again, seeming his old self. "Healing is where you find it, sometimes, you know. I don't believe that she's dead," the high one said slyly. "I think I would know if she was."

Prey-Pacer, as taken aback by this as by the burst of fire, felt his mouth drop open; he tried to reply but Zarhan simply held up a finger and said, "You have your tribe. Tend to them." Then he kicked at the guttering remains of the mock-allo, stood up, and went off. After a while, Prey-Pacer shook his head and did the same.

The next morning Zarhan was gone. He had taken only those few things that were his alone—a few pelts, the spear he almost never used. All of the wolves were still there.

The remaining high ones were as upset as the Wolfriders had ever seen them. Rellah in particular seemed to hold Prey-Pacer responsible. "We were few enough," she accused, an uncharacteristic flush rising to her face. "Now we are even fewer!" None of the Wolfriders was quite sure whether she was referring to the entire tribe, or to the high ones themselves, but no one ventured to interrupt her anger. "Why did he go? What did you say to him? What did he say to you? Go after him—track him!"

Prey-Pacer was calm in the face of Rellah's outburst. "No. He goes his own way now. I think—he went to find a measure of healing . . ." he began, when the high one interrupted.

"Healing? I could have given that to him," she said.

Prey-Pacer looked directly into her eyes; had she been a Wolfrider, it would have been a challenge-stare, but now it was simply Prey-Pacer's assurance and calmness. "No. You could not give him what he seeks." And then he let her eyes go and turned to the day's tasks.

"Then tend to your fires, Wolfrider, now that he's gone," Rellah said in a low voice, but no one heard her.

Zarhan wondered if he had made a mistake. He had ever so quietly slipped away from the Wolfrider camp several nights ago, and while he was grateful that no one had followed him, he was still a bit surprised. He must have reached Prey-Pacer, then, he thought. Good.

But the high one was no wolf, and no Wolfrider. His senses were not those of a tracker, and for days he had been pursuing nothing more substantial than a feeling. So far he had managed to avoid the occasional allo that still roamed the grasslands beyond the Wolfriders' woods. Though he knew he had not covered the ground a Wolfrider could, he was certain he was a distance from the camp. He was not certain in which direction it might lie, for he had not paid much attention to the path of his wandering. Sun-goes-up, sun-goes-down meant less to him than the itch at the back of his mind that told him that his lifemate was still alive somewhere. He wondered whether or not he should listen to the itch. Where did it come from, anyway?

He had felt the shock of Rahnee's wounding by the allo; it had been a silent thunderstrike in his mind. But there had not been anything that felt like death. Of course, Zarhan realized, he did not know what another's death felt like. If it meant only the release of his lifemate's spirit from her body, there might be no sense of it at all. Then too there was the question, if Rahnee was still alive, but hurt, how had she gotten away from the allos? How had she gotten as far as Zarhan's hunch seemed to be leading him? Alone with his thoughts, living on late-summer berries and the occasional small animal reluctantly killed, prodded by his vague feeling, Zarhan pressed on.

Two nights later, Zarhan was awakened by the touch of something lightly nuzzling his ear and throat. Sleepily he tried to brush whatever it was away and was rewarded by a low, throaty growl.

"Yaaah!" Zarhan's cry was as undignified as it was involuntary, and as he thrashed blindly, he struck the thing that had waked him. He heard another growl, louder and sharper this time. By the light of a nearly full Mother moon, he got a glimpse of his tormentor. *A wolf?* he thought. *Have they found me?* and then he was knocked flat by something falling across his chest —something alive.

For a timeless moment, all Zarhan could sense was the dark shape atop him, pinning him to the ground; hot breath in his face, the smell of fur, and a constant rumbling growl convinced him that he'd soon be some beast's meal. Gathering what wits he could, he focused his thoughts on the bulk above him. There was a quick hissing noise and a horrible yowl of pain and suddenly the creature was off of Zarhan and was scampering about in the moonlight, sometimes on two legs and sometimes on four, slapping at the back of its neck. Two wolves—now Zarhan could see they were wolves —danced with the thing.

Taking advantage of his momentary freedom, Zarhan quickly gathered together the glowing remains of his sleep-fire, threw more wood on it, and set the pile blazing brightly. He hoped, now that he had a chance to think, that the flames would keep the intruders away.

Instead, the creature that had jumped him now came up to the fire, its movements slow and stalking. It heel-sat across the crackling twigs from the wary high one, watching him. Then it spoke.

"My daughter."

The voice was more growl than anything else, but the words were clear. Zarhan's eyes went wide and he peered at the figure in the flickering light.

"Yellow-Eyes? Timmorn?"

The creature grinned, sharp teeth gleaming in the firelight. Zarhan stared, disbelieving. He had last seen Timmorn many turns ago, on the night of what had become Rahnee's first chief-feast. But his memory of Timmorn was still clear, and he was hard-pressed to match the past memory with the present vision.

Timmorn had become even more wolflike than Zarhan remembered. The golden fur was shaggier, and the old chief seemed as comfortable moving about on all

21

fours as walking on two legs. The eyes, the piercing moon-golden eyes were more luminous than Zarhan had ever seen them, and even Timmorn's face seemed subtly changed, the nose and jaw starting to stretch into what could only be a wolf's muzzle.

Yellow-Eyes? Zarhan tried again, sending this time.

Timmorn rumbled. "No. Hurts. Smell daughter on you. Where?"

"Um. I'm—looking for her. I'm sorry for burning you. You surprised me."

"Cub—daughter." Timmorn seemed to have forgotten about the stinging burn Zarhan had given him. The high one also realized that talking was more painful for the first Wolfrider than it ever had been.

"She's not here. She was hurt, very badly I think, two eights and some days ago. She didn't come back to the tribe. Some of the others said she was dead, but I don't think so." Zarhan felt himself starting to ramble; what could he say to this strange Timmorn? What had caused the change that he saw?

"Felt cub's hurt. Was looking for something. Came to find her." The two wolves came up beside Timmorn, one on either side. As he spoke he scratched them behind the ears. "Cub mate?"

So he had sensed something too, Zarhan thought. It could be a good sign. What had he asked? Had Rahnee mated, or was Zarhan her mate? The answer was the same in either case.

"Yes," the high one replied. "When you left the tribe. The hunt disappeared as well, and we had to survive without them." Zarhan smiled at the memory. "We managed. We had cubs of our own, she and I. I guess I've changed myself from those first days. I want to find her, if she's alive to be found."

Timmorn cocked his head to one side. "Change," he said. "Why change? Why me? Wolf."

"Yes, you're more wolf than I remember, that much is certain. But how? Timmain was your mother; she came with us. She was the only one with the power to shapechange completely. She became a wolf herself, but she was never able to reverse it." Zarhan cupped his chin in his hands; an idea was forming in his mind. "But even in wolf form, she was full elf. Your father, though, was a true-wolf. Timmain never had another child. So you are the only one who could ever be!" Zarhan smacked a fist against his palm; Timmorn jumped. "You are the only one in the world who has the blood of both elf and wolf in equal measure. And your mother was a shapechanger; I wonder if you received any of that and we never knew. You sit right on the edge. Something, it seems, has pushed you over."

Timmorn did not respond, so Zarhan simply watched him for a while. The wolf chief buried his face in the ruff of each wolf, nuzzling the animals. In turns, the wolves poked at Timmorn with their snouts, vying for attention and licking his face. To the high one, Timmorn seemed lost in his own world.

Zarhan wondered what that world was like. Did Timmorn float on waves of wolf-scent and sound the way Zarhan's kin lost themselves in contemplation of infinite time and space? Did the eternal memory of the high ones have its counterpart in some timeless thread of wolf-thought? Zarhan looked up, beyond his little fire into the midnight-dark sky to the stars shining overhead. His people had heard the cosmic music of the endless universe; what, he wondered, was the wolfsong that now danced in Timmorn's veins?

"Do you ever hear my song?" Zarhan wondered out loud; Timmorn cocked his head at the voice. "And if

you do, does it change you the other way?" As gently as
he could, even though Timmorn had rejected his sending earlier, Zarhan attempted to convey to Timmorn the
emotion and experience of the starsong as it still sang in
his own mind. Timmorn looked uncomfortable. Zarhan
sighed. "What does it matter, anyway? You're looking
for whatever you're looking for; I search for my lifemate. That's all there is for now."

"Daughter cub chief?" Timmorn asked. Then he
seemed to remember something. "Find name?"

Realization dawned in Zarhan's eyes. "That's right.
You left before she found her name. It's Rahnee. Rahnee
the She-Wolf." Timmorn grunted, a satisfied sound, and
Zarhan continued. "She was chief, and a good one." The
high one smiled to himself, thinking for a moment of the
many times that the relationship between lifemate and
lifemate conflicted with that between chief and tribes-
man. "But when she . . . disappeared, her son became
chief. Is chief." Zarhan paused, thoughtful. "I don't
think she can return, if she is alive."

The two spoke of other things as the stars wheeled
overhead, but at last quiet settled between them, punc-
tuated by the crackling of the fire. Timmorn seemed to
withdraw into himself, as if wrestling with some private
dilemma. Lost to the world, he rocked back and forth on
his heels. He was father to his daughter, but the She-
Wolf was an outcast now, without a pack, as he was.
Which would she need more, father or mate? And what
of his own feelings? What of the new/old thing that this
cub-mate had sung to him?

The night passed. Zarhan, try as he might to stay
awake, found himself hypnotized by the flickering of the
flames and Timmorn's rhythmic movement. He was
sure he dozed more than once.

Finally Timmorn spoke. "Find mate. Take wolves

—help you." Half-asleep, Zarhan watched as Timmorn touched his head to each wolf's head, as if communicating something. The wolves growled and whined, but only briefly and gently, and then they lay down with their noses between their front paws. Zarhan tried looking into their eyes, huge and deep in their darkness, to see what was there, but it was no use. He fell asleep.

The daystar was well up in the sky the next morning when he awoke. The wolves were still there, watching him, waiting for him to move, to resume his search. But Timmorn was gone.

Time passed; the world was green. Once again new life rioted across the land. Colors and scents that had been hidden by snow or locked away by frost spilled forth in a tide that flowed northward day by day. Caught up in the tide, part of it, came the hunters.

For many days the wolves had been following the great herd of treehorns. The spring birthing season had been a good one, and the grazing herd had grown huge, to nearly half again its numbers of the previous autumn and winter. Now, in their leisurely migration back into more northern lands, the treehorns had come to a broad valley, fertile and awash in new grasses, running roughly in the same direction as the path of the moving beasts. The glen was bordered by cliffs that were old and tumbled, and was home to what appeared to be a curious structure of rock piled high upon rock, rising out of the center of the wide valley floor.

Neither the wolves nor the treehorns paid any attention to the odd formation, for it was simply there and did nothing. So at ease, in fact, were the deer-beasts, so content to champ moist grasses and clovers in the warm sunlight that they did not seem to mind when the wolf-pack, as it did from time to time, surged in close to the herd. The two groups, herd and pack, flowed in and around each other like two liquids, swirling gently though never mixing. When the wolves, having exhausted their bowing and scampering play with several of the treehorns, made their move to cut a yearling from the herd, the beasts nearby the calf formed a circle of protection, but the rest of the placid grazers barely noticed. That sort of thing had happened before; it was happening again. The wolves broke the defense; the unlucky calf, beset leg and throat, went down; a ripple of reaction passed through the treehorns closest to the kill, and then it was over as the wolves settled in to feed. The doe felt its loss for a while, and then forgot, and in the midst of plenty, the herd afforded its diminution easily.

For the wolves, life was as careless and as generous as it ever got. Not that the winter they had just come through had been so terribly cruel; it had not, but no creature ever chose hardship and desperate foraging over ease and a full belly if it had the choice to make. And even though most of the wolves in the pack lived in the continuous now of wolf-thought, and were content with a present existence that felt like forever, there were a few who could sense a difference, a few whose brains and minds were host to hazy memories of winters past that were harsh, misty impressions of cookfires and strange, pale companions who walked on two legs.

The pack fed lazily in the afternoon shadow of the monumental tower of rock; there were no snarls of challenge, no bared teeth of defense. Each wolf had its portion and no wolf went hungry, for the food was plentiful and had been for many days; each animal seemed to know that life might continue in this wide green valley for time unknown.

One of the wolves, a female, cloud gray with white face markings, was among the last to feed. She was a shy one, low in the order of the pack. Even so, she was able to take her fill of the warm meat, and then she loped off to explore the immediate surroundings. Perhaps there were smells to roll in and bring back to the others, but first there was the tall thing to look at. The thing that grew out of the floor of the valley and was neither grass to roll in nor tree wood to sniff for scent, but rather was stone that hurt the paws to walk on. The wolf spent a long moment peering with golden-yellow eyes at the piled stones, then snuffled at some of the boulders that lay scattered around the base of the thing. She thought that she caught the scent of something that was not part of the valley, puzzled a moment, decided that it wasn't important, and sneezed violently to clear her nose. It was just a pile of stones. As the gray wolf turned to saunter back to the pack, her gaze was drawn by the lengthening shadow of the rock spire, up the gentle slope of the eastern side of the valley. There, at the top of the bluff, among the weather-worn crags, someone was watching.

Once, ages ago, the valley had been new, carved by some great chisel of ice that had torn a raw, ragged wound into the rock and soil of the world. The gap had been deep and bounded by rocky cliffs that were steep and sharp. But time, wind, and rain, while they might never heal the wound, had softened the scar, so that now the valley was broad and gentle, and the cliffs mere nubbins of what they had been. In places they were worn completely down to the level of the valley walls; in others, tumbled outcroppings of stone grew out of the grassy slopes, rough perches from which other eyes might view the scene of treehorns and wolves below.

"Why are we here?" growled one of the watchers, a brutish, sharp-toothed creature whose name might have been Threetoe. He shook his head and thick mane of hair, which made him seem more like a wolf than an elf or anything else, and gestured with his spear at the scene below. "Wolf-pack. Treehorns. So what? Look at them. They run like a river, they bring the kill down. The wolves know how to hunt, and so do we. They know how to live. I should be with my pack, or they should be here. This, now, is a waste. If I had the hunt with me, we'd all feast."

"No, you've missed it all, thinking only of your stomach," replied another, who was tall and slender, with fair skin and long hair the fiery color of sugarbush leaves before they fall to the snows. This one's name could have been Zarhan, and he said, "Don't you see it? Not the wolves and the creatures that they kill—*there*, down there. The palace, the sky-mountain." He pointed a slim finger at the tower rising from the valley floor. "That's what we were, it's what we are. Even you! How long have we been here? How long since we were cast here, homeless?" And as he spoke, he saw the sky-home as it had been, spires radiant with magical energies, delicate and powerful machineries thrumming, elfin travelers, beautiful like Zarhan himself, moving stately to and fro. He turned and took hold of Threetoe's shoulders. "How long?" he shouted.

Threetoe snarled and bared teeth at the touch, but rose to the challenge of the other's words. "How long?" he mocked. "That's not my care. There's no time in me, only the song. The song is enough." He grinned, not a reassuring sight. "And you, you liar. You don't have any more to care about time, or a useless pile of stones, than we do. Or than they do," he spat, giving a jerk of his head toward the wolves down below feeding on the yearling's carcass. He shook free of Zarhan's grip.

The tall elf looked down for a moment, and then back

into the valley. "It's not the same," he said softly. "You've lost what we once had."

"And you never had what we do now, and never will," Threetoe shot back.

"Must he?" a third voice joined in, female. "Must we?" The silver-haired speaker stood suddenly behind the two elves, lithe, with Zarhan's unworldly beauty, but with the feral eyes of Threetoe. "Must it be one or the other? Must we choose between the songs?" she asked.

"She-Wolf," acknowledged Zarhan.

The elf-woman smiled. "Is it She-Wolf, then? Have I no other name? Did I not succeed in finding my name? Did I fail to love you—both of you, all of you as I was told to do?" Her voice grew harsh. "Was I unable to bring all the scattered children together again?"

Threetoe laughed, an unpleasant sound. "You couldn't do it anyway. You're weak. Not enough wolf, too much of *that* one," he said, poking a finger into Zarhan's chest. "Too much of his useless magic keeps you from hearing the real song. The hunt's all there is."

"No!" Zarhan shouted. His face, enraged, started to lose its delicate beauty; his eyes seemed to blaze. The air around him grew warm. "You needed the old powers. You wouldn't be here if we hadn't helped, before your song was ever sung. Don't forget, as you lose yourself in your wolfsong, that my other name is Fastfire." And he burst into flame, a shimmering figure all ablaze, standing there.

"You'd starve without us!" howled Threetoe, who himself began to melt and shift shape until he was no longer elf, but completely wolf, bristling and snapping. He flung himself at the burning Zarhan.

The She-Wolf stood, watching impassively as the two, struggling, tried to consume each other, and said in a low voice, "I have two names, too. You've forgotten, or

29

you never knew. *Two* names!" Her voice rose. "Two! The songs in harmony! Do you know them? Have you forgotten already? The names? Do you know? Do you knooooow?" And her words trailed off into a howl of agony, of torment, like that torn from the throat of a trapped animal.

Down in the valley, the gray wolf heard the howl that came from the cliffs, where she had sensed someone observing the pack. With her keen eyes she saw the sole elf, the only one who had ever been there, half-hidden among the crags. She saw the golden figure rise up, put its hands to its head, and howl again to the sky in pain and madness. Then the wolf watched as Timmorn Yellow-Eyes bolted from the tumbled slabs as if pursued, and disappeared over the lip of the valley.

After a time, tugged by a curiosity she did not understand, the wolf followed.

The world was iridescent, fragments of rainbows flashing brilliantly in his mind. As he ran, aimlessly, to exhaust himself, Timmorn realized that he could no longer remember when the dreams had begun. Had they first come to him after he had left his daughter, the She-Wolf? (No, he scolded himself, she has a name now. Call her by her name!) How long had the dreams been inside him as he ran with the hunt? How long had he been with the hunt? He couldn't remember. But remembering was never important before. Timmorn ran.

What had the dreams done to him? he cried to himself. The memories came in fragments: the flame-haired one, singing in his mind of stars and endless time, unforgiving awareness; the song that he'd tasted in the blood of Valloa who became Murrel; the joy of timelessness and prey-scent in his nostrils; times spent doing nothing at all except to think, bored and exhilarated at once. What had Zarhan said? You sit on the edge? The edge is too sharp, it cuts me! Timmorn's mind howled. He ran.

They both spoke of songs, his mind said. Wolfsong and starsong. He had heard them both, and now they both shouted within him, warring. Endless present fought against endless future and past. Sky battled earth. Elf fought wolf. Finally Timmorn Yellow-Eyes, exhausted, fell to the ground in a wide meadow of soft grasses. Gradually his gasps became breaths, and he slept.

The gray wolf found him asleep; his trail had been so easy to follow. For a while, the wolf stood by Timmorn, gazing at him, a softness in her expression. Then she gently licked his face, and lay down next to him, her head touching his. Soon she too closed her eyes.

Even deep in weary slumber, Timmorn's senses were keen. As he slept, he dreamed, and the scent of the wolf entered his dream.

The first thing he felt was surprise. **Mother. It is you,** his mind said.

Yes, cub. I'm here, she answered. **I saw your shape as you ran, recognized your scent, followed you.**

In the dream, Timmorn saw his elfin mother as she had been before he was born, as he could never have seen her. She was tall and beautiful, radiant with strength.

Why, Timmain? Why the dreams? Why the pain where there was none before? Why do I fear the dreams?

The answer was a sigh, as gentle as the faintest breeze, as old as time. **This world made my choice for me, even though I made the choice. To survive, I became wolf—but I cannot change back. The blood is old though my form is new and strange. And old blood and

31

new made you. But for me the song is the wolf's for the wolfsong becomes louder each day. I am all of this world now.**

Timmorn's dream-self was a child once again, and he beat his small fists against something he couldn't see. **But you don't feel the pain! The wolf sings at me and pulls me one way, and the stars sing at me and pull me another. Who am I? What will I be?**

There is no one else like you, my cub, and there will never be. Both of the bloods run equally in your veins, and only now have they both found their power. Watch with me, she said, and took his hand. Together, the two floated into the sky until it seemed they were midway between stars and forest.

She continued. **The wolf dreams in the present time, of prey chased and killed, and of mates won. The elf, child of the stars, dreams far and wide, of frightening gulfs. You have some of my power within you, though it slept until recently. It saw your dreams. When you dreamed of wolf, it made you more wolf, and when you dreamed of elf, it brought you closer to elf.**

The dream-Timmain touched her son's eyes, and suddenly it was as if all the hues and tints in the world swirled before the child's gaze. Gauzy shapes flitted to and fro in the colors.

Once, Timmain said, **we all had the power to change as we would, to be whatever we wished. We could take on endless forms, or no form at all.** A parade of creatures, few of which Timmorn recognized, crossed his view, and he knew that his mother had been all of these and more.

But we learned a great truth, she continued. **We discovered that having too many choices is the same as having no choice at all. We chose form over no form, and one over many. It pleased us.** The swarming polychrome multitude of shapes gave way to the image once again of Timmain. She touched his face and smiled sadly. **This is who you were,** she sent. **Only you can choose who you will be.** And as Timmorn watched, she changed as a wisp of fog might, blown by the wind, into something that looked for just a moment like a wolf, and then disappeared.

Timmorn's dream-self floated alone now in darkness. He was no longer a child. Voices called to him, from below and above. Starsong and wolfsong.

He looked upward and saw the great sky-mountain as it once had been, the way Zarhan Fastfire had sung the image into his mind, magnificent and cold between the stars. His eyes beheld marvels of shape and form on numberless worlds; he ran his fingers over glistening devices and felt the tingle of magic.

He looked downward and saw a world of heat and cold, pleasure and pain, of droughts and full bellies, of uncertainty and uncaring. He filled his nose with the scents of fresh-killed meat and mates who longed for him. His ears heard the wind in treetops.

He chose.

Timmorn awoke much later, after the daystar had set and the night sky was bright with stars. He was alone. He stretched hugely, trying to remember the dream he'd had. For a moment, a scrap of memory seemed to say that dreams had recently plagued him, torn him. But the memory faded almost as soon as it came to him, and Timmorn realized that he was hungry. For many things.

He stood up, handsome and straight on two legs, his mane golden in the starlight. He moved, limbs flowing with the liquid grace of his father. He looked into the sky and saw the stars. They were beautiful, and Timmorn could almost imagine a faint, vaguely compelling song coming from them. Then he grinned widely, threw his head back, and sent a wild song howling upward in answer. "I am Timmorn," the wolfsong said, as the singer loped into the night, "I am here, and I am now!" The world was clear.

Love and Memory

by Lynn Abbey

The red-haired elf approached the crest of the hill. His arms hung limply at his sides and he sat down with a great weary sigh. His life, like that of all the Wolfriders and elves, had been wrenched through sudden, dramatic changes, but while everyone else seemed to be recovering their equilibrium, Zarhan Fastfire felt himself slipping deeper into his own lonely world.

At first he'd resisted the descent into melancholy, but as the days multiplied his efforts had become less sincere. His closest acquaintances—Fastfire had no friends—cast sidelong glances his way and even his son seemed uncomfortable around him. Of course, that was Prunepit—the child never relaxed except with the wolves.

Prunepit was the last of their children, the least of their sons. He was a nondescript youth, a bland leavening of otherwise distinctive parents, and he had inherited few, if any, of their disparate talents. While their other children refused to linger in their mother's shadow, this one had remained. He'd borne his mother's acid impatience without complaint and seemed devoid of all ambition. Then, in a few tumultuous days—between the blinking of the two moons—he'd gathered everything into his arms and held it tight.

Prunepit was chief of the Wolfriders now, the second of Timmorn Yellow-Eyes's lineage to bear that honor. He'd led the band to victory over the saurian beasts and

Recognized the most beautiful female of his own generation. He'd taken a new name for himself, Prey-Pacer, and held it in a way that was uniquely his own—as all chiefs must. But most importantly, and most painfully, for Zarhan Fastfire, the red-haired man who held himself apart from the moonlit chorus rising in the valley, he'd replaced his mother in the Wolfriders' hearts.

That was the way with the Wolfriders. The blending of elf and wolf, which enabled Timmain's descendants to survive on this cool, green world left walls within their memories. Their off-world, alien heritage was obscured by the sheer physicality of their wolf-blood. They were superb hunters and foragers, but they neither remembered nor aspired. The Wolfriders dwelt in a world where past, present, and future were melded into a single *now.*

Their chief was gone; long live the chief.

Zarhan Fastfire dwelt with the Wolfriders; his children were Wolfriders but he, himself, was the youngest of the elves—the last and least, perhaps, of those now-mythic unfortunates who had been stranded here many generations ago. He remembered all that had been lost, and nurtured that emptiness within him. Zarhan knew he was no more like his ancestors, now solemnly referred to as the high ones, than the Wolfriders were like their wolves. The high ones had had no bodies; he could not imagine anything but his stable flesh. They had traveled between the stars and through time itself; his feet would never rise from the ground nor deviate from time's natural rhythms. Still, his inherited memories were his ambition; he measured himself against the unknowable.

Through many long, pleasant seasons Zarhan Fastfire lived among the Wolfriders. He had his magic, and he had been the chief's lifemate, but he held no special place of his own. His fellows all tolerated him, as he

tolerated them, but when the She-Wolf had been lost
—crushed beneath saurian talons—no one had looked
to her lifemate for guidance or leadership.

Rahnee!

Her name burst out of Zarhan's thoughts. Guided by
an intelligence that understood, instinctively, how the
world moved and curved, it shot past the Wolfriders'
camp into the emptiness. It came to rest in a more
profound emptiness that bothered the elf like a loos-
ening tooth.

The She-Wolf was dead. The Wolfrider hunters had
seen her fall beneath splayed and taloned feet and,
though they had not been able to retrieve her body, they
were certain she had not survived. Her white wolf,
Silvertooth, mourned as only those wolves who had lost
their elf-friend mourned. There could be no doubt that
Timmorn's daughter was dead.

Yet Zarhan doubted. He had felt a sudden death
before, when Enlet was swept away. He could not
describe what he felt when the She-Wolf's soulname
descended in the emptiness, but it wasn't death. Enlet
was dead, but Zarhan could still feel his father's fire; he
could not find Rahnee at all. He confided in Murrel and
Samael Dreamkeeper, the eldest of the elves. They
regarded him with wide, distrusting eyes and began
avoiding him altogether.

Pure-blooded elves were immortal. For them death
was outrageous and unnatural. They did not discuss it;
they barely acknowledged its existence. Zarhan's odd
pursuit of his lifemate's spirit was yet one more example
of the general failure of the pure elf-blood to adapt to
this world, and yet one more reason why it was just as
well he'd remained the youngest elf for a very long
while. When the time came to choose a new chief, the
other pure-blooded elves preferred slow, awkward, and
ordinary Prunepit to his morbidly curious father.

Rahnee!

Fastfire's passion and essence poured into the sending. His hair, undulled by the years and still as red as the setting sun, lifted upright. Every muscle lent its strength as his magic dug into the grass beside him, withering it. Unconsciously he brought his knees to his chest and tucked his head down, rolling onto his side like a newborn, until there was very little of Zarhan Fastfire left on the knoll. He trembled, his lip grew dark where he had bitten it, and shrill keening vibrated in his constricted throat.

Not since Timmain had shaped her self and soul into a wolf had an elf fought so hard against the magically inert reality of the world of two moons. The fur of Zarhan's tunic steamed and shriveled. He shimmered as his body struggled to contain the heat of his efforts. Then, his strength utterly depleted, he fell back into himself and lay motionless with only a faint smile on his lips to proclaim he had succeeded.

He'd gone beyond emptiness and beyond death into a formless place that was all blackness and despair. He'd called her name, and received an answer. He did not perceive his own name formed from her thoughts, but the sense of frost and ice that always marked the She-Wolf when she was in the grip of her wolfsong. Zarhan couldn't pull her out. He disengaged his thoughts and called his soul back—only to discover the greatest oddity of all: Rahnee, daughter of Timmorn and granddaughter of Timmain, was still very much within the *now* of this world. She was far away, and moving farther away, but she remained a living presence.

Moonlight passed beyond the knoll and the valley. The Wolfriders ceased their chorus and, flesh against flesh, retreated to their private bowers. Zarhan relaxed and slept. He awoke before dawn, refreshed and ready to begin his search. The valley was quiet. He crept down to his shrub-walled lair to collect his few possessions, confident that no one would notice his passing.

It didn't take long for Zarhan to make his traveling bundles. Rahnee had left no mementos behind and years of life with the Wolfriders had all but purged Zarhan's elfin need for possessions. He gathered a handful of jewel-bright pebbles, a bone-flute carved into the shape of a wolf, and an ivory comb on which he'd scratched his lifemate's profile. Together the items barely filled a small pouch which he slung from his waist. He took his fishline and a handful of briar hooks and his hunting weapon: a hardwood pole that served both as a staff and a spear. It was summer and he needed nothing more, but he pulled a thong-wrapped cloak out from under the bushes and set about making it more compact.

"You're leaving now?"

Zarhan leaped to his feet, more startled than anything else, and stared blankly at Wreath's smiling face. "I . . . It seemed . . ." he stammered.

"How very wolflike."

There wasn't anything friendly or complimentary in her smile, but Zarhan's curiosity roused itself anyway. "How so?"

"You can't guess?"

Zarhan's auburn hair fell across his face as he looked away. He didn't have the wolf-blood, he had never adapted to the constant petty challenges that flashed among the younger Wolfriders. Wreath, who was both younger and smaller than he, had cornered him in his own lair. The elf had to force himself to look at her.

"I cannot begin to imagine how your mind works," he said in the dry, lofty tone he knew irritated the Wolfriders.

"There's no place for you. You're too weak to challenge; you've lost your place beside *her*. What else can you do but run away?"

Zarhan nodded. She was right, or close enough to right that it didn't bother him to concede the point. It was Wolfriders like Wreath that made it possible for him to leave without any regrets. Not that she was a typical Wolfrider.

Wreath's mother was Laststar, Rahnee's full sister, but no one knew her father. The two sisters quarreled a bit, though everyone, including Fastfire himself, quarreled with Rahnee sooner or later. Then, one spring day, some fifty turns before, Laststar had walked out of the camp. She'd stayed away for five turns. She came back riding a mean-tempered, but beautiful, gray wolf and an equally mean-tempered, beautiful daughter riding on her hip. The wolf was gone between the blinking of the moons, but Wreath remained. It had been Recognition, Laststar said, and she never said anything more.

The She-Wolf hadn't liked the little girl and had watched her with cold, hard eyes. Zarhan knew his lifemate would have broken the youngling, if Wreath had ever challenged, but the child was as intelligent as she was beautiful. Wreath never failed; she never tried where she could not triumph. Zarhan looked deep into Wreath's eyes and knew that she was far stronger than Prunepit, and that she would never challenge his son, either. Wreath had everything she needed, and her children would undoubtedly lead the Wolfriders eventually. Recognition—if not her own ambition—would see to that.

Fastfire almost smiled, and almost felt sorry for her. He started to congratulate her, but something very different rose through his throat. His groin pulled taut. He felt his skin grow warm.

"Aiyse?" he whispered, only half-believing what was happening.

Wreath's eyes widened in panic. She turned away slowly, and turned quickly back to face him. "No," she pleaded. "I Recognized Prune-Pacer; I made him chief—"

Zarhan threw the bundled cloak back under the bushes and tossed his staff beside it. She was beautiful, ravishingly beautiful, and he wasn't about to sicken himself fighting the most primal of elfin urges. He never had before, and he'd had more than a little experience with the gut-passion the high ones had bequeathed to their flesh-and-blood descendants.

"Recognition isn't perfect," he explained, pulling his tunic over his shoulders and throwing it on top of the cloak. "It's your father's blood. It's something special; something the Wolfriders need. But Recognition isn't perfect, Aiyse. Sometimes it pulls toward the wolf, not the high ones. We used to call those the hunt, and many times they were deformed. You Wolfriders don't have to worry about the hunt, the She-Wolf saw to that. But Recognition is a legacy of the high ones; it works best when it strengthens the elfin part of the Wolfriders. If the wolf part is too strong, if the wolf Recognizes, then the hunt might be reborn, so you Wolfriders don't always have cubs when you Recognize. Probably you can't bear my son's cub, so Recognition asks if you can bear mine. I have no wolf-blood to confuse Recognition's goals."

There was a look of pure horror in Wreath's eyes as he took a step toward her—but it was only in her eyes, and after he touched her, she closed them. The demands of Recognition were onerous only when resisted.

The secluded valley was still quiet when they rolled apart from each other. Wreath's nearly white hair spread around her shoulders in a thin, pale blanket. Though the morning was pleasantly warm, she shivered and hugged herself. Zarhan reached beneath the bushes for his clothes and pulled out the rolled-up cloak as well. After slitting the thongs with his knife, he spread the thick fur over her.

"Why now?" Wreath whispered, digging her fingers into the cloak but not looking up at him.

Fastfire shrugged into his tunic before answering her. "Why? It is as you said. I'm leaving now. It's Recognition's only chance. The high ones live within us, and they are not foolish."

"But what shall I do?"

A surprised laugh got past Zarhan's lips. "Why should you do anything different, Aiyse? Nothing has changed, has it?"

"Perhaps you shouldn't leave—"

"What? Should I stay behind so you can make me chief instead? No, Aiyse, you were right. My place isn't here, and your place is with my son. I won't be back and he'll never know if you don't tell him. And, Aiyse, we both know you won't tell him."

Wreath pulled the fur cloak tight over her head. Zarhan tied his belt over his hips and picked up his staff. He left the lair, the valley, and the Wolfriders without another word and without looking back.

The Wolfriders had journeyed to the limits of their hunting range to confront the saurians. The only familiar trails led back toward their usual prowl grounds. Zarhan had sensed his lifemate far to the north and east. In an eight-of-days, he had followed her into unfamiliar territory.

It was the first truly warm day of his journey. The land was overgrown. Zarhan was just as glad not to be carrying the bulky cloak though his wiser self knew he would never be able to kill a great bear on his own to replace it. He calmed his wiser self with the knowledge that winter was a season and a half away and, for the moment, the least of his problems.

Though Fastfire was a competent hunter, he was a reluctant hunter. His hunger had to reach desperation before he could harden himself to the death echo he heard when his spear thrust home. In the past, before Timmain had turned to the wolves, the successful hunter-elves were more than a little crazy. The high ones had not killed or hunted for their food. Zarhan's own father, Enlet, who hunted with fire, had been consumed by his own magic. Rahnee admitted that she, and all Timmorn's descendants, were aware of the death of their prey, but that sense of awareness was bound within the wolfsong and did not drive them to insanity, blood-lust, or cruelty.

Zarhan knew he walked a narrow path anytime he fixed the spearhead to his staff. If he stalked a huge predator like the great bear, his greatest danger would come from success. At the moment of its greatest pain, the beast would be far stronger than he, and a perverse sort of Recognition might erupt. The hunter could be caught in his prey's death or, worse, commit a sort of vengeful suicide. While Rahnee was chief, Zarhan hunted as little as possible; instead he'd become the foremost of the tribe's fishermen. His mind was not attuned to the emotions of cold-water creatures—if, indeed, they had emotions at all.

The thought of rich nut-flavored fish made Fastfire's mouth water. The thought of the cold water in which he'd find fish was pleasing as well. The afternoon had progressed from warm to hot. Bits of grass and seeds worked their way inside his clothing where they itched incessantly. The elf turned away from his straight course and headed downslope.

He found a brooklet and followed it until it merged with a larger, swift-flowing stream. Minnows and insects abounded in the deeper pools. While he watched from the banks, a meal-sized shadow cruised downstream. Zarhan left his clothes on a sun-warmed rock and plunged into the stream. The fish, large and small, vanished while he frolicked and splashed the salt-sweat from his body, but they came back when he stood quietly at the entrance to a shallow pool.

The minnows returned first, navigating fearlessly between his motionless legs, then the meal-fish. Zarhan scooped an armful of water into the air. Before the black and green creature could flop back into the water, he was on the bank beside it. With both hands firmly wrapped around its slick tail, Fastfire smashed its head against a rock, then settled down to enjoy his meal.

Zarhan picked his teeth with a discarded bone. He gathered his clothes. There was ample sunlight left for continuing his journey. Too much sunlight. It was still hot, and his belly was full. He swished his tunic through the cold water and looked around for a suitable lair. He chose a many-limbed tree and set about twisting branches into a nest. Lulled by the hot sun, the lapping stream, and a good meal, Zarhan sank into a doze.

He awoke with red sunlight beating on his eyes and a strange sense of loss, as if his dreams had been empty. Zarhan tried to recall his dreams, but all that emerged was Rahnee's reproachful face. Twisting his arms and legs securely into his nest, he tried to reach her as he had before leaving the Wolfriders' valley. The branches around him trembled from his efforts, but his sending fell short. He thought of climbing higher, but his legs were deadweight. It took all his wits and care just to climb safely down from the tree.

His lifemate's face was still there in Fastfire's thoughts. He rubbed his eyes. She sparkled and, for a moment, transformed into Wreath. There was a strong family resemblance between the two women, and a complete opposition of personality. Where the She-Wolf was concerned, he, like everyone else, was of hopelessly lesser stature. She fulfilled her chief's duties with a grim determination, seldom showing affection and never showing favoritism. Prunepit, Bright-Eyes, and her other children had had a chieftess of great competence, but never a mother. Zarhan was her long-suffering mate, not her partner—though she sought no other lovemates and flew into a hearty rage whenever he suggested that she might be happier alone.

Fastfire had Recognized the She-Wolf before she was born; he had known her soulname almost as long as he'd known his own. Their first brush with irresistible attraction had not begun with a moment's passion, as it did for Zarhan with other women, but with a challenge. Zarhan had forced the She-Wolf's soulname into her consciousness, creating a balance between her wolf and elf natures. Challenge had become the foundation of their passion; their children were conceived in prolonged emotional storms.

Rahnee and Zarhan's life together was exhilarating, in its own reckless way, but it was not what anyone, elf or Wolfrider, might have expected. Usually, when its imperatives were fulfilled, Recognition left a serene, almost smug, satisfaction in its wake. Often Recognition produced a bond that lasted a lifetime, but when it brought two incompatible natures together, the partners—or victims—went their separate ways as soon as possible. The strength of the bond between the She-Wolf and her lifemate was exceeded only by their dry-tinder tempers.

For Zarhan, this failure to achieve compromise and cooperation within Recognition's wisdom was a harsh light that illuminated his fall from his ancestor's grace. He wanted something more from his inheritance, and he wanted the assurance that he was a worthy inheritor. There were no flirtations in the fire-haired elf's life. His trysts were sanctified by Recognition, or they did not happen. He was attuned to the finest quiverings of the imperative, and he courted them assiduously.

Not surprisingly, Zarhan had Recognized a good

many of the Wolfriders, mostly in sudden, lusty interludes. Sometimes there were children, often there were not, and each partner looked forward to the next lightninglike encounter. There never had been any regrets, except with his lifemate and now, more profoundly, with her niece, Wreath.

When Fastfire recalled Wreath, he unconsciously brushed his hands over his tunic and thought about plunging once again into the cold stream. It had been Recognition, all right. He knew all the symptoms and was unresisting, as usual, but they'd felt nothing for each other but contempt, even at the height of their passion. Zarhan imagined his high one ancestors frowning out of memory and he flushed with shame.

The Mother moon was full. Fastfire waded into the torrent, hoping to wash Wreath's face from his mind. Without the daystar to warm his back, the elf was all too soon aware of the icy origin of the stream. He clambered onto the bank with his teeth chattering. His mind's eye still focused on Wreath, though its field had expanded to include the warm cloak he'd left around her shoulders.

He wouldn't be cold now, if he hadn't left her alone in his lair then, or so said the tensing muscles in his groin. Zarhan shook his head, but the fiery memories would not slacken. He got up from the bank and began to run in the moonlight. Temptation lured him back toward the Wolfriders' valley. He resisted and ran in a great circle, shivering until physical exertion overcame Recognition's pull.

Fastfire was panting when he flopped down beside his staff at the base of his nest-tree. Wreath's allure was gone. He tried once again to find Rahnee, but failed. His thoughts went not half so far as they'd flown earlier. Rasping his fingers deeply into the bark, Zarhan slowly hauled himself back up to his nest.

Waves of futility and despair washed over him as he

sank into the webwork of branches. The returning Wolfriders swore they'd seen Rahnee broken beneath the saurian's talons. He had never been comfortable with her and yet he clung to the belief that she had somehow survived. He was willing to cast aside all logic and walk to the frozen shores of the Muchcold Water to find her. Perhaps the other elves were right to doubt his sanity. Before he fell asleep, Zarhan had begun to doubt it too.

He dreamt of the She-Wolf. In swift-moving vignettes, she emerged from the forlorn group called the first-born —the children of elfin mothers Recognized by Timmorn Yellow-Eyes. Fierce and loyal, she was the archetypal Wolfrider. She brought the first-born back to their mothers' heritage, and she brought the first of the telepathic wolves from her father. And though Fastfire had Recognized many Wolfriders, she never Recognized anyone but him. Through the dream she stared at Zarhan with eyes as dark and turbulent as a thunderstorm.

There is no one for me but you, she seemed to say.

Fastfire writhed in his sleep and threw his arm over his closed eyes. *It is what the high ones intended for us. Recognition is the way we inherited, but the wolf-blood damaged it. Now everything moves toward restoring what was lost. I do what our heritage commands. There is no room for loyalty or peace.*

The image faded slowly. Zarhan saw Timmorn Yellow-Eyes—more wolf than elf—rise out of Rahnee's melting face. The half-breed snarled, then he, too, began to fade. The wise, elegant Timmain shifted free of her son's features. Fastfire heard the high one laugh as she shifted free of physical form and vanished amid a cascade of starlight.

Zarhan was awake and staring at the night sky. The moon had set, the forest was still except for the sounds his trembling body made within the nest. He yearned to take his dream to Samael, the oldest of the living, who might explain it to him; but Samael Dreamkeeper was with the Wolfriders. Zarhan's arm flailed drunkenly across his body, seeking the She-Wolf who should have been beside him. The arm slammed against a waist-thick branch and he clung to it.

Rahnee!

Fastfire's sending did not soar away from the tree, but wrapped close about him. Recognition was a minor itch compared to the ache in his heart. He pressed his cheek against the branch and tried to imagine her rather than the rough bark. Loneliness burned all else away. He embraced her in the darkness, squeezing ever tighter until need exploded in a single burst of ecstasy.

Gasping, sobbing, Zarhan Fastfire fell back to the branch-web of his nest and lay still.

Zarhan remained by the stream. He moved with a dreamer's grace and was fortunate that no larger predators chose to fish or bathe near his tree. The She-Wolf was in his thoughts constantly. Their lives flowed past his mind's eye and Fastfire realized how much he had become like the Wolfriders as the seasons twisted away. Though he could recall events in almost any season, they were meaningless vignettes. He had to force himself to relive the past before he could recapture the emotions of the past—which was what the Wolfriders did when Samael Dreamkeeper brought forth his dreamberry bowl.

For two days the past returned to life in Zarhan's mind. He crouched beside his tree with his arms folded over his face and tears streaming from his eyes. He leaped into the cold water, laughing at some private joke or rediscovering a happy moment—but Fastfire was joyous rather less often than he was sad as he remi-

nisced. There was more to Timmorn's children than
wolfsongs or soulnames, and he hadn't seen until it was
too late.

After a few more days, Zarhan made peace with
himself. He sent his thoughts, and his rediscovered
emotions, to Rahnee with new urgency. But he had no
more success than he'd had before. He lingered one
more day, drying fish, then set out once more for the
northeast.

Fastfire was well beyond any territory where the
Wolfriders had hunted, but he was not in unfamiliar
territory. The green forests of this world extended many
days' journey in all directions. Each glade was unique;
each hillcrest view a little different from the last, but the
elf continued his journey without undue concern for the
danger of the unexplored woodlands. When his dried
fish was gone, he found another stream. Each night he
found a safe tree for his nest. Every third or fourth night,
when he was well fed, he confirmed that his course
brought him closer to Rahnee's mystery.

The Mother moon had blinked and summoned her
child beside her. Nights became dark, and the days as
well. The leaves showed their silvery undersides and
squalls punched through the tree canopy. Zarhan
trudged against the weather for the better part of two
days, then he gave up. Soaked and tired, he sought
shelter until better weather returned. He pushed his way
into an evergreen thicket where the wind was tamed and
the water fell in easily avoided sheets from dense
branches.

A doe springhorn and her fawn were already in the
thicket, and a handful of smaller animals as well. They
regarded Fastfire with wary eyes, but the rain had
washed any meat-smell from him and they were content
to remain with him in the shelter. He built himself a
small bed of pine needles, then tried to get some sleep.

Zarhan remained awake—quiet, still, but awake —just like the other animals. The dreary day became a dreary night. Lightning crackled somewhere beyond the thicket. It had rained almost a whole day; there was little danger of fire, but lightning was dangerous even without fire. A tree crashed to the forest floor. All eyes were wide in the darkness, ears lifted and noses high, but the wind remained moist. They relaxed, a little.

The elf did not try to find Rahnee that night, nor was he surprised that the forest felt ominous. Trees were dying. The forest dwellers were losing their homes, perhaps their lives. A bedraggled tuft-cat made its way into the thicket. The smaller animals, ravvits and mice —its normal prey—chittered and scrabbled over the slick pine needles. The cat simply sat grooming itself and the grove became quiet again.

Before dawn the storm passed to the south. They began to leave the thicket. The tuft-cat went first; then the springhorn and the other grazers; Zarhan was last. The sky was already a pale aqua when he saw it above his head. He was hungry, but he wouldn't hunt here —not after sheltering with the forest's feral life. Planting his staff at each long stride, he hurried away, hoping to find a stream.

Fastfire's mind was on his empty stomach. He was moving quickly and taking little note of the animals he passed or their mood. He heard a flock of black birds. The birds didn't leave the meadows to fly deep into the forest unless there was a carcass to be gleaned. Zarhan thought of the storm and walked toward their raucous chorus. He was not above scavenging himself.

The birds had come for gleaning, all right. But the carnage laid out before Zarhan's eyes had nothing to do with the storm. Four healthy wolves, adults in their prime, had been tossed to their deaths. They'd been ravaged while guarding their pack's kill—an elderly springhorn whose mauled carcass was raked with truly monstrous gouges. The black birds, death-birds, grew quiet when Zarhan approached, but they didn't fly away. Now, while he watched with dry throat and clenched fists, the boldest of them scurried to a lupine corpse to wet its beak in blood.

Something broke within Zarhan Fastfire. His staff slashed and whirled through the air, scattering the birds to the safety of high branches. He shook his fist and yelled at them, but they knew they were out of his reach and would not retreat farther. Fastfire was hoarse before he gave up his futile shouting.

Zarhan's anger, and his sadness, surprised him. He had no special bond with the wolves. Rahnee's wolf-friends merely tolerated him and he gave them wide berth if he crossed their paths without his lifemate beside him. In fact, he harbored a secret, unspoken resentment that Rahnee lavished more affection on her wolf-friends than she did on him. Moreover, he understood the rightful place of the birds and other scavengers in the forest's order: If they did not glean, then life would quickly drown in a sea of death.

But Fastfire could not bring himself to leave this handful of wolves to their naturally ordained fate. He went from corpse to corpse, closing eyes, arranging bodies in more serene postures, and covering wounds where he could. They had been a small pack: three males and a female—and the female was milk-swollen. There were cubs somewhere, or there had been. They would have hidden their den well; a Wolfrider might have found it, but not a clumsy-eyed elf like him. He could only hope that a nursing female had survived, or that the cubs were old enough to fend for themselves, though he knew wolves well enough to know that neither was likely.

The black birds ventured down from the trees. He

scattered them again, then sat alert against one of the trees. The immortal high ones had bequeathed no mourning customs to their descendants; the Wolfriders had not had time to evolve their own. Zarhan Fastfire kept a lonely, empty vigil at the edge of the grove, grappling with emotions he couldn't quite name.

Late in the afternoon Zarhan had stumbled upon a purpose for his vigil. The creature which had killed but not fed, which had killed out of all proportion to its hunger, was a creature which should be purged from the forest. It was huge and powerful, that much could be easily read from the carnage it had wrought, but it was unhealthy. Zarhan Fastfire found sufficient audacity within himself to vow that he would set this corner of the forest to rights again. He told himself there was no risk; a malignant creature could not corrupt his mind for his motives were pure. He'd wait for the beast to return—he was certain it *would* return—then he'd kill it.

Time and time again, Fastfire whirled his staff at the black birds, driving them away from their feast. By late afternoon they surrendered and abandoned the grove altogether. They were creatures of daylight, for all their inky, iridescent feathers, and would not linger in the deep forest once sunset approached. Fiercer beasts did the night's gleaning.

Zarhan watched the last bird wheel across the circular patch of open sky. He should have left himself. When they were in groups his kind, elf and Wolfrider alike, were night-dwellers, but alone they traveled by day and made themselves secure after the daystar set. This grove could not be made secure so long as there was blood and meat lying within it. The instincts of a lifetime counseled him to move on, to move on quickly. He resisted them.

He took the heavy spearpoint from his pouch and

lashed it into the notch at the top of his staff. He found a Y-shaped branch and lashed that a handspan behind the tip. It seemed a feeble weapon to raise against a beast that had sundered a wolf-pack, but it was not his only weapon. The Wolfriders had fought the saurians with fire, but they'd gotten their fire the hard way—the only way they could—with pitch, tinder, and sparks. In the end, the Wolfriders feared magic a bit more than they feared fire. Though they knew he, Fastfire, could call flames with his mind's eye they had not sought him out. And he had not offered to hunt the saurians with them. Their hunt had been successful. So would his.

As the light faded from the grove, Zarhan wrapped the branch with damp grass and brown pine needles. His magic and the damp tinder would hold fire against the beast's breast until fur and flesh kindled. It would be a vicious, cruel death; but he did not think of that. Zarhan Fastfire had made his vow, he would succeed and his sanity was already frayed when he settled against the tree trunk to await the beast's return.

Dusk became starlight filtering into the grove. The wolves and the spring-horn vanished into the dark forest floor. An owl took position in the tree above him. This was its favorite hunting grove. But nothing an owl could kill would enter the grove this night and, reluctantly, it flew on. Zarhan braced the spear between his legs. His mind wandered, searching for the tainted one—luring it back to its kill.

Nothing answered, nothing came. The evening hunters rested. The midnight forest was silent.

Zarhan jumped when he heard the sound. He was shamed to realize that he'd dozed off. The spear nearly fell to the ground before he caught it. Unconsciously, the elf held his breath until he heard his heart pounding in his ears. His sleep-dulled senses had neither identified the sound nor fixed its location in the darkness. If it was not repeated he'd never know exactly what had awakened him.

Relax, he counseled himself, summoning his lifemate's face and hunting poise in his mind's eye. *If it's there, it will sound again. If it isn't anything, it won't.*

It did. Two sounds, a wail and a snarl, merging together in the darkness to Fastfire's right. He cast his thoughts out cautiously. There was madness and pain, fear and pain, hunger and pain, swirling in the still, midnight air. With the spear-tip thrust forward, Zarhan left the grove.

The beast and its latest victim were quiet, but the elf held their position in his mind. Perhaps the beast would feed tonight, as it had not fed before. If it did, then it might be distracted, and Zarhan was not so confident that he scorned to take his enemy unawares. As he moved closer he heard smaller sounds: low growls, rasping breath, and the tread of something heavy across the decaying leaves on the forest floor.

A sphere of emotion loomed before Fastfire, challenging him to pass between the last trees. He hesitated, changing his grip on the spear and swallowing hard through a constricted throat. The beast hadn't killed; it held its victim at bay. One more step and he'd be within the duel. The beast's blood-lust, rage, and madness would squeeze around him; a challenge far more deadly than any the Wolfriders offered. Zarhan touched the place in his mind where magic rested and, confident that he could touch it again, took the last step.

Fastfire's eyes were useless. The beast was huge, black, and formless; its victim invisible against the forest floor. He thrust the spear into the dark mass of the beast and thought *fire*! Bright fingers of flame leaped up from the dried grasses, bringing faint light into the battleground. The beast was a great bear, and the elf had struck it high in the shoulder. It batted at the annoyance. Zarhan clung to his fire mantra as he was flung away from the spear. The bear was ancient. Its muzzle was almost white and its right eye was clouded by a cataract. Almost blind and crippled by age, it lived by terror and intimidation rather than the harvest of its own hunting. More important for Zarhan, the age-stiff bear was unable to reach around to tear the flaming spear from its shoulder.

With a stunning bellow, it turned, lurched toward the tormentor it could reach. Ignoring his aching ribs, Fastfire poured his soul into his magic. The flames contracted and turned yellow, then blue. The beast threw itself sideways, breaking the spear and rolling on the fire. Once Zarhan had said he could only bring fire where fire could naturally occur; he was no longer bound by that limitation as the bear's agony merged with his own magical frenzy. The bear was dead, but the fire did not stop.

Zarhan was one with his magic. His soul left his body and danced with the blue flames.

On the far side of the fire an undersize wolf licked the gouges in her side. She struggled upright, planting each unsteady foot with the utmost caution. Her left hind leg buckled. She bared her teeth at her hindquarters. The den was behind her, and the two cubs she would have died defending. Instinct told her to return to them. Trembling, she bit the air, and took a step in the opposite direction.

She hurt, and she was afraid of fire, but she kept moving until she reached Zarhan's side. Her nose moved over his shoulders and face, then, with a sigh, she dropped to the ground beside him. The elf responded to neither her whining nor her licking. She stretched her neck across his shoulder, touching his chin with her nose, then she waited for the fire to burn itself out.

*   *   *

55

Zarhan's magic had set him free. He'd broken away from the confines of flesh and shape; he had no intention of returning. He tasted the power of his ancestors.

I am a high one, now, Fastfire told himself. *This is how it was; how it should be. Freedom from the needs of flesh. Freedom from feeling and emotion.*

The blue flame became a narrow pillar ascending to the treetops. It shimmered in the moonlight and almost vanished before collapsing into a blue and yellow corona above the bear's diminishing body.

The elf had deceived himself; he'd been seduced by his own magic. He wasn't a high one. He was still bound by time and shape, but he'd exchanged the flesh-and-blood body that could sustain itself for the greed of flame. Enlet's face formed in the flames beside him, and Zarhan saw there were tears in his father's insubstantial eyes.

We who did not choose flesh, cannot choose to abandon it.

Preserved in magic's flame, Zarhan's father's dying thoughts filled his mind and with them came knowledge of the terrifying choice that he must now make: the ultimate truth about his father's death. The blue flame would burn until the bear was utterly consumed, then it must find a new source. Zarhan could consume his own discarded body, or the injured wolf lying beside it, or, sooner or later, the entire forest—if he chose to continue his existence—or he could let the flame be extinguished. There was no third choice. There was no abandoning flame, no returning to flesh. Only a simple choice existed: consume life or end life.

Father, why, in all the times I've sought your spirit, did you never tell me?

Enlet was gone. The blue fire shrank until it was a tiny hand of flames, conserving life as best it could. Zarhan was grateful that none of his children had inherited his magic; that he would not fail to warn them as his own father had failed to warn him. It was a small consolation. Very small. Fastfire wonder if it would be enough in the moments to come when there was nothing left of the bear. He wondered if he'd be able to resist the need to live. But wondering made the flames burn higher. The elf's mind retreated into empty meditation and the flames all but disappeared.

The wolf struggled to sit up. She tasted the air, then gave a little growl at the bear's charred corpse. Wolf eyes couldn't perceive the sapphire mote of flame, but a wolf nose could. She raised her head for a lonely, frustrated howl, but her torn flesh protested so she growled a little louder instead. It would be a long wait.

Dry leaves fluttered down from skeletal branches; conifers cloaked themselves in their darkest greens in readiness for the long, icy winter. A pale-blue firefly darted back and forth over a black-ash circle at the center of a quiet grove. The female wolf, her wounds long since healed, sensed that the waiting was finally over. She yawned and stretched to her feet, nudging the pale shape beside her with her nose. It was cool, but it wasn't meat; her waiting hadn't been in vain.

The little mote of fire shunted frantically above the ashes. The wolf stepped gingerly onto the crunchy surface. She yipped and put a paw out to block the speeding not-insect. It changed course abruptly and skittered between her hind legs. Her wolf mind understood *game* and *play*. She hunkered down and chased after it, scattering ashes as she matched its unpredictable movements. The dark circle blurred; the blue speck became confined, catchable. The wolf touched it with the moist tip of her nose and it vanished.

* * *

Zarhan Fastfire had dwelt in emptiness for a small eternity. His consciousness had atrophied; the final realization that the fire was dying was no more real than a dream. He had a sense of desperation, frenzy, and mourning, but nothing personal—not even the final blackness.

There I go, he thought, *I just died. I'm dead now. Dead . . .*

Something didn't seem quite right. Zarhan muzzily chewed on the idea of death for a while, getting his strength back, restoring the habits of consciousness. He'd never given afterlife much thought. Whatever else the high ones were, they weren't philosophers, and neither were the wolves. Still, it seemed that death should have been more final, more different than it was. Death shouldn't resemble the tingly prelude to a toe-snapping sneeze . . .

Or perhaps death was a sneeze—he was new to thanatology.

He decided he'd have to think a bit more about the nature of death and afterlife. He found some comfortable-looking light, sat down, realized what he'd done, and tumbled into profoundly real confusion. The only reality was disorientation—and his little world of light was getting more real every moment. It no longer seemed likely that he was dead. He careened beyond memory and beyond imagination. His consciousness had resurrected itself. He was Zarhan Fastfire; he was terrified.

Zarhan cried out, uncertain if he was thinking within his own mind, sending his thoughts elsewhere, shouting from his throat, or if it made any difference at all. Like a child, he called for his parents; like a Wolfrider, he invoked the name of the shapeshifter, Timmain. His wails had some reality. They resonated through this empty universe and, suddenly, Zarhan was not alone.

Timmain descended from the light at the center of this world. Zarhan recognized her because she'd lived in his parents' memories. From their images Zarhan knew Timmain was beautiful, elegant, and serene; he recognized her, but he had only known her shadow. Zarhan had knees, and he fell to them in the presence of a high one. Reflexes he'd never suspected took command of his muscles. He crossed his wrists and extended his arms toward her.

My lady.

Timmain's sensitivities crowded around Zarhan; this was, after all, her personal world. The young elf had always known that the high ones had chosen their shape; now he learned why elves and Wolfriders looked as they did. There were patterns to this world: an aesthetic written in the lifecodes of every intelligent creature born here. Expressed in one form, large eyes and slender limbs should bring forth the parenting, protecting instincts; expressed in another form it should foster awe and obedience.

So the high ones had been very careful, adapting their form to the lifecode pattern of this world, but something had gone terribly wrong. They had been slaughtered, not revered, when they stepped from their sky-mountain, and they had been unable to correct their errors. Zarhan's ancestors had been unable to adapt to the world at all until Timmain surrendered completely to her shapeshifting magic.

Rise up! Timmain commanded. **Do not remind me of what has been lost!**

Her sending echoed with anguish, frustration, and a handful of other emotions—none of which were pleasant and none of which made it easier for Zarhan to uncross his arms or rise to his unsteady feet. He understood how she felt, seeing him—one of her own kind —making the ritualized gestures, but it took every mote of self-discipline to keep from kneeling again when he looked into her eyes.

Where . . . Where am I? he stammered.

Timmain was nonplussed. Her eyes widened and, for a fleeting instant, the white brilliance of her world fractured into a thousand shimmering colors. **You saved me.** The unity of her world was restored as her thoughts grew stronger. **You preserved my life. I waited and preserved yours.**

Zarhan felt himself slipping away from her. The high one pushed him away from herself, away from the light, toward darkness. The elf felt all the panic he had not felt when he'd thought he was dying. He feared the empty darkness beyond Timmain's world, but mostly he feared losing her.

No . . . Wait . . . he sent, and was surprised to find the pressure abating. **Don't send me away. We— We are the same, aren't we? Shouldn't we stay together?**

Stay together?

The Wolfriders loved to remember the tale of Timmain shaping herself into a wolf. It was their favorite dreamberry reverie, but they seldom remembered to its conclusion. Timmain had not come back from the wolves. She'd sent her son, Timmorn Yellow-Eyes, to be the father of the Wolfriders, but she'd followed the wolves deep into winter and never returned. The elves —Zarhan's parents, aunts, uncles, cousins, and friends —called Timmain's story a tragedy and her transformation a sacrifice. Watching her struggle to maintain the unity of her world and thoughts, Zarhan Fastfire saw the truth in their words.

Perhaps we could help each other?

Unity returned in a disdaining rush and Zarhan felt himself further diminished in her eyes. **But we have helped each other. We have preserved each other; there is no more that we could do—**

But we are the same, Zarhan repeated, aware that his thoughts were petulant and childlike. **We are high ones. We should stay together.**

High ones! The bright world pulsed with Timmain's bitter laughter. **By guiding powers, what is a *high one*? I am not a high one, nor are you, I think.** The high one—for Zarhan knew no other way to describe her—used that lofty mode of thought which so infuriated the Wolfriders. Zarhan blushed with shame, but she continued. **You were born here. Your lifecode is marked with this two-mooned world. You *bowed down* before me. How could we be the same? Why should we stay together?**

Fastfire's mind was filled with what Timmain had seen: a gawky youth, still a child as she understood living and maturity, offering his liquid-eyed reverence to her. It was disgraceful, disgusting, unworthy of a people who roamed immortal between the stars. Had he been a shapeshifter, Fastfire would have shrunk and transformed himself into an insect or a worm. But Zarhan wasn't a shapeshifter, and, forced to stand in a shape he had not chosen, he wasn't without a claws-locked, desperate sort of courage.

You are Timmain. You shaped yourself into a wolf so your children could adapt and survive. I am the father of your great-grandchildren. You will not abandon me, and I can learn what you can teach me. We could become friends—

She cut him off with an open-mind scream. **No more of friends. We were betrayed. We lost everything. You can*not* imagine what I have done or will do. We lived for friendship, for harmony within diversity; we did not need to worry about survival. We had friendship and loyalty to hold us together across eternity. We had peace; we had forgotten violence and passion. We journeyed between the stars. We threatened nothing and, in turn, we feared nothing. And we were so terribly wrong—

**We were betrayed from within, by our pets and helpers; we were betrayed from without, when we were stranded here before humans had evolved to understand the message already written in their lifecodes; and we betrayed ourselves . . . We did not think we could fail, so we had no contingencies. We tumbled from the sky, unable to prevent the destruction of our home—unable, even, to bring it down in hospitable lands where we might have repaired it and ourselves. No, the humans dwelt in the wreckage of our home, and when they left the ice followed. We awoke to find ourselves trapped in an ice-locked place and time where our magic did not work and our very shapes inspired hatred—

It had been so long . . . Those of us who survived the wreckage had forgotten what it was like to be a prisoner of time and place. It was a time of rediscovery; it was not pleasant. Children and parenting. Recognition, not for community and diversity, but for survival. Too much has happened, *child* Zarhan, for us to be the same, or friends. Do you know what would happen if you lingered?

Zarhan did not know, then was not certain, and, finally, resisted the knowledge with all his might and will. He should have guessed, but she thrust the knowledge into him. There was nothing she, nor her lifecodes, needed from him. Recognition would not engender from her deep psyche. But there was much in her lifecodes that had never been shared; much that had been added since her transformation. Recognition would come, resist it though she might. She would bear another halfling child—and she had already given too much of herself.

There seemed no end to Timmain's resignation and woe. Zarhan could not, in fact, imagine what Timmain had lost if she were, indeed, the only one whose living memory moved between the stars, but he understood why she might seek refuge in the eternal *now* of the wolfsong. It might be better to be blind than to see what you might never have again.

I shall not linger, then, he assured her, setting one foot behind the other, moving away from the light.

Timmain's slender, elegant shape drew in on itself as Zarhan retreated. Her long hair was no longer a tawny cloak descending past her hips, but rough textured fur. High cheekbones became long cheekbones as the cold of the unknown swirled around Fastfire's back. Her eyes shifted last—among wolves and Wolfriders only Timmorn had his mother's yellow and gold eyes—but they grew peaceful as they silvered.

The star-traveler rejoiced as the wolfsong opened to her. Her howl carried Fastfire through the darkness.

Zarhan became exquisitely aware of his body. He ached from the soles of his feet to the roots of his hair. Even his eyelids protested as he struggled to raise them.

It was autumn, and he had lain in the grove through two dances of the moons. The way his arms and legs felt, he might have lain there for whole turns, but his clothes hadn't rotted away, so he knew it was dances, not turns. Though why he hadn't starved to death was something only Timmain could have explained, and she was gone.

Getting to his feet took Fastfire the rest of the day. He'd had to go slowly, unlocking a muscle at a time. His fingers and toes had to function before he could move his hands and feet. He nearly fainted when he sat up. By the time he took his first stumbling step it was dusk and hunger pangs had triumphed over muscle aches. There was a ravvit just outside the grove—Timmain's parting

63

gift. He devoured it raw, as the Wolfriders would, then slumped into an ordinary sleep.

Morning found the elf clearheaded and shivering. He remembered the bear and the blue flame, his encounter with Timmain, and the winter cloak he'd left with Wreath. There was a new concept rooted at the back of his mind: hubris, the tragedy of pride.

His abortive magic had tainted the grove. Nothing —not browsers, predators, nor gleaners—had approached the seered ground where Fastfire had consumed the great bear. The world of two moons rejected magic. The ashes were a putrifying wound that would never heal. Already they radiated a dark miasma. Most creatures would continue to be repelled, but some would be drawn and Zarhan could imagine the malignancies that would emerge from such a joining.

He raked the ground as best he could, carrying the ebony motes to the abandoned wolf den. He weakened the den's roof and rolled stones over its entrance. It was better; it was the best an elf could do, but the taint was still there. Had Zarhan not discovered hubris, he might have tried to purify the grove with fire. But his mistakes could not be eradicated. The high ones themselves had not come lightly to this world and now he'd added his own bit of darkness to theirs.

Hubris went beyond the abuse of magic and the rape of the forest. Zarhan Fastfire saw how he had lived, how wishful emulation of so-called high ones had turned him against himself. It was not simply that he considered the Wolfriders to be a long step down; Fastfire rejected the other pure-blood elves, as well. He deluded himself into believing that this rejection made him purer, nobler than the rest—and he saw confirmation of this in his Recognition conquests.

He had taken something sacred, the long-term instinct

for survival among his kind, and profaned it with his own petty needs.

Zarhan turned away from magic as much as he could. It was autumn, though, and he had neither cloak or weapons, nor the means to get them. He did not send his thoughts questing for his lifemate again, but only clung to the hope that she was still to the northeast. The elf had purged the high ones from his thoughts, and was no longer certain he was worthy to find her anyway.

The weather grew colder and he traveled less as it did. Half of each day was dedicated to gathering enough wood to keep him warm through the night. He tried his hand making spear-tips in the firelight, but he did not even know what sort of stone to use. He caught fish, ate berries, and wondered if it might not have been easier to burn out like a flame. He began to wonder if the timelessness of wolfsong was not the best way to confront a life without hope or growth.

He was disabused of that notion before the Mother moon blinked again. Timmorn Yellow-Eyes and two wolves came to him in the middle of a clear, cold night. Though he spoke with some difficulty, the eldest of the Wolfriders made it clear that there was neither blessing nor peace in subjugating his elfin self beneath the wolfsong. Timmain, who was purely elfin, might become a true-wolf, but none of her descendants had inherited that ability. Her son walked a knife edge between elf and wolf, between clear-mind and crazy.

There was little Zarhan could offer his one-time chief. They sat beside each other—Zarhan huddled close to his fire, Timmorn protected by his mother's russet-fur legacy—staring at the darkness twice as much as they talked.

"Only the wolves are happy," he said as Timmorn's companions chased sparks from his fire. "Maybe we should not even search for happiness or wholeness. Not within ourselves, anyway. We have too much of one thing, and not enough of the others. But I think the younger ones are happier . . . if that's any consolation to you. Your grandchildren make friends with their wolves and each other. They live from one day to the next; their lives are reckless and they die young. But they're happy, I think . . . ."

Timmorn scuttled around the firepit until he sat at Zarhan's side. He made a fist that left two fingers extended. "Happiness like this," he affirmed as he crossed one finger over the other. "Or this." He clasped Fastfire's hand in his own and squeezed it tight.

Zarhan squeezed back.

Timmorn grinned and released him. "Understand?"

The elf nodded, shook his head, then shrugged his shoulders. "I understand it's not that simple. Not for me. The She-Wolf spoke of a Wolfrider's Way, but there is no Way, only lonely, twisted paths. And I've gone astray; Recognition and my dreams kept me moving when I ought to have kept still."

"Recognition!" Timmorn's eyes blazed in the firelight. He scratched himself and flicked something into the flames. "Many times, Father. Like wolf."

"But I'm not a wolf. I'm not a high one. I don't know what I am, but I'm not a Wolfrider. I wasn't even chief." He recalled his last morning with the Wolfriders, his last bout of Recognition. The images flowed between them.

Timmorn's eyes widened. "So, too. Too much good thing. Wrong-head reason. Right time leaving." He threw a sympathetic arm over Zarhan's shoulders. "The same for me, the same for me. No focus . . . no *self*. Better now. Maybe too old, eh?"

Zarhan stared into the fire. He'd never considered the possibility of outgrowing Recognition. He'd resolved not to pursue it any longer, but he hadn't abandoned hope that it would still find him. Life would be less complicated, less interesting. Besides, in his heart of hearts, Fastfire generally liked the skyfire romances that grew in an evening and vanished with the sunlight.

Then the She-Wolf's face came unbidden into Zarhan's mind.

"Find her! Find She-Wolf. Find Rahnee," Timmorn commanded, sweeping aside Zarhan's image of his daughter and replacing it with the younger face he remembered.

They lived so long, aged so slowly that Zarhan had forgotten how much being chieftess of the Wolfriders had changed Rahnee during the turns of her ascendance. He'd forgotten how young she'd been when he'd begun to suspect that the soulname he'd heard since childhood was her soulname. She hadn't wanted to be chief. In her own mind, she'd been less suited for responsibility than Prunepit. Leadership had been thrust upon her, just as Zarhan had thrust her soulname into her.

Fastfire looked up. Timmorn was smiling, looking more elflike than he had since emerging from the darkness. Looking very much like Rahnee's father.

"You do it. But you stay with her, where she is. Time passes for being chief, yes; time comes for peace, yes, too." He clasped Zarhan's hand as he had before and squeezed it until the elf smiled and nodded.

They didn't talk of Rahnee after that. Timmorn didn't talk much at all. He listened avidly as Fastfire related a smattering of events, smiling or frowning whenever appropriate. The eldest of the Wolfriders sat straighter as the night wore on. What little he said was easier to understand—or perhaps it was just that Zarhan, himself, was dizzy with exhaustion.

At any road, Zarhan didn't remember falling asleep, and when he woke up, Timmorn was gone. It hadn't been a dream, though. Not by a long shot. The two wolves who had been traveling with Timmorn lazed not two good leaps away. Fastfire might not be a Wolfrider, might not even like wolves, but he couldn't be completely ignorant of their ways. He knew that, regardless of whatever commands Timmorn had given the pair, challenge and submission were the only rules a pack understood.

The wolves stood, stretched, and regarded him with gray, intelligent eyes. Zarhan stared back and they yawned. He extended a cautious hand and they bounded forward. The larger one bowled him over and the smaller commenced a leisurely examination of his flesh and clothes that left no part unsniffed or unprodded.

The elf was terrified, and knew it was death to unveil his fear. He retreated into himself and hoped—almost prayed—the wolves would grow bored before he *had* to move. The big wolf cocked his head as Zarhan's mind drifted away from his body, then he closed his teeth ever so gently over the elf's nose. Zarhan couldn't breathe; he returned to physical consciousness and willed his lips apart. The smaller wolf pressed her cold, wet nose against his sensitive ears and exhaled.

Zarhan had steeled himself to withstand pain and terror, but he had no defense against a tickling minx. A burst of laughter exploded from his throat. He saw the incompleteness of his life flash before him, but the wolves released him unharmed.

So that's the way of it, he thought, scratching between the big male's ears. *It's all fun and games to you.*

The wolf whined and pushed forward. He stared up at Zarhan pleading to succor those many other itchy places he could not reach with teeth or claws, but his elf-friend did not understand. In frustration, he lifted onto his hind legs and stared evenly into Zarhan's eyes.

"No," the elf commanded, wrapping his hands around the wolf's forelegs and making a futile attempt to push him away. The animal's flesh was firm and smooth beneath his fingers. There was no dew claw pressing against his palm. **No. Down.**

The wolf bared his teeth and sang, but he got down as well. Zarhan knelt down and rubbed the big male's forehead, still unaware of the itchy places on the wolf's shoulders and under his chin. The animal twisted away and snapped at the air.

I cannot hear you. You can hear me, but I cannot hear you—can you understand that? Your ancestors ran with the hunt, but mine never ran with the pack. I cannot hear you.

Fastfire had little hope the wolves would understand. The Wolfriders, themselves, were not entirely comfortable with the notion that some of the elves could send to the wolves without, in turn, being able to hear their replies. Fastfire's doubts seemed confirmed as the big wolf took the elf's ankle in his jaws and growled deep in his throat.

For a brief moment, Zarhan sent dark thoughts winging after Timmorn, then called them back. The yellow-eyed chief was too troubled by the mixture of elf-blood and wolf-blood in his veins to have misled the wolves deliberately. And though he could not perceive their primal emotions, Zarhan was not without empathy for them: They were at the mercy of their vestigial elfness as much as any Wolfrider suffered from the wolfsong. They did not choose to bond with him, it was almost another form of Recognition.

We can be friends, but you will have to be very patient with me. I will never make a very good wolf—

Zarhan wished he knew how the Wolfriders communicated with their friends. He could feel himself taking

69

refuge in the lordly paternalism that irritated them so much, and yet that *was* the way the pure-blooded elves thought. Or at least, he realized, it was the way *he* thought. Emotions were for the blind passions of Recognition; thoughts—the sending of thoughts—were reserved for that part of him which had aspired to be a high one. There was very little in him that was just Zarhan Fastfire, just a lonely elf who'd wandered from the Way.

Belatedly Zarhan extended his hand toward the big male. The wolf was agitated and wary, but he let the elf touch the rough fur across his shoulders. Zarhan closed his eyes and grappled with the habits of a lifetime. He remembered how Rahnee played with her wolf-friends; he imagined himself to be a wolf-friend. He embraced the wolf stiffly, not yet able to relax with himself or the animal. His fingers penetrated to the soft, thick fur of the wolf's inner coat. He scratched vigorously and the wolf leaned into his embrace.

He found he did not need wolf-blood to share the animal's pleasure. When the smaller wolf whimpered in his ear, Zarhan opened his arms to include her and buried his face between them.

Elves had never been adept at giving names. Among them, names were found or taken. Children were born with soulnames, if the elf-blood ran true. Wolf-friends declared theirs—or so the Wolfriders said. Fastfire thought his new companions had names and wished to declare them, but he could not fathom them. He called the pair Big One and Little One, and they did not seem to mind. They hunted for him, played with sparks from his fire, and slept beside him to keep him warm during the late-autumn nights.

With the wolves at his side, Zarhan continued northeast. He made it clear to them that he would not grow a warm winter coat, and they took exquisite care with the kills they brought back each morning. He scraped the skins as best he could and bound the aromatic pelts around his hands and feet. Gradually an ill-fitting cloak grew: ravvits, mask-eyes, and squirrels. Once they brought him a young forest pig he fashioned into a cap with front legs tied beneath his chin and hind ones trailing down his back. Chill breezes blew through the knotted and poorly sewn seams, but Zarhan prized the unseemly garments more than the bear cloak he'd left behind.

In his own way Zarhan Fastfire joined the wolfsong. He led the two wolves, but he did not think about their destination. He hoped that Rahnee was still alive, still to the northeast, but he did not look for her with his mind. The world shrank to his immediate perceptions, the perceptions of feral creatures preparing for winter. Zarhan's life was simple as it had never been before. He slept with his feet by an embered fire and his head pillowed on a wolf's flank, and he never dreamed.

Or he hadn't dreamed since leaving the blue fire.

It was a cold night—the coldest thus far in the season. The skies had turned leaden, darkness had come early and completely. A bitter, moist wind blew down from the north and, though Zarhan positioned himself downwind from the fire, he could not get warm. He sat up and wrapped his patchwork cloak tighter. The Little One woke up and whined her concern; the Big One was out hunting.

Winter's coming, he sent to the Little One. **There's snow in that wind, you wait and see. The forest will be white by this time tomorrow—** Zarhan never knew if they understood any of the words spewing out of his mind or if, as he suspected, it was the act of sending itself which calmed them. Either way, the Little

71

One stretched out again and he lay down against her. She tucked her nose alongside his; he inhaled the musky warmth of her breath.

His dream began with musk and darkness. Fastfire was back in one of the many dens he'd shared with the She-Wolf. They'd been quarreling about something trivial, something he couldn't remember, and she'd given him her cold back to sleep with. He sought to break the tension in the only way he could imagine. His arm snaked over her side; he kissed her shoulder and pulled her closer.

The She-Wolf growled—a wild, fearsome sound that echoed through the cramped den. Zarhan's temper rose to meet hers. He gave a sharp tug to her shoulder. It was not his estranged lifemate who rolled over, but a wolf in full fury. Jagged claws raked Zarhan's naked skin. Fangs clamped down over his shoulder, shaking him against the hollowed dirt sides of the den. He tried to defend himself but his elfin magic deserted him and his fists were useless against her strength. She threw him down and he lay bleeding in the darkness.

This is a dream. This is all a dream, he told himself. *I'll wake myself up. It will be over. Just a dream. WAKE UP!*

But Zarhan's will had deserted him along with his magic. The dream would not end and the wolf was on him again. He cried her name and with his final strength embraced death and his lifemate. Fastfire passed beyond pain, and beyond the dream. There was nothing in his arms, and nothing but a sad ache in his gut.

I'm sorry, Rahnee. I never understood you, never loved you as you loved me. Forgive me. Nothing stirred in the emptiness beyond Zarhan's dreams. He sent her name again and again.

I'm here.

It was her: her soul's voice within his mind. The

contact terminated and Zarhan was awake. He tried to reestablish his connection to her, but the dream had exhausted him. He hugged the Little One and told himself it had been real, not his imagination.

She's not far, he insisted, wrapping his thoughts around Rahnee's image as he sent them to the wolf.

The Little One whined and licked at his nose. He held her tighter before burrowing back beneath his patchwork furs.

Morning came with no promise of sunlight or warmth. The sullen clouds seemed scarcely higher than the treetops and the forest was unnaturally quiet. Big, lazy flakes of snow were falling by the time Zarhan had eaten the ravvit the Big One had brought for him. The Little One raced from one white mote to the next, her eyes growing brighter as they melted on her tongue. She was young enough to be delighted by winter's novelty, a sense her older companions could not share. Snow was falling heavily by the time Zarhan buried his night-fire. The Little One began to shake the white rime away, just like the Big One.

The flakes tinkled as they descended through the bare trees, and seemed to make more noise than their feet on the thin blanket of snow. Not long after they began the day's journey, Zarhan stopped to strip green withies from a willow stump. He had a feeling he'd be needing a pair of snowshoes before long. The Big One, too, sensed that serious winter had begun. Twice he tried to urge his elf-friend off the trail toward granite outcrops where sizable cold-weather dens might be found.

Each time Zarhan shook his head and sent Rahnee's image into the Big One's mind. The brindled gray wolf would growl in the back of his throat and lower his head until it jutted straight out from his shoulders. Fastfire saw the challenge implicit in the wolf's eyes and posture. He didn't dispute the Big One's wisdom, nor did he respond to it. He kept walking, letting the male wolf fall behind for a while.

They usually rested at midday, but, with the snow, light and time both seemed frozen. Fastfire called a halt when he felt tired. The snow was already above his instep, not deep enough to bother the wolves, who bounded away into the forest without him, but deep enough to turn his crude boots into frigid lumps. He hunkered down in the lee of a large tree and picked the ravvit clean. After knotting the pelt onto his left sleeve, he set about warping the withies into teardrops. He wove the mesh with his fishline and wondered if he could convince the wolves to hunt such oil-furred prey as muskrat or pouch-rat until he had enough for a decent pair of boots.

Fastfire had one shoe almost finished when the wolves returned. The Little One forced her way into his lap; the Big One danced stiff-legged a little distance away. Zarhan knew they were both agitated, but it wasn't until the Little One took his wrist between her teeth that he understood that they wanted him to follow them. He was sure it was another request to settle down in a warm, dry cave, but though the Little One was scarcely full-grown, she could easily splinter his bones. The elf had no choice but to follow.

He was growling a bit himself as they led him along briar-walled pathways that snagged his cloak. Bursting with impatience, the wolves shot ahead, leaving him to follow their trail.

His face and hands were bleeding from several thorn scratches when the Big One's snow-muted howl came back to him. **This had better be good,** he sent in reply.

It was—and more astounding than anything he'd seen or met in his long life. There was an arrow aimed at him when Zarhan emerged from the briar patch, and an elf

he did not know behind it. Clear blue eyes met his own
and the bowstring grew taut.

"Who are you?" the stranger demanded, a woman by
her mid-pitched voice.

Zarhan was too stunned to reply. His memories went
back through Timmain to the sky-mountain itself, but
they had never promised he'd meet elves he did not
already know. Wreath's face mocked him from memory,
as well; he should have known better, should have
believed Rahnee could not be alone. Laststar had always
said she'd Recognized Wreath's father, but Zarhan had
never put the thoughts together correctly in his head.

"Who are you?" she demanded again. The arrow rose
to point at Zarhan's heart.

Zarhan gaped. Clearly his ancestors had passed a
single language along to their children, but they had not
left a communal name. Once, not long ago, Zarhan
might have called himself a "high one"; now that rang
hollow. Elves was a word they'd gleaned from their
enemies, the five-fingered hunters, and Wolfriders was a
term the strange woman could not possibly understand.
It didn't occur to Zarhan to simply give his personal
name, and even if it had, it seemed unlikely that any
coherent sound would get past his paralyzed tongue.

The stranger's fingers were getting dangerously
twitchy when all attention was diverted to the Big One
as he crashed out of the brush and ran between them.
The woman shifted her aim.

"No! Don't shoot him; he's my friend!" Zarhan
shouted. He waved his arms to attract her attention, and
got more than he bargained for. The Big One hadn't
been running for the pure joy of it. The woman had two
companions, each armed as she was, and all of them
now aiming at him. The Little One broke cover and ran
straight for his arms. A third bow-wielding male now
took aim at Zarhan's chest.

High ones help me, Zarhan pleaded to his memory. **Timmain, Timmorn . . . Rahnee!** He was poised between panic and absurdity, unable to believe they'd actually loose the arrows; unsure how to prevent them. The Little One bared her throat and begged for protection. Panic began to overbalance absurdity as Zarhan's fears expanded to include the wolves. Then memory responded to his plea.

Cheseri. The name came to Zarhan on the familiar pangs of Recognition. **Cheseri,** he sent through the snow and followed it with his own name.

Cheseri's face drew inward with doubt. Her eyebrows tensed as thought shot between her and her companions.

"Zarhan? Zarhan Fastfire?" she asked.

He nodded and they lowered their bows. Her companions, young men of evident pride and skill, came closer.

"You look . . . *diseased*," one of them said, indicating Zarhan's ragged cloak and, especially, the uncured, knotted hat binding his tender ears against his scalp. "We couldn't recognize you."

Fastfire's hair was almost as stringy and aromatic as his hat when he pulled the forest pig's pelt off, but he shook the red braids down anyway. What was important was that they did know him—and that could only mean one thing. "Where is she? How is she?" He reached out to take the other's hand and receive his thoughts, but the young man retreated.

"Kelagry!" a black-eyed man chided as he stepped forward to take Zarhan's hand between his own. "Have you no manners?"

Fastfire watched the aforenamed Kelagry shuffle his feet through the snow, then the immediate world fell away as he shared thought-images with the black eyes. He saw his lifemate as these strangers had first found her: broken, almost lifeless. They thought she was dead, but these elves had death-customs: rites of remembering

76

and fire. They carried her away from the trampled meadow toward a place appropriate for mourning, and then they'd realized a stubborn spark of life lingered in her helpless body.

As the high ones had fire magic to pass on in a diluted form to their distant children, so too they had passed along a healing magic—but none of these four strangers was a healer and no healer would have spared much hope for Rahnee's crushed back. Rahnee had healed herself, drawing on the shapeshifter talent implicit in all of Timmain's descendants. While she did, the four strange elves had cared for her like a newborn. She was better now—able to talk, able to feel with her fingers and toes, though she was still confined to her bed.

Zarhan prepared a wave of gratitude, but it was shunted aside by the rest of the stranger's sending. He found himself inundated by memories and traditions akin to, yet very different from, his own.

The strange elf sharing with him was Merolen, the leader of this much-reduced clan. Like the Wolfriders they were the descendants of a desperate handful of survivors; like the Wolfriders, their lives had been changed by the march of the saurians. They had suffered more directly than the Wolfriders had. The huge marauding beasts had leveled their village and left only these four youngsters, who had been hunting, to survive. For two turns of the seasons the quartet had harried the saurians with vengeance, then they'd found Rahnee.

The She-Wolf had given them hope, Merolen sent, and reminded them that the elfin way—for they had also adopted the descriptive name from the five-fingered ones—was life, not vengeance. They had already learned much from the Wolfrider chief, not the least of which was her faith in her full-blooded lifemate.

We are very grateful to have the wisdom of the high ones with us—

Fastfire felt his hand begin to burn with embarrassment. Like Kelagry, he stared at his feet and began to pull away. Merolen held him fast and blunted his shame with a leader's smile.

"Of course, Rahnee might still have been a little fevered and not quite herself when she spoke of you. The high ones *I* remember were very fastidious. Never rancid. So, I imagine you're just an elf, like us. I imagine I'll know for sure once your ears are clean again." He released Zarhan and turned to the others. "Cheseri, Kelagry, Delonin"—he nodded to each of them in turn—"this is Zarhan Fastfire—or it will be in a little while. Now we are six strong."

They led Zarhan along a stream to a pair of mud-walled huts, the first freestanding structures the red-haired elf had ever seen. He stared in slack-jawed amazement, but Merolen's clan had other wonders to reveal. They heated water in hollow things that looked like huge seed-pods and felt like stone. They took his worn-out clothes away and replaced them with patterned garments that were made from twisted hair, not leather. They offered him a spicy, pungent milk they said came from the same square-eye animals that produced the hair, then they offered him spongy white stuff, laced with dark lines and pressed between leaves. They claimed it was *cheese* and made from square-eye milk, not fungus, as Zarhan at first guessed.

It was more than Zarhan could believe, but he ate it gratefully and tried not to scratch where the hair-clothes chafed against his skin. He used his own comb on his matted hair, but had to admit their reddish metal knife was better than his teeth for removing the most stubborn tangles.

"You *have* met the high ones, haven't you?" he whispered to Merolen. "They taught you all this, didn't they?"

The clan chief shook his head sadly. "We were five eights strong when the lizards came, with eight times that many square-eyes in our herds—but we weren't high ones. The Trickster died long before I was born, he was the last who remembered the sky. He taught us much, more than four can remember or use. It is good we have found more of our kind. Now we can have hope, instead of vengeance."

The sincerity in Merolen's eyes made Fastfire uncomfortable. He looked around the room and saw that the other three were watching him as well. "Can I see Rahnee now?" he asked, wanting to be alone with her—or at least away from these strangers.

Cheseri offered him a heavy blanket, then led him through the snow to the other hut. She untied the leather but let him enter by himself.

I'll be out here if you need me, she assured him, and let the leather drop.

Zarhan's eyes took a moment to adjust to the darkness. He found a small firepit at the center of the hut and kindled it quietly with his magic, then he went to the wall where his lifemate rested. Merolen's sending had conveyed some sense of the extent of Rahnee's injuries, but it had not prepared Fastfire for the sight of her.

The She-Wolf was shrunken and frail within the bed they had made for her. Her breathing was so shallow, Zarhan might not have noticed it at all. Only her white-gold hair, unfurled across the blankets, retained any hints of her extraordinary beauty.

And they said she was much better, much stronger, than she had been when they'd first taken her into their care.

Zarhan hesitated before brushing a lock of her hair

79

away from her fragile, yet still familiar, face. Her *dark-violet* eyes flickered open and took several heartbeats to focus on his face.

"I knew it was you," the She-Wolf said, though Zarhan would not have been able to understand her if she had not sent her thoughts beneath the words as well.

Her smile was lopsided. Fastfire realized she was still almost completely paralyzed. He caught the undercurrent of her desire and reached beneath the blanket to take the hand she struggled to raise.

"I couldn't believe you'd just die—"

"The Wolfriders . . . Are they all right? Do they need me?"

Fastfire squeezed her fingers gently and shook his head. "Prunepit's become Prey-Pacer. He led the Wolfriders in a glorious hunt against the saurians. You'd have been proud." There was a calculated risk in telling her that the Wolfriders had a new chief. He thought he'd lost when she grimaced, but then she sent clearly into his mind.

It's over. I don't have to go back. I was so afraid I'd have to go back. That the Wolfriders would be broken like Trickster's clan. When I finally woke up and recalled that you had been seeking me, all I could think of was that the Wolfriders needed me, when all I needed was you and Silvertooth— Her eyes widened as she caught the moment of sadness that escaped Zarhan's closely guarded feelings. **Silvertooth?**

She was badly hurt and she had nothing left to live for—

The wolves are gone, then. A tear rolled across her cheek, something the chieftess would never have allowed. But Rahnee was no longer the chieftess, and she did not have the strength to live without emotions. **I've been dreaming of you and Silvertooth, my high**

one and my wolf. The balance of me.** She looked away as another tear slipped free.

Now you know I couldn't have come this far alone. There're two wolves outside, and they're desperate for an elf-friend.

Fastfire extended his mind, trusting that the Big One and the Little One weren't far away, and trusting that Merolen's elves would understand. He asked for too much. The wolves came. They bounded through the leather door and brought a radiant glow to Rahnee's eyes. Cheseri came too, with a black-stone club raised above her head. Zarhan sprang to his feet, catching her wrist before any harm could be done.

Earlier, before any harm could be done to the wolves, Fastfire had pulled Cheseri's soulname from her while she had an arrow pointed at his heart; now he had her in his grasp.

Zarhan! she sent with an undercurrent of surprise and confusion.

He found himself on the cusp, and ready to tumble down the familiar path that would change confusion to Recognition.

Zarhan? An echo filled with resignation and tinged with sadness.

Fastfire released Cheseri's arm. "I'm sorry," he said loud enough for Rahnee to hear. "I didn't mean to frighten you. The wolves won't hurt her. She's told you about the wolves, hasn't she?" He fought free of the tension in his groin, and channeled his resolve into a sending of pure determination.

Cheseri lowered her arm and blinked. "Wolves," she said slowly. "Yes, she's told us all about the wolves." She rubbed her forehead with her empty hand, then peered into his eyes. The fire was gone. "I'll go back outside. Call me if she needs anything."

Zarhan let a triumphant grin cover his face once she turned away. He'd conquered Recognition—or at least he'd conquered his need for it. He was still smiling a gentler smile when he returned to Rahnee's bed and knelt between the wolves.

"I call them Big One and Little One, because I couldn't find anything better—"

You came back. Her hand slipped free of the blankets and fell into his own.

He gathered it up and held her fingers against his lips. **We can start again, beloved.**

Songshaper

by Nancy Springer

They called him Hummer, because hum he did, practically from the day he came out of the womb. When he was small, his mother, Moonwisp, had only to turn her sensitive, pointed ears to know where he was at any time, even when he slept. Later, when he grew to be a stripling and started riding out after deer with the other young elves his age, his humming spoiled every hunt. He could not seem to stop himself for long, even to stalk the game. He hummed as regularly as most elves breathed. Finally, when the prey had been alerted one too many times, his companions refused to take him with them any longer.

Hummer sometimes droned tunelessly under his breath, sometimes hummed more intently, though the melodies he produced seemed to have meaning for his ears only. Often he seemed far away, his large dusk-gray eyes gazing as if he had been eating dreamberries, though in fact he seldom did. He seemed not to need them, or he seemed always to be dreaming, even under the light of two good hunting moons, with the tribe gathering and the game afoot.

"Never mind, Hummer," his lifelong friend Brightwing said to him, touching his cloud of brown hair before she went off to track the deer with her wolf-friend and the others. "You don't mind, do you?" she added anxiously.

"Not a bit," he told her. It was the truth. After Brightwing and the other striplings rode away into the benighted forest, Hummer settled himself in contentedly on the lowest branch of a large oak, and there he lounged. As always, he hummed. He felt no disappointment, for he sensed he did not belong on the hunt; he felt that he belonged where he was. He had taken passage, he knew his soulname, and though he had growing yet to do, to some extent he knew what he was meant to be . . . Humming, he seemed to see colors and images in his mind. The silvery flash of a huge flying thing, and willowy forms, elves, yet not elves such as he knew. And the slender four-fingered hands stroking fire out of snow—

"You sit and stare like a treewee!"

The words came to Hummer dimly, as if from another world. Blinking, he focused on his father, Blade. The sturdy elf stood scowling up at him—though Blade seemed always to scowl. A scar ran across his face from the outer side of one eye to the opposite side of his mouth, a death-white scar left from human torment at a time when the Wolfriders had been without a healer. It had taken one nostril of his nose and curled his lip in a constant sneer. Hummer could tell little from his father's slashed face, but from the strong hands gripping the spear far too tightly he knew that Blade was annoyed with him. Though he never meant to, Hummer seemed somehow always able to annoy his father worse than red ants or stinging flies.

"But even a treewee has more sense than to make so much noise," Blade added grimly.

Coming out of dream as he was, Hummer saw his father as if seeing a stranger, noting Blade's hard muscles and scarred chest. Battle scars. And the frowning brows, the keen look in Blade's dark-blue eyes, the proud way he held his head—everything about the older elf looked toughened always, Hummer knew, even in sleep. Older—Blade was not so much older, really, not yet bearded like some of the Wolfrider elders, but he seemed old and hard to his son. Life had aged Blade quickly. Life and humans.

Always, since he could remember, Hummer had wanted only to please Blade, and usually he had failed. But no harm trying one more time. "Father," he asked, "what is it you want of me?"

Somehow the sincere question seemed to anger Blade more. Hummer saw his father's forearms bulge as Blade gripped the spear-haft yet harder.

"I want of you some sense of what it is to be an elf and not a bumblebee, for a beginning!" snapped Blade. "You are not fit for hunt or fighting. How will you be of help to your tribe?"

Others would hunt. And there was no fighting with the humans at the time; there had been none for many turns, not since the Wolfriders stayed on the roam to elude them. But Hummer did not say either of these things to his father. He gazed at Blade, trying to understand. And as he thought, as always when he thought, he began to hum.

"Stop that humming!" Blade ordered. "Come down here."

Hummer scrambled down from his tree. His father's angry stare on him made him clumsy, or even more clumsy than usual.

"Get your bow," Blade told him. "By the high ones, you are going to learn to hunt and not hum."

And Hummer went to do as his father had said, but slowly, so that Blade sent sharply after him, **Move!** Hummer moved, but he was humming, for he was thinking, and his thoughts were somber. He had believed he was starting to know what being an elf might mean for him. He had felt the soul-stirring inside him . . . and he had heard his father's voice. And the two were telling him opposite things.

"Hunting after all?" Moonwisp asked in surprise as he reached past her to pull his weapon from the tree hollow where it was kept.

"To please Father," he said quietly.

She looked at him as if she understood, but did not reply. Perhaps she also had tried to please Blade, in her time.

In fact, Hummer did not please his father, that hunt. Concentrating on not humming, he could not concentrate on anything else. And his wolf-friend, Moth, seemed to sense his inner reluctance and ran sluggishly. Even at the best of times, it annoyed Blade to be near Moth. He disliked the name Hummer had given the wolf. Hummer had been only a cub, and the wolf a fuzzy, playful, blundering half-grown creature still in its puppy fur. Moth, Hummer had called the wolf for its color and its fuzz and its flitting. But it had seemed to Blade somehow soft, such a name. Hummer should have called the wolf Strongjaw, or Slash, or Graydread.

But the wolf was named Moth, and ran on little faster than its fluttering namesake might have gone, and Hummer, looking about him at shifting leaf-shadow and the way the moonbeams crisscrossed each other and puddled like bright water on the forest floor, began for the twentieth time to hum. **You are useless!** Blade exploded, though not aloud—he was too good a warrior and hunter to shout aloud. Hummer clutched at his head; the sending had dizzied him worse than any shout. And his father set heels to his mount, Toughpaw, and sped away.

Hummer went back home and put away his bow; and

when his father came back without game at dawn, Hummer avoided him; and when Blade came looking for his son the next night to attempt a hunt again, Hummer was nowhere to be found. He had hidden himself, for he had a sense of what he must do—though he had never intended to do it so quickly. The process was nearly as futile as pulling at a starflower to bring it into bloom.

But if his father was to understand, Hummer had to try.

For several days he appeared only to eat. Where he slept, Moonwisp no longer knew, but she knew also that he was growing; she did not ask. She watched Brightwing, and saw that Brightwing's face looked merely puzzled, nothing more, when Brightwing sat with Hummer to eat, and after that Moonwisp was puzzled as well.

In fact, Hummer was not sleeping much, night or day, though he often dreamed. And by the time of the next fullness of Mother moon and the next howl, he had something ready to offer. Something ready to lay before his tribe, his chief, and his father. Mainly his father.

When his tribe-mates tilted back their heads for the ritual chorus, and Hummer ceased his humming to join his voice with theirs, his howl found melody and words.

Ayooah, ayooo! Under two moons
The mountain flew down, to the high ones' dread;
Ayooah, ayooo! Under a strange sky
The humans slew some and the others fled.

The tribe fell to shocked silence to listen, and Hummer's voice faltered. But he sang on with an effort worthy of a warrior facing battle. It was hard, pulling his dreams into words so that the others could share them and keep them, pulling his hums into melody, laying dreams and melody before the others like a naked cub, newborn.

Under two moons the elf magic flowed
And mingled with the wolves of this world.
Ayooah, ayooo! The cold snow tingled,
Ayoo! The warm fire glowed.

The song was a poor thing, and Hummer knew it. Years of humming and dreaming later, he could have done better. Likely none of his tribe-mates understood what he wanted to say, this night. But thinking of his father, he had known he had to try. Blade had to understand what Hummer was or could be, what an elf was.

An elf is magic and an elf is flesh,
A wolf's bone, a hunter's blood,
But when Wolfriders sing—

"Cease your noise!" Blade roared.

Hummer blinked his way back from the dream, tilted his chin down from the howl cant, met his father's dark, angry eyes. The others looked uneasy, as if they had just witnessed something embarrassing. Even Prey-Pacer. Even Moonwisp, even Brightwing. And Blade was furious. None of them had understood, none. But none of them mattered to Hummer as much as Blade.

"What do you mean!" the scar-faced elf exploded at him. "Spoiling the howl with your uncouth noises!"

And facing that familiar wrath, Hummer wanted to hum, to comfort himself in dreams. But he knew humming would only anger Blade further. So he spoke instead.

"It is for the chief to say if I have done wrong at the howl!"

The force of his own words startled him. But Prey-Pacer, not reacting to his tone, said levelly, "Hummer has done no harm. I find no fault."

"Well, I do!" The wrath-blood had flooded into Blade's face so dark that Hummer could see it even in the moonlight; against it the disfiguring scar showed like a slash of skyfire against storm clouds. The elf raged, not at his chief but at his son. "My son, and you have never given me anything but shame! Soft thing that you are, you think you know what an elf is! You—"

"An elf is what an elf is! We are Wolfriders, and our Way gives us that freedom!" Hummer had never shouted at his father, but he was doing so now, in front of the entire assembled tribe. "But you will not give it to me! Nothing I have done in all my life has ever pleased you."

"Bah! You dare to call yourself a Wolfrider?"

Hummer stood panting, for suddenly it had all come clear and sharp to him; his future teetered as if on a knife's edge. And Moonwisp was by him, and Brightwing, both trying to comfort him and hush him, but he looked at neither of them. When he spoke again, he had made his decision, and his voice was as level as the chief's.

"Father, you give me a choice that is no choice: to be what I am, or to try to be what you want me to be. And I am telling you now, I am what you see. Myself. The one you call Hummer. I cannot be otherwise."

And Blade answered, "Then I am telling you, stay far from me."

In horror Moonwisp cried out, "Lifemate! No!" And Prey-Pacer said sharply to Blade, "Think what you are doing! You would banish your cub?"

Blade stood silent. It was no easier for him to take

back words he had spoken than it would have been to call back a flung spear.

Though if Hummer had sent to him then, even so much as a single word, **Father,** Blade would have tried. But because the anger of all the years had suddenly found voice in him, had peaked into a thing hard and sharp as a spearhead, Hummer did not send to his father or give him time to struggle with his pride. He said, "I am going," and he turned away. And within a few moments, though his mother pleaded with him to stay —and though he knew he could have stayed, and no one would have driven him away, least of all Blade—he nuzzled her and rode away on Moth.

He rode with a hard set to his jaw. He did not weep, and he did not hum. He did not hum all night.

Nor did he hum the next day, or for days and nights thereafter. All humming seemed to have gone out of him the night of the howl.

He traveled fast and hard, as if someone or something was pursuing him, and Moth felt his mood and loped willingly. Dawn and early daylight they traveled, resting in a thicket only at the height of the day, then traveling on when the sun was still up, though low. Nighttimes, Hummer stopped only long enough to let Moth hunt, and the wolf shared the kills with him. Small game —ravvits, shadow-tails. A wolf hunting alone could not bring down deer. Within a few nights elf and wolf were both growing thin from hard travel and poor feeding.

Hummer reached the edge of the forest and saw the mountain peaks rising, the mountains he had seen only in dreams. They were as lovely as he had ever imagined them, but he looked at them and felt nothing but a hardness like their own. He got off Moth and sent the wolf away to hunt, then climbed the stony slopes. The stones would show no trace of his passing, and there were many ledges and crevices, good hiding places. On one such ledge, the next day, Hummer lay and watched as his father searched for his trail far below.

He had known Blade would be after him. And his father had waited, it seemed, no more than a day before following.

Hummer watched his father retrace a cold trail into the forest, searching for him, then turned his back and faced the mountains.

They were beautiful, the mountains. His eyes knew it, and he gazed on them for the next several days and nights as he and Moth struggled up the rocky slopes frothing with small, strange flowers. No need to travel so quickly now that Blade had lost their track. Time enough to rest, time enough for Moth to hunt the small, ravvitlike creatures that lived in the rocks. Then up the bare rock above the flowery ledges to the mountaintops, and the gap that led beyond—and then Hummer saw the plains, billowing into blue distance.

Days and nights to follow, he saw bristle-boars feeding on the rocky foothills. He saw mad-horns and serpent-noses moving like brown monoliths on the plains, gathering at the waterholes, their skin thick and tough as leather armor, their tempers uncertain. He came down from the slopes anyway, and set foot in the seemingly endless lushness under vast sky, and saw the grass-feeding leapers and the small spotted wildcats that fed on them, and felt a pain in his throat, and knew that he would never hum again. But he would sing of this place, of this world beneath two moons.

His bow rode on his shoulder, unused all this time. That day when they rested Hummer took it and strung it and plucked the string—it made a humming sound. As Moth lay nearby he twanged it and sang aloud of the forest and mountains, the plains and the Muchcold Water far to the north and the two moons that spilled their white beams on them all, pulling the words out of his heart. It was not easy, and singing left a pain in his heart worse than the pain in his throat. Yet he knew he would never stop singing.

He looked long into Moth's yellow eyes when he was done. "If only my bow had more than the one string," he said at last, not sending, for his thoughts were not thoughts a wolf-friend could understand.

Red wolves roamed the plains. Hummer and Moth could hear their howling at dusk, their yelped signals at night as they hunted. Many wolves together could pull down a bison, though often with loss of blood. And a bison made more meat than even a pack of wolves could eat. Hummer and Moth followed the pack, fed at the kills. And Hummer knew that the warm guts, from which bowstrings could be made, were always ripped out and gobbled first.

He looked at Moth and thought—thinking no longer made him hum; whatever had made him hum had now gone deep and came out in different ways. "We must find a place where there are deer," he said. "These great horned beasts are too large for just the two of us to kill, Moth. Also, I will need wood. And ashes, or else white dirt." He sent the images to the wolf's mind, and Moth panted contentedly by way of reply. He did not need to understand why Hummer wanted to find these things. What his elf-friend wanted was what Moth wanted, without need of reasons.

The mountains still showed gray-blue at the edge of the plains. Hummer and Moth veered toward them.

That night a mad-horn charged them, and only Moth's burst of speed kept them alive. The hurtling beast passed so close to them that Hummer could see the gleam of the small, rheumy, red-glaring eyes. It was not the first time on the journey that Hummer had learned the meaning of danger. One day on a sunny mountain-side he had awakened to find a poisonous snake coiled on a rock by his head. There had been sting-tails hiding in the rocks as well. Longtooths roamed the plains, the only predators that dared attack a great tusked serpent-nose. Hummer loved to watch the great cats stalking, but he knew they could kill him with a single swipe of one clawed paw, just as a serpent-nose could turn him to dirt with one trampling foot. He rode with every sense alert, and with every escape he loved life more. When he stopped to rest, when his wolf-friend stood guard, he sang, pulling words and melodies out of his soul.

He and Moth came to a flat, white pan in a hollow of the plains, and Hummer took handfuls of the white dirt in a ravvit-skin pouch. Days later, the elf and the wolf reached a place where plains turned to small hills, where copses of slender, rustling trees stood on the hilltops and Moth lifted his head and pricked his ears, scenting deer. Then Hummer strung his bow to use it for the first time that journey as it was intended, concentrating fiercely on the hunt. With Moth's help, he killed a yearling buck, and sickened himself, for he made a bloody business of it, needing three arrows to bring it down. Moth lapped up the blood and wanted to feed, but Hummer would not let the wolf feed until he had taken the deer's guts for his own use.

Do not eat these, he told Moth, and Moth whined, for the intestines were a delicacy. But Hummer repeated the command, then skinned the deer and used the hide to carry the unwieldy guts to where a trickle of water ran.

It was good to be back again in a forest of sorts —though not anywhere near the great forest where the Wolfriders roamed. Still, trees were trees, and Hummer felt a deep contentment even as he struggled with the messy business of cleaning the guts and cutting them into ribbons. While the fouled water of the hillside spring cleared, he scratched a hollow in the nearby ground. There he laid his strips of intestines, and he soaked them with water from the spring, then sprinkled on the white dirt he had brought from the plains.

He let the things soak for hours, throwing on more water and white earth from time to time, guarding them from birds and scavengers while Moth, bloated with deer meat, lay flat on his side and slept. When Hummer judged it had been soaking long enough, he took the guts strip by strip, rolled them into strings between his fingers, and hung the strings from low branches to dry, then guarded them some more. He had cut a green sapling with his knife, and as he stood guard he bent and whittled it into a bow smaller than a hunting bow.

By the time Moth woke, Hummer was exhausted and peevish. **I'm almost ready to string it,** he grumbled at the wolf. **Thanks for all your help.**

Moth, who considered that he had been of considerable help, nevertheless did not snarl, but sat silently and watched as Hummer did incomprehensible things with two, three, four strings and a bow far too small to kill anything but the smallest songbirds. Then Hummer made noises with his fingers on the strings. Smothered noises such as a wet cat might make.

"Puckernuts!" Hummer exploded, throwing the crude bow-harp off amid the trees somewhere, and for a moment the elf looked as if he might either roar like his father or weep. But he did neither. He flung himself down on the ground where he was and slept.

When he awoke, he went to find the harp and looked at it carefully.

"Well," he remarked to Moth, "I will have to try it again."

He tried it again and again, many times again, so many times that he learned to shoot deer with only one arrow. He used that first bow as a fire-bow, to make the fires that gave him ashes, and he built himself a stone-lined basin in the ground in which to soak the guts. For a full dance of the two moons he and Moth stayed in the region of deer groves and small hills while Hummer made bow-harp after bow-harp.

And as he worked Hummer sang, shaping his songs, the chosen words, the rise and fall of the music, as intently as he shaped the harps.

And when at last he had made a harp with eight strings, some of which hummed in a lower pitch, some higher, and all of which pleased him more or less, he sat down to shape songs and harp together into oneness.

He sang of red deer and black-neck deer and wolves and the world of two moons. He sang of the high ones and Timmorn and Timmain. He sang of Recognition and lifemating and lovemating and an elf's love of tribe; he sang of an elf's valor in the long struggle against the humans; he sang of things that he had seen in vision and things that he had seen in fact. Bristle-boars. The shining mountain that had flown down from far cold sky. Brightwing. The stars, the stuff of midnight stars pulsing in his blood. Blade—in a way he sang of Blade. He sang of the Wolfriders.

> Bone of elf and blood of wolf
> And dust of distant stars are we,
> Tree-shapers and spear-makers,
> Deer-hunters, moon-howlers,
> And warriors fierce if need be,
> And dreamers of things we cannot see,
> And dreamers.

The bow-harp purred like a great cat, hummed like a bumblebee, sang like the forest in a high wind. Moth lay and listened. Even the rustling copse seemed to fall silent to listen. And sitting in beneath those slender trees, under the shadowy light of two fingernail moons, Hummer sang at one with the harp, sang like a demon spirit out of the dark and like a winged messenger out of the past, sang with his heart in his voice, his self open like a night-blooming flower, his soul naked like a lost cub.

> *Wanderers are we,*
> *Stalkers in the mighty forests,*
> *Wolf-howling, night-prowling,*
> *Roamers in a strange, hard world*
> *Where cold and claws and humans hurt us—*

Something moved in the shadows of the copse. "Stop!" a voice said harshly.

Hummer blinked his way out of the trance. Blade stood before him.

"No!" Hummer cried. "No, go away!" Knife-thrusts of pain seemed to strike him at the sight of his father. He bent double with pain, and his mouth stretched with weeping, he who had not wept when he had left the tribe—but singing, he had laid himself open, made himself vulnerable; there were no defenses left for him. "All you do is hurt me!" he shouted at Blade, taste of tears salt in his mouth. "Go away from me!"

Blade said, "I'm sorry."

The rough edge to his voice was not harshness, really, so much as—huskiness. The older elf spoke nearly in a whisper. "I shouldn't have said that. I don't want to hurt you, ever again. It's just that . . ."

Hummer saw the sheen on his father's scar-twisted face. Tears in Blade's eyes, as in his own.

"Your music," Blade said, struggling with the words. "It pierces me like spears."

Hummer sat with his harp in his arms, his mouth moving wordlessly. In a moment Blade came over and dropped to one knee, awkwardly, in front of his son.

"You will be a new sort of shaper in our tribe," he said

softly. "A dreamshaper, a songshaper. You will give us howls fit to live in legend. You shape the stuff of heart and mind as others shape wood." Blade's voice shook, saying that last.

Hummer lifted one hand from the harp, reached out his string-callused fingers and touched his father's face, feeling the warm, wet tears, feeling the tough whiteness of the disfiguring scar. "But you can scarcely bear to hear me sing," he whispered. "Why?"

Blade flinched back a moment, then held his ground. "The songs call to me," he said.

"Of course they call to you. You are elf." Hummer laid his hand once again on his harp.

"It is—it is more than that." And Blade, the warrior, met his son's eyes as if fighting his most difficult battle. "They call—to what I could have been. Memories—I try to forget. There was—there was singing in me once, also, Hummer."

"But—but I have scarcely ever heard you sing, even at the howls!" Hummer knew that his father growled more than howled when the tribe sang to the moon.

"There was fighting to be tended to." Blade spoke with difficulty. He had never been much for long speaking, not since Hummer had known him. "Fighting with humans, always. I told myself I would be of more use to my tribe as a warrior. And then—when they captured me—"

He could not go on. He never spoke of that time. But Hummer, gazing, still half in the trance of the night and the singing, knew his father for the first time with a songshaper's vision and whispered, "Yes. Yes, I see."

Blade's soul, injured, long-unhealed, twisted awry by its wound just as the scar twisted his face.

"It withers," Hummer murmured.

"It kills," said Blade starkly.

"Not you. You're too tough." And with an odd,

entranced sureness Hummer picked up his harp. "Father. Stay here, listen. Do not go away." And he started to play.

"No," Blade whispered, inching back. "Stop."

Hummer gazed levelly at him and started to sing, pulling the words out of himself. New words, a new song, meant for his father alone.

"Stop," said Blade. His voice shook. "Please."

Father, Hummer sent to him as he sang, **it is a gift for you, this song, the only gift I can give you. Take it, please. Accept it, surrender to it. Let it into your soul.**

"I—I cannot! Stop!" Blade crouched in a shadow, shaking as if he was a frail thing, a leaf battered by a wind of song. His son's song. He had told Hummer to stop, and the cub had not obeyed him—

"Stop!" he roared. The warrior rose, spear gripped in a strong hand, every muscle taut for combat. Being the warrior was the only defense Blade knew against—

The music-storm of bittersweet beauty, bringing back all the heartbreak, all his aching longing for—just such music, just such beauty, once his to hide within himself, so deep inside, no elf knew; and now—gone, all gone, the humans had bled it away with their brutal knives; and the worthless cub—needs must remind him . . .

With a wild yell more than half a cry of pain, Blade lifted his spear and rushed at Hummer.

The songshaper watched him come, and played, and sang on as he had been singing, about a certain elf's valor in battle and courage under torture and the love of a mate named Moonwisp . . . and as his father rushed him he mind-spoke without moving from the place where he sat, **Father. Where is your true courage? Open your soul, find it.**

"Aaaah!" Blade stood over him, spear raised and

spear and spear arm shaking with rage, his tormented face dark and his scar corpse-white with rage.

Hummer looked steadily up into his father's half-crazed face, all the while singing, and the harp sang like a wildcat, a waterfall, a lovestricken woodland bird . . . and Blade threw down the spear, shaking worse than ever, shaking with sobs, and stopped Hummer's music in the only way he well could: by pulling the youngster, harp and all, into his arms. And Hummer laid down the harp and embraced his father.

"Let me see," he said softly.

"What?" Blade's voice, muffled; the elf had hidden his face against his son's shoulder.

"Let me see if it is true or if I dreamed it . . . Look at me, Father."

Another test, Blade thought. Very well. He had made the cub wretched often enough; he could be miserable for once, and honest about it. He lifted his head and braved his son's gaze, knowing what a freak he must look, with his face twisted by his weeping as well as by the scar, the hateful scar, his blasted eyewater turning it glistening, fishbelly white . . .

On Hummer's face, tears as well. But they looked fair as dew on the youngster's smooth, pale face. The cub's dusk-gray eyes, rapt. His voice, when he spoke, hushed, halting, as if he bespoke a mystery.

"I—thought so. I saw—the change. It—it melted in the tears and washed away, it is gone as if it never was." Hummer once again lifted a harper's hand, touched, and Blade felt with an unaccustomed shock and thrill the touch of those long, sensitive fingers above his mouth, felt through their touch the smoothness and newness of his own skin. No scar tissue had ever sensed touch so. Even before he lifted his own hand to his face, he knew.

"Gone," he whispered. "Songshaper, it's gone!"

99

"I can see that," Hummer said with a cub's joyous mockery.

"You young pest, the scar is the least of it. Gone, I am telling you! The dead place in my soul—gone as if it never was! Washed away by your song. Healed."

It was a matter too great and too eerie for much speaking. And both elves felt exhausted, even though the night had not yet neared dawn. In a warm huddle on the ground they fell asleep, pressed against the fur of the two wolves who guarded them. When Hummer awoke, near midday, he found his father missing. But Blade had not gone far away. At the pool below the woodland spring the elf knelt, studying the reflection of his face in the surface of the water.

He gave Hummer a bemused look as the songshaper knelt beside him. "I look like you," he said.

"No, you have that wrong, Father." Hummer flashed him a merry glance. "I look like you."

They drank, then washed, then went back to Hummer's camp and ate dried meat and foragings. At dusk they mounted their wolf-friends and departed, knowing without saying it where they were going.

"There was no need to come after me, you know, Father," Hummer said quietly into the night after a while. "I would have made my way back to the tribe soon enough. I am a Wolfrider; I am nothing without the others. I just needed—a little time apart."

"But there was need for me to find you," Blade said gruffly. "Not for your sake. For mine."

They rode on in silence. Hummer stroked the coarse, gray fur of Moth's neck and watched the moonbeams sheening the grasses, the sky. And Blade watched him, seeing the dreaming look in his son's wide, dark eyes.

"You no longer hum," said Blade. "I—I almost miss it."

The youngster stopped dreaming and grinned at him. "I think not."

"Not entirely," Blade admitted. "Nevertheless . . . I am sorry for the way it left you."

"Never mind. I sing now."

"And I will sing with you, Songshaper."

From that time forth Hummer was called Songshaper, the Wolfriders' first such, and all later songshapers were of his blood. But there were none quite like him again, for his singing could send the listeners to heights of pride and wells of sorrow; singing with his harp he could heal the soul waste or draw tears out of a tree. Many of his songs were passed down for generations of Wolfriders, but no one could sing them as he did. And those howls became legend, the howls when Songshaper sang for the Wolfriders with his father singing by his side.

The Search

by Christine Dewees and C.J. Cherryh

Rain fell steadily outside the Wolfrider's cave, as it had fallen every day between the last blinking of the moons. The ground had already swallowed an elf-high snowpack and refused to swallow anything more. Deep, cold puddles blanketed the clearing in front of the cave; steadily streams dripped down the rock walls. Lovemates complained that their bowers were filling with mud and the wolves' thick fur was spiky with water.

The old ones—those born before Timmorn brought the wolfsong to the tribe—said it had been like this before, but the greater number of Wolfriders couldn't clearly remember a spring that was so miserable. And dangerous. The drinking stream not far from the cave had crested above its bank before the rain started. Oaktree said that now the whole tribe standing side-by-side and holding hands couldn't span the raging torrent.

The beaver dam was long gone, and the beavers too, though they were tough animals and might be somewhere waiting out this miserable weather. Other animals were not so lucky. Pouch-rat and mask-eye carcasses had washed up along the bank. Dampstar said he'd seen a bloated forest-pig whirl by with its legs sticking up like branches, but that was Dampstar and he was not above exaggerating. Still, many of those who lived in the forest had lost their lives as well as their homes this spring.

Spring: the season that should have been full of life and hope and sunshine.

Then the rains slowed to a drizzle. Cubs took instant advantage of the slight improvement in the weather. They darted outside where their playful shrieks were less apt to be rebuked by a short-tempered adult.

"The sky's turned *blue*!" little flame-haired Skyfire announced, racing to the mound of furs where her mother was trying to nap.

Wreath looked up, ready to scold, then—when she saw the bright blue patch beyond her daughter's shoulder—she smiled. The pair joined the others who were edging outside as if to greet a long-wandering friend.

Prey-Pacer, the chief, set his flint knappers aside but did not leave the cave. He went instead to a sheltered niche where Owl sat weaving pine-needles into useless, wondrous shapes. The quiet Wolfrider had seemed a natural choice to replace Samael Dreamkeeper when the old elf had departed on his last journey; if he wasn't a dreamkeeper, he was, at the very least, dreamy.

"There's blue sky overhead," Prey-Pacer said gently to avoid startling the youth. "Do you think that we're through with the rain?"

Owl set his lacy creation on a ledge. Without smiling, nodding or otherwise acknowledging his chief, he went to the entranceway. They called him Owl because he moved so silently, and stayed so still when he wasn't moving, and he stared at things as if he had a special knowledge of them. Now he stared past a rainbow in his wise, owlish way, until even the patient Prey-Pacer felt his fingers start to twitch.

"Well? Shall we celebrate?"

The chief blinked when Owl blinked, and when he opened his eyes the youth was facing him again.

"Too soon," Owl said, heading back to his pine needles. "There's still lots of rain up there."

Prey-Pacer sighed. If Owl said it was going to rain some more, it probably would. The youth didn't have weather magic—not in the sense of being able to influence the weather—but he had a canny knack for predicting it. Many a hunting party had learned the hard way that Owl *knew* about rain or snow.

"I think, then, that we should spend the night with dreamberries," Prey-Pacer said as he followed Owl into the shadows. "Everyone's going to be snappish when it starts up again." Owl nodded without looking up from his intricate handiwork. "And let's strive for something cheerful?"

Owl looked up, blinked slowly—his all-purpose gesture which meant anything from "yes" to "you must be kidding"—then picked up another long, flexible needle. Prey-Pacer could only hope for the best as he joined the rest of the tribe outside the cave. In truth, the Dreamkeeper could only influence the stories and visions that the dreamberries called forth. Even Samael had not been able to control them.

The blue patch lingered, shifting slightly as the afternoon waned but always staying about the same size and directly above the trees opposite the cave. As sundown approached, Prey-Pacer began to hope that for once Owl might have been wrong, but the breeze that sprang up as the blue patch darkened to mauve was heavy with the scent of rain. The chief was not alone in the entranceway as the clouds began to squeeze the patch shut.

"If only I could see a star again," Skyfire whispered wistfully from the ground beside his feet.

Prey-Pacer reached down to ruffle her hair and assure her that the stars would shine again when she jumped up and pointed at the now-violet knothole in the clouds.

"A star! A star! Look everybody!"

The chief's hand fell limply to his side. No ordinary

104

star glistened in the patch of sky. It was large and very bright, yet somehow not as brilliant as the stars. It shed sparks behind it and seemed to tumble through the sky. Breath caught in the tribe's collective throat, fists clenched, and knuckles grew white.

"A sky-mountain . . ." someone gasped. A hoarse chorus affirmed and repeated the notion. A sky-mountain such as their ancestors had riden so catastrophically to this world. It awakened faint memories in the depths of their minds where the dreamberry visions dwelt. Ancient hopes and fears, voiceless and unnameable after all these turns of the seasons, welled up within each of them.

Then, while no one could breathe or take their eyes away, the star burst apart like an old pine tree struck by skyfire. The motes flared as bright as the daystar and were gone. The patch of sky was empty.

Someone began to sob uncontrollably, then another joined in, and another—until the whole tribe was oppressed by a sense of loss. The clouds rolled together to hide the heavens' nakedness. Prey-Pacer felt anguish swell in his throat, and a pressure against the fingers of his hand. He looked down into Skyfire's tear-streaked face.

"It's *gone*," she wailed and buried her face against the chief's thigh.

Prey-Pacer would have picked her up and carried her away to comfort her privately. She was, after all, his daughter. But Wreath, for reasons of her own, had never chosen to acknowledge their Recognition. To the rest of the tribe Skyfire was only Wreath's love-cub: cherished equally by all the adults. The Wolfrider's chief could not single her out without slighting all the others who needed their chief at this moment.

He patted her hair and was prying loose of her arms

when the rain came down in a flood and the forest echoed with a single, sharp boom of thunder.

"Inside," Prey-Pacer told her, giving her a gentle shove in the right direction then turning his attention to the rest of the tribe.

The old ones—the full-blooded elves—seemed physically stunned by what they had witnessed. The chief had to shake Newwolf by her shoulders to get her moving, and he had to shout at Talen to break that elf's trance.

"I could feel them," the elf said as tears gathered in the hollows beneath his eyes. "They seemed so close I thought I could touch them with my mind—"

Talen's voice wavered. He was already drenched to the skin, had begun shivering, but he took no note of his discomfort. Prey-Pacer grasped the old one's arm and guided him out of the rain.

The chief didn't understand. The tribe had endured its share of tragedy—true tragedy: hunting parties that never returned, challenges that turned ugly and sent the loser beyond the horizon forever, children who perished along the path to adulthood. They'd mourned and gone on living, that was the Way. They never stood around numb to the world. And an exploding star wasn't a tragedy. Still, there was no denying or ignoring the grief that had set its roots throughout the tribe, Wolfriders and elves alike.

Dreamberries wouldn't be enough . . .

"I'd like to have a fire," Prey-Pacer said to Marrek, but loudly enough that all within the cave could hear. "A good-sized fire to keep us warm right here where the stone juts out . . ."

It was a request that jolted each Wolfrider out of wolfsong. Fires had been a rare thing since Prey-Pacer's father had departed a long, long time ago. It was an elvish passion; Timmorn's Wolfriders wanted nothing to do with cooked meat or flaring branches, and the Wolfriders dominated the tribe now. But it seemed to the chief that only a fire in front of the cave could undo the effects of the exploding fire in the sky.

Marrek had already gone off in search of tinder, while the other full-blooded elves were looking for wood that might burn. The rest of those who lived in the cave —Wolfriders and first-born—brightened to the thought of being warm and dry again, even if only on one side at a time. Prey-Pacer had guessed right, but then, it was a chief's duty to guess right.

"And dreamberries as soon as the fire's built. To-night's a night for being somewhere else . . ." The chief turned to tell Owl, but the youth was already gone.

It wouldn't be a real howl—not with a bonfire blazing in their midst. The wolves would not join them and neither would some of the Wolfriders. There were a handful, mostly young hunters, who scorned even the softness the cave represented. They dwelt in tree-hollows and improvised lairs except in the depths of winter. The chief's son, Swift-Spear was among their number.

Swift-Spear had a chief's soul, but not a chief's head—or at least not yet. He'd challenge his father someday, if he didn't take his young companions off to their own holt first, but not tonight. He and his friends did make a point of staying well away from the orange-yellow tongues of flame, and that—in a way—made for a more pleasant gathering.

Owl came to the circle last, bearing an age-darkened wood bowl which he carried from one person to the next. Dreamberries were precious at this time of year. They were stored in special skins filled with amber honey and doled out as the ocassion demanded. Every-one was allowed two berries—no more, no less; the chief receiving exactly the same as the youngest cub who had not found his name. But what the bowl lacked in quantity was adaquately replaced by quality.

The berries were sweet and tart at the same time. They filled the mouth with a delightful tingling; they were meant to be savored slowly. Owl took his after everyone else and squatted down to enjoy them while staring into the flames.

Prey-Pacer felt the rich nectar coat his throat with warmth and softness. He swallowed; the feeling spread to his belly and from there to his fingers and toes. He looked out past the flames where the rain still fell steadily. He looked past the rain and the whole of elfin memory hovered before him. The other Wolfriders joined him. Their minds touched as their bodies touched and they waited for the Dreamkeeper who would guide them.

They grew impatient, and finally the chief separated both his selves from the others and looked for the storyteller. Owl hadn't moved—hadn't seemed to breathe, or swallow or blink since putting the berries in his mouth. Prey-Pacer waved his hand in front of the young Wolfrider's eyes; there was no response. He was ready to resort to more drastic measures when, of his own volition but still oblivious to his surroundings, Owl began to talk.

"This is a story of the beginning—"

Prey-Pacer hurried back to his place in the circle. He merged into the not-quite-here, yet not-quite-there world of the storyteller. A sense of the story should have welled up in his thoughts, but instead there was only rainbow formlessness. The chief, like the other Wolfriders, was confused and uneasy. Newwolf reassured them:

This will be a story that has never been told before, the elf sent with considerable excitement.

The chief sighed and was content, if not precisely comforted. It had been such an unusual day that it was almost inevitable that the dreamberries would churn to unmarked depths. He strove to admire the misting colors of memory and bid the wolfsong within him to be still.

The untold story began with images; the Wolfriders were scarcely aware of Owl's occasional words. First and foremost was the dazzling image of the sky-mountain itself. Like the burning star they had seen through the clouds, the sky-mountain trailed fire as it came to the world of two moons. Like the burning star, it vanished into darkness—and then there were the high ones.

The Wolfriders lived not merely in the present, as their bonded wolves did, but in a world where all that could be known was known to all, and where all that could not be known was irrelevant. Even the full-blooded elves possessed little of the trait the five-fingered ones called *awe*. Yet insofar as there was awe—or something which made the individual aware of his or her small size within the vastness of life, time or space—then that feeling was directed toward the high ones. In jest and in solemnity the tribe swore by Timmain, their ancestress and savior, and though no one could put words around what they had felt when the burning star vanished, that, too, owed as much to awe as it did to grief.

So it was not surprising that this—a story about the beginning, about the high ones—did not unfold as other stories did. Owl was the sole and infrequent speaker; no one else sent nuances to enrich the communal vision. No one else could. Owl, himself, faltered as the potent dreamberries led the tribe down an obscure trail.

They found themselves in the dreary final days of a long winter at a camp that was, somehow, less vigorous than their own.

They were hard times, Owl interjected. **The Long Winter was on them.**

The old ones grunted and nodded their heads. **The Long Winter,** they chorused. **It was in the middle of the Long Winter that Timmain became a wolf.** They put forth the image of the Long Winter, with its creeping rivers of ice and its endless vistas of snow, and then they put forth the image of Timmain, the high one.

Timmain was golden in their memory, as she was golden in all the stories the Wolfriders knew, and loved, about her. Her face hovered above the white-shrouded camp. Reflexively the tribe yearned to find peace and serenity in the tableau, and were brutally turned aside. The hollow-eyed men and women of this dreamberry tale were not high ones but merely tall.

Owl cleared his throat and spoke hesitantly, using words that had long been forgotten by the tribe: *malaise*, *alienation*, *negritude*, and *anomie*. The Wolfriders, young and old, heard the sounds and understood them only as they described the dreamberry tableau. In their own minds the words were simpler: *waiting-for-death*.

Prey-Pacer struggled to free himself and his tribe from the morbid vision, but he was thoroughly caught in its oozing web. Rescue came from Swift-Spear and his boon companion, Graywolf.

The wolves are sick!

So they did not shake off the aura of the dreamberries, but carried it with them. They moved like bears after their winter sleep, and they seemed more interested in what had happened that in what was happening. The young men flexed their hands into impatient fists.

"The cubs are dead or dying!" Swift-Spear shouted at his father.

Prey-Pacer rose unsteadily to his feet. The wood stank and hissed where drips from the overhang touched it. They'd forgotten much about building a fire. There was more smoke than light and he had trouble seeing the faces of his tribe. Owl was there, still staring fixedly at the scarlet embers, and Drum—but where was Skyfire?

"It was a dream," he protested. "A dreamberry tale! They can't die."

With a feral growl rumbling in his throat, Swift-Spear strode into the fire circle. He thrust his arms forward and held a dark, shapeless thing before the chief's face.

"The *wolf* cubs, my chief!" Swift-Spear's voice was deep and dangerous: challenging.

Nostrils flared and lips parted as the Wolfriders tasted the air, confirming that death rode in Swift-Spear's arms. Prey-Pacer sent his thoughts away from the fire to the forest and the mind of his wolf, Snoweater. The young male scarcely responded to his sending so consumed was he by the presence of wolf-death.

Why? Prey-Pacer sent, unaware that his despair went far beyond Snoweater's mind.

The Wolfriders got to their feet slowly, their minds distracted by contact with their wolves. The animals seldom came to the cave, and with the long rains many had not seen their wolf-friends for several days.

"Why didn't they tell us?" Mist cried, and shared the knowledge that her wolf was dying. She disappeared into the rain, with only the sound of her wails to say which way she'd gone.

"Why didn't you listen?" Swift-Spear accused those who remained.

Prey-Pacer had no choice; he surged forward, locking stares and minds with his son. Anger, not intelligence or even knowledge, drove Swift-Spear's tongue, but it was challenge just the same, and at this delicate moment Prey-Pacer could not let it go unanswered. He battered at his son's sense-of-self, summoning the sense-of-chief he so seldom felt himself. The effort took all Prey-Pacer's strength, one day it would not be enough, but tonight it was. Swift-Spear's head and shoulders slumped forward.

Graywolf's eyes went wide and brilliant amber in the firelight. The old ones, the elves, had called him "Hunt" when he was born, and turned away from him. And the young man was a hunter, but of the wolfish kind. He ran free and wild, with only Swift-Spear to call a companion. And now Swift-Spear was trembling. He glanced at Owl, his twin who had gotten all the elfinness he seemed to lack, but Owl—who had no wolf—was still dreaming his story.

He tugged on his one friend's sleeve. "Swift-Spear, you must tell them!" But Swift-Spear was rapt in his humiliation.

Prey-Pacer took the dead cub from his son and laid it in Graywolf's arms. "You tell us, Graywolf," the chief said as gently as he could.

No sounds came from Graywolf's mouth, nor thoughts from his mind. Prey-Pacer reached out to reassure the young man. Graywolf shrank back and Prey-Pacer thought better of the notion. The chief reached out for Snoweater, but again his wolf did not respond. Taking a spear from the pile beside the cave mouth, Prey-Pacer followed Mist into the night.

Rain made the forest too dark for even a Wolfrider's comfort. Despite the urgency of his mission, Prey-Pacer was forced to walk slowly. He felt his way around cold, slimy tree trunks, trying to hold onto the faint thought-echo he felt in Snoweater's mind. At last he reached the rocks where the pack laired. He could smell them and feel the heat of their bodies, but there was nothing in his mind to say that these were the tribe's wolves and not some wild pack.

He found Snoweater's smell and followed it. There was a black mound that had Snoweater's shape and scent, but when Prey-Pacer approached with open mind and arms, the wolf lurched at him with a snarl.

They did not tell us because they do not know us! Mist's despair filled his mind. She came cautiously toward him through the rain; there was blood-smell about her. **Darkwater does not know me!**

The wolves were not so vital as the Wolfriders. They lived their lives more quickly and were prey to illnesses which did not plague their riders. The rump end of winter, when the snows were gone but the trees were still bare and the game animals had not yet brought forth their young, was the worst time for the wolves. Every year a few died, or were driven away from the pack and lost to their elf-friends. That was the Way, and no Wolfrider would interfere, but this was different. The whole pack was mind-lost to the tribe, cubs had already died and sickness was heavy in the air despite the rain.

Prey-Pacer summoned his strength again and blanketed Snoweater with his sense-of-self. The brindle wolf snarled; he bent his neck in submission. Then, finally, he relaxed and knew his elf-friend. Snoweater opened his mind and shared his agony with the friend he had forgotten. Prey-Pacer fell to his knees.

The sickness had begun with a pain in the belly that made standing impossible. Wolf instinct was to vomit the vileness out, but the sickness was too deep and retching had brought weakness, not relief. Some of them had gone to the water, and they were the ones in the worst condition, like Darkwater and the other females who had passed the sickness quickly to their cubs. Instinct had failed them, and they were ready to die.

Prey-Pacer lifted Snoweater's head onto his thighs and sheltered the exhausted beast from the cold rain's steady miseries. Snoweater whined and thrust his muzzle weakly along Prey-Pacer's arm. The bond between them was renewed, the wolf was content, but the Wolfrider chief demanded more.

He doubled over until his forehead rested against Snoweater's ear—as if bringing their minds physically closer would strengthen their sendings. Then, though he was no healer, he sought knowledge of the sickness and its cure. Snoweater began to tremble; Prey-Pacer stroked the soft fur beneath the wolf's jaw but did not slacken his quest.

He became enmeshed in the true wolfsong: a step beyond place and time where wolfish thoughts swirled in an endless circle. His question could not be asked within this wolfsong, nor could it be answered, then his mouth was filled with the taste of sour-bark leaves.

Were time and place different, the pack would have sought out the sour-bark tree and gorged themselves on its leaves. But the nearest sour-bark was too far away for the weakened animals, and there were no leaves at this season anyway. So wolfsong prepared them for death. Snoweater struggled free and crawled away.

"Did you learn anything?" Talen asked.

Prey-Pacer realized that the tribe had followed him to the lair. They'd stood in the rain while he'd delved into the wolfsong—even the full elves who could not share their thoughts with the pack.

"They are sick, and dying, and we can do nothing to help them."

The other Wolfriders—some beside their wolves, others still held at bay—met his mind with mourning sadness.

"There is nothing to even make them more comfortable?" Talen did not come any closer, but there was no mistaking the compassion in his voice.

"I have searched with Snoweater. He would seek the leaves of the sour-bark tree, if he could. I think . . . he thinks they would help, but there are no sour-bark leaves."

Someone stumbled forward in the darkness. "They won't need the leaves!" Willowgreen said with a gasp as she tripped over something and fell onto Prey-Pacer's shoulder.

The old ones were no good in the dark. They didn't have night eyes, and they never learned how to see with their other senses. Prey-Pacer was displeased that Willowgreen had left the cave; he was annoyed past anger that she would gainsay the wolfsong.

"If we get the bark, I can mash it and heat it in water until the water has the flavor and strength of the bark. Then the wolves can drink it. It will work better than leaves—"

She was clinging to his shoulders, still awkward on the mud-slicked ground. Prey-Pacer was half of a mind to send her and all the other elves back to the cave, but he said instead: "You have never tried healing the wolves before. Why now?"

His tone hurt her. **Because of the others,** she sent, conveying with the thought the memory of the burning star and the sad-looking elves of the dreamberry story.

"We've got to let her try!" Graywolf shouted, his love of the wolves overcoming his deep-seated distrust of Willowgreen and her kind.

Prey-pacer frowned and turned away, stood with his arms locked together and his senses folded in on himself. He had never had overmuch dealing with this elf—with young Graywolf—whose strangeness melded very much with his own son's. Graywolf was an accident, a thing too much elf and too much wolf at the same time to be acceptable to either: yellow-eyed and bridle-haired elf with teeth disquietingly different. That part of him Prey-pacer could tolerate. It was the inner contact

115

that turned up the real differences, the wolvish-elvish mix that was just a shade crazy, just a shade unstable —*loner,* his senses always said. A loner-wolf was an unhealthy one: not part of the pack. Pack-leader should kill it, be rid of it, at least drive it away. . . .

But being elf and not wolf, he did not. And it attached itself to his son and made him strange. . . .

If his son should take the pack, this halfling—would be pack-second. And even if, in the way of things, *he* would not see that day—he did not like the thought.

And Willowgreen—afraid of the wolves, afraid of the wolfriders, afraid of everything—sent that child off to the woods and likely she would not come back. One more life lost. . . .

But not to try—

Graywolf had said it.

For the *wolves,* Graywolf had said it, who loved nothing human; and the softhanded healer had said it, who had no love of the wolves.

For himself, Prey-pacer said it, who had no love of either Graywolf or Willowgreen; but being their chief he did not send it; he smothered it and sent instead, without even looking their way. **Graywolf. Bring the things she wants.**

He got no organized sending back. A flood of tears and fear from Willowgreen: of all the wolfriders Graywolf was the one she trusted least; a cold dismay from Graywolf, a recollection of the floods.

A cold sense that his chief might well be rid of a boy he had never liked. But Graywolf consented, a simple **Yes,** and a desperation. His wolf was among the sick. Prey-pacer had not picked that up before. Goldeye was coughing, the first hints of what had spread among the pack; and even if Goldeye had been hale and strong, the wolf would have been no help in this. Graywolf only worried that Goldeye would lose heart without him. But he had spoken on impulse; and Prey-pacer had chosen him—and overthrown Swift Spear, who might have helped him.

Very quietly, very deep beneath it all, a wolfish sense of suspicion—**You'd be glad to be rid of me . . . to rob your son of help. . . .**

But that was not supposed to come to the surface. It was in Graywolf's distress and his own, so closely matching Graywolf's that he caught without either of them intending it; and having read what he was not supposed to have read, he was embarrassed, and no little put off his balance.

You are wrong, he sent privately. **Name who will go with you. Or *I* will go instead.**

No. Graywolf's sending was equally tinged with embarrassment and hurt pride. **I will bring back what she wants. I want no help.**

Regret, Prey-pacer sent, only the feeling. But he got nothing but hurt feelings back from Graywolf, who turned and left, splashing through the mud and the sudden spate of rain.

In the edge of his sight, Willowgreen, who put her hands on Snoweater. He felt his wolf-friend's anger, felt the threat and sent it:

Leave him alone. Go back to the cave. And thought to himself: *Useless as a healer.*

Everything is useless.

He saw Willowgreen's face pale and drenched in the flicker of lightnings, saw the hurt in her eyes. Perhaps the battle with his son had opened his sendings too wide. Perhaps it was just that Willowgreen took his simple order amiss. He saw her break into angry tears, and leap up and run.

Perhaps he should order someone after her, to be sure she got back safely. But he was a grieving wolf-rider among other grieving pairs, sure that, however well-meant, no half-thought idea of a young elf was going to avail anything, and that Graywolf's prideful bravery was wasted—a waste, perhaps, of a life as well, in the flooded riverside, in the dark—because a young fool of a healer had intervened with creatures she neither understood nor ever cared for. . . .

That was what offended him.

Perhaps it was the fight with his son. Perhaps it was that, after all, they grew more and more wolflike, and more pragmatic and more fatalistic. Disease came. Death came. Some were going to die. Like Snoweater, he wanted to be let alone, and wanted no high ones' gentleness and no outcast's help, and no flank attacks from his unruly son.

So the rest of the wolf-riders, who separated quietly and went where they were needed, in quiet, feral and fatalistic as their wolf-friends.

Something was wounded and desperate. Graywolf smelled it in the rain-soaked air or heard it in his too-quickened mind: he was not sure. But it was a hurt of the mind and the heart and it was anger too: he smelled that or he felt it, and knew by the feel of the mind it was elf and it was tracking him.

So he threw back at it a **Who are you?** and stopped cold when he got the full flavor of the sending.

What's the matter? he asked, thinking perhaps there was something urgent Willowgreen had forgotten to tell him. **What more do you want?**

He received nothing of sense. Only the anger, and a feeling so keen and so sharp and painful he winced—but the elves closest to high ones had that about them . . . powerful, sometimes too powerful when they were distraught; and he felt that in the Healer and waited.

Peace, he sent to her, and got back **anxiety** and **mistrust.**

Which was always the way of things.

So he closed off the deeper levels, waited in the shelter of an old tree.

She found him, following his Presence to that same tree—arrived soaked and pale and panting from her run. **Prey-pacer,** was part of her sending; **useless** and **anger** were the unintentional thoughts she spilled. And **wolfling, no friend of mine.**

"I'm going with you," she said, and there was silence where the spillage had been. Her clothes were torn. So was her skin. The forest itself resisted her.

The Healer—wanted to do her own herb-gathering. Graywolf stared at her in the lightning-flicker and thought, baffled, that it might be a healer-matter. Or simply that she trusted him no more than Prey-pacer did, and that her honor would be affronted if he failed to come back and if wolves died for her failure to see to the matter. That was no matter to him. But the wolves were, and it made sense to him that a Healer might know what she wanted and how she wanted it.

Besides, she was half a high one herself, and no one's effort was good enough for that breed, not even Prey-pacer's.

So he nodded, and waved a hand toward the way ahead, lowering his head, because he was tired, he ached from the cold, he wanted no fight with her. He had not the strength to spend on it, if there was the river ahead.

And of all elves who disliked him, the high ones were chiefest.

Abomination, they called him.

He called her Healer, and showed respect, because that was the Way things were.

The water had a voice in the dark. It said Death, and Cold, and Force, and when they came down from the heights it spoke louder, a sound that sharp elvish hearing could not precisely hear as sound, but a rumbling that might be the whisper of the forest or the constant thunder or the earth echoing it.

It's the River grinding stones in its belly, Willowgreen sent. It was too loud. A voice lost itself in the constant noise.

And Graywolf saw the thing with a shiver in his bones and a reckoning that for pride's sake he had undertaken something more than any elf could do.

They might do it, he thought, if they took days and days and walked down to the lowland where willows were abundant on *this* side of the river. But here—

He did not ask Willowgreen what to do. There was no time to spend going downland. There was no choice. He simply started walking numbly down the tree-covered slope, and, perceiving Willowgreen stumbling again, reached out without thinking and gave his hand.

We can't cross that! she said.

We can't cross anywhere else, he sent back. He showed her his memory of a trail, on sunnier days. It was what they were following, except the rains had made it muddy and treacherous, and the wind had blown down branches to hamper their passage. He showed her his memory of a way down from the cliffs, where he remembered the willows on the other side. And perhaps with that came his understanding that she could never cross it; or perhaps it came from her. He had difficulty, tonight, sorting anything out. He only went because he had to, because without him his wolf-friend was dying; and he had not sent to tell him where he was going or why he had deserted him.

But Goldeye would have dragged himself along the trail to follow him. He knew that.

And Willowgreen never could. Never could feel that bond. He did not understand her. But he thought: *Maybe pride is enough for her*, because that was mostly what he knew of the high ones and their ilk.

She stumbled again, over a tree root or some such thing. He supported her patiently, thinking, in a numb haze: *Fool.*

But the noise was more and more, and he saw the water now—the very cliffs were ripped further back, trees fallen into that boil.

"High ones," he murmured, who had the evidence of *their* helplessness on his right arm. "Stay here," he said, and sent.

And let her go and heard her call after him: "Graywolf!"

He looked back. **You can't cross this,** he sent. Not hurtfully. Not to argue. It was only plain fact. He wondered if the willows of the far shore had even survived, or if they had been torn up and carried away, old giants that they were.

Wait! she sent, *sent,* with a force that shook him; and of a sudden he *knew* what the Healer knew—

—knew the unwholesomeness in himself, like that in the wolves, knew the Healer's concern for him, impersonal and cold as the river, knew the sources in the rain-washed plants at his feet and all about him, like lights that did not shine, but they were *there*, ineffectual against the death that was in the wolves—

—that was in *him*—

He staggered on the slope, caught his balance in the mud and the rain, and understood that he was more than weary, that he had felt it for days and thought it was the cold, the lack of food, the hardships of the storm. It was the way it had come on the wolves—them never understanding, wolf-like, that their strength was ebbing and their faculties were fading—

One just died, that was all, bewildered by the matter—

Except she took that from him and showed him his weakness.

Why? he asked her, offended. The tribe hated

121

him. But none of his enemies had pursued him so far. Prey-pacer had given him the chance he had believed in—

Willowgreen had never loved the wolves. She was their enemy. Kill the wolves and the way of the high ones survives—

—till the elves die—

Hate you? her sending came, with a shudder. **Fool. Look, look, I cannot hold this—**

There was health by the riverside, a glow in the mind, not the dark—

He *felt* it—the health that could save him: he knew its direction in the night, perceived it as clearly as he knew the difference between sky and earth—not that it shone brightly, not that it shone at all. Only by her touch at his mind he knew what would save him and save the wolves. . . .

And he knew where it was.

He went, stumbling on the slope, sliding in the mud, sitting down and using his hands to stop himself until he could rise up and walk a space.

But *it* was there, continually, *it* was there in the dark; and he knew it.

He heard the water singing, louder and louder. There were other things than elves that lived there. There were creatures that survived in that dreadful place. There were things fouler than trolls—that would like to lay hands on an elf.

He slipped. It was toward the *wholeness*. That was why he fought so little; and he felt betrayed when he shot out over empty space and plummeted into the water—

Willowgreen! he called out, pragmatic, because he was dying, and she should know, if there was any good and any help in her. **Find it!**

Because he could not.

But he saw the *wholeness* then, not with his eyes, but

122

with the sickness in him . . . saw it looming ahead of him like a wall in the flood.

He felt a bruising force. He might have died then, except he heard the voice saying, **I need you. The wolves will die. Answer me.**

So he did. He fought to find the air again. He clung to the old willow the flood had torn up and thrown crosswise to the current. He saw himself through her eyes, and he knew that the small figure clinging to the forest giant was himself. It was through her eyes he saw himself draw his dagger and fight his way to air, where the flood poured over the trunk of a willow old as the forest—

He touched the wholeness. It was there under his hands. He drew his dagger and hacked away at the trunk, understanding—he understood as if other hands were directing his, that it was the inner bark he sought. That it was life he was holding to, and that the arm which was going numb had to hold, and somehow he had to use the tree for a bridge to shore.

He *saw* where to hold. He knew where the branches were, and he was beyond pain. He just held on, and crawled, clinging to branches that stabbed, battered by cold water until he had no feeling in his limbs—it was vision which guided him, when he had none, and he crawled out past an agony of branches until he was in shallow water. . . .

Come *on!* she sent, pulling at him with her mind, and finally with her hands, her grip slipping on wet, chilled flesh. ***Move!***

Image of dying wolves. She felt the feeble surge of determination in him, that moved him to the shore.

He hated the water. He *hated* it. He wanted to die on land.

It was what she used, the way she had used his

sickness to find the cure, the way she had known, standing in the band of wolfriders—first that he was afflicted, and then that Healer-sense could use that affliction.

—Healer-sense. The half-wolf had the taint: the healer saw the cure.

He was useless now. He was a hindrance to her. She could take what he had gathered and go back to the tribe, save the wolves, win her place.

But she took hold of more than what Graywolf tried to offer her: she pulled the half-elf with all the strength she had, and when he was on the shore, in the mud, sat and cried, for reasons she did not understand.

Finally she moved and shook at Graywolf and sent:

It's no good if it doesn't get back. What a shame —to have won—and to lose. . . .

He moved. The effort hurt her heart, it cost so much.

But there was no gentleness that would serve between them. There was no love, nor even liking.

He moved because his wolf-brothers were threatened. Because the Way of the wolf-riders was threatened. There was not enough elf left in him to worry about his own death—only about the pack.

And Swift Spear—

—not-wolf and friend.

She felt more than she wanted of Graywolf, sitting there on that bank, in the misting rain. **Move,** she sent to him. **Move. Lives are at stake. Everything is—**

And she felt more than she wanted of Graywolf's heart, when he thought of his wolf-friend and his elf-friend, and when, driven by something more than a Healer's skill, Graywolf stirred.

Chew the bark, she said, stripping out the soft inner lining of the willow. It was talismanic: her namesake, willow. And she was half-afraid of him, sick as she was, as afraid as she was of the wolves, and loath to touch his mind and his motives that deeply. **Do what I tell you. . . .** And hard upon that, in anger and fear: ***I can't travel the forest! Not alone! I need you!***

It was with the most extreme effort that he kept his feet. He was not sure that he was walking in the right direction, except he *felt* the unhealth that matched his own. He felt the loathing too, of the elf who thrust her slight strength under his arm and pulled at him when he faltered, saying with her mind: **Keep going! Keep going! Don't sit down, I can't lift you!**

Can't and can't and can't was this elf's whole attitude —except where it involved her pride, and *that* was tangled up in her healing-gift. A self-important elf, blood of the high ones, proud of her heritage and proud of her gift, and despising the wolves and the wolf-riders —despising *him*, most of all. That he had spoken for her offended her. That she saw him likely to fail and to humiliate her in Prey-pacer's eyes—that had driven her to him in the woods; and it was a concept of humiliation so strange to him—as if death in her presence was a deliberate affront to her sanctity—

It was a high one whose mind touched him and drove him and held him. Willowgreen used him for a spell to find the tree; she used him now for a spell against the woods; and she relied on him because she feared him —and knew him harmless to her—and feared the forest more than she feared him.

Mad, he thought. Other elves shied from intimacy with *his* thoughts, and accepted *her*. He did not understand. He was offended, himself; and resentful that she wrung so much pain from him, even if he was grateful that she was there to keep him on his feet—he was half-crazed himself, and knew nothing except the pain in his legs and the blur of branches and the constant need to climb and struggle on the muddy slopes.

He knew finally the presence of other elves —Wolfriders. He was falling, and expected no help, but someone caught him. **Goldeye,** he sent, feeling the wolves in the woods round about.

He felt the answer. He lay still for a moment, then thought that he might have the strength to get to Goldeye, because his wolf was too weak to get to him.

But elves around him sensed what he wanted and took him there. It was the only kindness he wanted. He lay down with his wolf and slept until someone brought Goldeye a potion to drink. Goldeye refused, but he insisted, so his wolf-friend drank. They gave him a leaf-cup of it too, and he realized then it was Swift Spear who had brought it.

Better, he thought. He wanted nothing to do with the rest of them. He settled down with Swift Spear by him and slept.

The sun was out, finally. Wolves basked in the warmth, cubs rolled and romped. The wind that chased the clouds brought warm air, and the first breath of spring was on the forest, when the new growth would begin to hide the scars of winter flood.

Prey-pacer watched the changes. Watched them in his son, the sullen thoughtfulness that came of failed ambitions; in his daughter, growing rowdy and tending to challenge her year-mates for room.

The halfling never changed. Graywolf was silent as ever, turning away the tribe's tokens of gratitude. So he got what he chose to have, and perhaps did not care. The line between elf and wolf in him was strange, and sometimes what resulted was alien to both.

Perhaps Willowgreen should have enjoyed more

warmth than she got. But she hated the wolves. She made her tonics and her potions and her medicines that saved them, and could not speak to the wolves and jumped in fear when jaws snapped or a growl warned her of offended dignity. The Wolfriders could never love a Healer like that, even though they wanted to. She was Old One, and she distrusted them. Everything she did was because of that: her chief was a Wolfrider and she wanted a place for herself and she wanted honor. Preypacer had lived enough centuries and seen enough of her breed to know that kind of mind, and to avoid it when he could.

Even if it had saved them.

Graywolf was the one he regretted. But there was always the unwholesomeness about him, of a kind of wolf and a kind of elf he knew—the over-the-edge ones. And he wished that he could drive him away from his son.

It would seem mean-spirited to do that—now. He could not even justify it to himself. And he tried, High Ones, he tried, to be just.

So he existed with things-as-they-were, even if it would have been wiser to take the wolf's solution—and kill the odd one. That would have been better done —long ago, before there was a grown mind to contend with, before the halfling attached to his son and sought too high a place.

No one had chosen that situation. Not even the halfling.

He recollected the star that fell. It seemed ominous, Owl's dream-speaking. Perhaps it was the sense that the spring was only beginning and there might be more storms, more of winter. Maybe that was what the star foretold.

But it seemed to set a mark on all these things—the plague, the dream, the rivalries and the rescue. And the quarrel with his son and with the halfling and with the Healer. Sometimes an elf nearing the end of his days —saw over the edge, into time to come.

That was the shape of his dread.

As if—by injustice he could right a wrong before it happened.

But that was not the kind of mark he wanted to leave on the tribe either. The very act would change them—if he did murder, or if he even banished the halfling. *And* his son. That act would become precedent as vile as the things he feared for them.

It was the way of foreknowledge. One *knew*. But there was no way to use that knowledge. Every path led the same from here.

Every one.

Genesis

by Richard Pini, Lynn Abbey
and Marcus Leahy

The forest surrounded Two-Spear with its sounds and scents, its movement and temperature. Each breath evoked in him life's ever-fresh sense of adventure. The air was alive with the sweet scent of the kill and the pack's howl of satisfaction. It was the world; it was the *now;* it was wolfsong.

The pack was large now, with many wolves and Wolfriders running behind him, following his cries. Two-Spear grew strong on the vitality of his tribe. His half-sister, Skyfire, rode her wolf as if she could dance upon its back. Graywolf clapped strong legs around his wolf, laughed, and raced against the wind. It had been a good chase, a clean kill, and Two-Spear was content.

Through his hunting leathers, Two-Spear felt his wolf-friend's rippling muscles and the pounding of his great heart. No-name was the fiercest of the wolves, and he ran as if he would challenge the forest, the sky, and the daystar itself. Though No-name was Two-Spear's wolf-friend, the wolf had always been mysterious and unlike the other wolves. There was no real love between the bond-mates, just wary respect and the certain knowledge that they needed, and were right for, each other. Each believed that he was the strongest of his kind, tolerated no defiance—but only Two-Spear was a chief.

No-name was an outcast, whose presence the other wolves endured for the sake of their elf-friends.

The air got cooler as the dawn grew closer. Two-Spear brought the Wolfriders' exuberant race to a halt. Some wolves and Wolfriders flopped to the ground, their sides heaving. Two-Spear waved three of the younger Wolfriders ahead to scout a clearing where they could rest through the day. He leaned against No-name's shoulder, their sweat and musk becoming a blended, tart perfume. The wolf nuzzled Two-Spear's wrist, and the chief scratched behind No-name's ears.

There was no thought or consciousness, just action and emotion. Each moment came as easy as breath, as welcome as clear-running water. It was wolfsong, and the Wolfriders had basked in its innocence for three generations since Timmorn had formed their tribe.

Silence was broken by a fear-tinged sending from the young scouts. Two-Spear sniffed the air, and found no cause for alarm, but the scouts' fear was genuine. He sprang onto No-name's back and set off to help them. The chief found his young scouts in a stream-pierced glade that seemed perfect for their day's rest. But the trio had not noticed his approach; they were transfixed by something on the ground between them.

Two-Spear slid from his wolf and joined their small circle. A moon-shaped, moon-colored object reflected the dawnlight. He knelt down to examine it more closely and, though it was half-buried in the stream-bank, a low growl rose from the back of his throat. Two-Spear didn't have to touch the ivory object to know what it was. It was the skull of his enemy, the skull of a human.

No-name pushed forward and nosed at the skull. It rolled free to reveal a gaping hole in its underside. No-name whined, and slunk away. The five-fingered hunter had met its death by violence. Perhaps it had fallen against the rocks, or perhaps it had been killed. Humans could be killed; Two-Spear himself had proved that.

The Wolfrider chief looked up at the scouts. He saw fear and awe on their faces. They had not been born when Swift-Spear became Two-Spear and savaged the five-fingers' village, but they had remembered his deeds when the dreamberry bowl was passed. He had led the Wolfriders then, and these three expected him to lead now. Two-Spear got to his feet.

This is a good sign, he assured the scouts, and those Wolfriders who had remained behind resting with their wolves. **A place where the five-fingered ones have died is a place where we may rest in safety.**

The scouts relaxed and the remaining Wolfriders came to the glade. The kill was gutted and shared. Yet the feast that night was not as sweet to Two-Spear as the many before. They were near the edge of their hunting range; the air was thick with strange scents. It was time for the hunters to return to the rest of the tribe. They had been gone—

Two-Spear was uncomfortably surprised to realize that he could not reckon how long they had been gone. Time bothered him. He lived each day to the fullest, but they swiftly blended into the liquid past of wolfsong. Had it been a moon-dance? Or had it been a hand of dances? He struggled to grasp time's movement through his life and recalled the bush that grew outside the lair he shared with Willowgreen. It had just put forth leaves that were the same color as her willow-green eyes. The leaves above him were dark green now, so it had been a season, more or less. Spring had become summer, and, though Willowgreen was his lifemate, the chief had not thought of her since she'd stood beside that bush and said good-bye.

She was pleasant in his mind now. Two-Spear smiled at her image and settled down to sleep. No-name came to curl beside him. The great wolf was shivering slightly; his fur was stiff and raised. The Wolfrider sent comforting thoughts, hoping to calm him, then drew his thoughts back. Wolf-thoughts were rarely clear, but No-name's had always been filled with his fierce, aggressive identity. Tonight the wolf was disquieted; his mind was tinged with dread.

Two-Spear threw an arm around the wolf and saw what the beast saw: his eyes focused on the crushed, bleached skull. Hunkered at wolf height, surrounded by wolf-thought, the skull was more than the sad relic of a dead enemy. It was an omen, a warning that said the next trail would be dangerous.

The chief and his wolf-friend were the only ones who noticed the skull now. The other Wolfriders seemed to have forgotten it, and the fear it had initially inspired. Except Graywolf, and he thought about the bones only indirectly, for he noticed the miasma of dark, troubled thoughts swirling around Skyfire. Two-Spear's greatest triumph, his vanquishing of the human village, had been her moment of greatest shame. The pair did not, could not, agree about the five-fingered menace. Skyfire would never agree that the Wolfriders might know safety in a place where elf or human had died.

Huntress Skyfire met Graywolf's stare, then looked away. As it happened, Graywolf was right; she was thinking about Two-Spear. And she was, like her brother, thinking about time. The passage of time was not an elusive mystery for her. Each day was different, true, but life itself was not expected to change. Skyfire remembered what she needed, forgot what was unnecessary or ill-fitting, and relied upon the dreamberry bowl to keep the Wolfrider heritage alive in her mind. The past was, indeed, liquid, like clear water; no matter how deep it got, it did not obscure the bottom, unchanging truths of a Wolfrider's life.

The red-haired Wolfrider knew her brother's world was not so well ordered as her own. Two-Spear brooded; he became mired in his worries. Skyfire could not understand what caused the clear waters of her brother's memory to become clouded, but she had learned to predict when it would happen. Whenever a tribe-mate died, whenever a human relic was found along the path, and especially when death and the five-fingered ones merged, Two-Spear became as one trapped in a nightmare. Except he lived the nightmare, and it seemed to her that he lured the whole tribe behind him.

She glanced back over her shoulder and saw that Graywolf was still watching her. She repressed a sigh; that one was even harder to understand than her brother. She looked around for Oaktree, who would gladly lair with her, but Oaktree wasn't alone. Skyfire settled against her wolf, much as Two-Spear did, and tried to get some rest.

Two-Spear looked up at shadowed beings that were taller than anything he'd seen before. They flickered in unnatural red light; they seemed made of stone, or harsher substances. Lightning erupted from their hands and their eyes burned with a lust for death. They were not silent, but shouted as the ground gave way beneath their feet.

Within his nightmare, Two-Spear tried to run, to hide, though his tribe-mates moved forward without him to confront the death shadows. But he could not run; he was surrounded by a sea of stone that hemmed him in and pushed him forward to join the others.

Two-Spear writhed. *This is not real, not happening*, he

thought. *It is a dream!* He knew it was true, but his fears would not leave him for, though, it was a dream, it was not *his* dream. He could not will himself awake from it.

The shadows marched relentlessly. The Wolfriders fought as only the desperate could. Shadows fell, but others rose quickly to take their place, and nothing rose to replace the fallen Wolfriders. Then skyfire fell upon Two-Spear himself and he howled with his fear. Crying in pain, he raced through the stones and leapt behind the shadows, beyond the dying elves. He threw himself into the abyss, and he fell knowing he might never hit the ground, might never awaken to hunt again. His howls went beyond the dream.

Two-Spear's cries woke the whole camp, but not No-name who thrashed in unison beside him. Only Graywolf dared to move past the wolf to wake his chief. Two-Spear started at his friend's touch. He groped for his second spear, his man-hunting spear. The camp fell silent, except for his labored breathing. For a moment Two-Spear glared at the other Wolfriders, then he straightened, smiled, and cocked his head to one side.

Even chiefs have nightmares, he joked.

The Wolfriders laughed weakly and Two-Spear ignored their nervousness. He also ignored Graywolf's concern and Skyfire's lock-sent demand for an explanation. But he did not sleep again before nightfall, and as the Mother moon rose, he began the journey back to the tribe.

It took a blinking of the moons to get back to the tribe's settlement. Two-Spear pushed the wolves and the Wolfriders remorselessly. The image of the human skull haunted his mind's eye and left him no peace. He wanted to see his lifemate again, to bury himself in her arms, before he confronted the omen's meaning.

Home for Two-Spear's tribe was a pleasant glade, deep

in the forest where five-toed feet had never walked. Home was where the elves without wolf-blood, an equal number of Wolfriders, and their children waited while the season's hunters prowled the woods. Animal-hide tents clustered around a spring-fed pool on one side of the glade. Drying racks exposed fresh hides and dried fish to the daystar. The tribe prepared for the winter even though summer was at its height.

The hunters sent greetings to their friends, families, and lovers well before the wolves bounded into the glade. Everyone had set aside their usual tasks to welcome their return. Two-Spear leaped from No-name's back straight into Willowgreen's arms. He laughed as her hair fell around his shoulders and, for a moment, they were the only two in the glade.

That moment vanished. He was the chief, after all, and it was only natural that everyone had something to say to him—even those who had ridden with him all season. With his arm still around Willowgreen, Two-Spear waded through the crowd toward the eldest of the tribe: the pure-blooded elves who remembered a time before the Wolfriders.

"Talen, I'm glad to see you," he said, causing the others to fall back just a little. "You're looking well." The chief's voice lifted at the end; the true-elves never changed.

"Well enough," came the gentle answer. "Our home has been peaceful all season, Two-Spear."

Two-Spear relaxed and smiled sincerely, but before he could reply another of the old ones stepped in front of him.

"Well enough, but no thanks to you." Rellah's condescending voice shattered the chief's homecoming. "Once again you come back well fed and nearly empty-handed. Perhaps we should be grateful that you take your hunters away so this empty part of the forest does not have to feed them. It was four dances this time. How long will it be next? Six? Eight? A turn? How long before we should worry about you? How long before you forget about us completely?"

Two-Spear's smile faded. "I thought I was doing you a favor." It wasn't true, not in the least, but it shut her up, and that was all that mattered. Rellah was a thorn in his side that could not be removed. His fingers dug hard into Willowgreen's side and he pulled her away.

"But you were gone much longer than you promised," Willowgreen said gently. "We had all begun to worry. *I* had begun to worry about you."

"You should never worry about me," he replied. "What could happen to me?"

His lifemate looked away. Two-Spear was entirely serious; the only answer he could tolerate was "nothing," and Willowgreen could not lie to him.

But Two-Spear took her silence for agreement. "Besides," he continued, "it didn't seem that we were gone all that long."

Willowgreen bit her lip. *How long has he been like this. He is at peace only when he is lost in wolfsong.* She had turned to him for his strength and intensity, she who was among the most timid of the old ones. They had balanced each other at first, and she'd hoped there would be real sharing after he'd vanquished the human village. Instead, each long turn of the seasons had taken him further away from her, from the elves—even from the Wolfriders. Only Graywolf seemed to understand him, and no one understood Graywolf.

"Come, there is something I'd like to show you," she said, hoping the invitation did not sound forced. He said nothing, but followed her to the far side of the pond. "Well, what do you think?"

"It's very pretty," he said, looking out at the blue-green water.

Willowgreen swallowed her disappointment. "No, here . . . right here, at your feet."

Two-Spear stared at the ground, then looked at her, raising one eyebrow.

"The plants," her voice rose in exasperation. "What do you think of the plants?"

Again he looked down. Now he could see that the area had been scraped clear and that vining plants had sprouted in unnaturally even patterns. Here and there along the vine stems were fist-sized sickly green balls. "Yes, very pretty," he said, with no real attempt to conceal his disinterest.

"Two-Spear," Willowgreen shouted. "I *made* them grow here! I took the flat nutlike things from the ones we gathered last autumn, and I put them here. In this one place we'll gather more punkins than we would searching for them in the glades."

He thought he understood. "Ah, nuts make plants!" He was surprised that the anger did not fade from her eyes.

"No, no!" She lifted one of the globes and shook it before him. "Food. Regular dependable food! We don't have to grub through the forest. We can grow our own."

The Wolfrider chief took the unripe punkin and squeezed it. He remembered the orange-ripe fruit; he didn't like the texture or the flavor, though it was nourishing. Humans ate them, just as humans cleared the forest to plant things in straight lines. "Ah, yes, it is good to know where to look when the hunger-time comes. We could save meat for the wolves—"

"Not just the hunger-time," Talen interjected, surprising the two. Neither had noticed him following them to the growing-patch. "Such as these will be useful when you hunters are gone. Willowgreen's discovery will let us safely stay in one place for greater lengths of time."

"I don't understand . . ."

"We dare not kill every day; already some animals have vanished from this part of the forest," Willowgreen explained. "And we dare not move for fear you will not be able to find us."

"If you had not returned," Talen continued. "If disaster had overtaken you and the other hunters, these fruits, and others we have nurtured, would have sustained us until we gave up hope for you."

Two-Spear stood up, his mouth was hard. "The hunters provide all the food the tribe needs! We always have."

"The hunters provide for the hunters!" the elder said with uncharacteristic sharpness. "We are grateful that you've brought us black-neck and forest pig—but it will be gone before you leave again, then how else should we survive while you are gone. Are you the tribe's chief, or merely the first of its hunters? Why must the chief lead the hunt when Skyfire has been chosen as Huntress?"

Two-Spear stared at Talen. "How long"—his voice was rough—"how long have the elves, and the others, felt this way?"

With his point made, Talen's voice softened. "Several seasons. It has been . . . many turns since you have led hunters off for less than a dance of the moons."

The chief looked at Willowgreen. She nodded, then looked at the ground. He looked past Talen to the glade where the tribe was already preparing for a feast. He saw the sleek, lithe hunters, and he saw that they seemed a bit more robust than the clean, carefully clad Wolfriders and elves who had remained behind.

"We will move the whole tribe to where the hunting is better," he said, still watching the glade. Moving, though, wouldn't solve the tribe's problems for long. The Wolfrider tribe was as large as it had ever been; as large as it ever got before a handful of young Wolfriders got the urge to move off on their own. It had happened

138

before, but he had not expected it to happen again so soon. He had not expected it to happen at all while he was chief. "There are so many of us," he whispered.

"Since the five-fingered ones left this part of the forest, we have faced only the natural dangers of the world. That is why you did not lead us away when the big kills became scarce. We thrive here—"

"Do not be so gentle with him!" Rellah joined the group. Her silvery eyes were hard, and there was something akin to satisfaction in her voice. "We thrive like a too-large hive of bees. Twice we have watched the young ones swarm away—and our chief does not even notice that even his precious Wolfriders are not here when he returns from the hunt. Oh, yes, we remain behind, we old ones, we elves.

"You are Timmain's sacrifice, Timmorn's promise —and we wait for you to return. And we remember that it has all happened before. Hunters and elves; the wolf-blood and the elf growing apart, not together. This time there are no first-born, and this time we will have Willowgreen's crops."

Two-Spear looked to his lifemate for support, but she would not meet his eyes. Among wolves and Wolfriders the gesture meant acceptance, but among elves it meant shame.

"It is true," she said softly, still not looking at him. "You have become more wolf and you've led the Wolfriders away from us. It would be different, if we could bond with the wolves, but you know we never can. Changefur has Recognized Marrek, do you understand what that means?"

Her lifemate shook his head.

"*Elves* are being born again," Rellah explained. "Not since Timmorn came to us, have we Recognized each other, only Wolfriders. Talen and I—"

Talen laid a restraining hand across Rellah's arm.

"Timmorn Yellow-Eyes left when he could no longer hold elf and wolf together. You must decide, Two-Spear, are you chief of the elf-blood or the wolf-blood?"

Two-Spear had no answer for that. He turned from the three and walked into the woods, his clenched fist the only sign of his rage. A rage he directed solely at himself, for he was the chief, and he had not noticed when the other Wolfriders had left, and he knew his responsibility was to the elf-blood.

In his mind he saw the crushed human skull lying in the grass and in his heart he recalled the bright promises he had made as the human town burned. Promises he had done nothing to keep. Promises that were being replaced by his lifemate's carefully nurtured punkins.

Skyfire watched him leave, as she had watched the entire conversation. She had heard none of it, but she didn't need words to gauge her brother's anger. Two-Spear had made her the Wolfrider Huntress, a hollow dignity since he led all the hunts, but she had the right to know what was wrong. And something had to be wrong.

The Huntress took a step in her brother's direction, then reconsidered. She already knew what was wrong. Two-Spear himself was wrong. She pulled a lace from her jerkin and ground it into the mud by the stream. On the pretext of needing a new strip, she went to speak with Rellah.

Two-Spear put the tribe behind him. The woods were cool; a light draft flowed through the leaves. The small sounds of the forest hummed a song as sunlight wove among the leaves. It was gentle now, but the chief knew that sudden death and violence was never far away. This was his world, and he was the master here—as he had once proven to the humans. It was a wild place, full of the unexpected, and it had never been suited to the orderly, tame elves. But the world was wider than this. There were mountains and plains and lakes that the Wolfriders had never explored. Was this the best place for his tribe, the best place for him?

Is it here, he thought, *among the ancient trees where we have always been? Is this where the old and the new can be joined together? Or is there more . . . ? A place where elf and Wolfrider can be themselves and yet be together?*

Once he had shamed his sister, Skyfire, when he claimed that he could not be content with the life of a wolf, that he and the Wolfriders were meant to be more. He had thrown his spears into the air, at the stars. He had staked his claim to the future, but he had not followed it. He had promised but, like the other Wolfriders, he had not *needed*.

Two-Spear sat down with a thump, leaning against an oak. Above him the light and wind and leaves fought each other. The scents of the forest called to him as nothing else could. For how long had he listened to the song of the wolf, the dance of the forest, and to nothing else? It was tempting; it was all that he loved, but in the end it wasn't enough.

He was the strongest. He was the chief of the tribe because none could stand before his will. His leadership was absolute, no one could best him at his chosen skills. He was the best among the Wolfrider hunters, and they prospered as he did, but it wasn't enough.

The tribe was more than hunters. There were the old elves, who had no wolf-friends, and children, and even Wolfriders in whom the elf ran thick and who preferred a quiet life. He had been chief of the Wolfriders because leading came easily to him. He led the hunters because hunting satisfied him as nothing else did, but he was no longer chief of the entire tribe.

He remembered his dream. The tribe had gone out to fight, to die, without him. Worse, he had run away from them. It would have been bad enough if he had been a chief like his father, taking each day as it came, but he was Two-Spear and he had made promises. His success as a Wolfrider, as a hunter, had weakened him; he would have to overcome his weakness.

I must become like this old tree: hard outside, harder inside. The hunt is lost to me forever.

Two-Spear stood up; he knew what he had to do now. Moving to another part of the forest wasn't enough. It was time to keep his promises. He had sworn to build what had been lost out of memory, to replace the sky-mountain, to fulfill the Wolfriders' destiny. To make a single home where the wolves could hunt, where the old ones could live their lives in tranquility, and where the Wolfriders could find their future.

It was time for him to become the chief he could, and should be.

And to make this world his own.

Two-Spear remained in the glade with the tribe only a few days. He was anxious to put deeds behind his renewed promises. He, who had never felt the prick of time on his conscience, was suddenly aware how quickly it passed and how little of it there might be. The old ones assured him that the tribe could feed itself for as long as necessary, but the chief looked at the ripening punkins. He remembered their mealy taste and texture, and knew he had to get moving. He had to find the home for his tribe before Wolfrider bellies rebelled against orange mush.

"Must you go so soon?" Willowgreen whispered as they lay together one last time before he said he would leave.

"Yes."

"But alone? Surely it would be safer . . . less lonely to take some of the Wolfrider hunters with you?"

"No. No-name and I will hunt and travel alone."

"You carry your confidence like a spear," she said softly. "It is the weapon you use to hold me away."

Two-Spear didn't answer. She was right; he could not tell her that he'd decided to travel alone for only one reason: fear. His new resolution was an uneasy burden that threatened to slip from his shoulders. He feared that with the Wolfrider hunters beside him, he would shuck the burden off and slip again into wolfsong. He feared that the next time he succumbed to the wolfsong, he would not remember to come back. And these were only a few of the things he could not tell his lifemate.

He certainly could not tell her what he had decided beneath the oak tree. She would not understand why he must become hard inside and out. She would laugh when he said it was not enough to be the strongest in the tribe, that now he must prove himself the strongest in the world.

She would say it was arrogance and pride, though those were elfin traits and had no place in his thoughts. If he'd had arrogance or pride, he would have resisted the nagging anxiety at the back of his mind; he would not still be dreaming about that human skull. Except it wasn't always a human skull anymore. Sometimes it had high cheekbones; sometimes it had her eyes.

He could never tell Willowgreen, or anyone else, that it was the true elves' softness that drove him. The Wolfriders could survive here, but the elves could not. Deep in his own mind Two-Spear knew that if he failed to find the right home, the safest, strongest place in the world, then the elfin race would die, taking his lifemate with it.

Two-Spear pulled Willowgreen closer. He covered his face with her sweet-smelling hair, not for memory or longing, but, once again, from fear. She might see, *someone* might see, that he was not half so clever, nor half so sure as he pretended. He nuzzled her neck gently, feeling the pulsing of her heart through the tender, soft skin.

In the end it was because of his lifemate that he would keep going. It was for her that he would find a way. It was for the moment when he felt the softness of her in his arms; when the daystar lit her hair; when she thought he was unaware and watched him with bright, adoring eyes. He would sacrifice for those eyes, as Timmain had sacrificed. He must make it safe and warm so that never, never, would he lose those eyes.

Willowgreen knew he was deep in his own thoughts and was glad that he was unaware of her tears. They were not tears of pain, or even fear—as he would have believed—but frustration.

I love him, she thought as his hands wove over her body and she contrived to make herself comfortable. *He is the best of the Wolfriders, the strongest, the most daring. He is all those things I am not, all those things that I need. How can I not love him? How can I not lose him again and again?*

Two-Spear loved her in his way, she knew, but his way often turned brutal and selfish. His strength made everyone else feel less strong, less necessary. His strength had sparked a slow-burning fire in his sister; it inspired Graywolf with awe. Each tribe-mate drew something different from Two-Spear's unwavering strength. Willowgreen, herself, was filled with a special sort of loneliness that she must always hold in silence.

There was so much Two-Spear didn't understand, so much he did not see. He was different, not like herself

144

and the other elves, and yet not like the Wolfriders either. Willowgreen knew that he, too, felt a special sort of loneliness. It was his way. No matter where he was, or with whom, her lifemate was always alone.

She thought—hoped and prayed—he was searching for himself, for peace such as the elves and other Wolfriders had discovered since he'd chased the humans from the forest. But what kind of peace could a man like Two-Spear find? And what would be left for her . . . ?

Huntress Skyfire stood with the rest of her tribe-mates at the center of the glade. Two-Spear was leaving and taking no one with him but No-name, his wolf-friend. Her brother was agitated and moody—even more so than usual—and she, certainly, would be glad to see the back of him. For a hand of days, he'd been making preparations and making solemn pronouncements.

He'd told the tribe they should consider Talen and Willowgreen their chief in his absence, and he'd reconfirmed her as the Huntress of the Wolfriders. It was all very strange, as if he felt that his words, and his words alone, made something happen. As if no one would hunt without his say-so, or the tribe would be guided by those who weren't the strongest or wisest after him.

Skyfire had tried to talk to him, and had been angrily rebuffed. He had his own demons and, seeing what they were doing to him, she wasn't all that unhappy to leave him alone. All she'd been able to gather was that her brother thought he was going to find something that would change the world and the Wolfriders forever. It was not a pleasant thought.

She turned and saw Graywolf watching her. The Wolfrider made no secret of the fact that Two-Spear had told *him* to keep her from causing trouble. Skyfire didn't like it, but she understood it. They were both Prey-

Pacer's children, but Prey-Pacer raised two broods. Two-Spear, Swift-Spear then, had always been chief's son and even though his parents had never Recognized, the Wolfriders were prepared to accept him as chief. Then, not long before he left, Prey-Pacer admitted that he and Wreath were Recognized.

Huntress Skyfire was Wreath's daughter.

She'd been too young to challenge her brother at the beginning, and not at all certain she wanted to be chief. She was old enough now, and strong enough—which was why Two-Spear felt such a need to keep an eye on her. She liked being Huntress, and she didn't mean to be a troublemaker, but she couldn't accept Two-Spear the way the others could.

It was the wolf-blood, Rellah had told her, and the next time she and her brother crossed, it would be death-blood unless Two-Spear backed down.

Graywolf had taken a step toward her and, rather than deal with him, Skyfire gave her attention back to her brother. The Wolfrider chief had raised both his name spears above his head, but his voice was soft and the tribe had to move closer to hear his final words.

"I will leave you with this," he said. "I have made promises to you as your chief." He looked at Rellah as he spoke. "Promises I have not kept. But the time has come to once more take hold of a dream." He stood up straighter.

"This world of two moons will be ours; we will be part of it, and it part of us. There is more for us here than we have, more that is meant for us. These things we will find. We need more than food, or shelter, or even hope. We need more than we have had. We need to find our destiny. And that, my children, is what I am going to find."

With that he leapt upon No-name and raced off into

the woods. The tribe watched him go in silence, with strange, unreadable expressions on their faces. No one wanted to be the first to speak.

And so, once more he goes off on a dream. Rellah lock-sent to Skyfire.

It is madness, she replied in the same way.

Never before had a chief referred to the tribe as his children. Never before had anyone presumed so much. Skyfire was not alone in her sense of puzzled outrage, but there were those who would follow Two-Spear to the ends of the world. She looked at Graywolf, who was so wolflike and should have minded being called a child, but his eyes were filled with admiration. She looked at Willowgreen, and her eyes were filled with a sad, empty love.

It is madness, the Huntress repeated to herself, and stalked off in the opposite direction from Two-Spear.

Two-Spear had no clear notion of his destination, either in a physical place or within himself. The Wolfriders had always lived in glades or caves, so it was most comfortable to think he'd find what he was searching for in such surroundings. But he knew he'd never find what he needed in a place where he'd set his feet before. He knew he had a long way to go when he guided No-name toward the daystar's resting place.

No-name moved quickly through the undergrowth, faster than Two-Spear had asked him to, and unwilling to slow down. The chief could tell that No-name was bothered by something, but he could make little sense of the wolf's confused mind-pictures.

The Mother and child moons completed their dance, and Two-Spear continued in one direction. No-name grew more and more agitated, but the Wolfrider had gained no more insight into his bond-mate's thought.

147

When they hunted it was not what it once had been. Neither much enjoyed the kill, and they did not sing after feasting. Two-Spear had no choice, it took considerable strength of will to resist the wolfsong. And No-name—if No-name had reasons, he wasn't sharing them.

An eight-of-days had passed before the nightmare rejoined them. It had the same substance as before, though this time it seemed harsher and even more relentless. The two woke up howling, they simply faced each other. For the first time Two-Spear realized whose dream it was that he shared.

So the mighty No-name has known fear, the Wolfrider sent, but the wolf turned away.

And so it went. Each day the forest became thinner, the land more hilly and dry. Each night the wolf spun his nightmare, trapping Two-Spear in a red-shadowed world. Always the same dream. Always the same fear.

Then one day the trees ended and the two stood on a bluff overlooking a great plain. It was full of strange sights and even stranger scents. Great beasts roamed the high-grass plain. They moved in herds that dwarfed Two-Spear's imagination. They were more numerous than the stars on a clear winter night. Never had he seen so many animals in one place, and he began to believe he was on the right path.

No-name sat on his haunches and howled once, a terrible longing in his cry.

We need never be hungry again, Two-Spear sent as he knelt beside the wolf.

No-name stared out at the plain, pawing the ground restlessly. **Home.**

Two-Spear nearly leaped up. Wolf-friends sent feelings and images, not fully formed words; they had enough of the elf about them for the bond to be made, but no more. And if a wolf were going to send words, Two-Spear would have guessed that No-name was the least likely to do so. **What do you mean, *home*?** he shot back.

But No-name did not answer. The wolf's mind was cloudy and impenetrable as it had always been.

Two-Spear led them down to the plain and kept them on their course. The wolf's nightmares came with a regularity that was almost boring. Neither awoke in howling fear anymore, but neither slept well. They had little patience with each other, but they kept moving together.

No-name had remarkable knowledge of the plain. It was the wolf who chose what they would hunt and how they would hunt it. The wolf warned Two-Spear away from unfamiliar berries. He taught the Wolfrider to outwit the great longtooth cats, and how to drive off the unfamiliar scavengers that haunted their kills. It was a knowledge the wolf could have only if this were truly *home* to him.

Two-Spear sent to the wolf regularly and directly, but No-name never responded. The wolf seemed to know the plain, but there was no satisfaction in his knowledge. No-name became moodier with each rising of the day-star. He trod the ground as if he expected it to betray him. Every day, before their march began, the wolf would give his single, mournful howl.

Two-Spear no longer rode above No-name's shoulders, but walked silently beside him. He was tired; the muscles in his legs cramped and begged for rest, but Two-Spear kept moving. Life itself became a dream, a part of the nightmare.

The high-cheekboned skull glowed in a halo of sickly yellow brilliance. Its eye sockets loomed large, drawing the Wolfrider chief into an endless, black mystery. He could not resist . . . He *did not* resist; this was what he had been looking for.

The memories, and hopes, and dreams of Two-Spear's human enemy had long since sunk into the dirt. Nothing within the skull's dark dream revealed identity or personality. A few faint emotions, signifying nothing except, perhaps, loss, floated in the emptiness. Two-Spear sighed, and the sound echoed through the cavern of bone.

There was silence, and then there was a roar. Everything changed. Two-Spear was in the forest, and great cats were pursuing him. They growled deep in their throats and the underbrush cried out as their claws carved through it.

Two-Spear thought there might be three of them, but he couldn't linger to be sure. The pulse of fear was known to him, but this was a new, intense terror. With a howl of his own, the Wolfrider turned and ran deeper into the forest than he had ever gone before.

The cats followed with more endurance than cats should have—but this was a dream, and nothing was as it should have been. Two-Spear ran for his life. The trees became blurred shadows beside him. His heart said that there was sanctuary ahead. He gave his last strength to weave between the trees. He fell to safety just as the claws grazed his back.

The beasts couldn't follow him into the blue-green clearing. They paced beyond the trees, constantly veering inward, and always rebuffed. Two-Spear watched them while his blood cooled. He was breathing normally before he was convinced they would never find an entrance. He looked away from the cats, and his heart began pounding again.

The sanctuary was larger than he imagined—and he was not alone within it. At the center of the clearing was a circle of dancers. The dancers were elves, but their beauty surpassed Two-Spear's imagination. They were small and delicate, with wings that mimicked a flower's crown of petals.

Their minds were closed to him, but Two-Spear approached and entered their circle. He towered over them, but they had no fear. Then there was something behind him and he turned.

She was more beautiful than anyone he had ever seen. She was too beautiful to be alive; she was flawless, perfect. Two-Spear gathered her in his arms, holding her tight as she pressed against his body. She was warm and sweet, and her arms closed around him, both strong and soft. His eyes forgot the dancers; his ears forgot their song. He yielded to the world that grew between them.

Then the soft, perfect body became hard and cold. Its arms stayed locked around him and when Two-Spear opened his eyes he saw the dancers coming forward, building a wall with their bodies, preventing his escape. He dared to look at the beautiful face; it had all but melted away. The soft flesh and magic eyes had sloughed off, exposing dry and brittle bones.

She wasn't dead—by the Mother moon and her child—the leering skull wasn't dead. It looked clear through him to his soul, and called his name.

Two-Spear fought as he had never fought before. He fought free of bones and free of the clinging wall the petal-winged elves had woven around him. He fought free, and then he fell into the void. Her voice followed him and, as she had been, her voice was perfection.

"Why have you let my people die?" The voice was not cold, as he thought it would be, but gentle and full of tired wisdom.

There was a horrid squeal: the sound of something hard crushing through bone. There was a sad wind whipping about him: the cold wind that takes a child to its final sleep. Cries howled around the Wolfrider chief as he heard her people, the purest of the elves, die in agonizing, uncountable ways. Hearing was worse than seeing, for the sounds were so poignant, so easily understood, that his mind could not turn away from the story they told.

They fell from the sky, and Two-Spear fell with them. They screamed as the fibers of their bodies caught fire, and Two-Spear screamed with them. They languished in the dark cold, and Two-Spear languished with them. Finally, their wills gave out and they turned to dust, and Two-Spear began to turn with them.

Suddenly the transformation stopped, and blue brilliance replaced the cold dark. Within his visions, the Wolfrider wondered what could produce such a light, then he realized he was in the presence of pure memory. The blue was the color of elfin memory, of the high ones' memory, and it contained the heart-spirit of all those who had died. There was no thought within the blueness —no fear, either—but unfathomable serenity.

The heart-spirit of the elves, the distilled essence of their memory, flowed slowly to the world of two moons. It cast a faint-blue aura through rocks, trees, and streams and subtly, enduringly, changed the fabric of the world.

Two-Spear saw that there were many places where the blue aura had collected and deepened. He named them spirit-pools; and the brightest of them called his own name. The Wolfrider dipped his dream-hand into the gentle blue pool. It quickened to his touch, and he knew it was *home*.

Two-Spear woke up as a soft moan escaped through his lips. No-name lay beside him, still trapped within the dream—within the old dream. The chief knew he had broken through the barrier of nightmare to end the dream truly. His mind's eye could see a faint-blue nimbus on the horizon. There was a quick flare, and then it was gone. The chief shivered as his fear-sweat dried in the thin night breeze.

There, he thought, *there is where I must go, where the dead have guided me. I will find the past there, and the future. I will conquer time along with everything else.* He curled his arm beneath his head and closed his eyes. The fear was gone, but the sad, perfect voice lingered.

"Why have you let my people die?"

It took three more days to reach the place where the blue magic had flared. Two-Spear pushed No-name hard and himself harder to reach the source of his vision, the home of truth. They entered a desolate part of the plain, where sandstone jutted upward like hands toward the sky. The land was rutted with streambeds, but now, at the end of summer, only a few ran swift or clear.

On the afternoon of the fourth day, Two-Spear led No-name down a wide, shallow canyon. He knew he was close. His skin tingled and his heart beat loud in his ears.

There was a lively stream at the end of the canyon; there were trees here with soft, green leaves. The mud was pocked where animals of all types had come to drink. And across the water rose the ruddy flatland that he had seen in his dreams. He stared at it a moment, then, quietly—without a word or thought to his wolf-friend—Two-Spear waded into the stream.

No-name whined but did not follow. The wolf seemed to know what lay ahead, nestled on the flatland of the plateau. It could not have been conscious thought; it was knowledge grown out of his dreams, out of the accretion of familiarity that had begun when Two-Spear led him out of the forest and onto the plain. His chaotic mind shied away from what it knew, and rebelled against knowing more. The dark wolf sat on his haunches, and would not cross the water.

No-name did not howl, or shiver, or growl. He was not especially frightened or angry. He had chosen, in his own way, to dwell with this elf. He could not follow and he could not leave; he just waited. Once he bit the air as a coherent thought formed in his mind: Was this the strong one? Was this the one who would triumph where all the other elves had failed?

Two-Spear felt his wolf-friend's eyes on his back, but he did not turn. He did not understand the wolf; he did not need to. Long experience had taught him the meaning of that haunted look in No-name's eyes. A chief knew when not to ask the impossible, or he did not remain chief. He had shared No-name's nightmare for many dances of the moons, but the wolf had not seen the blue brilliance of elfin memory and magic. Perhaps the wolf's destiny did not lead to the flatland; his did.

The plateau was ancient and weathered. Its sides were fairly steep, but well creased with age. Two-Spear climbed quickly, carefully. He restrained his curiosity and minded where he put his hands and feet, rather than let his thoughts leap ahead. He kept his eyes lowered until he could stand up straight.

At first his eyes were dazzled by light; he saw darkness and light without detail. He saw the dream-skull yawning at him. He shivered uncontrollably and blinked. He overcame his eyes' confusion and saw what was truly there. Another plateau, invisible from the canyon below, rose from this one. The ground on which he stood was vaster than he imagined it would be, and seared by the daystar. The second plateau of red sandstone glistened with the heat, and the great hollow in its side was what Two-Spear had mistaken for the skull.

The cave evoked deep memories and called to Two-Spear as if it had waited for him since the morning of time. It was alive . . . no, not alive, but filled with

mystery and the essence the Wolfrider had felt in his
dream. He hesitated and it seemed to him that the deep,
sad blue of elfin memory winked in the darkness.

Lost, it seemed to say. But Two-Spear knew the
message wasn't for him; he was no longer lost. He held
his spears tight and strode toward the darkness. His
back was straight as he entered the cavern. It was cool
and serene within its shadows, and not as dark as he'd
expected. Faint light powdered the air around him. He
could not see the ceiling or walls, but he guessed the
second plateau was very nearly hollow.

Best of all, he heard the sound of running water deep
against the back wall. Thirst replaced all other thoughts
and curiosity. He pushed deeper toward the water,
unmindful of darkness on either side. But even
this single-minded pursuit was set aside when he saw the
waterfall.

Sunlight flowed with the water from a hole in the
ceiling of the cavern: a silver-blue thread beginning and
ending in darkness. A gnarled monument of shining
stone rose out of the pool. The water was crystal clear;
the milky stone basin reflected the color of the unseen
sky. Two-Spear was filled with a sense of wonder and
awe greater than anything he had felt in any of his
dreams: This was real.

He did not disturb the shimmering water but followed
the overflow stream that led, like an arrow or a spear in
flight, through the darkness. The walls echoed his soft
footfalls and, by the changes in that sound, Two-Spear
knew that he descended through a narrowing tube. The
stones beneath his feet were slick and dangerous. Again
he set his mind against curiosity and toward caution.

Two-Spear lost track of time—but not in the empty
way of wolfsong. Now he felt time's passage, and distrusted it. His mind said the daystar had hardly moved

since he entered the cave. His heart said he might be lost here forever.

Once, he dislodged a stone. It filled the darkness with its tumbling, startling him and a myriad of bats. The pinging creatures flew by him in a cloud, their leathery wings whispering through the air. They never touched him, but they frightened him nonetheless, and it was several long moments before he could breathe easily again.

The light had vanished from the stream he followed. The passageway was darker than the longest winter night. It was a darkness Two-Spear could feel on his skin like sweat. The Wolfrider had never been comfortable in caves and now he felt the weight of the world pressing in around him. He fought a wave of panic and continued downward.

Two-Spear's mind cried out for light and freedom. He became careless and fell hard on his rump, the spears fell from his hand. On his hands and knees, he searched for them, then stayed on all fours as the passage steepened.

He didn't believe the light when he first saw it and needed to touch his eyes to convince himself they were open. Standing upright, Two-Spear took a step toward the glowing cerulean disk.

It was a deep pool, a bottomless pool. It was the spirit-pool of his dream: the resting place of elfin memory and magic. The clarity and intensity of its color belonged to another world. Two-Spear hunkered down and approached it cautiously. He prodded the water with his hunting spear, and did not touch bottom. The water ran back along the shaft, covering his fingers.

It was cool, but not cold, and it made his skin tingle. He could contain his excitement no longer.

"Ayooah!" he howled. "I have found it! I've found the

resting place of the elves!" The unseen walls of the cavern tossed Two-Spear's voice from side to side. *Elves . . . elves . . . elves* amid the tremulous call of the wolf.

Then another voice seemed to join the chorus: a sad voice. *Lost*, it whimpered, and the Wolfrider chief shivered.

Heart pounding in his throat and spears clutched grimly in his fist, Two-Spear climbed back to the main cavern. He could feel the elfinness of the darkness now. It welcomed him, yes, but it saddened him as well. The blue pool existed because the elves did not. It was beautiful, but it was the tomb of their heart-spirits. Somewhere, he knew, he'd find the tomb of their bodies.

It took a while, finding other passages and coming up short in blind tunnels, and there was the nerve-wracking danger that he might become disoriented and lose his way in the darkness, but Two-Spear persevered. And once again, when he found it, the tomb glowed with its own light.

The skulls, clearly elf skulls this time, lay in two faintly luminous piles at the center of a side cavern. Perhaps once they had been arranged in a deliberate shape, but that had been long ago, and now they were just heaps. Not so the object the skulls flanked and illuminated with their pale-blue light. That was built of stones, each carefully shaped and fitted together.

The Wolfrider had never seen anything like it. He couldn't imagine its purpose, but it didn't radiate the soft, sad magic of the skulls, and surely the skulls had been placed beside it.

Lost. The haunting whisper filled the cavern.

This time Two-Spear understood. He knotted his hands over the highest stones and wrenched one loose with more difficulty than he'd expected. It soared into the darkness and hung there a long time before striking the wall. He found his voice. It was ragged and painful, but it was not filled with grief.

"Revenge! I will have revenge for this!"

He reached for another stone.

Revenge!

It was the second sending No-name had perceived from his elf-friend during his vigil on the near side of the stream. The first had been a cry of exaltation. It had been pure elfin joy, and he had ignored it. This one, though, was something he knew, something that reverberated in the twisted canyons of his own past.

He stood, stretched, and crossed the water.

No-name trotted past the sharp creases where Two-Spear had climbed to the flatland. He plunged into the shadows without hesitation and found the place, hidden from casual eyes, where a switchback trail had been carved into the sandstone many turns before. The wolf didn't have memory, not even in the uncomfortable sense that Two-Spear understood. He had a sort of certainty, like bubbles rising through water, or images overlapping and coming suddenly into focus.

He could not have said, if he could have said anything at all, when he had padded up these stones before. But his mind said that they were *there*, so he found and used them. These feelings were stronger than simple image memory. No-name refelt, relived, his past. All that had happened here, happened again for him as he climbed the switchbacks.

There had been laughter and kindness here, enough to have impelled him into the long struggle from the darkness of his wolf-birth to the light of the elves. No-name whined as that light—that pure, beautiful, agonizing light—shone once again in his mind's eye. It penetrated into the deepest shadows of his wolfness and proclaimed anew that there was more.

Long, long ago the mixed-blood wolves had not bonded with elf-friends. Some of them had remained together until Timmorn Yellow-Eyes led them to his daughter, Rahnee, but most of them had run free. They were strong, smart, and long-lived; they rose swiftly in the ordinary wolf-packs they encountered. The elf-blood faded, usually, but sometimes it did not.

Sometimes the elf-blood concentrated and a wolf was born who *remembered*. No-name was such a wolf. He'd led his pack, and outlived them. He'd wandered through the dark mists of wolfsong, not quite knowing where he was going, not quite knowing what he was looking for—until he'd wandered across the plain and up the switchback trail.

The changes had begun here, incubated by the elfin light. Selfness had been awakened here, proclaiming that the was more than an animal—but less than an elf. The light shone brightly, but it did not invite him across the threshold. Not even the elves could penetrate shape's prison to see that his mind could think and reason, and command the world about him.

No-name was panting hard when he reached the flatland, though not from physical exertion. The reliving had exhausted him, and there was much more to go. The promise had been broken. He trembled as the first twinges of bitterness raced along his nerves. The bitterness had twisted him since that betrayal. The bitterness swallowed his sleep with nightmares and had long since filled him with hate.

All he could do now was howl against the agony that bitterness had built around him. He could have been more, but the elves hadn't seen, and then they had gone away.

He *remembered* the night that the elves had died. It was the night that his hopes had died as well. He remembered, and he hated the destroyers even more than he hated the elves. The smell of their flesh, their sweat, their blood, freshened in his nostrils. They were there in his mind's eye, as they were in his nightmares. Their long, hard claws ripping life from the elves.

And he had run away.

No-name opened his throat and howled. The sound rose and echoed in the mouth of the cave. It was a strong sound, a mad sound, and it pulled him backward . . . upward . . . until he stood on his hind legs.

But he was a wolf, not a man. His body was not balanced for two-footed walking. No-name snapped at the air, leaping, looking for a throat. He longed to drown his hate and rage in some enemy's spurting blood. But he was alone, without any enemy but himself. He bit at his tail, because he could not bite the hurting place in his mind. He raged at his wolfish self imprisoning his meager portion of the elfin magic, but it was thick, black ice.

His anger turned toward the elf he had followed to this reawakening place. No-name had followed Two-Spear because Two-Spear was metal-strong, and because he blazed a trail with human blood. Ah, *that* time had been sweet. Ravaging the village had been satisfying in a way no hunt could ever be. Savage killing, not for food but for vengeance, appeased a not-quite-wolfish passion and rage.

No-name and Two-Spear had unleashed their wrath upon the humans just once, but that had been enough to lure No-name into a cautious alliance with an elf again. Now Two-Spear had led him back here. No-name remembered and understood as much of that night as he had ever understood. Nothing could strengthen his hatred of the humans, but Two-Spear—who had led him here, who had reminded him of what had been lost, and what could never be gained—had inflamed his hatred of the elves to blazing fury.

The wolf crossed the line from light to shadow. He inhaled the elf-scent, the death-scent. The tenuous truce that had made Two-Spear his elf-friend burned away, replaced by an aching desire to *be* an elf. The image of the Wolfrider chief was foremost in his mind and a clear thought coalesced: *Him I hate most of all.*

No-name was ready when Two-Spear walked out of the cave into the dwindling sunlight. The elf's mind was bright with many wondrous things: things No-name could not share. He sundered them with his rage.

Strongest! the wolf sent, and the elf staggered back from the power of his thought. **Strongest!**

Two-Spear shook his head. The day had been filled with strange, unprecedented knowledge. He could not, at first, determine the source of the sending which had shattered the bright peace in his mind. For a moment he thought it might be the spirit-pool itself, affirming his vow of revenge—then, he saw No-name's eyes.

The wolf was wolf-friend no longer. There was hatred and unnatural cunning in those red-reflecting eyes, but though he became instantly wary, Two-Spear had no notion of the depth or cause of the wolf's sudden madness. He knew that a whisper of elfinness within the wolf made bonding possible, but it did not make a wolf-friend more than a wolf.

Wolves are strongest!

Two-Spear reeled backward, and No-name leaped for his unguarded throat. The elf abandoned thought himself. This was challenge, and his instincts rose to meet it. As once he had challenged a five-fingered chief, Two-

Spear howled and met the wolf's attack. The flatland seemed to shudder as their howls mingled and each sought to rip the other's life away.

Strongest, the wolf sent as his teeth tore elfin flesh.

Betrayer!

And so they both fought that which threatened them the most. They tore at each other, leaped, and rolled on the ground. Two-Spear did not use his spear. They fought as wolves fought, in a scarlet chorus of wolfsong.

The air about them was streaked with the red of spraying blood. Bits of skin and fur were ground into the sandstone dust. The battle had gone beyond challenge; there would be no survivor. There could be none. Each warrior was bent on the destruction of the other; each would sacrifice himself if the other could be made to die a single heartbeat sooner.

It was madness, and it was just as well they were alone on the flatland, for no sane mind—be it elf or wolf, or somewhere in-between—would dare to witness it. The daystar closed its eye and the fight continued in darkness.

Their weakened bodies slowed, but not their minds. The fight was over, in a mortal sense, for each bore wounds that could not heal. And each ignored his wounds, his pain. They flailed in silence, each determined to be the last to die. Simultaneously their blows failed to land and they fell heavily apart. Their savaged bodies had a moment of rest, and their minds a moment to know that the next lunge would surely be the last.

No-name could barely fill his burning lungs. The world was dimmer than it had ever been, yet his thoughts had never been clearer. If he could not triumph as a wolf, then he would surpass himself and would become something more.

Power was there for the taking. Blue elfin magic, distilled within the ground, responded to No-name's call. He sucked the magic into himself and keened to the empty heavens as it raced through his body. Bone and muscle twisted, tore, and healed, forming itself in the image of No-name's hate. He pushed himself to his feet, to *two* feet, and loomed over the elf.

Two-Spear gasped as the apparition arose. No-name was no longer a wolf, and no longer near death. He had become a crazed exaltation of that the Wolfriders might have been, all that Timmain had desired them to be. No-name's muzzle sprouted long fangs, his eyes glowed a bitter red, and his clawed hands were man-shaped.

But Two-Spear was Two-Spear, and in his inmost heart he knew he could not be vanquished. He kenned what the wolf had done, and delved into the spirit-pool himself. It was elfin magic—magic of this world now —and it belonged to him. It cascaded through his veins, clear and sharp, like a river of crushed quartz. It cut and bit; it purified and strengthened. The Wolfrider chief rose to his feet, more than equal to No-name's challenge.

I know your name, Two-Spear thrust into his enemy's thought. **You are *Fear*.** He paused for a moment and sealed the power of his words with the power of his eyes. **And you think fear is enough. But I tell you that it takes more than strength and cleverness to be chief. It takes laughter and love, and a knowledge of righteousness. It takes more than nightmares. It takes the black fire of destiny. And I tell you, betrayer, that *I am your chief*.**

Once more they lunged together. No-name carried the rage of this world with him; the need—the ability—to take what the puny elves had brought here, and make fearsome use of it. Two-Spear, though, carried hope and the almost-forgotten potential of his people.

They both had drawn upon the latent magic of the spirit-pool. It strengthened them, but it had not truly changed them. No-name had hands and clear thought, but he did not make them his weapons. He was as Two-Spear had named him and he fought with a blood-crazed fury. Two-Spear fought with intelligence and cunning; he eluded, feinted, and struck with darting, deadly accuracy.

No-name did not suspect he was losing until a great weight descended across his back. It was the weight of the Wolfrider chief squeezing the air from his lungs. It was the weight of the world pushing him back into the wolf. He used everything he knew, everything he had been given, in an attempt to throw the elf to the ground, but it was not enough.

The elf held on, slowly choking the life out of his greatest enemy, his betrayer, the betrayer of elfin magic. He felt No-name's ribs give way. The beast wasn't fighting anymore. The pathway to the wolf's mind was clear and open. Two-Spear squeezed harder and plunged into the morass of No-name's being.

Two-Spear quickly understood how the fight had begun. He saw how madness had warped No-name's feelings, turning them back on themselves until love and hate were no different one from the other. It was the same with the wolf heritage and the elf heritage; the essences were tangled beyond unknotting. Then, at the very core of No-name, at his beginning, the essences separated; the blue of elfinness veered off from the red of the wolf, of the world of two moons.

Within the tragedy of No-name's mind, Two-Spear encountered the beginnings of truth: For a Wolfrider to belong to the world of two moons he must accept the unresolved mixing of elf and wolf. It was not a surprise, Two-Spear had always known it in his heart; now he knew it in his head. But there was another truth revealed

by the branching of elf away from wolf: Death belonged
to the wolf, and to the world of two moons.

The elfin heritage did not die. It did not know
sickness, or the decline of age. It could be killed, but it
took the wolf to kill it; death did not come naturally to
the elves as it came to the wolves. Wolves were born,
lived, and finally died. No matter what they did, they
finally died. As the Wolfrider accepted the wolf within
his being, so, too, he accepted his death.

Two-Spear thought he'd uncovered the answer to the
puzzle of time. He withdrew a little to study it.

No-name was silent as consciousness slowly slipped
away from him, as darkness surrounded him, and the
completness of his defeat became manifest. He had
taken the elfin magic into himself, had been transformed
by it, but he had not become an elf. His man-shaped
hands were not elf hands, and would again become
paws. The tendons in his legs had already begun to
contract. He struggled to form a single word, before it
became too late.

"Lost. Los-s-s . . ."

The word swirled around Two-Spear, deafening him
until he withdrew all the way, and heard it as it was
meant to be heard. It churned with all the sadness and
rage that blended together and were the wolf. It was
more than a dual-natured being could contain. He could
have killed No-name before he took up his burden
again. Two-Spear could have killed both the elf and the
wolf, but he hesitated, and then it was too late.

Lost.

A perfect voice repeated the word and Two-Spear
collapsed on top of No-name. The sad, gentle magic
slipped free and vanished like quicksilver into the red
dirt of the flatland. He felt no flush of victory. He had
taunted the wolf at the beginning, claiming that a true
chief would know what was right. Panting and ex-

hausted, Two-Spear still believed that a chief would
know, but he no longer knew if he had been right or if he
was truly a chief.

Would he have done anything different if he had been
No-name? If opportunity glimmered, offering the promise that he could be more than he was, wouldn't he have
fought with all his strength and will to get outside the
boundaries of his life? And, in the end, wasn't the
greatest tragedy simply knowing that the boundaries
existed? To know that there were challenges that could
not be met? To be trapped in a body that was less than
the mind that governed it?

Two-Spear sighed as the magic dwindled. He would
have done what No-name did, but the greatest tragedy
remained his own. He had fought a wolf's battle, in
wolfsong and in blood. The purest elfin magic had
merged into his body; he'd used it to augment the wolf,
not the elf. And it was too late to try again.

It is easy, he thought, *to be the strongest. It is easy to
wrest power and mold it to my vision. But with strength
there is no resting, only more strength. I could only face
No-name as he faced me: strength for strength, tooth for
claw. With strength there is always challenge. And challenge is not the elfin way.*

Two-Spear was filled with a sadness more profound
than any he had known before. His entire being was
bound up in strength, just as No-name's was. Strength
was what Timmain had gotten for the Wolfriders when
she'd chosen the wolves. It seemed she had sacrificed her
elfinness for strength.

The Wolfrider reached out to touch the wolf's blood-
stiffened fur. *It is too easy to be master. If I am to be chief
for the elves, I must set aside what is easy.*

He sat upright through the cool desert night. He
thought about strength, about killing and dying, and

about being chief. He made peace with it before dawn; his own sort of peace. A path became clear in his mind: The greatest leader understood the frailties of others and protected them from their weaknesses. The greatest strength lay in forgiving. Two-Spear forgave the wolf who had attacked him and knew, once again, that he was indisputably the strongest.

When morning came the wolf bared his throat to his chief, but Two-Spear, newly clothed in the power of compassion, turned away. He wanted no other creature's submission. He understood No-name's weakness, just as he thought he understood the weakness of the elves, who did not die but could be killed. He would provide a safe haven for all of them, because he was strong, but he did not need their submission, because he was stronger.

"I will find a way," he said gently to the wolf. "I will find a place for you as well."

The wolf did not respond and Two-Spear said nothing more. The new insight he had into the paths of strength, the way of a chief, forbid him to reveal his weakness to those who were less strong. But deep in his heart— despite the long night, the revelations, and the promises; despite the terrible glory of his battles with men and beasts—there was only one thought: *He betrays me still.*

It was hot and painfully bright on the flatland. Two-Spear had been drained by the events of the past day and night. He had found what he wanted: a home for the elves, but he couldn't bring them here. Not yet, at least. Not while elfin skulls framed human stonework.

He returned to the softly glowing tomb-cave and asked advice of the skulls. "Why did they kill you? Why did they put you here? Is this where you want to be?"

They did not answer him, but, in the end, Two-Spear needed no answer. He knew he could not leave the bones of his unknown kin within the cave—if only because humans had put them there. Gingerly he picked up the first of the skulls and carried it to the light.

All day long Two-Spear shuttled skulls from the tomb-cave to the light. He buried each separately, making a great circle around the upper plateau. They looked outward, he made certain of that.

"They will watch over us," the chief told No-name. "They will guard us so our enemies do not again catch us unaware."

No-name just watched and waited. He thought clearly, but he thought like a wolf. He had been defeated. When the elfin magic drained away, so had much of his bitterness. He would never become an elf, and he would never be quite like the wolves—even the changed wolves who bonded with the other elves. He remembered what he had been, and he remembered what his much-wanted hands had resembled.

It was a sad sort of peace, but it was more than he'd had before.

The daystar had slipped behind the cavern plateau by the time Two-Spear finished his grim, self-appointed task. His body ached with exhaustion, but a voice at the back of his mind said there were still tasks he must complete before he could rest. Leaving No-name and the skulls to guard the entrance, Two-Spear returned to the tomb chamber.

Without the faint luminosity of the elfin bones, the cavern was black and cold. The unseen walls radiated a chill that seemed to speak of great depths, impenetrable darkness, and knowledge still hidden in the realm of the dead and blind. If it was fear that Two-Spear felt, then it was a new kind of fear. It was a fear that could not be named, and could not be fought with the weapons of either elf or wolf. Like a rain-sodden cloak, it weighed heavily on Two-Spear's shoulders and surrounded the Wolfrider chief with a thick blanket of lassitude.

He waited for the blue light of elfin memory, but, of course, it never came. He had removed it and placed it in the ground outside the cavern. Once, as his senses strained against the emptiness of the cavern, he thought he heard the harsh chanting of human voices, but before he could impart meaning to their words, the sound vanished. Later he was sure he heard the cry of a lone hunting wolf. That could have been imagination, or it could have been No-name. It wasn't repeated.

Yet he waited. There was something more here. He needed something more. There had to be another sign, another vision that would complete this odyssey. Two-Spear was not content with bits of insight that ultimately raised more questions than they had answered. He believed the cavern contained *the* answer, and he was determined to wait until it unveiled itself.

His eyes were useless, and his ears had already played tricks on him; the truth finally came to the sharpest of his wolf-senses: his nose. He caught a change in the slow-moving air currents of the cavern. A scent of long ago: the fear-stink of his enemy, the humans, and the dusky tang of charring wood. And, woven through it all, the acrid smell of blood. Blended together they were the scents of elfin annihilation.

As soon as Two-Spear named the scent, it changed. Now he smelled the milk-breath of young cubs: broad, green leaves spread beneath the daystar; water flowing over mossy rocks. There was only one word to describe the mingling of these essences: Willowgreen.

The scent of her filled the cavern, and Two-Spear's lungs. It was the scent of her herb-rinsed hair drying in the sunlight; her breath warm and delicate against his skin. Thought of her filled the chief's other senses until she was almost there, barely hidden in the darkness. The Wolfrider's body throbbed in anticipation of her lovemaking. Willowgreen.

She gave her love to him alone—not to the chief of the Wolfriders, not even to Two-Spear, but to a sense of himself that resided beneath all names and responsibilities. He took his strength from her love, and she gave love endlessly. She was weak, like all the elves, but her capacity to love him—to give him strength—gave her unconquerable strength in return.

Love, endless love. Weakness, yet strength from weakness. Death, but only through violence. Even we *would not die without violence . . . Yet without violence, without killing, we would starve. And if we do not perfect our ways of killing, then surely the humans will slay us as we sleep. It's there in No-name—blind hatred for anything that doesn't need to die.*

We can never live with the humans. They can never accept us. Yet if we fight them on their ground—as I fought No-name—then we risk the elf within each of us.

Two-Spear flailed the darkness with his fists, striking the shaped stones the humans had left behind. This, then, was the truth; he held it in his mind. But having the truth was not quite the same as understanding it, or knowing the right thing to do with it. He could almost sense a path, but it was a path only Wolfriders could follow. Timmain had endowed her children well. It was just possible that Wolfriders could keep their elfinness intact and hold the humans at bay. But that wasn't possible for the older ones, for the elves.

After all, wasn't that why Timmain had chosen the wolves in the first place? So her children would not die as those in this cavern had died? The Wolfriders were the way for the elves to greet the future on this world. But because of the Wolfriders, some of the old ones had been protected by their children and had survived—so far. And as long as the Wolfriders were successful in protecting the old ones, they would never die. Elves *never* died, except by violence.

They had died, of course, one by one. There were only a few of them left. The rest were remembered only in the dreamberry tales. The Wolfriders couldn't protect them against everything; nature itself was violent here. But he'd protected them better than his father, or Rahnee, or even Timmorn himself. No elf had died since he had driven the humans from the forest. He'd made them safe.

And now they were having cubs! There'd been no elves born since Timmorn's day. Only now when he had made true-elves safer than the Wolfriders—who had to face the dangers of the forest and the hunt, even when the humans were no threat—were they having cubs!

Two-Spear wrapped his arms tight around his chest. Wolfriders would die to protect the elves. The more elves there were, the more Wolfriders would likely die until . . . Until what? What would happen if there were more elves than Wolfriders? Perhaps he should speak with Talen and the others and explain why there could be no more elves. It was harsh, but true; Wolfriders were the future, not elves. The Wolfriders would do their best, but the old ones had to accept that it was their fate to die.

Then Two-Spear thought of Willowgreen. They'd never had cubs, but he'd not given up the hope that they would. In his mind's eye he could see their children: little girls who looked exactly like their mother. He couldn't bear the thought of losing her or them.

The truth finally became a path he could follow.

He'd bring them here—elves, wolves, and Wolfriders alike. The Wolfriders could hunt, and the elves could plant their seeds. There would be food enough for everyone, no matter how many elfin cubs were born. And he'd keep them safe.

Two-Spear's hands closed again over the shaped stones that would not come apart. If the humans could do this, so could he—but he'd do more. He'd make a wall all around the flatland and guard it with elfin magic. It would be a place where elves could move freely, and where violence could never enter.

He saw it in his mind's eye and knew the vision would remain stronger than wolfsong. It was finally time to go home.

The journey back across the plains and through the forest exhausted both Two-Spear and No-name. They traveled faster, with their destination firmly in mind, but it was not the pace that sapped their energy. Neither was the same as he had been when he left the forest glade. The journey back to the familiar was, emotionally at least, a steep, uphill climb.

There was little pleasure in the familiar for either of them. No-name was more an outcast than ever. He felt his elf-friend's sendings, though he did not respond to them, and would not respond to them. They were still bonded, but they were less than a pair. Insofar as the wolf retained the ability to think clearly, and insofar as he understood the grandiose plans that Two-Spear thrust into his mind, No-name did not think he would follow the chief back onto the plain. The peace he had found after his defeat was to tenuous, too bitter, to endure that strain again.

Two-Spear hardly noticed the changes in his wolf-friend. In the highest parts of his mind, he had forgiven the wolf for his weakness and betrayal, as a chief should forgive weakness in his followers. But he hadn't forgotten it, and there was no trust between them. So long as

No-name behaved, Two-Spear didn't need to resolve the conflicts in his own mind; and Two-Spear quickly became adept at not noticing most of No-name's behavior.

Besides, he was overflowing with plans for the future. Not once during the long journey had he slipped into the muzzy timelessness of wolfsong. His mind had been clear and orderly. The elf was strong and master of the wolf within him. Not even Rellah would be able to match him for sheer single-mindedness.

He imagined the old one's face after he told the tribe his plans. She'd hardly be willing to believe that a Wolfrider could find answers that had eluded elves, but he'd prove it to her. Her mouth would look like she'd bitten into something sour, and a thin smile passed over Two-Spear's lips before the image faded from his mind's eye.

His pace quickened.

There was a celebration when Two-Spear and No-name returned, one of the last of the season. Summer had become autumn while they'd been away, and autumn itself was waning. Preparations for winter had been made. The meat-drying racks were heavy; caches had been set along the most-used trails, and all those adept with a needle or quill were putting the final seams in warm winter clothing.

Any other time Two-Spear would have been pleased by such industry, now he caught himself scowling. Heavy furs weren't going to be necessary at their new home and they couldn't carry half the food that had already been smoked or dried. It was a waste; worse, it was a warning that it might be difficult to get the tribe to move so far.

Two-Spear wasted no time, and made his pronouncements at the first feast-meal he shared with them. He asked for the dreamberry bowl, and told his tale with their intoxicating assistance. He didn't share everything;

173

he passed lightly over No-name's rebellion and said nothing at all about the skulls. With sendings, gestures, and words he described the plateau and its cave. He showed them that it was remote from the forest and the humans, but that the plains supported vast herds of heavy-footed beasts just waiting to be hunted.

It is the safest place in the world for us, and it will be our new home, he concluded.

The same berries which had made it easier for Two-Spear to share his vision with the tribe made it acutely possible for him to feel their skepticism. Rellah did indeed look like she had a mouthful of puckernuts, but her thoughts were not the sour admiration he'd expected.

It is too late in the season for such a journey, she grumbled. **And there is nothing there that we don't already have here.**

It was the home of elves before! Two-Spear fairly shouted through his thoughts. He battered Rellah and all the others with his memory of the spirit-pool, but still he did not share the tomb. **It is destined to be our home for the future!**

Two-Spear felt them all withdraw into their own thoughts. Destiny and future were unfamiliar, uncomfortable thoughts to be shoved into their minds. Willowgreen had said that not all seeds could grow in all types of soil, and the chief saw that she was right. His tribe, even the old ones, were not prepared to accept the truths he had discovered. He had made a mistake in revealing it to them so quickly.

Chiefs could make mistakes, he decided quickly. It was natural to forget the weakness of his followers; dangerous, perhaps, but understandable. He would not make such a mistake again. If neither Wolfriders nor elves could face his truth directly, then Two-Spear would guide them to it, as the wolves sometimes guided a straggler from the herd. As long as he learned from his mistakes, Two-Spear could tolerate them.

He let the dreamberries lead the Wolfriders down other paths for now. The cavern had waited a long time. It could wait until spring, or longer.

Dreamsinger's Tale

by Janny Wurts

The spring grass grew long and lush in the glade, and a
brook where peepers shrilled in annual courtship ran
close by. There, Huntress Skyfire flung herself down,
panting and hot after a long run through the forest. She
drank and splashed cold water through her hair, then
shed her bow and her spear and her sweaty, winter-
musty furs and rolled onto her back. Mother moon
peeped like a needle of bone through the leaves. Skyfire
regarded its thin crescent and sighed, not quite content.
Something was missing, lacking, *not right*. Hard as
she ran, fast as she could shoot an arrow into fleeing
prey, she could not quite catch up with whatever it
was.

Her wolf-friend, Woodbiter, arrived at the clearing.
Old now, and surely where he had once been full of
antics, he had leaves sticking in his coat. With his ears
canted back, he crouched in the grass, panting also. The
breeze that wafted through his fur carried the scent of
something dead.

Rolled in a scent patch. Again, Skyfire sent. She
wrinkled her nose in distaste.

Woodbiter regarded her with unwinking yellow eyes.
Go hunting now. The wolf's image held the savory
taste of hot blood, the thrill and the kick of prey as his
jaws closed and snapped the spine.

No. Skyfire rolled onto her elbows, irritable as a
she-wolf past her heat. **No.** She was hungry, but

hunger was not what drove her. She would go hunting, but not now, not tonight.

Woodbiter endured his elf-friend's gaze for the span of a heartbeat, then whined, rolled, and showed the pale fur of his throat to appease her aggressive mood. **Hunt alone,** he sent. When the Huntress neither answered nor forbade him, he sprang up and slunk off into the forest.

Skyfire hammered his fist into soft spring soil and flopped with her chin on her elbows. The *not right* feeling persisted. Though she tried, she could find no name for it. This was no anticipation of danger, like the moment when the prong-horn's charge caught a spear-thrower off guard. Neither was it a feeling of threat, like the packs of human hunters who sometimes wandered too near the holt. Skyfire twisted two grass stems between her fingers. Decidedly, this was not even the faintly giddy feeling one got after eating too many dreamberries. She frowned at the brook, and watched the moon's broken reflection frown back. She could not say why she was here, lying idle in new grass when her belly growled with hunger. Well after nightfall, the tribe would be wondering why their chieftess did not appear to lead the hunt. Yet Skyfire made no effort to rise. She would not take up her spear. Some instinct as deep as earth urged her to linger.

She plucked a grass blade and chewed the stem, only to spit it out because it tasted sour. In the stream the shape of the moon rippled on as if nothing was wrong. The peepers shrilled in a forest that seemed touched by strange, waiting silence; not the quiet of approaching predators, but a sort of stillness that caused the hair to prickle. In that moment, with discontent sharp as a thorn in her side, Skyfire first heard the singing.

The melody touched her first, high and sweet and filled with the vitality of growing things. Skyfire tilted her head, tense and listening. She sniffed the air, but smelled no taint of humans. Belatedly she noticed that this song held none of the grunts which passed for language among the five-fingers. Perhaps in sound, perhaps in sending, this singer used no words at all, only notes laid out in brightness and light. Each lilted phrase filled Skyfire with a pure and innocent joy. Without quite knowing she had moved, she found herself on her feet. The song drew her as nothing in memory had ever done before.

Only the sternest habits of survival made her remember the spear, bow, and quiver lying in the grass. She paused to gather them up, though the delay made her ache. The sweaty fur garment she had shed no longer seemed important, so she abandoned it. Clad only in thin leather tunic and cross-laced boots, Skyfire slipped into the dark of the forest.

As only an elf or a wolf could move, she followed the elusive song through thicket and draw. Yet the singer eluded her. Between the black boles of oaks, over ferny hummocks and marshy hollows, he walked and left no marks. Neither branch nor briar nor deadfall seemed to slow him. Huntress Skyfire shook her bright hair in annoyance. She was considered a fine tracker, lacking only the nose of a wolf to unravel the most difficult trails. She hurried, silent and adept and forest-cunning, and determined as never before; but somehow, the uncanny song caused her native grace to abandon her. Scratched on twigs, scraped on thorns, she felt clumsy as a five-finger, and as foolish. Yet to stop or even slow down was to lose the music that even now filtered through a copse of saplings. The melody ran flawless as stream water, describing delight that bordered the edges of pain. Skyfire ran. Breathless, she twisted around tree branches and half tripped on roots and vines. Still the singer evaded her. His melody drew relentlessly farther ahead, until at length it became no more than the memory of beauty, the fading essence of dream.

Skyfire cursed and stumbled to her knees in moss. Tired, confused, and even hotter than before, she rubbed at scratches on her spear arm. The discontent which had troubled her earlier intensified, became a disappointment near to sickness. She jabbed at soft earth with her spear-butt. The silence, the terrible absence of song, left her aching in a way that knew no remedy.

Around her, night had begun to fail. Gray light shone between branches and new leaves, and birds awakened singing. Soon humans might be abroad, dangerous to any elf who foolishly stayed in the open. For once Skyfire did not care. Crossly she threw herself prone, her chin cupped in her fists. She did not move as the world grew golden with dawn, nor when the sun speared slanting through the boughs, striping her shoulders with warmth. Furious at her own folly, yet helpless to free herself of yearning, she lay and frowned until her head ached and her thoughts spun with hunger. The music pulled at her still. The memory did not fade before the *now* awareness of her wolf-sense; notes spilled and echoed in her mind until she wanted to weep, bereft.

Woodbiter found her at midday. The wolf had fared well on his hunt and his belly was gorged. He had dragged his kill beneath a fallen log, then urinated upon the place to mark it; the cache was not far, and still fresh. Yet meat would not assuage the emptiness left by the singer. Skyfire refused her wolf-friend's offer.

The animal sensed her discontent. He licked her eyelids in commiseration, and finally curled in the shade to sleep.

Skyfire left him there. Irritable and alone, she arose and retraced her trail from the night before. The path of her run was clear, a swath of torn leaves and twigs freshly challenge of survival seemed somehow less keen. The lilt of the song stirred within her at odd moments, like an echo never entirely lost. And as was her habit in the old days of Two-Spear's strife, Skyfire wandered often. Perhaps not by chance, she found her way back to the clearing. There, yet again, she waited for something she could not name.

This time clouds shadowed her vigil. Rainfall slicked her hair on her shoulders and dripped coldly down her back and groin. She shook herself like a wolf, licking irritably at the runoff. Long hours she listened between the patter of droplets over leaves, but no song reached her save the shrilling of peepers in the damp and the puddles. Shivering, saddened, but never quite miserable enough to leave, Skyfire finally dozed.

The song returned in her dreams. Notes tripped and spilled between thorn brakes where no rain fell, and the forest lay dappled with sun like high summer. In dream, Skyfire leaped up and pursued. The song flowed like sending, and images swept through her sleeping mind. Though the singer used no words, his music spoke of other times, of taller, fairer elves than those who ran with the wolves. They wore beautiful, many-colored clothing. Beyond them Skyfire beheld strange dwellings, then stars sprinkled uncountably across blackness deeper than night. She saw suns that blistered her eyes, and moons silvery as the trinkets that humans cut from mussel shells. And yet there was sorrow beneath the beauty of this song. Woven through the strangeness and wonder of the images lay a memory of cold, like death. In the dream, Skyfire started. The stars and the moons snapped. Many times she had stepped carelessly on soft soil and left the imprint of her booted foot. Although she searched and sniffed, she found nothing of the singer. His melody haunted her. Once when she might have stopped to spear fish, his memory stung her haplessly onward.

In time, the daystar lowered and the birds flew to roost. Exhausted, and hopelessly in thrall to the singer's dream, Skyfire stumbled and fell. She caught herself short of a bang on the head; and there, between her hands, found the impression of a bare foot. The track had four toes, clearly made by an elf. Yet Skyfire knew at once that none of her own tribe had trodden here. Precisely between the hollow of toes and heel, there bloomed a flower entirely out of phase with the season.

Astonishment overwhelmed Skyfire, and her breath caught. For no reason she could name, she knelt by the blossom and wept. Then, as if the release of emotion had snapped the dream's hold on her mind, she acknowledged the sending from the holt which had sought her for some hours. Most oddly, it was Twigleaf, the youngest cub in the tribe, whose call reached her first. Skyfire returned reassurance of her well-being. Then, with weariness similar to the feeling of waking from dreams of escaped prey, she rose and returned to lead the hunt.

For an eight-of-days, the chieftess ran with the pack as always. The rough way of the Wolfriders and the song of their mounts as they howled before the hunt stirred her, made her heart lift and the blood race through her veins. Only now the abruptly vanished, and dark against the silver-ice light of new dawn, she beheld the singer.

He stood before her, clad in gray. A wolf of the same hue lolled at his side. The eyes of wolf and rider were eerily alike, deep and light as mist. But the elf-singer's hair was black, hanging tangled and unkempt down his back.

Convinced she had awakened, Skyfire surged to her feet, all grace and speed and anger. Nobody, wolf or elf, *ever* sneaked up on her like that, far less a stranger in territory hunted by her tribe and pack.

Yet even as she raised her spear and called challenge, the singer and wolf both vanished. Skyfire checked. The dream dissolved around her and she woke in reality, to chilly rain and daylight. Her breath came painfully to her chest. On the ground, where in the dream the singer's feet had trodden, the grass grew sere and dry as autumn. A single oak leaf lay caught between the stems, not the new soft green of spring, but colored red as blood.

Skyfire gasped. She brushed the dried grass with her hands and shivered. This singer of dreams was surely part throwback. The magic of the old ones ran deep in him.

The storm had split into broken clouds, and the leaves dripped sullenly by the time Skyfire returned to the holt. Most of the tribe lay in tree hollows, sleeping, but a few of the young ones tussled like wolf cubs in the shade. One just barely an adult watched over their play, her hands weaving baskets out of rush.

"Been stalking black-neck deer?" Sapling taunted. Her fingers stilled on her handiwork as she tossed back pale hair. "Or maybe something bigger than a deer stalked you? Looks like you spent the night holed up in a thicket."

Skyfire bent and snatched a rush. "Close."

"Barren hunt?" asked Sapling, quick enough to grab back her stolen green. Such teasing had been part of her life since she was a cub.

The chieftess shook her head, but the ravvit she had caught and eaten on her way home had not left her sated. The dreams and the singer were driving her to distraction. Even her wolf noticed her ribs, as if she was gaunt from the season of white cold. As Skyfire reached the

tree which held her sleeping hollow, she sensed the
concern of Pine, who sometimes lay with her after the
hunt. She never confided in him, but the fact that she
was troubled had been noticed. Yet Pine's embrace
offered no comfort. Chilled and confused as Skyfire was,
she did not wish the warmth of a lovemate. A strange elf
walked the forest, one who belonged to no pack, and
who owned depths not seen in cubs born for many
generations. He was Wolfrider, surely enough, but different in ways not easily understood. Skyfire sensed trouble. If she told the rest of the tribe of the song-dreams
and their maker, the wolf in them might precipitate an
outcome that could not be controlled. Though pack
ways and pack actions served well in matters of survival,
Skyfire struggled to balance instinct against a drive that
ran deeper than curiosity. She realized she must track
down and confront this singer without help from the
other Wolfriders.

The limbs which led to her hollow were smoothed
with many climbings. Skyfire pulled herself upward out
of habit, her mind preoccupied with unfamiliar concepts. Against her nature, she must plan, for the tribe
must not suffer for her pursuit of the singer. She must
lead the hunt through the night, and then in the gray
hours before daybreak, slip away.

The hollow in the tree was dim and invitingly cool,
but Skyfire did not sleep. Curled in her furs, her bright
hair wound damply over her shoulders, she wondered
how an elf could track a shadow. For the singer was
shadow, a figure spun of dreams. In the depths of his
gray-silver eyes she could easily become lost.

The mild weather of spring quickly gave way before
the darker foliage and the stronger sun of summer. Like
most elves, Skyfire abandoned use of her sleeping hollow
altogether, preferring to curl up like a wolf in the

dappled shade of a thicket, her body against cool earth. But while the winds stilled, and prey grew fat and plentiful, and the Wolfriders became sleek with easy hunting, their chieftess grew lean with muscle. After the nightly kill, she ran, until she could traverse the dense forest in silence at speed. She learned not to thrash through briars, but to twist and duck and dodge through the narrowest of openings without slackening stride. She practiced leaping over streams, from rock to fallen log, to banks treacherous with moss. Her feet became very sure; for the first time, Woodbiter had trouble keeping up.

Gray-muzzle, she teased once, as the two of them lay panting in companionship in a forest glade. She licked the corner of his lips in the manner of one wolf showing affection for another.

Woodbiter's eye rolled and met hers. **Killed deer,** he sent in wolfish reproach. Except for rank, distinctions were never made between members of the wolf-pack once a cub reached adulthood. A wolf either hunted successfully and held his own, or else failed to survive.

Skyfire slammed playfully into her wolf-friend's shoulder and tussled, rolling over and over upon the ground. As elves, her tribe handled life with little difference. Hardship made no allowance for individuals who were not strong. Such was the way of the wild. But as Skyfire wrestled with her wolf in the midsummer heat, she thought upon the singer's dreams. For the first time, she wondered whether Timmain's sacrifice, which first mingled the blood of wolves and elves, might have been made in the hope of something more.

That night the hunt went well. Early on, Spearhand brought down a large buck. Then Skimmer and his wolf, Brighttail, flushed a herd of prong-horns. The Wolfriders leaped eagerly in pursuit. By the time the two moons lifted toward the zenith, there was feasting. Skyfire did not gorge on the meat with the others, but ate sparingly and wrapped a second portion to carry with her. Then, leaving her spear in Sapling's care, she tightened the strap of her quiver and settled her bow over her shoulder.

Going? sent Woodbiter. He licked his bloody muzzle and raised expectant eyes.

Skyfire returned the image of the clearing by the brook. By that the wolf understood she would spend another night running, or perhaps simply sitting by water staring at nothing. He chose to remain with his kill.

Huntress Skyfire twisted her red hair into a braid. Aware that she prepared to embark upon another night of wandering, her tribe-mates did not ask why. Neither did they try to go along, as once before they might have. Skyfire did not explain her leaving. If a wolf-chief wanted solitude, he drove off his subordinates with snarls, not affection. Skyfire could be as fierce in defense of her wishes. No elf in the tribe cared to provoke her wrath as Two-Spear had, on the day she had challenged him for leadership.

Yet the more distance Skyfire set between herself and the members of her tribe, the more determination deserted her. She paused, leaned against a tree, and rested her cheek against rough bark. She had heard no singing for many eights-of-days. All her practice at running and her nights of vigil had led her no closer to the strange elf than the time when the peepers called. Soon the forest would change. Frost and cold winds would strip the green from the leaves. The season of white cold would follow and the struggle for survival would force an end to her search. Recalling the marvels in the singer's dream, Skyfire clenched her teeth in frustration. Somehow she knew that if she failed, the lost feeling inside her would never be answered.

Accordingly, she tucked her bow more comfortably across her shoulders and began to jog. Tonight she paid no attention to landmarks, but traveled without purpose or direction. She might encounter humans, or even one of the clearings where they set snares for game, but this once caution deserted her. The singer's long silence drove her, aching, to recklessness.

Skyfire ran. The familiar paths, the known trees, the territory hunted by the wolf-pack, all fell behind. Breathless, weary, the chieftess would not rest. Deer started out of her path, and night creatures looked up from their hunting. Still she ran, while stars blinked endlessly between the leaves overhead. The earth jarred over and over against the soles of her feet, and her bowstring rasped blisters on her shoulder. Still the chieftess ran.

Her breath came in wrenching gasps. She did not stop. Not until her legs failed her and she tumbled headlong into old leaves. The musty smell filled her nostrils, and skeletons of veined stems caught in her hair. Skyfire rolled miserably onto her back. Her frustration skirted the edges of despair, but she was too spent even to curse.

She could do nothing at all but lie still and listen to silence until her ears stung under the weight of it.

In time her heart stopped hammering and her breathing slowed. Something stirred in her mind and she heard a faint drift of melody. Skyfire shut her eyes, uncertain whether her imagination might be tricking her as had happened so many times before.

But the singing grew stronger. The melody turned and interwove like a waterfall, intricate beyond understanding. Skyfire rose up on her elbows. Longing woke within her. Feeling tears burn behind her eyelids, she pushed at last to her feet. She did not feel the protest of her tired body as, once more, she started to run. The singer's dream enfolded her senses, drew her irresistibly like a moth toward flame.

Skyfire no longer saw trees, or the night-dark vista of forest. She ran through a waking dream of wide, open plains under cloudless sky. The stars seemed close enough to touch, and the wind held a bite of cold that burned her throat as she breathed. Scents of many descriptions filled her nostrils, intoxicating in their detail. Skyfire sniffed deeply. She realized that she ran with the senses of a wolf, even as Timmain had done generations in the past. Yet though her limbs might seem clothed in fur and her body that of a beast, still her mind was not entirely animal. The compassion, the gentleness, and the sorrow of her ancestors reverberated through her being. As she raced on four pads over the plain, she shared echoes of Timmain's thoughts.

Then the singer's melody changed. The dream of sharing wolf-shape faded and turned deep and sad and lost. The cold deepened. Snow fell, a whirling maelstrom of flakes that smothered the memory of summer or stars. Frost cut cruelly into flesh no longer clothed in the protective pelt of the wolf. Skyfire cried out, painfully rubbing fingers that were thinner, longer, and more delicate than those she had been born with. She experienced the past suffering of the first ones, and the crippling confusion of minds accustomed only to contemplation. Terror ripped into nerves she never knew she possessed.

She cried out, stumbled, and fell waking into the icy reality of a snowdrift. Cold shocked her back into memory of self; around her, the singer's melody sang of despair that approached madness.

Skyfire rolled until the end of her bow no longer hampered her legs. She shook icy flakes from her lashes and hair, and stood upright with a shiver. The music seemed very near, and it pulled at her heart without surcease. Around her the trees drooped under a hardened burden of ice. Summer stars shone faintly through the cold. Skyfire blinked. Unquestioning as a wolf, she shook off the muddle left by the chill and pressed forward. The snow deepened. Before long she labored through drifts that rose to her chest. But her efforts brought progress. The melody grew stronger as she went; the spell of the singer wove inescapably through her being. Whether she risked death, she would not stop now.

The way grew more difficult. The snow acquired a hardened, glassy crust of ice that cut at her fingers and toes. Skyfire was not dressed for such weather. Her flesh gradually went numb. She shivered uncontrollably, and longed for the stoic presence of Woodbiter at her side. Still, harsh as her own straits seemed, nothing prepared her as she scrabbled over the final rise in the snow and beheld the singer at last.

He sat with his head bowed over crossed arms, bare feet buried to the ankles in the pelt of his gray wolf. Black hair hid his face, trailed in unkempt tangles over shoulders clad thinly as Skyfire's. He did not shiver, though his fingers seemed frozen and bloodless as quartz. His song surrounded him with magic. Thick as mist, the spells he sang brought cold deep enough to crack stone, and grief enough to make the trees weep.

Skyfire hesitated as if struck by a blow. Then, before she quite realized she had reacted, she was running, sliding, flailing down the steep drift, to tumble breathless at his side.

The gray wolf looked up and growled, its eyes all

silver-bright and wary. For once as brash as her brother, Skyfire dared its wrath. She recovered her footing and addressed its uncanny companion.

Who are you? Though she had not planned, her words came out as sending.

The singer looked up. Eyes identical to those of the wolf met hers, and it seemed for a breath that the earth stopped turning.

Then his song changed, flowed without break into sending. The melody itself framed answer, describing him as Outcast, wild as the bachelor wolf who runs with no ties to a pack. Skyfire, listening, heard a melancholy that made her spirit ring with echoes. The song described more than an elf with silver eyes, more than a hunter who roved alone. The chieftess of the Wolfriders heard silence more deep than sky, wind more free than storms, a spirit more solitary than the terrible moment of death. She knew then that she had been gifted with this elf's soulname, and in the depths of his silver-ice eyes she saw her own self reflected back at her.

Kyr.

There, in an unseasonal enchanted snow, Huntress Skyfire became Recognized by an elf who was a stranger, and who conformed to no law and no pack. More terrifying still, the melody this outsider sang held all of the exhilaration, and all of the pain, and all of the twisted madness that the magic of the high ones became heir to on the world of two moons.

Even through the compulsion of Recognition, Skyfire sensed danger. The spell the song wove was not gentle, but filled full measure with remembered tragedy from the past. The effect was compelling enough to wound, and both she and the one fate chose for her mating were entangled in its threads. One of them must free the other, and of the two, the singer was most lost in his dream. Recognition offered no choice in the matter. Skyfire reached out to the singer, but never completed her touch. The gray wolf's warning became a snarl of rage and his muzzle lifted over bared teeth.

The despair of the singer's spell only hampered. In desperation, Skyfire sent to the beast, her image all strength without threat. The wolf did not respond as a pack member would. Mad as his outsider master, he rose and advanced on stiffened legs. Skyfire sensed the tautening of muscles beneath the silver-gray pelt. The wolf was preparing to rush her, and she carried no spear to defend.

Only her bow remained to her, hung uselessly across her shoulders; if she made the slightest move to free it, the stranger wolf would charge. Skyfire knew better than to attempt to flee. The spell slowed her reflexes and the snow would mire her. The wolf would sense her disadvantage. That would inevitably provoke an attack, and she had no desire to die with fangs sunk into her neck from behind.

She glanced to the singer, but no help awaited her there. Snow flurried over his dark hair, and his eyes were mirrors of grief. Song and sorrow had overwhelmed his senses; his magic ran out of control.

The wolf growled again. It shifted onto its haunches. Aware she was out of options, Skyfire snatched for her bow. The string barely cleared her shoulder as the great beast sprang. He was larger than Woodbiter, and young. Skyfire raised the frail wood, tried uselessly to stave off his rush. Fangs closed over the shaft and splinters flew. Then the chieftess was borne down beneath hard-muscled weight and gray fur.

She ducked to protect her throat. Battered into snow, she rolled. The terrible jaws clacked over her head. The wolf pressed for another snap. Skyfire twisted and managed to jab a knee into the animal's ribs. The wolf snarled in rage and tried again. Once more she dodged its teeth. Her quiver banged into her thigh, spilling stone-pointed arrows treacherously over the ground. If she rolled in an attempt to throw the wolf off, she risked becoming impaled. Yet she had little chance if she hesitated. The wolf caught her braid in its teeth and worried, slamming her head from side to side. She punched at its eyes, missed, and caught a glancing slash from a fang.

The wolf scented blood and attacked with renewed fury. In danger of severe mauling, Skyfire braced against its chest and sent, **Submission-fear-fury-submission.** She hammered the beast's mind with her self-awareness, the irrefutable knowledge of her right to lead. She had challenged for dominance, and won. This stranger wolf *must* back down before her, or else kill, or be killed in turn. Such was the way of the wolves.

Skyfire gritted her teeth, the scent of her own blood strong in her nostrils. She knew no fear, only determination; this the wolf sensed. Its great heart faltered. Skyfire sensed its instant of unsureness. She twisted, used a wrestling trick and threw the heavier animal down. At once she went for its throat. Her nails caught its flesh and twisted, hard. The breath rasped in its throat. It lived now only by her sufferance. Her green eyes stared into ones of silver-gray, elf and wolf both equally savage and fierce.

Then the wolf went limp. Its lips stayed turned back, but it arched its neck to farther expose its throat. Skyfire gave the animal an extra shake to enforce her moment of victory. Then she backed off.

The air felt very cold. Grazed, disheveled, and bleeding from her slashed wrist, the chieftess licked at her hurt. She watched the gray wolf warily, but it rose with its tail down and settled on the far side of the singer. Only then did Skyfire realize that the terrible song had stilled. She looked around to find the black-haired elf senseless in the snows his magic had spun. But the dreams of the past which inspired him had dissipated. His awareness was dark as the night.

Skyfire shrugged her torn tunic back into place. Stiffly she regained her feet and went to him. His eyes were open and empty as clouds. Outcast he had named himself; but to Skyfire he was Dreamsinger, and would remain so, though he had no pack to name him. Slowly the chieftess knelt at his side. She cautiously extended a hand, and this time the gray wolf did not challenge. Her fingers bridged a gap of empty, wintry air, and touched.

His flesh was very cold. Skyfire sent thoughts of urgency into his mind, and could not reach him. His magic had carried him perilously far. He would return on his own, perhaps, but unless he wakened soon he might freeze. The possibility filled Huntress Skyfire with a new and uncomfortable dilemma.

The way of the wolf-pack urged her to leave. Survivors did not burden their resources; to be encumbered by the helpless was to invite a pointless death. Yet the dream of the singer had poisoned the familiar, pushed Skyfire's awareness beyond the limits of experience. Though taxed by the rigors of her night-long run, and shaped by the same wild laws which had arbitrated her dispute with the wolf, the chieftess hesitated. Skyfire found herself incapable of leaving the Dreamsinger to die.

Surely Recognition might cause such madness. Partially reassured, the chieftess caught the stranger beneath the shoulders. The gray wolf whined, but did not interfere as she half lifted, half dragged him over the heavy drifts. The Dreamsinger was slight, perhaps the same build as Sapling. Yet the Huntress was tired, and the snow hampered her steps. Leaving her arrows and broken bow, she labored over the ice with her burden until her feet stumbled beneath her. Her strength was long-since spent. Somehow she continued. In time the magic of despair fell behind. The stars overhead lay pale in the glow of dawn, and green ferns and moss cushioned her steps.

Skyfire lowered the Dreamsinger in a clearing and flung herself down by his side. Whether or not there were humans, she could go no farther. She curled on the ground beside the strange elf and slept. After pacing with uneasiness the gray wolf curled on the opposite side of his elf-friend and buried its muzzle beneath its brush.

Huntress Skyfire awakened to song. Sunlight dappled her shoulders and eased the ache of her cut wrist; yet even summer's warmth seemed thin beside the joy in Dreamsinger's melody. The chieftess stirred, and found eyes of unearthly silver intently watching her. The black-haired elf seemed poised, as if for flight; only the ties of Recognition prevented.

Speech itself seemed an intrusion, a sour note against a magnificence of song that no living being might dare to spoil. **Come,** Skyfire sent. She raised her arms toward him.

The outsider elf hesitated. Outcast, the song defined him, and a thread of sadness slowed the cadence.

"No." Skyfire smiled, for the moment as sure as bedrock. "Dreamsinger." Though the ways of the pack and the vision of dream might war inside her, the call of Recognition obscured them.

For a moment the fey elf did not move. All his years of wandering cast a current of doubt between them. Skyfire smiled, uncaring; and the pull of longing overwhelmed. The Dreamsinger answered the name he had been given and gathered Skyfire into his embrace. His song swelled around her. For an instant she knew the wild joy of Timmain running with her wolf-mate; then the pound of blood in her veins overturned the dream. The notes of the spell shifted afresh, transformed the clearing to a place of new spring grass that was softly perfect for mating. Skyfire had known the exertion and thrill of the hunt. She had killed for food and for survival, and lived the fierce way of the wolf-pack. She had howled in moonlight, and chipped winter ice for drinking, and gnawed upon bones when her stomach was hollow with hunger. The life of the pack contained all there was to know of death and survival. But in Dreamsinger's arms the Wolfrider chieftess learned gentleness, and that one thing overturned all else.

Dreamsinger traced her many scars with light fingers. His song spoke now of healing, and places where elves need not kill. Skyfire heard, and ached with the terror of the unknown. This dream which lacked the howl and the hunt tore away the familiar, left her adrift without bearings. The Dreamsinger sang of the past, lost forever, or of a life impossibly far into the future. Skyfire caught her fey mate close, for his body was warm and listening caused pain. Yet little comfort came to her. He was the song, and his strangeness brought conflict beyond bearing. The pull of Recognition would not let her leave, not let her run and join Woodbiter, and find refuge in the pack. She could not go; in time she no longer wanted to. The Dreamsinger's strange magic touched her spirit and wove irrevocable change.

After the mating he caught up her fiery hair and gloried in the color, which promised both sunset and dawn. As he braided the shining length of it, Skyfire looked up past his head and watched a tree burst spontaneously into blossom. The scent made her languid and content, until the Dreamsinger's spell changed key, as, inevitably, it must. He belonged to no pack. As outcast, he must leave her, or risk the leadership she had won from Two-Spear at such cost. Dreamsinger's music encompassed the brightness and sorrow of that. Released from the drive of Recognition, and caught in contention between ways, Skyfire pulled free of his arms, unable to speak.

The aftermath of their joining was bittersweet. The Dreamsinger pulled on his ragged clothing with his back turned. Before the afternoon was spent, his gray wolf arose and slipped away with him into the forest.

Evening fell, and the moon rose. Skyfire sat amid drifts of falling petals. Woodbiter crouched at her feet, insistently proud of finding her; she had strayed very far from known territory. The old wolf's sides heaved as he panted, yet occasionally, in concern, he would turn his muzzle and lick at the cut on his chieftess's arm.

Skyfire scratched absently at his ears. She was hungry but had no inclination to hunt. The woodland silence oppressed her, filled her with a strange, numb emptiness that the way of the wolf could never fulfill. She would bear a cub to the Dreamsinger; such was the fruit of Recognition. But his song and his dream might leave her with more than offspring, if she was bold enough to risk leading the tribe into change.

For by the way of the wolf, Dreamsinger was outcast. The magic of the high ones ran to madness within him. Rightly the earlier generations had driven him out, for compassion and dreams of peace had no place in pack life. Yet Skyfire had shared his visions. She had experienced the hopes of Timmain, and through them she understood that her ancestress had mated for more than the toughness and savagery of the wolf. The ancestress had wished to pass on hardiness and forest cunning, yet retain the bright dreams of the first ones. All of this had been lost over time. Skyfire's tribe lived only the way of the pack, and not an elf among them questioned why.

The chieftess rose restlessly to her feet. She drew on her boots, and blossoms fell like snow from her shoulders. She considered the cub she would bear from this mating. It might inherit its father's fey madness. By pack law, it also might suffer and be driven away into solitude. Skyfire flicked her braid back in frustration. By then she herself might not remember the song and the dream, for the wolfsong eroded the memory. This minute she perceived very clearly. If the tribe continued as it had, they would have nothing to offer their cubs but hardship and hunger and the changeable luck of the hunt. Something precious stood to be lost, perhaps without chance of recovery.

Dreamsinger himself held the answer. He wandered the forest in exile, hunting what he could forage, and driven relentlessly by gifts that had potential to kill him. Yet he had not died. His madness had harmed no others. Skyfire might bring him into the holt, and ensure the continuance of the dreams his songs inspired. But to do so defied pack law. For that the Wolfriders would challenge her, force her to fight and fight again until all had submitted to her will. Her chieftainship might be lost. She might be defeated by another, and earn death or even exile without hope of reprieve. The thought of sharing Two-Spear's cruel fate filled her with distress. Woodbiter sensed, and whined softly by her knee.

Skyfire stroked the wolf's head, but not to offer reassurance. **Find Dreamsinger,** she sent.

The wolf hesitated. Sharply impatient, the chieftess drove him forward. She had learned a thing worth fighting for, worth even the risk of total loss. Elves might hunt with wolves, and share the hardships of survival.

But Dreamsinger had showed her another way, neither elf nor wolf, but a glimpse of Timmain's wise vision. Skyfire chose change. She slipped through the thickets like the wild creature she was, her ears listening keenly for distant strains of a song she still could not distinguish between the sending of an elf, or true sound.

Summer Tag

by Allen L. Wold

There was still morning mist in the forest as Raindance, Suretrail, and Sunset moved quietly and quickly from tree to tree. Their eyes searched in all directions, their ears were tuned for any sound of pursuers, or of their quarry who, since the trail was not that fresh, might be anywhere. In spite of this, they carried no weapons, other than their knives, and they tracked their quarry without the aid of their wolves.

Raindance, tense as a bowstring, was in the lead. Her short amber hair was damp with more than mist. Though it was still early in the day, she and the others with her had already seen action, and she knew that one misstep could cost her and her companions. The trail was faint, but she spotted a bent leaf ahead, a sure sign that she was leading them right. She raised one hand briefly to signify that she'd found the way.

Suretrail, two paces behind her, and responsible for making sure no one came at them from the sides, had seen the leaf before Raindance had, but he had said nothing, as this was her lead. Two paces behind him Sunset, as brilliantly dressed as if this were a normal day, kept watch at their back. She tried not to breathe too loudly in the near stillness, and struggled to identify each of the small noises she did hear, to make sure none of them was someone on their trail, even as they pursued another.

Though the elves did not have any weapons, they each

carried an elaborately carved *taal*-stick, as long as an arm, in special slings at their belts. That was part of the risk of the day, since the sticks were no defense against any aggressive animal they might inadvertently run across.

They came to the edge of a shallow ravine, where more firs than maples grew. The slope was steep, and the elves looked down together. It was a good place for an ambush, but there seemed to be nobody there.

"Which way?" Sunset asked as she scanned the tree-limbs overhead. She was nervous, though no stranger to this kind of hunt.

Suretrail glanced up the ravine, then down, then across again. There, on the far side, was the mark of elfin passage, but he said nothing, waiting for Raindance to report it. She did.

"Straight across," she said. Her voice was only a whisper. "But it looks like they doubled back." Around them, except for the normal chatter of squirrels and birds, the forest was silent. "How many?" she asked Suretrail.

"Three, I think." He, too, was whispering. "We're gaining on them."

"Quiet," Sunset hissed, and they all crouched lower as they listened.

The birds off to their left had gone quiet. They held their breaths as they tried to sink into the all too scanty cover on the edge of the bank. But whatever had disturbed the birds must also have stopped moving, for after a moment the chirps and other bird sounds returned to normal.

Suretrail breathed more easily now. It had been hard for him not to take the lead from Raindance, as good as she was. He wished Sunset had not been so intent on living up to her name and had worn something less brilliantly colored this morning.

"Let's move," Raindance said softly, "and see if we can't shorten their lead."

"And," said Sunset, "leave whoever is following us behind."

With one more glance around, in case of ambush, and specially careful of a dense tangle of wine-berry vines hanging from a pair of gigantic cedars on the far slope of the ravine, they left their resting place and descended the steep but shallow slope, then hurried up the other side.

Lonebriar, as he was known then, high in that very tangle of vines, kept still as he watched the three elves cross the ravine. He had had a tense moment when it had seemed that Suretrail had looked straight into his eyes, but apparently the older elf had not seen him after all. Lonebriar had never intended to ambush them from here anyway, he would make too much noise coming down through the vines, and would lose all surprise. He was willing to be patient, to wait for just the right place before making his move.

He did not stir until the three elves on the ground below had disappeared from sight, and almost from hearing, and even then he kept to the treetops as well as he could as he left his hiding place and moved to intercept them. He did not follow them directly, but paralleled their line of travel. It wasn't his trail they were following—those others had gone by sometime before. And besides, it was Raindance he wanted.

He moved quickly, being as quiet as he could, away from the three below in an arc, and then back again, hoping to cross their path some distance ahead of them. But even as he chose his place he heard them turn aside. What for? he wondered. He dropped down to the ground to look for the trail they had been following and couldn't find it. He hadn't followed that other trail far enough, and had missed a turning.

By now he could no longer hear the all but unnoticeable sounds of their passage. He feared that he had lost them and started off in pursuit. The forest floor was more open here, which gave him less cover, but it allowed him to be as quiet as he wanted to be. When he saw a slight movement perhaps fifty paces ahead, he took to the trees again, and ran along the higher branches—oaks here—hoping for a good place to make his move, and in his hurry almost revealed himself to the three elves. He stopped and ducked back behind the high trunk and listened.

There was no sound of movement below. He peeked around the trunk, barely wide enough this high up to conceal him, and saw the three, crouched in some tall weeds, barely visible from his vantage point. They must have heard him, since they were glancing almost directly at him. He very slowly moved back out of sight and waited, listening as hard as he could, until he heard the subtlest of rustles from below.

But if he let them get away from him again, he might not have another opportunity for a long time. He had to take a bold chance. Once again he moved on in a direction which he hoped would take him ahead of their line of travel, until he came to a single smooth snake vine dangling down. He looked at it for a moment, weighing the possibilities in his mind. Its lower loop ended only three elf-heights from the ground. Yes, this would serve him very well indeed. Especially since he was well concealed by the foliage of the branch on which he crouched. He gripped the vine and waited. It was a tricky move, and a risky one. If he didn't make a count this time, he would lose his only chance. And it seemed that his plan was going to be tested, for there they were, coming toward his tree, with Raindance still in the lead.

It was all he could do to wait until they passed —marvelous luck—directly beneath him. He gripped the vine with one hand, took his *taal*-stick from its sling with the other, then stepped off the branch and slid, a bit too fast perhaps, down the vine to land just two paces behind Sunset.

The three heard him as his feet hit the ground, and, startled, started to turn, but he leaped, swung his *taal*, and struck Sunset a glancing blow on the head. Without a pause he spun and even as Suretrail turned to face him struck him on the shoulder. Raindance was just beyond Suretrail, and Lonebriar leaped for her too, but she was already standing in a face-off crouch. He pulled up short.

"Where did you come from?" Suretrail exclaimed as he burst into laughter.

"Owl pellets," Lonebriar said with a frustrated jerk of his *taal*-stick. "I could have gotten you two anytime, it was Raindance I wanted to count."

Raindance was laughing too as she straightened from her crouch, but Sunset was rubbing her head ruefully.

"A bit rough, there," she said. "Were you in those wine-berry vines back there by the ravine?"

"Way up high," Lonebriar said, "but that was just to spy you out."

Suretrail was looking up at the snake vine from which Lonebriar had descended. "If you'd come down just a moment earlier," he said, "you'd have gotten her."

"I know," Lonebriar said, "but I got greedy at the last minute. Sorry if I hurt you, Sunset."

"Not the worst I've been hurt today," she said. "That was a good move."

"Who are you following?" Lonebriar asked his three friends.

"Hornbird and Puckernut, I think," Raindance said, "and Grazer."

"I haven't seen them all morning," Lonebriar said.

"I got Grazer once," Suretrail said, "when he had to

stop and send Smoke back to the holt. The poor wolf just didn't understand that he couldn't play with us today."

"Can I join you?" Lonebriar asked.

"Sure," Sunset said, but Raindance shook her head.

"I think I'd like to go off on my own for a while," she said.

So she left them, and Lonebriar, Sunset, and Suretrail went on, skirting the far edge of the part of the forest they'd designated for counting *taal*.

Fawn was not old enough to go out with the elders that day. She felt old enough, but she didn't yet have her adult name. She was the oldest of the cubs, but still her parents, Grazer and Dreamsnake, had told her she had to stay near the holt. It was little comfort that her mother, too, had elected to stay behind to take care of the children. Her father was out there having fun, while Fawn had to make do, playing with the younger cubs.

Of course, once she started the game she forgot about the elders. Right now she was sneaking through the fern brake, across the stream from the holt. Beyond the edge of the head-high ferns she saw Sundrop, just about to take refuge in the same place. Fawn leaped out with a shout and tagged her, fair and square. Sundrop, surprised, burst into a scream of laughter. Fawn laughed too.

Then the two stood back-to-back for a moment. Fawn yelled, "Now!" and they ran away from each other as hard as they could. Fawn counted two eights of paces, then ducked behind a tree, hoping to get out of sight before Sundrop could turn around and start chasing her, but Clamshell, quite a bit younger than she, was already there and waiting for her. He tagged her with both hands, and laughed at her surprise.

He's going to be good when he gets a little older, Fawn thought as they stood back-to-back. That was an important part of the game, as was racing away from each other a counted two eights of steps when the winner of the last tag gave the word.

This time Fawn kept running until she got to the white rock, a large outcropping of massive stone, and ran around behind it, almost afraid she'd find somebody there waiting for her. But luck was with her, there was nobody there this time. She stopped a moment, looked quickly over her shoulder, then climbed up the rough, white face toward the rock's flat top. She kept low, in case anybody was watching, and paused on top to catch her breath.

From up here she could see Greentwig, almost as old as she, come sneaking around the rock from the willow wood right next to it. This would be an easy tag, she thought, but before she could make a move, Sundrop dropped down from an overhanging branch and got him.

Poor Greentwig, Fawn thought, he's tagged nobody so far this morning. But he seemed to be having fun in spite of that.

Fawn watched as Sundrop and Greentwig stood back-to-back and raced away from each other. Greentwig went right back into the willow wood, but Sundrop ran away from the white rock through clear forest, so Fawn dropped down from her hiding place to chase after her. She ran so fast that she caught up with Sundrop before she finished her count of paces and tagged her as she ran past. But Sundrop must have heard her coming because she turned just then and tagged Fawn in return. Both were surprised.

"I thought you were Greentwig," Sundrop said, laughing.

"He's in the willows," Fawn told her as they put their backs together.

But before they could race away from each other,

Greentwig came screaming out from behind a tree and got them both.

"Good score!" Fawn told him. She was very surprised; Greentwig was hardly ever clever enough to think of doing something like that.

"I heard you chase Sundrop," he said. His smile was as broad as if he had actually accomplished something. "It's my first tag, and a double, too."

They all three put their backs together, and on Greentwig's word raced away in different directions. Fawn ducked into a clump of berry bushes, where the foliage was so thick she couldn't possibly be seen by anyone outside the bush. She crawled through the low, clear space near the stems, then felt someone tag her hard on the ankle.

She turned in utter surprise, nearly scratching her face on the low branches, and saw that it was Sprig, the youngest of the cubs.

"I was waiting here all the time," Sprig said, laughing so hard he couldn't crawl out of the bushes. They giggled together, then worked their way clear of the berry bushes and stood back-to-back. Sprig's head barely came up to Fawn's shoulder blades. He gave the word and they raced away.

This time Fawn kept running until she was far away from everybody else, then she circled around the outside of the area they'd marked as the territory of the game, until she heard a squeal coming from the hollow in the bend of the stream. She approached carefully and saw Clamshell and Greentwig just beginning their race.

She followed Clamshell as he left the hollow and turned past the triple stump, until Sundrop jumped out from behind the dead cypress and tagged him. But instead of running on up to them, Fawn stopped short while she was still concealed by a tree trunk. Clamshell and Sundrop hadn't seen her, so she waited until they stood back-to-back, and then raced in and tagged them both before Sundrop could give the word.

"That's not fair!" Sundrop shouted, stamping her foot.

"Yes it is," Clamshell said, while Fawn danced, laughing, around them both, eager to be on with the game. Sundrop pouted for just a moment, then joined in their laughter. Then they put their backs together, Fawn gave the word, and they raced off again.

Lonebriar, Sunset, and Suretrail were taking an easy time of it. They had counted *taal* several times in the short while they'd been a team, but each had been counted in turn more than once. Now they were on the far south side of the *taal* area, and seemed to have lost track of everybody. At least, they hadn't seen another elf for long enough that they felt safe in letting down their guard. It gave them a chance to catch their breaths, but if they'd really wanted rest, they'd have stayed back at the holt, or gone fishing with Bluesky and Starflower. It was action they wanted, and so they were heading back north toward the center of the *taal* area. Their casual movement meant that they were vulnerable, but at the moment that was all right with them.

When they first heard the commotion, off to one side, they all had the same thought and went immediately up into the low branches of the oak under which they were passing. Even as they hid themselves in the thick foliage they realized that it wasn't elves they had heard, not the sound of somebody counting *taal*, but more like an animal hunting. But the sounds, half whistle, half bark, were not like those of any animal with which they were familiar, so with only a few quick glances to each other by way of communication, they went back down to the ground to investigate.

As they neared the noise they heard a wood pig squeal

in pain, but somehow more agonized than if it was just being killed by a predator. They gave up caution and hurried on until they came to a small clearing, where they found two swordfeet—animals like giant birds covered with green scales instead of feathers and grasping claws instead of wings—attacking a very small wood pig. It was the calling of the swordfeet they had heard while in the tree. No wonder they hadn't recognized the sound.

One swordfoot was a large adult, the other a nearly grown juvenile. Swordfeet hardly ever came this far north and, in fact, only Suretrail had ever seen them before, when he and some others had gone eight-and-two days' journey to the south long ago during a bad, dry summer of no rain and no game.

He was just as fascinated as Lonebriar and Sunset as they watched the two creatures leaping at the small animal. The great claws on their hind feet, which gave them their name, slashed at the poor animal over and over again. The wood pig was bleeding from several deep wounds, but still too quick to let the swordfeet get a killing blow. As he watched, Lonebriar felt a strange sensation in his mind, like a sending, but different.

The larger of the two swordfeet was taller than an elf, but had been crippled at some time and was not as agile as it should have been. The smaller one, nearly as tall as Lonebriar, was quicker but clumsy. Together they kicked out at the frantic, dancing wood pig, sometimes leaping over it for a better blow, working together to keep it from getting away, chattering at each other in their strange voices.

Eventually the wood pig tired, and the younger swordfoot got lucky. It lashed out with a powerful kick and its long talon caught the wood pig just under the shoulder. The blow tore through skin and ribs, ripping the animal open so that its insides fell out on the ground.

As if they were very hungry, the two intruders from the south immediately started tearing the wood pig apart, even before it was fully dead. The strange sensation Lonebriar was feeling became stronger. It was thin and sharp, almost a taste in the back of his throat. And while it was like a sending, it had no content, other than a feeling of great hunger at last being satisfied.

But in their fascination with the killing, and their excitement, the elves had gotten careless and had let the wind get behind them. The swordfeet suddenly caught their scent and, jealous of their prey and chirping angrily, turned toward the elves and leaped to attack them.

The elves were taken by surprise, and discovered that they were a lot nearer the swordfeet than they had thought they were. The swordfeet made two great leaps toward them before the elves realized what was happening, and they had to scramble to get out of the way. Each elf jumped in a different direction, which fortunately confused the swordfeet for just a moment.

But it was only for just a moment. The swordfeet were incredibly fast and quick, and immediately turned their attention to Suretrail, who barely managed to get up into a tree before it was ripped apart by the swordfeet's huge talons. Lonebriar and Sunset, while they had the chance, decided to follow suit, and each climbed the nearest tree.

The swordfeet, frustrated, dashed from one tree to another and back again, but soon gave up since the elves no longer presented a challenge to their prey. As they returned to eat up the wood pig, too small really for a decent meal, Lonebriar felt the sending sensation again, like an acrid taste in his mind, not very strong but very clear.

Let's get out of here, Suretrail sent to his companions. The others agreed wholeheartedly. Quickly they worked their way higher up into the trees, and then away from the creatures at their meager meal. When they were far enough away to pose no further threat to the swordfeet, they returned to the ground and headed on toward the center of the *taal* area. Lonebriar felt the odd sending diminish, until at last it faded away altogether.

He started to tell the others about it, but Suretrail was talking very earnestly with Sunset about what to do about the swordfeet.

"We can't just let them run around up here," he was saying.

"But there are only two," Sunset said, "and the older one looks like it won't live very long."

"That's as may be," Suretrail said, "but they're both female, and the younger one looks like it's carrying young. If she has her litter up here, we'll have more trouble than we can handle."

"A few swordfeet won't be much competition," Lonebriar said.

"That's not the point," Suretrail answered him. "The trouble is, swordfeet attack anything—deer, big cats, wolves, elves. I saw healthy adults kill a gray bear. They're fast, and strong."

"These two don't seem too impressive," Sunset said.

"They are not a good example. Another problem is that wolves can't smell them—or at least they don't pay any more attention to swordfeet than they do to lizards and small birds. And swordfeet are smart, very smart. But they are different from other hunters, they don't think the same way a wolf does, or a cat. No, we can't let them stay up here in our hunting grounds. And if more swordfeet came north, we'd have to find a new place to live."

"So should we go back," Lonebriar asked, "and destroy them now?"

"Tomorrow will be soon enough," Suretrail said, "but

destroy them we must, and the sooner the better. But
right now I want to find somebody to count." He patted
his *taal*-stick and grinned.

Raindance inched her way through a tangle of
thornbushes, moving so quietly that a robber-bird just
four arm-lengths away didn't notice her. She knew there
was another elf nearby, maybe two, though she had seen
or heard nothing so far. She was good at the game, had
counted many times with her *taal*-stick, and had not
been counted once herself yet. Graywing had once said
that she thought that perhaps Raindance could sense
other elves even when they weren't sending to her, but
Raindance didn't agree with that. Maybe it was smell.

She paused to listen, heard the robber-bird, now
behind her, preen its deep-blue feathers, heard something that sounded like a fox, some way off, digging up a
mouse burrow, heard a slight rustling up in a tree ahead
of her, just a scratching. She looked up toward the
sound, like tiny claws on bark, and saw a squirrel
running along a branch. There was something about its
movement—

She looked back along the way the squirrel had come,
and heard a chattering there, where another squirrel was
scolding at something concealed among the oak leaves.
Nearby was the ball of leaves that was its nest, and
farther out on the limb were, yes, two elves—Freefoot
and Shadowflash. Raindance let her breath out slowly
and watched them for a moment, then backed away, just
as quietly and carefully, until they were out of sight.

She circled around their tree, far and fast, until she
was well ahead of them and, she judged, on their line of
movement. Then she climbed a tree of her own. She
went high up, as high as she could, then out on a limb
which overhung a lower branch which, she hoped, would
be the one Freefoot and Shadowflash would take when

they went by. There was a free drop between her limb and that one. Now all she could do was become a part of the tree and wait.

After a few moments she heard the faintest of sounds approaching—bare elf feet on treebark. She did her best to become even less visible, and even more silent than she was. And her guess, if that was what it was, had been correct. First Freefoot, then Shadowflash stepped out onto the branch below her.

When they were directly underneath her she dropped down to their branch. She landed just behind them, and struck them both, one right after the other, with her *taal*, even as they were reacting to the impact of her landing. Freefoot, in fact, was so startled that he nearly fell out of the tree.

"Easy," Raindance said, laughing, as she helped him regain his balance.

"What did you do," Shadowflash asked, "fly?"

"Just watched the squirrels," Raindance said. "Who are you tracking?"

"Suretrail," Shadowflash said, "and Lonebriar and Sunset, if we can judge by the marks."

"At least," Freefoot said, "we know Suretrail has two others with him."

"I left them together a while ago," Raindance said. "I suppose they could still be teamed up. Can I join you?"

"Sure," the other two said together.

"There's Suretrail's mark, right there," Freefoot went on, pointing to a tiny disturbance in the bark of the limb a few paces farther on.

They followed the trail, which went down from the tree at last. Shadowflash, as the longest sighted, took the lead, while Raindance kept on the alert for anybody who might have been following them. After a while the trail began to get vague, and they all had to work hard to follow it. So intent were they on this task that they almost stumbled across a bear cub before they were aware of it.

"Not good," Freefoot said. The mother bear had to be nearby, and none of them wanted to deal with her if she thought they were a threat to her cub, so they backed away from the little animal, who was not at all afraid of them, and who indeed seemed to want to play. But before they could get fully away, two strange green scaly creatures, as big as elves, jumped without warning out from behind a fallen tree behind them.

The larger of the two swordfeet misjudged its leap, and its huge talons missed Freefoot, but it hit him with its body and knocked him to the ground. Shadowflash was not so lucky. The smaller swordfoot caught him a glancing blow on his right side with one great claw, ripping through his jacket and the flesh beneath.

Raindance had little time to think, but she was nearer Freefoot. She leaped for a branch that nearly overhung her chieftain, then swung from it, aiming a two-footed kick at the swordfoot adult which was about to attack him again. She hit it on the shoulder and knocked it away even as it was jumping.

Shadowflash, meanwhile, had recovered enough to be able to jump on the juvenile, just above its kicking feet, and struck at it with his knife. But the swordfoot's scales were tough, and his blows hardly scratched it.

The adult swordfoot had turned toward Raindance, who was still swinging from her branch, and raised one foot high to kick at her. The momentum of her swing just barely took her out of its way. Freefoot got unsteadily to his feet, drawing his knife as he did so, and stabbed at the swordfoot, aiming just under its foreleg. The blade bit through the softer skin and scales there, but did not penetrate the ribs. The swordfoot leaped away and turned to face him again.

Meanwhile, Shadowflash was having trouble hanging

on to the juvenile. It jumped and twisted and threw itself about, and at last threw Shadowflash to the ground. With almost the same motion, the creature turned on him.

At the same time Raindance was taking advantage of the adult's momentary distraction to swing away to the ground, but she was so concerned for Shadowflash, who was stunned by his fall, that she fell clumsily herself, and that left the larger swordfoot free to pursue Freefoot, who now was trying frantically to get away from it. Raindance lurched upright, then froze—as did everyone else—at the roar of a large animal thrashing through the undergrowth nearby.

It was the mother bear, about which they had forgotten in the fight, which came crashing out of the brush toward them—and they were between her and her cub.

Freefoot was directly in the black bear's path as it charged, upright on its hind legs, forepaws outstretched, more than twice as tall as an elf. He tried to duck out of its way, but the bear swung one paw and knocked him backward, through the air and against the trunk of a tree. The adult swordfoot continued its attack by leaping at the bear, and slashed at it with both talons. The bear was saved from serious injury only by virtue of its dense fur.

Raindance had to choose and Shadowflash, this time, was nearer, so she jumped to his aid even as the smaller swordfoot turned away from him. But before she got to Shadowflash she saw the bear grab the larger swordfoot in a mighty hug, and couldn't help but turn to watch. It looked like the adult swordfoot would surely be killed, but the juvenile leaped high at the bear and struck her with both talons on the shoulder.

Shadowflash, without Raindance's aid, got unsteadily to his feet, and staggered off, away from the battle. With just a glance at him over her shoulder, Raindance turned her attention to Freefoot, who was lying very still at the base of the tree against which he had been thrown. She circled around the battling bear and swordfeet to him. Even as she did so, the bear swung a forepaw at the juvenile swordfoot and knocked it away, and the adult, which had not been unscathed by the bear's hug, attacked it again.

Raindance knelt beside Freefoot. He was unconscious. She grabbed him under the arms and dragged him away from the fight, in the same direction Shadowflash had gone. As she had to pull him backward, she was able to see the two swordfeet suddenly run away from the bear. The bear followed only a pace or two, then stopped to search for her cub, which was running toward her and squealing with fright.

Freefoot began to mutter and toss his head as Raindance pulled him up to his feet. She half carried him after Shadowflash, whom she found leaning against a small elm tree, unable to go any farther. He straightened up when he saw her coming, and tried to help with Freefoot, but he was too badly injured himself and was barely able to follow her away from the bear. They did not go far, but stopped when they came to a big, sturdy tree with low branches. Raindance pulled Freefoot up first, then helped Shadowflash clamber up after. They got themselves to the next higher branch with some difficulty, where Raindance propped Freefoot up against the trunk.

After a moment to catch her breath and to make sure her two companions would not fall, Raindance looked to their wounds. Freefoot had several broken ribs and was still dazed from hitting his head on the tree trunk. Shadowflash's wound was not deep, but it was very long and he was bleeding badly and in shock. Raindance bound his wound as best she could and tried to reassure him that the loss of his *taal*-stick was really not very important under the circumstances. She had lost her *taal*-stick too, though Freefoot still had his in his belt.

"We'll have to find them," Shadowflash insisted. His words were slurred, his shock was worse than she had thought.

"We will," she reassured him, "but later."

There was no hope for it. Freefoot and Shadowflash were too injured to move, and they needed healing right away. The only thing Raindance could do was to make sure they were secure, then hurry back to the holt for help and proper weapons.

Lonebriar, Sunset, and Suretrail were moving quickly through the *taal* area. They had seen or heard no other elf in quite some time, and were eager to find someone to pursue or elude. They went along through a stand of pines, which had carpeted the forest floor with a thick layer of needles so that nothing else grew between the trunks of the trees.

Lonebriar felt something tickling the back of his mind, like the memory of a dream that comes back unbidden. It was another strange sending like before, over almost before he could start to pay attention. It was—had been—sharper than before, and yet very faint, as if it had come from a great distance. He tried to puzzle it out, but the only sense he could make of it was anger and pain. He started to mention it to the others, but before he could speak they came to an open glade.

They stopped at the edge of the glade and looked out at the sunlit place. There was no cover higher than an elf's knee—all low ferns, flowers, thumb-bucket plants, and clumps of grass. It wasn't a very large glade, perhaps only a hundred paces across, but the verge surrounding it was dense—a good place for an ambush.

"Shall we go around?" Sunset asked. "If there's anybody watching and we go across, we'll draw them out."

"That's just what I was thinking," Suretrail said, "and that's why I think we should go out in the open and take our chances. It's no fun tromping through the forest all by ourselves."

"That's true," Sunset said thoughtfully. "And come to think of it, if we lay a good trail, whoever is following us will go through here too, and we'll be safe on the other side in ambush."

"Is there somebody following us?" Lonebriar asked.

"Where have you been?" Suretrail said. "Didn't you hear that branch break back at the draw?"

"I'm sorry," Lonebriar said, and started to go on to explain his distraction, but Suretrail and Sunset were already in the glade. He followed after.

They went across it quickly, keeping all eyes open in all directions at once but, almost with disappointment, they got to the other side without anybody jumping out at them. Once back in the forest they became more careful about the trail which, as a part of the *taal*, they had to leave for others to follow, and circled around just inside the verge of the forest, so that they could keep a watch on the open glade in case their pursuer was closer than Sunset thought. When they had gone about halfway back to where they had entered the glade, they paused to rest a moment and enjoy a little sit-down. Lonebriar was just about to mention the strange sending sensations when Stride appeared, at the side of the glade, right at the spot from which they had entered.

Stride looked out across the glade, even as they had done, and for a moment seemed to hesitate. Then her gaze went to the ground, and a moment later she started forward, with many glances from side to side, but obviously following their carefully laid trail.

The three elves in ambush did not speak nor send —sending would have been unfair—but a few quick glances from one to another, a few gestures, and their plan was set.

Suretrail, as quietly as he could, started to circle back through the woods toward the point where they had left the glade, going well in from the edge. Sunset, in the meantime, went on around the other way, and when Stride was nearly to the forest verge came out of the forest behind her, boldly but silently, and nearly caught up with her, just as she was about to enter the forest. Suretrail must have made some slight noise just then, because Stride, who had been about to turn around, hesitated a moment, and stared intently into the forest ahead of her, and did not see Sunset, who was in plain view behind her, but now frozen absolutely still. That was Lonebriar's cue. He went in the direction Suretrail had taken, but just at the edge of the glade, and so was able to see all that happened.

Stride waited by the verge just a moment longer, but the sound she had heard was not repeated. She felt nervous being out in the open like this, and hurriedly made her way in past the thick growth to the forest proper. She felt immense relief at being back in cover, and was about to turn around to see if anyone was following. She surely would have seen Sunset had not Suretrail, just at that moment, jumped out from behind a tree and touched her lightly with his *taal*-stick.

"Rats and mice!" Stride exclaimed, jumping involuntarily into the air. "Were you there all along?"

"More or less," Suretrail said, grinning.

"But I heard you—"

"I threw a nut," he said. And just then Sunset raced up from behind, leaped through the verge, and struck Sunset with her *taal*.

"Puckernuts!" Stride exclaimed. She had seen Sunset at the last minute, but hadn't been able to drop into the

217

face-off stance that would have invalidated the count. "Where did you come from?"

"Right out there in the open," Sunset said, laughing.

Stride was so perturbed she didn't even notice Lonebriar who, by this time, had come up behind her and was standing next to Suretrail. "That was a pretty clever move," she said to Sunset. And then Lonebriar touched her with his *taal*, and she jumped into the air again.

"Oh, come on!" Stride cried when she saw who it was. "Not you, too." But she couldn't help laughing herself now.

"Me, too," Lonebriar said, or tried to say through his own laughter. "What a blow! Count three in a row."

It was the best *taal* count any of them had ever been involved in that day, and they all enjoyed it immensely, even Stride. But they were having such a good time that they didn't notice, until it was too late, Moonblossom dropping down out of the tree right over their heads. She hit both Lonebriar and Suretrail with her *taal*, but Sunset and Stride were a bit farther away, and, though very badly surprised, managed to face Moonblossom off. But just barely, they were laughing so hard.

"Were you in on this too?" Stride asked her.

"No," Moonblossom said, "I was up in that tree the whole time."

"Why didn't you get the three of us," Sunset asked, "when we came through just a few moments ago?"

"You were being too careful," Moonblossom said, "and I was afraid to take the chance."

"You couldn't have picked a better time," Lonebriar said. "Too bad you couldn't have gotten us all, I don't think anybody's done that before."

"Raindance has," Moonblossom said, "the last time we counted *taal*, four summers ago."

"Well," Suretrail said, "we found the action we were looking for, and a bit more besides. Let's change partners."

"I could use some help," Stride said. "Why don't you and I go together for a while?"

"That's fine with me," Suretrail agreed.

"Then the three of us can make a team," Moonblossom suggested.

"I think I'd like to go alone for a while," Lonebriar said, "if that's all right with you two."

"It's okay with me," Sunset said. So they split up and went their separate ways.

Fawn was getting tired of playing tag. She was, she felt, getting too old for that kind of thing. After all, she thought she would be taking her adult name in not too many more summers, and elders didn't spend their time playing tag. She told Clamshell she was quitting, and went to find her mother.

Dreamsnake was busy in the treeless area between the stream and the clay cliff which gave Halfhill, the elves' holt, its name, and in which they had dug their dens. She was making pants for Sprig, and having trouble with her needles. They kept on breaking. They were all old, but there was no antler left to make new ones, and there would not be more until the fall. That meant she had to be especially careful in boring holes in the pants leather, and would have to stitch each seam twice, since the only needles she had left were small ones.

Fawn came up to where she was sitting cross-legged, and waited while she finished a thread of jumper gut. "I want to go out to the *taal* area," she said.

"Just a minute, cubling." Dreamsnake straightened out a new piece of jumper gut by running it several times between her fingers. It was fine enough for the needle she was using, but the needle had already begun to show a crack near the eye and she wanted to be careful with it, to make it last as long as she could.

Fawn waited a moment as her mother threaded the needle. The sound of the other cubs' laughter, coming from across the stream, made her want more than ever to be grown up. "Can I go?" she asked. "I'll be careful."

"Go where?" Dreamsnake asked as she picked up the half-sewn pants.

"Out to count *taal*."

"Oh, goodness no." She smiled up at her daughter. "You're not nearly old enough for that. Now let me finish this so Sprig won't have to go around naked."

Fawn wanted to argue the point further, but her mother was obviously so concerned for her sewing that she knew that to interrupt her further would only make her angry, so she wandered off, looking for Graywing or Glade, the only two other elders left at the holt, hoping that maybe one of them would give her permission to go.

She went upstream—which just happened to be in the direction of the *taal* area—but before she went very far she heard adult voices. There, just beyond the edge of the holt, were both Graywing and Glade, talking with Raindance. Grizzle, Raindance's wolf, was with her, and that made Fawn wonder, because she knew Raindance was counting *taal* and that wolves weren't supposed to be a part of the game.

"Hello," she called as she ran up to them.

"What is it, Fawn?" Graywing asked. Her face was troubled, and for a moment Fawn thought she had done something wrong.

"I want to go out and count *taal* with Raindance," she said.

"Oh, no," Graywing said. "You're too young for that."

"I'm nearly full grown!"

"And besides," Graywing went on, "there's been some trouble. Freefoot and Shadowflash are hurt. You'll have to stay here."

"I can help," Fawn tried to say, but Bentfang came bounding up to them just then, and Graywing turned away to nuzzle her wolf.

"Go tell Dreamsnake," Raindance said to Fawn, "that Graywing and Glade are going with me."

Fawn turned to Glade. He had often let her do things when the other elders wouldn't. "Please, Glade," she begged, "can I go with you?"

"Not this time," Glade said, and she knew by the sound of his voice that he meant it. He started to say something more, but Streak was loping easily toward them, and he turned his attention to his wolf.

Fawn couldn't understand their preoccupation. Raindance was saying something about litters, though it was not the time of year for wolf cubs, and what they could possibly have to do with anything was beyond Fawn's comprehension.

"Are we ready, then?" Graywing asked.

"We'd better get going," Glade said. He turned to Fawn. "Let your mother know where we are," he said, "and we may want you, too, when we get back."

"At least now we know," Graywing said to Raindance, "why Lightpaws left so suddenly a little while ago." Lightpaws was Freefoot's wolf.

But Fawn wasn't paying any more attention to what the elders were really saying than they were to her. She wanted so badly to go out and prove herself grown up that she could think of nothing else, not aware that her behavior was proving her to be the child she thought she wasn't.

So, being childishly selfish and feeling put off, she left the adults to their adult business and wandered back toward the bank. As soon as she could see Dreamsnake, bent over her work, she stopped and looked back just in time to see Graywing, Glade, and Raindance, all fully armed, go into the forest with their wolves.

She looked back at her mother. Dreamsnake was very busy, and not watching her. She was supposed to give her mother a message, but the opportunity was too good to miss. She would surprise her elders and show them how good a tracker she was. As quietly as she could, she ran after them.

She hadn't gone very far into the woods before Bouncer came bouncing up to her. Bouncer was her first wolf. She stopped to greet him with a nuzzle and a wrestle.

"You can't go with me," she told him. "I'm going off to count *taal,* and wolves can't play."

He sat up and looked at her, his head cocked to one side, almost as if he understood.

"Now you stay here," she told him, "and I'll tell you all about it when I get back." Then she ran off after Graywing, Raindance, and Glade. She knew approximately where the *taal* area was, since the elves who had gone off to play had planned its boundaries that morning before they left, but she wanted to practice her tracking skills by following the three elders. She easily found their trail, and then proceeded with more caution since, she knew, if she was caught, they would send her back home in disgrace.

Lonebriar had a strategy. First, he was sure that most of the other elves were in the northern part of the *taal* area, and he wanted to get to them as quickly as possible, to try to catch somebody by surprise. Second, he was sure that the companions he'd left behind would be coming after him, so, though he had to leave a careful if subtle trail, he wanted to get well ahead of them, circle around, and get behind them if he could.

When he had covered half the distance across the *taal*

area, he climbed up into a beech tree and paused a moment in a crotch to catch his breath and listen in case anybody else were nearby. But he heard nothing but the sounds he expected to hear if he were alone in the forest, sounds with which he was most familiar. Maybe, he thought, his strategy wasn't so good after all, if it left him with nobody to compete with.

As he got down from the tree he remembered the strange sending he'd felt several times that day. It had seemed to have come from the swordfeet, but he didn't know how that could be. He opened up his mind and tried to see if he could catch that almost-taste again, but nothing came into his mind but his own thoughts.

Oh, well, he'd have plenty of time to worry about it later. He tried to guess the best direction to go to find some elves to count *taal* on and went off, looking for a trail.

He hadn't gone more than a hundred paces when he found tracks—two elves. He examined the bent leaf, the torn bit of moss. That looked like Stringsong. A little farther on there was a scratch in the bark of a tree trunk. Catcher maybe. The trail wasn't very old. He put all thoughts of swordfeet and strange sendings out of his mind and went in pursuit.

Sunset and Moonblossom followed a trail into the marsh. It had not been a wet summer, but there was always standing water here, and the ground underneath was thick, sticky mud.

The going was especially tricky in the marsh, in several ways. Only occasionally was the ground firm enough to keep a footprint, and the rushes and reeds were always bent and torn anyway, so the marks left by the elves they were pursuing were hard to distinguish. Besides that, it was hard to move fast—the mud sucked at their feet, or the water was too deep, or the rushes too thick to push their way through. There were a few trees in the marsh, but they were either dead or spindly water willows, and in neither case any good for climbing. And to top it off, the mud and the reeds made it almost impossible to be quiet.

Still, this was the way the trail led, and crossing difficult ground like this was part of the contest. But at last, when they came to a bit of firmer ground, they were able to stop for a moment and listen. Up ahead, barely audible over the rustling of rushes, the screaming of red-wings, and the gentle sussuration of the marsh itself, they could hear what they were sure were other elves, their quarry perhaps, having as difficult a time of it as they.

There was a dead pine nearby. Moonblossom decided it was worth the chance, so she shinnied up the barkless trunk as high as she dared, both for fear of being seen and of bringing the rotten tree crashing down. Sunset stared up at her anxiously as she searched the marsh in the direction of the sounds. After a moment she froze in place, and then slowly slid back down to the ground.

"It's Quickthorn," she whispered to Sunset, "and Rillwalker. They're not that far ahead."

As quietly and as quickly as they could, they worked their way through the mud and rustling rushes toward the other two elves, and at last could see them, moving very slowly toward where the marsh merged with the little lake. But Quickthorn and Rillwalker were not taking any chances. Each was covering the other's back, so that they both were almost walking sideways. It would be impossible to come up on them by surprise.

Sunset had an idea. She touched Moonblossom's arm, drew her back just out of sight of the others, and whispered in her ear a moment. Moonblossom liked the plan, so they circled around until they were parallel to the others' line of travel, and at a place where there was a relatively clear stretch of shallow water leading away from where Quickthorn and Rillwalker were, they stood up.

"Where did you come from," Sunset said, not very loudly, but trying her best to sound surprised.

"I was waiting right there," Moonblossom said, "in that clump of willows."

"Want to team?" Sunset asked as Moonblossom carefully stomped around in the willows, making it look as if she had actually been there.

"Sure," Moonblossom said, and they hurried away up the clear stretch, leaving a muddy trail in the water.

They rounded a very dense clump of rushes and reeds, went on farther leaving a more than obvious trail, then doubled back to the clump. Moonblossom wormed her way in among the stalks of the tall plants, while Sunset went opposite, along a fallen log to hide behind the moss-covered stubs of its branches.

They didn't have long to wait. Sunset was barely in place, and painfully aware of a damp footprint she'd left on the log, when sure enough, Quickthorn and Rillwalker came up the trail.

Just as they passed her hiding place, Moonblossom jumped out of the rushes and tapped Quickthorn on the shoulder with her *taal*-stick. But Rillwalker, just a pace ahead, had time to turn and face off.

"I told you it was too good to be real," she said as Quickthorn ruefully straightened up from the crouch he had automatically fallen into.

"And you were right," he said, but where's the other—" But before he could finish, Sunset leaped out from her hiding place and lunged at Rillwalker, who was turning even then, and poked the end of her *taal* into her chest.

"Owl droppings!" Rillwalker said. "Can't even follow my own advice." Then she laughed, and the others joined in with her.

"That was a good trick," Quickthorn said. "Are there any more of you hiding in the muck?"

"Not that we know of," Moonblossom said. "I've counted ten *taal* today, how about you?"

"I can count only five," Rillwalker said, "but I've been hit seven times."

"Poor luck," Moonblossom said, "but I've been counted nine times—twice by Raindance."

"She got me once," Sunset said, "Lonebriar got me once, and Grazer got me once, but I counted nine *taal*."

"I'm even up," Quickthorn said, "done and got six times each."

"Has anybody gotten Raindance?" Moonblossom asked. Nobody had.

"She'd make a good target," Quickthorn said, "don't you think?"

"Do you suppose," Rillwalker said, "if we worked together, at least one of us could count her?"

"It's worth a try," Sunset said. "Somebody should get her at least once before the day is over, and it might as well be one of us."

Lonebriar was sitting near the top of a high rock, surrounded by the down-hanging branches of a beech tree that grew from a cleft halfway up behind him. He had been waiting there for a little while now, sure that his quarry would pass this way. He'd followed Stringsong and Catcher's trail until he'd noticed that it overlapped yet another, older track. So he'd circled around, gotten ahead of them, crossed their line of travel, and found that other track, which had led him here to the rock. It was the track of a solitary elf, he didn't know who, and it curved around the base of the rock. But Lonebriar had followed it no farther. Instead he had climbed up here to wait in ambush.

He had begun to wonder if he had made the right decision when a subtle movement back along the trail, in a stand of maple saplings, caught his attention. It was Stringsong and Catcher all right, intent on that other track he'd noticed. They came, cautiously, up to the base of the rock, but even as Lonebriar got ready to slide down its face and count them both, the two elves got suspicious, and he hesitated when they backed off a pace or two.

"There's been somebody else here ahead of us," Catcher whispered to Stringsong.

"They're going the same way," Stringsong said, "and this other trail is fresh."

"If we're lucky," Catcher said, "we can count them both. But isn't this first trail just a bit too obvious?"

They started to go around the rock the other way, hoping to meet their quarry face on. Lonebriar quietly changed his position so that he could watch, and then saw that their move had been anticipated—there was someone else waiting just a quarter of the way around, in a hollow in the rock. It was Smarthand; no other elf had quite that much girth. Lonebriar had not been all that careful when he'd climbed up; how had Smarthand missed hearing him?

It was a good trick, and Lonebriar grinned as he watched Stringsong and Catcher near the hollow. Smarthand could not see who it was that was approaching, but jumped out just as Stringsong came in view and jabbed him in the chest with his *taal*. Catcher, two paces behind, was able to face off in time.

"How long have you been waiting there?" Catcher asked Smarthand, laughing so hard she could hardly stand.

"I nearly fell asleep," the stout elf admitted with a

chuckle. He wiggled his *taal* under Stringsong's nose. "How did you fall for such a trick?"

"It was Catcher's idea," Stringsong said, poking at her good-humoredly with his own *taal*.

"You could have gone the other way if you'd wanted to," Catcher said as she eluded his stick. "Then you could have gotten both of us maybe."

It was time, Lonebriar thought, to make his move. The three elves were getting a bit silly, joking at each other, and might not notice the slight sound he made as he started to slide down toward them. He had almost reached the ground when Smarthand looked up, but Stringsong and Catcher were caught unaware, and he counted them both.

"It's you," Smarthand said, "who woke me from my nap."

"You should have heard me coming," Lonebriar said with a grin. "This makes my count eight for the day."

The three rescuers and their wolves entered that part of the forest which the elves had designated as the *taal* area, and had to pass through a depression filled with hand-leaf bushes. If Raindance did have a special skill in detecting animals or other elves, it did not serve her now, for without warning they almost stepped on the two reclining swordfeet. Even the wolves had not detected their scent.

The swordfeet were just as startled as the elves and jumped up, hissing and waving their long, clawed forelegs. Raindance staggered back into Graywing, but managed to throw her javelin at the larger swordfoot before it could attack, striking it in the chest. The swordfoot, already injured, fell sideways and knocked the smaller, younger one aside. That was when the wolves finally realized they had an enemy to deal with, and Grizzle and Streak leaped at the younger swordfoot, while Bentfang harried the older one.

Graywing recovered her balance, and she and Glade joined in the fight with their spears, while Raindance now had to use her ax. The swordfeet—old and injured, young and clumsy—fought like demons, leaping, slashing, kicking, even biting though that was not their way. Elves and wolves pressed them, stabbed and bit.

At last it was too much for the green-scaled monsters. Though the juvenile was only superficially wounded, it was inexpert at this kind of fight—one on one was more its style—and seemed reluctant to take chances. The adult was bleeding badly from several wounds, including a deep ax gash in its neck, and its previous wounds had already sapped much of its strength. As soon as there was a moment's pause, the swordfeet turned away from the elves and wolves and dashed off out of the bushy hollow and into the woods. The wolves did not try to pursue, nor did the elves, who were glad enough to fall exhausted to the ground and watch the swordfeet disappear through the distant undergrowth.

"You got her good," Glade said to Raindance, whose ax-blow it was which had caused the older swordfoot so much damage. "See," he pointed at the leaves of the bushes through which the swordfeet had run. They were spotted, almost sprayed with blood.

"Let's get it over with," Graywing said. She pushed herself to her feet and started after the animals, but Raindance grabbed her arm and stopped her.

"We can take care of them later," she said. "Right now we have to find Freefoot and Shadowflash."

Lonebriar, Stringsong, Catcher, and Smarthand were on their way back to where Lonebriar had last seen Raindance, in order to pick up her trail. They went by a slanting tree, one that had been blown halfway down in a

229

storm, long ago, but which had continued to grow until it was almost full size, though its top rested against its neighbors which now, too, had grown crooked. There they came across another trail and paused a moment to try to figure out who had made it.

"It's not Raindance," Smarthand said as he examined the all-but-invisible footprints on the smooth bark of the slanting tree.

"That's Fire-Eyes," Catcher said, "and it looks like Fangslayer is with him."

"Let's get Raindance first," Stringsong said. "I've counted Fangslayer once already."

Lonebriar wasn't paying much attention and missed what Catcher was asking him. "I'm sorry," he said. "What did you say?"

"I said, shall we still look for Raindance, then?"

"Yes, of course."

"What's the matter?" Smarthand asked. "Are you all right?"

"Yes, I'm fine, it's just—" He hesitated as he felt, once again, that strange almost-taste in his mind, which now he was sure meant that the swordfeet were not too far away.

"Well, let's go then," Stringsong said. "You have to show us the way."

"All right," Lonebriar said, but as they went he told them about the sensations.

"You ought to talk to Dreamsnake," Catcher told him, laughing gently as they went on.

It was a very dark and dense part of the forest where Suretrail and Stride were following, not so much a track—the undergrowth was too thick—as the vague sounds of other elves. It was impossible to be quiet here. But they weren't always sure whether they were trailing someone, or someone was trailing them, because sometimes the sounds seemed to come from behind them, or from one side or another, as often as from ahead.

Meanwhile Fire-Eyes and Fangslayer, not that far off in the same dark part of the forest, were nervously trying to get away from the sounds which they were sure were being made by pursuing elves. But sometimes the sounds were not so much behind them as ahead, or off to one side. The forest canopy was so thick here, and the forest floor so dark and tangled with shade-loving bushes and vine-stems, that it was easy for even an elf to get turned around. More than once Fangslayer lost his sense of direction. It was not a part of the forest the elves usually visited, except in winter.

And so the two pairs of elves stalked each other, all unknowingly. They got ever-more confused, sometimes mistook the sounds of other animals for elf sounds, and eventually completely lost track of where they were, or where the more open forest was.

Fangslayer was getting more and more tense with every passing moment. Suretrail was decidedly jittery. Stride was beginning to think that this wasn't any fun anymore, and Fire-Eyes was almost ready to call out and give up.

The two pairs of elves continued to become ever-more lost. They alternated between trying to be as cautious and quiet as possible, and being almost careless and quite noisy—for elves—in their movement through the undergrowth.

Once Suretrail and Stride tried to backtrack, but the forest became unfamiliar, and they had to admit that they'd lost their own trail. Once Fire-Eyes and Fangslayer thought they had found a clear trail for sure, only to realize after going twice past the same tree, with its distinctive shelves of fungus, that they had been following themselves.

The sounds of other elves, and maybe of other creatures too, continued to confuse them and at last they actually became frightened—wondering if maybe there was a real enemy out there. Each of them, privately, wanted to stop the hunt, but none of them cared to admit it to his partner.

At last, as it had to happen, they all came together unexpectedly, each pair meeting the other as they came around a huge tree from different directions. Their startlement was so great that they all leaped clumsily back from each other—Suretrail actually fell to the ground—shouting and waving their *taal*-sticks as if they were weapons.

"By the high ones," Fire-Eyes said, gasping for breath. "I thought we were done for there."

Stride helped Suretrail to his feet. "Let's get out of this place," she said.

"Yes," Fangslayer said, "I agree. At once."

They were so relieved to end the hunt that they didn't care that none of them had been able to count *taal*. Without further hesitation they started off, not paying any attention to which direction they took, so long as it got them out of the darkness. But even as they went, they thought they could hear . . . something . . . behind them . . . stalking them. . . .

Lonebriar, Stringsong, Catcher, and Smarthand, having finally picked up Raindance's trail where Lonebriar had left her, followed it to the place where she'd met Freefoot and Shadowflash.

"Now remember," Catcher said, "whatever we do, we count Raindance first."

"Maybe," Stringsong suggested, "if one of us makes a

try for Freefoot or Shadowflash, that will distract her and give one of the rest of us a chance at her."

"Let's see where we find them first," Smarthand said.

They followed the triple trail until they came to a place where the ground was torn up, and the foliage beaten down. And there were bloodstains. Lonebriar knelt by a large, half-dried spot. "It's elf-blood," he said.

As far as they were concerned, the game was over. They examined the ground all around the signs of struggle, looking for a clue as to what had happened.

"Bear tracks here," Smarthand said. His hands went to his waist, where he normally carried his two axes, one on either side, but, of course, he'd left them at the holt.

"They're too smart to tangle with a bear," Catcher said. "Something else must have happened."

Lonebriar was looking at some other footprints in the ground, dug in with such force that their maker could not be identified. And yet . . . he touched the track with a finger and felt, in the back of his head, a ghost of that strange sending taste he'd felt before. "The swordfeet were here," he told the others.

"Are you sure?" Stringsong asked.

"I can . . . *feel* them, sort of, in these tracks."

"You've been into the dreamberries again," String-song said.

"Maybe not," Catcher said. "Think about Dreamsnake."

"But she doesn't actually *send* to snakes and lizards," Smarthand said.

"No, but she *knows* them, maybe it's the same way with Lonebriar and swordfeet."

"Now is not the time to argue about that," Smarthand said impatiently. "Elves have been injured, we've got to find them, and find out what happened. Let's follow the blood, and hope that they're still alive."

"They were able to get away," Stringsong said.

"Maybe," Lonebriar told him, "or maybe the swordfeet ate them."

"So let's stop arguing about it," Smarthand said, "and go!"

But before they could follow the trail of blood, Lightpaws, Freefoot's wolf, came bounding up to them in obvious distress. The wolf didn't even pause to greet them, but sniffed around, smelled the blood, turned away from it—it wasn't Freefoot's blood, then—and dashed to another place where he started to whine softly, in the back of his throat.

"Easy," Catcher said to the wolf. "We'll find him, show us the way."

Whether Lightpaws understood or not didn't matter. Another wolf answered his howl, and they all ran in that direction as quickly as they could.

Meanwhile, Fawn had been having a hard time keeping up with Raindance and Graywing and Glade, and at last she decided to throw caution to the winds and just run after them. After all, they had not been trying to disguise their trail. She didn't understand that; she thought that leaving an all but secret trail was a part of the *taal*.

The elders seemed to have gotten awfully far ahead of her, as if they, too, had been running. No, their footprints were not that far apart. But they had been hurrying.

The tracks led her to a hollow where a bunch of hand-leaf bushes had been trampled down. What in the world had they been doing there? Then she noticed blood splatters on some of the leaves, and suddenly she was very frightened. Had they been hurt? Had they been hunting? She didn't have a weapon, and besides, whatever they had been fighting, it had left horrible huge

234

tracks in the ground. But there, their footprints went on beyond the place. She hurried after them.

It seemed to take forever, though actually it wasn't very far, but at last she heard movement up ahead and, now that she was away from the scene of the fight, she forgot her fear and remembered that she had wanted to prove to the elders how good she was at tracking. She became more careful about making noise herself, but still hurried on, until she finally saw Raindance, Graywing, and Glade, with their wolves, up ahead beneath tall trees, where the ground was clear enough to see a long way. They were moving quickly, but now she had no trouble keeping them in sight. She continued to play her game, always keeping a nearby tree between her and them as she ran after them.

She was able to close the distance to the elders, until at last they were so near that to go any farther would reveal her to them, so now was the time to try to tag them. She left the shelter of the last tree and ran toward them, trying to be as quiet as she could, but it wasn't quiet enough. All three elders turned toward her before she was halfway there.

"What are you doing here?" Graywing demanded. She sounded angry.

"I came to count *taal*," Fawn said. She was disappointed to have been discovered without even tagging one of them.

"We are not counting *taal*," Glade told her. He, too, was angry. "Freefoot and Shadowflash have been hurt, and there are swordfeet in the forest."

"She must have gone right by where we fought them," Raindance said. "Listen, cub, you are very lucky. If the swordfeet had come back while you were there, they would have had you for lunch."

"I didn't know," Fawn said. She suddenly felt very young.

"You'll have to go back to the holt," Graywing told her. "Did you tell your mother where we were going?"

"No."

"Oh, owl pellets. We can't just send her back alone, the swordfeet are between us and the holt."

"I'll take her back," Glade said, "and if any other elders have come in, I'll bring them back with me." Then he took Fawn by the arm and led her away.

Lightpaws didn't have to lead the four elves very far. The wolf bounded up to a huge tree, with low, overhanging branches, where Shadowflash's wolf, Snapper, was pacing and leaping, as if he were trying to get up into it. Not too far up, on one of the low-hanging limbs, the elves could see two forms, huddled and still.

"Freefoot," Catcher called up. "Is that you?"

"He's here," came Shadowflash's weak voice. "He's unconscious."

"Hang on," Stringsong said, "we'll be right up." He grabbed the lowest branch, out where it was just above head height, and pulled himself up.

Catcher and Lonebriar were just behind him, but before they could follow, something huge and black came out of the bushes beside the tree, came so fast that Smarthand, who was nearest, didn't have a chance. It was the wounded bear, angry and looking for trouble. She caught Smarthand utterly by surprise, and sent him flying with one great swing of her mighty forepaw. Smarthand crashed up against the tree trunk, and slumped down unconscious.

Catcher reached over her shoulder, her hand fluttering in the air where her javelin should have been. Lonebriar fell backward a pace, then ran to get between the bear and Smarthand, who was bleeding from his nose and mouth, as well as from the four long gashes across his

236

chest. Stringsong crouched on the limb, drew his knife, then dropped down on the bear's back and started slashing at the animal's face, its nose and eyes.

Which might not have been too smart a thing to do, because the bear turned around in place and, thinking Catcher was the cause of her pain, struck at her and hit her a glancing blow, which nonetheless sent her spinning to the ground. Stringsong was just barely able to hang onto the bear's thick fur.

Lonebriar knelt by Smarthand and touched him gingerly. The stout elf was still alive, though his breathing was ragged. Lonebriar left him, looking frantically around for something to use as a weapon, and heard a mewing from the bushes where the bear had been hiding. He looked and there was the cub, standing on its hind legs, excited and frightened by the battle.

Stringsong was still clinging to the bear, stabbing at it any way he could. Catcher was struggling to her feet, holding onto a dead branch, one end of which was broken and reasonably sharp. Smarthand was choking. Lonebriar looked at the cub, at the bear, then back at the cub. He didn't like what he was going to do, but elf lives were at stake.

Crouching low, hoping the bear wouldn't notice him, he ran to the cub and grabbed it. It was surprised and started to struggle. He threw it to the ground, pressed it down with his knees, then wrenched its ears until it cried out. Then, as the mother bear turned to see what was wrong, he stood and kicked it, not toward her but at an angle. It yelped with pain and crashed to the ground. The bear took two steps toward him, bellowing in utter rage, then the cub ran off and the bear, still wanting vengeance, decided instead to drop down on all fours and chase after it.

Stringsong leaped from its back at once and ran

toward Lonebriar who, having made sure that the bear was really leaving, had gone back to Smarthand. Catcher, staggering and holding her chest with one arm, got to Smarthand too, just as Stringsong did. The three elves turned their attention to their unconscious companion.

"Something's broken inside," Lonebriar said as he wiped the blood away from Smarthand's mouth and nose.

"Do we dare move him?" Stringsong asked.

"If we don't," Catcher said, gasping with the pain of her own battered chest, "the bear will come back and finish the job."

"Are you all right?" they heard Shadowflash's weak voice call down from the tree.

"No," Lonebriar said.

"I'll take care of Smarthand," Catcher said to Stringsong. "You help Lonebriar bring those two down. We've got to get away from here."

They could hear the bear, chasing its cub and bellowing, getting farther away, but they knew they would have precious little time before it returned. Stringsong and Lonebriar quickly went up into the tree, where they found Shadowflash, conscious but weak, holding onto Freefoot, whose eyes were open, but whose mind was elsewhere. They brought Freefoot down first, then Shadowflash.

"We need to get help," Lonebriar said. "We can't carry all three of them, and Catcher can hardly walk by herself."

"Let's find a place to hide first," Stringsong said.

So as best they could, they dragged their injured companions away from the tree.

It was getting late in the afternoon when Suretrail and Fire-Eyes decided to go one way while Stride and

Fangslayer went another. As much fun as it was counting *taal*, it would soon be dark and time to quit and go home for a more than welcome supper. But they were reluctant to give up too early. After all, not every summer provided them with so much game that they could take the time to just go out and burn off some fat. This year had been especially rich, even better than the last time they'd counted *taal*, four turns of the seasons ago.

Perhaps it was the time of day, or their hunger, but Suretrail and Fire-Eyes were not being as careful, or as perceptive, as they might have been. They were working their way around a juniper thicket when Moonblossom, who had been hiding there in ambush, jumped out and counted them both.

"That's twice you've gotten me," Suretrail complained to her. But even as he spoke, Stride, whom he'd thought he'd left behind but who had in fact left Fangslayer almost at once and had been following him and Fire-Eyes, ran up from behind, her *taal*-stick waving, and counted Moonblossom.

Suretrail dropped into a face-off crouch, laughing as he did so, but Fire-Eyes dashed off around the juniper thicket.

"What do you suppose has gotten into her," Moonblossom said.

"Go after her and fine out," Suretrail suggested. "I want to go toward the stream."

But just then Fire-Eyes came back around the far side of the thicket, and with raucous laughter and wildly swinging *taal*, counted both Stride and Suretrail, then ran off into the woods again.

Stride and Moonblossom glanced at each other, then grinned and, caught up in Fire-Eyes' wild mood, ran after her before she could get completely out of sight. It was a chase, and Fire-Eyes led them laughing around a batch of brambles where they all three, literally, ran into Quickthorn and Sunset, who were coming the other way. Everybody fell in a confused pile, and were laughing so hard it was some moments before they could get to their feet again. There was no count, of course.

But even as they were regaining their composure, Suretrail leaped out from a clear place in the briar patch and counted Fire-Eyes and Quickthorn, and Rillwalker dropped down from the branches overhead and struck Suretrail and Quickthorn with her *taal*.

Quickthorn had been counted twice in a row now, and was beginning to feel picked on, but Rillwalker was confused by their near hysteria.

Fangslayer, too, must have been confused, since he just walked up to them from another part of the forest and asked, "What is going on here?"

He failed to notice Sunset—though the others did not—who was tiptoeing up behind him. She reached out her *taal*-stick with an elaborate gesture and tapped him on the head, then burst into laughter along with the others.

In spite of this, Fangslayer was hardly startled. He rubbed his head as he looked at Sunset over his shoulder, a wry smile on his face. "I see," he said to Rillwalker, "that things are beginning to get a bit silly around here."

But even as he was speaking, Stride, Fire-Eyes, and Sunset dashed off, and then Suretrail and Moonblossom ran away, and then Fire-Eyes came swooping back from another direction and got Fangslayer fair and square, and Quickthorn too, though he might have argued the point, but missed Rillwalker altogether.

And so it went. In no time the *taal* degenerated into a hysterical parody of the cubs' game that Fawn had wanted so much to be too old for. For a little while, everybody was a cub again.

* * *

240

Lonebriar sat just inside the edge of a briar patch, his favorite place for solitude. Deeper within, made as comfortable as they could be, were the four wounded elves and the two wolves. Even Catcher, the least injured of the four, was sleeping now. For which Lonebriar was grateful. Ever since Stringsong had gone to the holt for help, Catcher had complained that either she should have gone instead, or should have remained on guard while both Stringsong and Lonebriar went, or should have gone with Stringsong. Lonebriar knew that this only showed that though she had been able to walk, she was in shock. But her constant muttering had made him uncomfortable. Now, at least, he had some peace.

They had chosen a briar patch not just because of Lonebriar's preferences. A tree would have been far safer, but Smarthand was so badly hurt that they had feared that the exertion of getting him up into a suitable branch would have hurt him even more, if not killed him. He, Freefoot, and Catcher all had broken ribs —and more—and flat ground was better for them to lie on. And the two wolves, Lightpaws and Snapper, couldn't climb trees. They were now lying near their companions, half-asleep but with their ears pricked for any sound.

The briar patch, Lonebriar hoped, would keep the bear from intruding, but he still felt vulnerable. He had sent a mental call for Blackbrush, his own wolf, and was waiting for him to arrive.

Catcher had sent for her wolf too, but she had been weak and in pain, and wasn't sure she had gotten to her. Smarthand, of course, had been unable to do anything. His breathing was still ragged, and shallow, and he had bled a lot from mouth and nose when Stringsong and Lonebriar had dragged him into the dubious shelter of the briar patch. If Stringsong didn't get back with help soon, Smarthand would die.

But it wasn't really the bear Lonebriar was worried

about, it was the swordfeet. He could feel them in his mind, the sharp almost-taste of their peculiar and involuntary sending. He felt hunger there, and fear, and pain, and anger—or at least, that was how he interpreted the images that were not images. The sensation flickered, and it was getting stronger.

He saw the swordfeet before he heard them. They were an eight times eight paces off, upslope from the briar patch, where the forest floor was relatively clear. Even from this distance Lonebriar could see that the adult was in a bad way. The two green-scaled hunters moved uncertainly, raising their heads now and then to sniff the air, but the larger swordfoot would pause every eight paces or so to sink into a crouch, as if she was very weak. Considering the wounds she had taken, Lonebriar was surprised she was still alive at all.

As quietly as he could, he crept back under the briar canes to where Catcher and Shadowflash were resting, and gently nudged them awake.

We're going to have company, he sent to them. He didn't know whether the swordfeet could hear a whisper or not, and he didn't want to find out just now.

Catcher came awake quickly, but Shadowflash moaned, and Lonebriar, who had not taken his eyes off the approaching swordfeet, saw the juvenile turn her head toward them. Catcher looked out of the briars and saw the creatures, then turned with a stifled moan of her own to quiet Shadowflash. But the damage had been done. And injured elves would be perfect prey for injured swordfeet. There wouldn't be much of a fight.

It was Smarthand's blood that finally made the difference. The swordfeet came closer to the briar patch, though apparently they could not see the elves concealed under the leafy, spiny canes. But even though there was no breeze, there was enough of a scent of blood in the air that the two swordfeet were able to catch it. Lonebriar could tell by their sudden tension and total attention. They did not run, but now they came toward the briar patch with eager determination.

Lonebriar felt sick. Aside from his knife he was unarmed, and though both Catcher and Shadowflash were alert to the danger now, they could not help him. The thoughts of the swordfeet, tickling in the back of his mind, were a combination of desperate hunger and raging recognition—they knew it was elves who had been the cause of their pain. And help—help was so far away.

Lonebriar crept to the edge of the briar patch and slowly stood up. He would fight them alone, and maybe he could hold them off long enough for Stringsong to come back. Behind him he heard the wolves stirring, but neither of them had fought a swordfoot before, and they did not recognize the enemy. The swordfeet kept coming nearer, but when the adult moved as if to attack from one side, the juvenile stayed with her, instead of taking the other side.

That, Lonebriar thought, might be his only chance to save his four companions. If he attacked the adult, the juvenile might just stay nearby to protect her instead of going into the briar patch alone. If he could keep them out here, he might be able to live long enough for help to come. Maybe.

Then the swordfeet's thoughts, tasting like sour berries around the edges of his consciousness, suddenly became stronger, as if they were sending directly at him. ˜Hatred!˜ ˜Anger!˜ ˜Hunger!˜ ˜Pain!˜ ˜Revenge!˜

Lonebriar grabbed at the thoughts, held onto them, felt them with his mind. He tried to send his thoughts back at them in the same way. ˜Stop!˜ he sent. ˜Go away!˜ And to his surprise, the swordfeet stopped.

˜Eating-time!˜ the adult swordfoot sent—or at least, that was what her thought clearly meant. ˜Sword-foot-killer!˜ the younger one sent.

˜Yes!˜ Lonebriar sent back. ˜Kill swordfeet. Power-ful elf. I defend my family as you defend your mother!˜ Or at least, that was the intent of the image he formed in his mind and sent at the creature.

Both swordfeet stood up a little taller, their heads twitching from side to side as they looked at Lonebriar. He could feel the more muted flavor of their private communication. They were surprised, uncertain. No other animal had ever spoken to them in their own language before. The younger swordfoot chirped; the older answered. *That* was their talking; they didn't know they were sending to each other.

Behind him, Catcher and Shadowflash watched in fascination and utter surprise. They did not know what was happening, only that the swordfeet had hesitated only eight and two paces away, and that Lonebriar seemed somehow to be communicating with them.

Which he was. He could not imitate their chirps, but he could put his thoughts into their strange minds. ˜Leave us alone,˜ he sent. ˜Eights of eights of elves coming. Defend to the death. Go away.˜

And the swordfeet went away.

Stringsong raced back toward the holt, sending a mental call for Ranger, his wolf, as he ran. He pulled up short when he saw, off at an angle through the trees, two elves with their wolves, hurrying back in roughly the direction he had come. He called out to them, and shortly stood talking with Raindance and Gray-wing.

He quickly explained what had happened, and they followed him back toward the briar patch. Ranger joined them just as they caught sight of Lonebriar, at the edge of the patch, suddenly sitting down and dropping his head into his hands. As they hurried up to him, Shadowflash and Catcher came creeping out from the briars.

"What's happened?" Stringsong gasped.

"It was the swordfeet," Catcher said. She sat down beside Lonebriar. Shadowflash just lay where he was, half out of the briar patch.

"Are you all right?" Raindance asked Lonebriar. She knelt beside him.

"My head hurts a bit," he said. "I think Smarthand is bleeding to death."

Stringsong, Graywing, and Raindance pushed their way in through the briars and found Freefoot, awake but very groggy, and Smarthand, who was lying in a pool of his own blood. Gently they dragged him out, then went back for Freefoot. He was very weak, had difficulty breathing, and was still quite dazed, but with any luck and enough time he would be all right. It was Smarthand they were worried about. The wounds across his chest had closed over. It was the internal injuries he was dying of.

"We should have brought Fawn with us," Graywing said, and told them about how the cub had followed them to count *taal*. Though still very young, Fawn was already showing signs of becoming a healer.

"We'll have to make drag litters," Raindance said. "So what's this about swordfeet?" She started to cut down long, straight branches.

"They came looking for us," Lonebriar said as he got to his feet to help. "They left just before you got here."

"You fought them off by yourself?" Stringsong asked as he peeled oak bark to tie the branches Raindance and Graywing brought him.

"It wasn't exactly a fight," Lonebriar said. He was still tired from his exertions and the strangeness of the swordfeet's thoughts.

"He *sent* to them," Catcher said, and told them what she had seen.

"They would chirp at him," Shadowflash added, "and he just stared at them, and then they went away."

"I wish I'd seen that," Freefoot murmured.

"I don't see how that's possible," Raindance said. She helped Lonebriar fashion another drag litter.

"I don't either," Lonebriar said, "but that's what happened."

"So Lonebriar is a swordfoot-talker," Graywing said. "Dreamsnake has a way with snakes and lizards. And Treewing can talk to birds. I've known a few other elves who had a special talent with animals. It's not very common, but it does happen now and then."

They continued to talk about it as they finished the three drag litters—Catcher was able to walk, and would have to—in part to keep their minds off what they could not help, Smarthand's pale-gray face and shallow, labored breathing. They then made harnesses from more oak bark so that Snapper and Grizzle could drag Shadowflash, and Lightpaws and Bentfang could pull Freefoot. Because Smarthand was so badly injured, Graywing would drag him herself, to be sure that his trip was as smooth as possible.

But Stringsong, with Ranger, and Raindance and Lonebriar had other business to attend to.

"The swordfeet have to be dealt with now," Raindance told the others. "You'll have to lead us to them, swordfoot-talker," she said to Lonebriar. "Can you do that?"

"I think so," Lonebriar said. "I wish we didn't have to kill them. I mean, I've *talked* with them."

"We'll do what we have to do," Stringsong said as

246

Blackbrush finally came in answer to Lonebriar's mental summons.

"I know," Lonebriar said.

Stringsong could sympathize with him. He'd had to destroy a wolf of his own once, when it had gotten the frothing fever. The memory still hurt, though he'd had no choice. Rage had bitten his father, Hickory, and the elf had died of the fever too.

Finally, when the injured elves were securely fastened to their litters and harnessed to the wolves, the three hunters went off in search of their prey.

Fawn was very subdued and contrite by the time Glade brought her back to the holt. He had explained to her about Freefoot and Shadowflash, and about swordfeet, and how important it had been for Dreamsnake to have known about it so that she could have sent more help if any of the elders who had not joined in the *taal* had come back, and how Fawn herself might have to use her fledgeling healing powers when the wounded were finally brought in.

Dreamsnake was cutting meat for the other cubs when they came to the bank. "Where have you been?" she asked. She put down the haunch of antelope and her knife and went to meet her daughter. "I've been so worried about you." She looked at Glade for an explanation.

"I've got to get back," Glade told her, then turned to Fawn. "I'm depending on you now," he said. Then he hurried back into the woods.

Sprig and Clamshell came up to listen as Fawn told her mother about Freefoot and Shadowflash, and how she had gone to count *taal,* and where to send any elders. Dreamsnake let her remorseful cub tell the story to the end.

"I'm very disappointed in you, cubling," Dreamsnake

said when Fawn had finished. "Fairheart and Fernhare were here while you were gone, I could have sent them out to help."

"I'm sorry, Mother," Fawn said. She was nearly in tears, and was little comforted when Bouncer came over to greet her.

"I know you are, cubling," Dreamsnake said. "But you must promise me that you won't run off like that again. You're just not old enough yet."

"When will I be old enough?"

"When you remember to do what you're supposed to do before you do what you want to do. Now don't go too far away. We're going to need your help when the injured come home. And you," she said to Sprig and Clamshell, who were giggling behind her, "it's time for your supper, and stop making Fawn feel worse than she already does."

Fawn felt very sad indeed. She'd been bad, she hadn't been as grown up as she wanted to be, as she had thought she was, and Sprig and Clamshell had witnessed her disgrace. Fighting back the tears, she ran off to where a low tree branch made a bridge across the stream, with Bouncer bouncing happily along beside her. On the other side, she went upstream to a large, flat rock where she sometimes went to sit and think, and there found Sundrop and Greentwig, talking quietly and trying to grab the little fishes that swam by in the water just below the edge of the stone.

"Where have you been?" Sundrop asked as Fawn climbed up on the rock beside them and sat down to dangle her feet in the water.

"I went out to count *taal,*" she said, and told them all about it.

Lonebriar, Raindance, and Stringsong followed the bloody track of the swordfeet. Raindance felt strange, not having Grizzle with her. Lonebriar and Stringsong had made Blackbrush and Ranger sniff the blood, hoping that they would recognize the smell, but the two wolves had shown little interest and paid little attention to the blood on the trail.

The trail did not run straight, but did go through more open woodland for the most part. There had been quite a bit of blood at first, though later it diminished, and from it Lonebriar could get a distinctive *feeling* of the swordfeet, not a smell exactly, though in his mind that was the way the image formed.

"I don't want to kill them," he told the others as they hurried along the trail.

"I know," Raindance said. "But what else can we do?"

"They're not evil," Lonebriar went on. "They're just being themselves, like any hunter."

"If we were south," Stringsong said, "in their part of the forest, then we'd have to let them be. We would be the intruders then. But they don't belong here, O Speaker to Swordfeet. We can't let them stay."

"I know that," Lonebriar said. "And the younger one is carrying pups. I could feel them in her when we 'talked.'"

"If she has her pups up here," Raindance said, "we'll never be rid of them. I'm sorry, Lonebriar."

"Just lead us to them," Stringsong said, "and we'll do what we have to do."

"I remember Rage," Lonebriar told him. "You couldn't let anybody else destroy him. It's the same now, I have to do this."

The trail descended into a lowland part of the forest, where the ground was wet and did not keep footprints. There had been no blood for the last few hundred paces, and they lost the trail. Blackbrush and Ranger were no help. Though they had smelled swordfoot blood, they could not follow the scent. It was almost as if swordfeet did not exist for them.

They tried to pick up the trail again on the far side of the lowlands, but found no signs. They then coursed back along both sides of the wet area, but without any luck. The swordfeet couldn't still be in that part of the forest, the elves could see across the whole of the lowland area, even though it was not small. The undergrowth was mostly mosses and a few low ferns.

"There was some hard ground over there," Raindance said, pointing, "they might have gone out that way."

"I think you're right," Lonebriar said. He could feel a tickling "smell" in the back of his mind.

"Are they sending?" Stringsong asked.

"Not the way we think of it, their thoughts just—leak out. But yes, I'm feeling them. The adult is in great pain."

"Let's go, then," Stringsong said gently, and Lonebriar led the way.

The tickle in his mind, the acid "taste" of the swordfoot thoughts, led Lonebriar across the hard ground and upslope to where the trees were very large, but very close together. There was no undergrowth here either. The tickle became stronger, but he remembered that, unless the swordfeet were "talking" directly to him, they would seem farther away than they really were, so he was cautious. Every tree trunk was a possible hiding place, the gently sloping ground had many shallow hollows and depressions. But he was concentrating so hard on the swordfoot sensations that it was Raindance who saw them first.

There they are, she sent to her companions, and pointed. An eight of eights of paces upslope, in a grotto formed by the trunks of two huge trees which grew almost out of each other's roots, were the two swordfeet.

The adult was lying down, her head upslope, the juvenile crouched beside her, her back to the elves.

She's dying, Lonebriar sent. His emotions were tangled like wine-berry vines. The swordfoot's thoughts were so alien, so strange, and yet it was a sorrow to him that she should be dying here, in a strange land she didn't understand, so far from her home. Swordfeet were terrible killers, so great a threat that elves could not share the same forest with them, and yet, because he could "read" their thoughts, he felt a kinship with them. The adult would not live long, but could he actually kill the younger one? And if he did, what kind of scar would he bear? Stringsong knew about that; he could help him afterward.

We only have to deal with the young one, then. Raindance's sending intruded on his thoughts. Lonebriar looked up. Stringsong was nocking an arrow in his bow.

I can't be sure of a kill at this range, Stringsong sent. **We'll have to get closer.**

They went as quietly as they could. Lonebriar's feet felt like they were caught in tangle-vines. When they were halfway up the slope, still too far for even Stringsong to make a sure shot, the juvenile jumped up and turned to face them. Its thoughts were like sharp smoke in Lonebriar's mind. Rage. Despair. Threat.

Raindance hefted her ax. The swordfoot kicked out at the empty air in defiance. Stringsong held his bow at ready. The swordfoot barked harshly. Raindance glanced at Lonebriar, saw that he had no weapon, and offered him her ax. The dying swordfoot raised her head and looked back at them.

"I'll cover you," Stringsong told Lonebriar.

But Lonebriar refused the ax.

"It's all right," Raindance said, "we'll do it for you."

"No," Lonebriar said, "I want to try something first." He stepped between his companions and started up the last of the slope toward the swordfeet.

"What are you doing?" Stringsong cried, alarmed.

"Just give me a few moments," Lonebriar said. The young swordfoot kicked at the air with both feet as he neared, but did not leave her mother's side. He was able to come within six paces of her before he stopped.

The older swordfoot hissed, but could not rise. The younger one lashed out again and again with one foot, but stood her ground. Lonebriar stood before her, feeling her hatred, her anger, her grief. Then he closed his eyes and *sent* to her, in her own special way.

˜I won't hurt you,˜ he sent, or simpler thoughts that amounted to the same thing.˜You are in no danger from me.˜

˜Enemy,˜ the swordfoot sent back.˜Destroyer. Food.˜

She was such a powerful animal. Her green scales, though dirty now, scarred, and spotted with blood, were large, brilliant, and glossy. Her huge hind-foot talons were perfect weapons, her grasping forelegs strong and agile, her needle-teeth perfect for grabbing and tearing flesh, sharper than a wolf's. Lonebriar let his admiration for the swordfoot form his thoughts. She had been so brave, so smart, so caring of her mother. In essence, what he sent was,˜I like you.˜

The swordfoot stopped kicking, and stretched her head toward him, as if to see him better. ˜Pain,˜ she sent. ˜Anger. Grief for Mother.˜

Lonebriar thought of himself as a terrible hunter, of the swordfoot as a terrible hunter, both hunting the same ground, both defending their own lives, their right to take whatever food came their way. The swordfoot echoed his thoughts, as if it acknowledged the truth of that.

Lonebriar formed an image of two great hunters in

competition, but, ˜I win,˜ he finished. ˜It is the way.˜ The juvenile's sending was simple acceptance.

Lonebriar looked into the large, yellow eyes of the young swordfoot, eyes like those of a snake. He almost heard Raindance and Stringsong, behind him, cry out as he went up to the creature and put out a hand to touch her, gently, beside her deadly mouth. The swordfoot reached up and touched him, too, in the same way.

For a moment, the elf and the swordfoot just shared their minds with each other. Then Lonebriar sent, ˜Go home now. But when you bring forth your pups, come back to me.˜

The swordfoot seemed to understand. She dropped her wickedly clawed forepaw from Lonebriar's face and looked back at her mother.

The adult was lying stretched out on the ground. Lonebriar could feel her mind, flickering, fading. The young swordfoot stepped up to her, sniffed at her, licked her wounds one more time. Then the adult died.

The juvenile straighted, looked once at Lonebriar, looked past him at the other two elves with a thought that they, at least, were fair game, then went away up the slope to the crest of the rise and out of sight.

"What happened?" Stringsong and Raindance asked together as they hurried up to Lonebriar. "You let it get away!" Raindance accused.

"I sent her away," Lonebriar said. He drew a deep breath and turned to smile at his two companions. "She's going home."

"How do you know that?" Stringsong asked. He was looking past Lonebriar at the dead swordfoot.

"I told her to."

"But it'll be back," Raindance said.

"Yes, after her pups are born, when they're old enough to travel."

"Listen, Talker to Swordfeet," Stringsong said, "I

think you fail to understand the seriousness of the situation. One swordfoot loose in our hunting grounds is bad enough, but if this one comes back fully grown with a half-grown offspring—"

"Four," Lonebriar said. "She's carrying four."

"You're crazy," Raindance said. She knelt beside the dead swordfoot, touched its great talons, fingered its foreclaws, rolled its head to one side to look at the terrible teeth in its half-open mouth.

"She knows me now," Lonebriar said. "She will come to me first." He stooped beside Raindance, then drew his knife and cut the two great talons from the dead swordfoot's back feet.

"How can you be sure?" Stringsong said. He kicked at the carcass. "We've got to hunt it down."

"No," Lonebriar said, "we don't." He stood up, the bloody trophies in his hands. "We shared minds, Stringsong. They are other, yes, but they don't know what lying is. They didn't try to fool us when they left the wet place, they were just looking for higher ground. They never hide except when they sleep. She—said —she was going back home. I believe her."

Raindance stood up beside him. She looked at the deadly, sharp, swordlike claws in his hands, each as long as an elf's forearm. "It's your responsibility then, *Talon,*" she said. "When the swordfeet come back, you have to protect us from them, even as you now protect them from us."

"I accept that," the elf who had been Lonebriar said.

"It's a great responsibility, Talon," Stringsong added.

"I know," Talon said. "That's fine with me."

"I wonder if this thing is any good to eat," Raindance muttered.

Talon, as Lonebriar would be known from now on, sat by the fire in front of the bank of the holt, surrounded by cubs. Only Fawn was not there, as she was with Raindance and Glade, who were tending to the wounded elves.

She was more than glad to have a chance to make up for her childish behavior that day, even though she was not yet very good at healing, and healing sometimes hurt. Especially with someone as badly injured as Smarthand. He was so broken up inside that she was afraid, at first, to even try. Glade suggested that she start with Catcher, and then do what she could with Freefoot and Shadowflash. Her success, little as it was for one so young, gave her confidence, and at last she put her hands on Smarthand again, and *felt* inside him. She lacked experience, but Raindance and Glade guided her, talked to her, suggested things for her to do. It took great effort, and a lot of courage on her part, but she succeeded in stopping his internal bleeding. By then, though, she was exhausted, and could do no more. At least Smarthand would live until morning, when she would try again.

Though it was full dark, Dreamsnake and Stringsong were the only other elders at the holt. None of the rest had yet returned from the *taal,* nor the few who had had not joined in from their other expeditions. They sat with the cubs, just as fascinated by Talon's story of how he had first felt a swordfoot sending, had fought with them, and at last had made friends with the young one and sent it back home.

"Is it like that with you and snakes?" Stringsong whispered to Dreamsnake.

"Sort of," she whispered back, "except snakes don't have much of a mind to talk to."

Talon had to tell the story several times, and answer all the questions Greentwig, Sprig, Sundrop, and Clamshell had to ask. The cubs delighted in using his new name whenever they could. For his part, Talon wasn't sure he deserved so much attention. After all, he had gotten his old name because he liked to be alone a lot. But there didn't seem to be any help for it.

He was relieved, then, when Sunset, Suretrail, and Fire-Eyes finally returned, tired and hungry, but laughing and obviously pleased with the day's events. Though, of course, he would have to tell the story all over again to all the elders, too.

"It was a great *taal*," Suretrail said as the three came over to the fire. "Everybody else will be here soon."

"Did you come back early?" Sunset asked when she saw Talon and Stringsong. "You should have stayed out with us. You missed all the excitement."

Stormlight's Way

by Nancy Springer

Stormlight stood at a distance, half-hidden in the shadows of the nighttime Everwood, clutching her spear as she watched Tanner comfort her cub. In her father's arms, little Goodtree wept huge, gasping sobs worthy of a mother's death.

"I—was—SCARED!" the cub managed between sobs. "It—its—antler—cut me!"

Child moon's light plainly showed that the cut was scarcely more than a scratch. Stormlight would have been embarrassed even to take it to the healer. But Tanner, heel-sitting with the youngster gathered to his chest, nestled between his knees—Tanner, the chieftain of the Wolfriders—held the cut arm in his work-roughened hands as if he cradled a broken bone. *And it's my fault, as always,* Stormlight thought bitterly, though in fact Tanner never found fault with her. *Wrong-ways thing that I am.* Tanner did not know it of her, that she had lied, that she had come back from her passage vigil without her soulname. No one but Stormlight knew that.

Nothing more than stick-thin lengths of limb and hair pale as flowerdown, Stormlight had been at that time. No more than a stripling, her breasts just beginning to bud, when she had looked at her chief one day—brown-bearded, puttering Tanner, old enough to be her father many times over—she had looked at him in youthful

257

defiance and felt her world shatter. Recognition. In that one moment it was all decreed for her, that she should be the chief's mate and bear his cub. She, scarcely more than a cub herself. She who did not yet even know her own soulname.

"But it is not fair!" she had shouted at Tanner, at her chief standing as pale and shaken as herself. "There should be lovemates for me, courtships, choosings! I have never wanted anything but to be free!"

You will be as free as I can make you, he had promised her, and he had not yet failed to keep that promise.

She had gone to take her passage almost at once, for an urgent hunger was on her that would not let her eat or sleep, that made her movements clumsy and her speech slow. Tanner had told her he would wait as long as need be until she was ready to accept Recognition and him, but she knew he was suffering as well. And though her youthful heart held him somehow to blame for what was happening to her, still she did not entirely dislike him. . . . Yet she had never credited herself with kindness in bringing her vigil to a hasty, unsuccessful close. Instead, she called herself coward, unable to prolong her own suffering, unable to discipline the whirlings of her mind. She went back within a few days and told herself it didn't matter. He knew her soulname. He whispered it to her that first time they lay together. "Myr."

She felt sure she could not attempt vigil ever again. Always she must keep her shameful secret.

I am Myr, she thought, listening to her sobbing cub. *I am Myr,* as she always reminded herself when she felt self slipping. She did not know whether the other elves sometimes felt self slipping or not. She did not know if they knew their soulnames in a way she did not. Hers meant little to her except as a reminder to be strong and secret.

"It—it had—big eyes! Looking right at me!"

The yelling of her cub made Stormlight want to hit something. She had often wanted to hit Goodtree, and the urge was another thing she had to be ashamed of, had to hide. No proper Wolfrider would ever strike a cub. But sometimes it seemed to Stormlight that she must either slap Goodtree or else herself yell as loud as the cub, and stamp her feet, and cry. How could she have a cub? She was still a cub herself. But nobody knew that. They must not ever know.

Little Goodtree bellowed at her father's chest between sobs, "It—it had blood—coming out its mouth. It died!"

Stormlight couldn't stand listening any longer. "Of course it died!" she shouted, striding toward her daughter and the cub's father. "It is meat for you to eat!" For if anything lay to Stormlight's credit in the tribe, it was that she had become a skilled and tireless huntress. She loved the hunt. Running the hot scent on the back of her wolf-friend, intent on the kill, she was a wolf, she always lost all other self for a while.

The cub burrowed her head deeper against her father's body and would not look at her mother. Instead, Tanner looked up at his young Recognized standing over him with her angry storm-dark eyes glaring, her fair hair flying like lightning. "The cub is too young to go hunting with you," he said mildly. He always spoke mildly, to Stormlight as to everyone, and because Stormlight felt herself to be unworthy, his gentleness enraged her. She slammed her spear-butt at the ground, burying it several finger-spans into the soft forest loam.

"I was orphaned younger than her, and hunting meat on my own!"

"Not treehorns, surely?" He said it with just a ghost of his half smile. She wished she could knock him over. If half the tribe had not been watching and listening from the shelter of nearby trees, she might have.

She lowered her voice slightly. "The cub must toughen, Tanner! This is a harsh world. You have—you have—" She faltered, because the language of the Wolfriders had no words, no concepts, for "coddled," "spoiled," "brat." The world of two moons and the rigors of a Wolfrider's life left no need for such words.

Little Goodtree, nestled against her father's chest, had quieted; in fact the cub had gone still as a fear-frozen ravvit, as if her mother was a predator. All Stormlight could see of her daughter was the sun-yellow curls at the back of her head. Hiding in the dark, she knew, were Goodtree's heartbreaking eyes, not midnight-blue like her mother's but green as new leaves, large and nearly luminous. The cub's green eyes and sunny hair had made Tanner wish to name her Goodtree, and Stormlight had assented. Ever since, she had wished she had not. It was a name as placid as Tanner himself. Stormlight did not want her daughter to grow up to be tame.

She wished her daughter would stop cowering. She wished Goodtree would look at her. She had wanted to take her daughter hunting with her; now it seemed that was wrong. She had never been able to do anything right for Goodtree, not since the day her daughter was born.

She remembered the birthing all too well. Because she was so young, so small, it had not been for her as it should have been for a Wolfrider mother. She remembered lying in the bed of furs in the midwife's tree hollow afterward, exhausted. "It will go better for you next time, little one," the midwife told her. "It is just that you are too slender, too narrow. You need a bit more growth." Stormlight's small breasts had made no milk for the cub. It did not matter, for there were other, older tribe-women with infants, they were glad to share, to take on themselves the care of the little newcomer while Stormlight's young body lay in the furs, slow to recover. Her cub was in no danger, Stormlight knew. But every time she saw her little daughter in hands not hers, at a breast not hers, she felt an odd pain in her heart.

There would be no next time, she told herself.

Yet within the year she took a lovemate.

Tanner had promised her freedom, and she made sure to take it. She left their cub largely to his care. When the lovemate left her, she turned to Tanner for a while, living with the chieftain and little Goodtree. . . . Tanner's brown eyes silently invited her to stay her life-long, and she fled, found herself another lover, drifted away again, returned to Tanner. . . . And so it had gone since, that she always came back to the chief and her cub—her only cub—but never for long. Something—something hot as tears always tore her away.

I have had my freedom, Stormlight thought, *but my own little one scarcely knows me.*

And looking at the cub nestling against Tanner's chest, she said harshly to him, "You have made a weakling out of her."

"You are tougher than blackthorn, Stormlight," said Tanner. "You cannot expect everyone to be as tough, least of all a cub. Perhaps Goodtree is more like me." He gave his Recognized the soft half smile she loved and hated, smiling as if he loved her, as if he would always love her, no matter how she stormed. Did he not know she was worthy of no such love?

"Puckernuts!" she exploded. "Go back to your stinking leathers. I will take the cub to the healer, if I must."

"But no one has said you must," he reminded her gently.

She could bear anything but his gentleness. "Of course you have not said!" she raged. "You would not say to a bloodsucker, fly away! I think you would offer it your arm! A chieftain, and you play all day with paints and leather! You—"

Tanner got up, setting little Goodtree on her feet; the

cub clung to his leg as he peered at Stormlight, reacting not at all to her words, but noting her flushed skin, the tremor of her lower lip, almost hidden behind anger.

Myr, he asked, a lock-sending for her mind alone, **what is wrong?**

Curse you! The reply seemed torn out of her. **Why will you not hate me?** She turned away from him, brushed through the tribe-fellows who stood frankly listening at no great distance, and strode away, bound into the woods to find her latest lovemate, Brightlance. Only when she was lying with him, filled by him, did she feel—not empty.

Behind her, she left mutterings.

Not from Tanner. He took Goodtree by the hand and led her off to play with leather at his side. But his going freed the others to speak their minds. "I don't know how he can abide her," declared Brook.

Several of the younger males agreed with him, and the young females, Stormlight's age or a little older. But an older elf shook her head, half-amused, half-disgusted. She knew that Brook and most of his cronies had "abided" Stormlight well enough when they had been her lovemates. She said, "Stormlight is unhappy."

The others looked at her, for she was Moss, the midwife, and when she spoke, she most often made sense. But this time Brook snorted at her. "Unhappy!" he scoffed. "Should we all be so unhappy, we could battle the humans away from Everwood with our scowls alone!"

The others tittered, but Moss said serenely, "She is very unhappy, and we ought to do something about it."

Nearby, a few heads nodded agreement. Other older elves drew near: Fallfern, Leaf, Watersong. Though not usually inclined to meddle, in Stormlight's case they felt they could. All of them had mothered her as an orphaned cub, and something in them sensed she was little more than an orphaned cub still. They would take her in hand. And though none of them owned nearly as many years as Tanner, they felt in themselves the authority of tribal elders. What they decided among themselves, short of war, they would do, for Tanner was a chief who seldom chose to lead his people.

"She needs to make up her mind to stay with Tanner," said Watersong.

"Just what I say," said Moss. "She's his Recognized. Poor thing, it happened to her so young that she set her mind against it, and she's been fighting it ever since. But it's time—"

"Past time she accepted it," Leaf snapped. "But there's this to think of. Do you think the tribe will accept her? As chieftess?"

"Don't see why not," said Fallfern, and many voices rippled together like water into a pool.

"She seldom quarrels with anyone except Tanner."

"Joygleam says she's cool as ice and keen as a new spear on the hunt."

"She's a bold wolf."

"She keeps the Way."

"I tell you this, she would make us a war leader, should we ever need one."

No one in the tribe ever remembered who had said that last, but at the words they all looked at each other, even Brook and the younger ones, and nodded.

It was Moss who first broached the matter to Stormlight, the following day, in the privacy of the midwife's tree hollow, and Stormlight's brows drew down like thunderclouds. "You don't know what you're talking about!"

Moss said, "I know what anyone in the tribe with half an eye can see: that Tanner loves you, and you love him. And you'd know it yourself, if you'd stand still long enough to notice."

"There are things you don't know," Stormlight said darkly, and though she would not quarrel with Moss —for she owed Moss a debt of caring—still, she shook her head no matter how Moss importuned her.

The next day Brook and some others approached her in the open, and she shook her head at them also. And for many days after that, for full turnings of the seasons, she refused all who requested her to be Tanner's lifemate and chieftess, sometimes with shouts, sometimes with a weary gesture. At times her tribe-mates sensed a wavering, a needfulness, in her. Therefore they persisted, no matter how often she stormed at them.

Truth was, their proddings echoed a half-hidden yearning inside her.

She drifted away from her lovemate, for Brightlance no longer seemed to fill her emptiness. But because the eyes of the tribe were on her she did not go back to Tanner as she would usually have done. She lived through a long winter alone, deeply alone with tribe-mates all around her, and felt the cold to her core.

"Myr," she whispered to herself sometimes, "I am Myr." It did not help as much as she would have liked. She did not know that other elves had shared similar difficulties, that the failed vigil had not been her only chance, that selfhood sometimes came later. These things she did not know because she had not asked. She had always kept her thoughts and her troubles to herself.

Every day one of the others urged her to be Tanner's lifemate, and in her heart she knew it was time. Nearly every unpledged male in the tribe had been her lovemate. None of them had helped her for long. But Tanner—Tanner was different. Perhaps he could . . . make her whole. . . .

And—there was the cub.

But every day pride made her shake her head.

Tanner watched as the seasons wore on; he was always aware of whatever happened within the tribe, though he seldom chose to intercede. He watched Stormlight, and felt for her, for he knew her fierce independence. The hidden Stormlight, the needful cub, he knew not at all, no more than the others did. . . . He watched, he listened, but never spoke—until one spring night, when Moss and Brook and the others made the mistake (so Tanner thought) of bringing the matter before the howl, where his authority as a chieftain required that he speak to it.

It was a sweet-smelling spring night, under two pregnant and swelling moons. The howl gathered in the beech grove on the brow of their longtime hurst. And yet one more time, formally, before all the tribe, Moss asked Stormlight to take Tanner as her lifemate and be a chieftess.

Near at hand, Goodtree sat with the other cubs, looking at her mother with great eyes. Stormlight felt the gaze of those eyes, and the shout of fury gathering in her throat broke apart, and her lips went dry; she wet them with the tip of her tongue. She moved them, trying to speak. But Tanner was speaking.

"No one has asked me of this matter," said Tanner dryly.

No one replied. Moss and Brook looked down at their hands, and Tanner did not see their secret smiles.

"Nor should anyone ask Stormlight of this matter. I made her a promise when we Recognized each other that she would have her freedom, and I will protect my promise. I, your chief, forbid you to press her—"

Before he could finish, Stormlight was on her feet, shouting at him. "I will protect my own freedom, thank you!" And she faced him within arm's reach, hot with fury, her dark eyes darker yet with fury.

No matter how often or for what varied reasons she stormed at him, it never ceased to astonish him. His eyes widened, and he nearly stammered, starting to try to explain himself. "I just wanted—"

"You wanted, it's always what *you* want! Nobody ever asks me what I want! Well, I will tell you what you are going to get, Tanner-chief-of-the-Wolfriders, whether you want it or not!" She stamped her foot on the forest floor, glaring at him. "I will be your lifemate, as I would have told you if you had troubled to ask me. I will stay with you from now on until one of us dies." And make your life a misery if you cross me, her tone said. The tribe burst into delighted cheers, and she turned on them. "Since that is what you all want!" she barked. Under the force of her glare they quieted, but they could not take the grins off their faces. Moss and Brook especially seemed gleeful almost beyond bearing.

"I told you!" Brook whispered to his coconspirator. "I told you as soon as he started to protect her from us she would side against him!"

"You were right," Moss admitted, smiling. "A bold gamble, well won. This deserves dreamberries."

"Later."

Amid the circle of the tribe, Stormlight and Tanner stood staring at each other. "I mean it," she said to him, softly now, all the spleen gone from her voice. "I will stay with you. I give you my promise."

"Fell me and tie me and fry me in a fire!" he said, his voice husky, and his hand reached out to her, and she did not back away.

Moss and Brook were not the only ones who had dreamberries that night. And in all the rejoicing tribe, the only one who seemed not glad was the cub Goodtree.

Somewhat older now, Goodtree was somewhat less prone to hysteria, though still sensitive, moody, more like her mother than she knew. On this night of her parents' lifemating, Goodtree broke the tribe's rule and went off by herself, wandering into the nighttime Everwood to brood.

Thus it was she who first saw the human warriors approaching, drawn out of their village at the forest's edge by the unaccustomed clamor the elves had made at the howl.

Humans. With torches and weapons. Humans, the one reason why she was not to wander alone in the first place.

Goodtree shivered at the sight of the Tall Ones, but did not disgrace herself by crying out or losing her head. Silently as a treewee she scampered up the nearest bole to the branches, and there she considered for a moment whether she might be punished. And then she put the thought away, clenched her small teeth, and sent.

Humans coming! Her sending included any elf not too drunk to hear. **Humans coming toward the hurst, with torches!** With some small satisfaction she considered that she was probably interfering with whatever it was her father and mother were doing at the moment.

Indeed she was. In a private hollow not far away, Tanner and Stormlight rolled apart and scrambled for their clothing.

"The cub!" Stormlight exclaimed.

"Stormlight! Wait!"

Tanner meant to have others go with her to fetch Goodtree. But without even a glance at him she ran off into the night.

Nor had she ever told him, even on this night of all nights, that she loved him. . . . Tanner quelled the thought. There was the tribe to think of.

Stormlight brought back the cub safely enough,

through the trees, just in time to quarrel with Tanner before his assembled warriors.

"No bloodshed if we can avoid it," he was instructing them. "No contact if we can avoid it. We stay behind, to protect the rest of the tribe as they flee. Do you understand?"

Before they could nod, Stormlight dropped with the cub in her arms, landing with a thump in front of her lifemate. "Flee!" she exclaimed, outraged.

"Yes, of course," said Tanner. The humans had become far too bold of late. It seemed to him that he should have led the tribe away long since, that he was selfishly to blame for not having done so. "Northward," he added. "We are to meet at Muchcold Water, at the river mouth. Go, hurry, take Goodtree."

Stormlight did not move. "Flee!" she repeated, scandalized. "This is our home! Why should we be driven from it? You take this cub, give me a spear, and I will fight the humans off myself!"

"The Everwood is well named," said Tanner quietly. "There will be other homes in it for us. I have no desire to see humans spill any elf's blood, least of all yours. Now go."

"I will not!" Stormlight flared. "What, and let the humans have it all? Our hurst? Your leathers?"

Goodtree hung uncomfortably in her mother's arms, her legs dragging, silently listening.

"Leathers be blowed!" Tanner exploded. There was not time for further squabbling. "Stormlight, I am your chief, and I tell you, take the cub and go!"

"What am I?" Stormlight shouted back. "Be chieftess, our people told me! I—"

Go, Tanner sent to her, a chief's sending to a challenger, and her ranting stopped with a gasp. She stepped back from him, shaking, then turned and ran. In no way could she contest him in such a battle, she who—lacked. She lacked something which made him strong.

Her cheeks flamed to the ears, she shook with chagrin, for she had showed before her chief and his warriors that she was strong only outwardly, that inwardly she had—no selfhood.

If it had not been for the cub, she might not have made the journey to Muchcold Water. She might have wandered off into the forest, like a moody youngster, and lost herself.

As it was, she joined a fleeing band, saw Goodtree to safety. And when Tanner rejoined her, days later, he seemed to think none the less of her. Nor did any of the others.

But the lifemating seemed to take its tenor from that first night: the lovemaking, but never that statement of love. The quarreling, the danger.

For many turnings of the seasons the tribe roamed the Everwood, seldom staying in any one camp for long. Most of the Wolfriders took well to the nomadic life. But oddly, Stormlight, in her way the wildest of them all, did not. She seemed to mind the loss of Tanner's leathermaking worse than he did. Whenever she spoke of the leathers he had lost, the tanning pits he would never be able to open, he shrugged, which enraged her. His art had brought them together, time gone by. It wrenched her to see him without leather in his hands.

She knew he cherished her, that there had never been any lover in his life but her. His silent, steadfast affection frightened her. She felt him prizing her as he had once prized his art. She felt him crafting her as if crafting a fine sheath of leather for a keen blade, taming her with gentleness as if taming a lone wolf, softly guiding her in the ways a chieftess should act and speak. Now that she had pledged herself to him, he no longer felt that he must guard her freedom. None of this she liked, but she remembered her promise. Sometimes she found her way past her fears, or became weary enough to forget them for a while. Sometimes things were good between them.

Until Goodtree grew to be a stripling.

Stormlight had tried in every way she could think of to mother Goodtree, and it had never worked. She could never feel at one with Goodtree. She could with Tanner, sometimes, because the thorn thickets between them were all Stormlight's, and she knew them well; sometimes she could slip past them. But Goodtree had thorn thickets of her own which verily seemed to move from day to day as the cub grew. Try as she might, Stormlight could never gather strength or wisdom to find her way through them, and whenever she approached her cub there was a mighty, briar-stinging tangle.

And never more so than when she tried to teach Goodtree the skills of the spear.

Stormlight had indeed become war leader as well as a renowned huntress. More than once the chieftess had led a picked band and skirmished with humans in an attempt to keep the Tall Ones out of the depths of Everwood where the elves roamed. Only when at hunt or war did Stormlight feel herself of any selfhood, any value, she, still carrying her shameful secret. Her skill with the stabbing spear gave her worth. This skill, above all others, she wanted to pass on to her only daughter.

"No," said Goodtree.

Her mother tried the soft ways first. "But look! I made this for you."

Goodtree did not move from the place where she sat or lift a hand to accept the proffered spear. "And I told you not to," she retorted.

"But I wanted you to have one. See, it is sized just for you."

270

Stormlight pressed the haft into her daughter's hand. Goodtree moved her hand away.

"No!" the cub declared. "I have told you and told you, no."

"And I have told you and told you, yes!" Stormlight abandoned the soft ways. Being a war leader had taught her how to give orders. "Get up!"

Goodtree did, but kept her hands down at her sides, away from the spear. "Take it," her mother commanded.

"No."

"*Take* it!"

"No!" Goodtree blazed with a sudden fury fit to rival her mother's finest tempers. "You can't make me! My weapon is the bow!"

Like a leaf turning in the wind, Stormlight turned from a war leader into a mother, perilously patient. "Timmorn's blood, youngster, *why*?"

"Because I am not the same as you!"

That hurt, though it was not meant to; it was merest truth. But Stormlight had no strength for truth. Patience left her as if blown away by a strong wind. Her fair brows drew down, stormclouds over eyes like dark, angry water.

"Because you are afraid to fight close, you mean!" The words hurtled out of her, darts meant to wound. "Because you are still afraid of coming close to a stag! The bow is a good weapon for a coward! It will keep you far from danger."

Goodtree felt tears stinging her eyes. Not now, she told herself fiercely, just this one time, please, let me not weep. Gulping, she stepped forward and yelled into her mother's face, "I am me! Why must you always try to make me like you? Why is nothing I do ever good enough for you!"

Astonished, Stormlight lost her anger for a moment.

She, the wrong-ways one, trying to make her daughter like herself? It was true, and heartbreaking, and laughable. She nearly smiled.

But Goodtree, fighting tears, raged on. "I don't want to be like you! You're proud and hateful and mean. You didn't think my father was good enough for you until you'd tried everybody else! And now all you do is yell at him. You're nothing but sourberries inside. You—"

Nothing—inside. . . .

Reacting like a hurt wolf snapping at a packmate, Stormlight drew back her hand and slapped. She saw Goodtree's shocked face, the green eyes widening, tears threatening, held in check, and she knew she wanted to make the cub cry. Goodtree had driven her half-mad with crying, seasons past; why would the youngster not weep now? Stormlight drew back her hand again—

"Stormlight!" Someone had hold of her arm. Tanner, of course. It would have to be Tanner. Some tribe-mate, hearing the uproar, had alerted him. And now he had caught her doing something truly bad, as she had always known must happen, wretched thing that she was. He had caught her striking a cub.

Not really a cub any longer, Tanner was thinking. Big enough to take her lumps. And in a shouting hysteria. He might have struck her himself, though perhaps not quite so hard. It had worked; Goodtree was sobbing, but not shouting any longer.

"No more," he told Stormlight.

Gentle, the words were gentle, as always. Would he never learn that she could stand anything but his kindness? He was shaping her again, guiding her toward steadiness, calmness, moderation. Something fiercely crackled in her mind. She looked into his serene brown eyes.

"That's right," she replied, her voice shaking and laden with bitterness, a branch bent fit to crack with sourberries. "No more." And she turned her back on his startled queries and walked away, taking with her not even her spear.

No more love. She had done wrong. No more lifemating. She had tried and tried, but Tanner's touch no longer served to fill her; it made her feel more empty than before. No more Myr. She had told herself for years that she was Myr, and it had stopped helping. No more struggling. No more—Stormlight. . . .

Because she wanted no one with her, she did not summon her wolf-friend. She walked. Steadily, spear-straight she walked toward the human village. Walking numbed the aching void inside her. She walked through the night, till sunrise found her within nose-shot of the noxious midden-heaps at the fringes of Everwood. Just beyond stood the human huts.

Stormlight's half-wolf instincts knew what she was doing better than her muddled head did, for at the first scent of the human place she found herself turning aside into the thickest cover. There, amid thornbushes—real ones, as well as those she had brought with her in her mind—she sat and waited.

It was not so much that she wanted to kill herself. It was just that she wanted—self, wretched hurting self, to die. . . . And no elf would come here to disturb her.

She sat through the day and the night and another day, without food or water, waiting for self to starve into nothingness. Human hunters went past, stinking their human stench, their gross feet thudding down within her sight, during the days. She paid them no heed. By the end of the second day, even when the half-grown ravvits scurried over her feet, she noticed nothing around her. She smelled nothing, saw nothing but inner visions.

She saw her parent elves—the parents who had died before she was old enough to remember them. She knew them for her parents, though their faces were strange to her, because she felt their love. She saw—her mother lying in childbirth, and herself coming from the womb, an infant, welcomed with rejoicing. She saw her parents riding away to the hunt, riding away to their deaths. She saw them kiss her before they went, and their kisses melted away all the thorns in her mind.

She saw—her own cubs, yet unborn.

She understood, she *knew*.

She knew soul. She knew Myr. Remembering nothing of Tanner, of her present life, she found the name for herself, and finding it, she found her center. She was Myr. She was cub no longer, but mother, strong mother, creator and protectress of new life. Loving and fierce, lover and warrior, she was Myr. She would have more cubs—now that soul and self had joined to make a whole, she could, she knew she could! She felt the motherseed awakening, waiting in her womb. She was Myr, the fertile one. She saw Tanner in her vision. He and she would have offspring, enough to swell the numbers of the tribe, more cubs than any elves had ever made before! He was old and wise, fit to father many Wolfriders. She was young and strong and *Myr*.

She came to self, laughing softly and dizzily, a springtime feeling in her mind, though it was the end of summer. It seemed unfitting that there should be thorns around her. All those within her had turned to white, sweet-smelling blossoms. It was time for her to go back to the tribe. To Tanner. Strength enough in her, now, to lifemate him as he had always been willing to lifemate her.

By good chance it was dusk, soon to be nighttime. No need to wait any longer. Stormlight crawled out of her hiding place and started back the way she had come. It seemed like a lifetime before that she had walked this way, despairing. . . . Droll, that it had never occurred to her that she was going to her long-delayed vigil. She giggled at the thought that she, the chieftess of the Wolfriders, had not known such a simple thing, that to take vigil was to let self die and be reborn.

Puckernuts! She was staggering even on the level, open ground beneath the trees. Weak from fasting. She would need help to get back to the tribe. Her wolf-friend—

But before she could send, someone hailed her mind: **Myr!**

"Tanner!" she cried aloud, and, sending, she exclaimed, **Lhu! Soulmate, I am here.** And within a heartbeat he was there, by her side, and Goodtree, both of them, her family, and her arms were around them both, and with a sending that encompassed them both she was sharing with them her happiness, her vision, her dream. I know who I am now, she was telling them, I am Myr! I am mother, I am love, I am strong and glad. And Tanner was embracing her and smiling, bemused, for it was no more than he had always known of her. "You foolish cub," he whispered as he began to comprehend that she had not known it herself. "You feckless, generous cub." And Goodtree was trying not to weep, and sending, **Mother, I'm sorry—**

Hush, Stormlight told her tenderly. **It was not your fault, any of what's happened.**

And a harsh voice cried, "There they are! Beast-eyes! I told you I heard demons snickering out here!" The warriors ran toward them, weapons upraised.

And the human stink hit them at the same time as the horror and shock of the thing, that they, Tanner and Stormlight and Goodtree, had been surprised flat-footed, in the open. And already the Tall Ones, three of them, had rushed almost within striking reach. They carried long, coarse cudgels, as if they were hunting the rats that abounded in their midden-heap.

Though weak from her vigil, Stormlight moved first,

for she was what she was: the protectress, and she thought first of the cub.

"Goodtree! Run, save yourself!" she cried as she sprang at the nearest human, her hunting knife stabbing; it was her only weapon. And to Tanner she sent, **The cub! Get the cub to safety!**

But Tanner was already busy with an enemy twice his size. And Goodtree, with a shrill yell, snatched her own knife from her belt and attacked the third human.

A clumsy, unskilled attack. It did no good. But, by Timmorn's blood, the little one was not afraid of fighting! Stormlight saw it all in a moment, in pride and terror, her cub's daring, and—and the club, swishing down—

She darted, and took on her own breast the blow that would have smashed Goodtree's back.

It broke her like an eggshell. She fell. But in the same breath the wolf-friends came, Tanner's and Goodtree's, and Stormlight felt Tanner snatch her up and cradle her to his chest as he fled. She felt herself floating somewhere beyond pain, nearing death. And before she went she touched Tanner with her mind to tell him one last thing.

Lhu. I always—loved you.

Myr, I always knew.

"Mother!" Riding, fleeing at her father's side, Goodtree sounded frantic. "Father, is she—dead?"

Beloved, Stormlight answered her, **in a moment I will be. Little one, do not grieve. I am a Wolfrider, and I have found my Way.**

A Very Good Year for Dreamberries

by Diana L. Paxson

*E*ven to elf memory the Everwood seemed old.

Its foliage had covered the hillsides since the great ice drew away. Men came and went in wandering clans. Elves had lived there also and then departed, leaving no sign of their passing to tell those who came after that they were not first on the ground. And yet those firstcomers did leave a legacy, for they wrought not with tools but with a desperate magic, and here and there a remnant of their power remained, mindless, formless, waiting for those who could shape it to return. . . .

In a hollow on a hillside lay one such pool of power. But even when the children's children of those who had created it came to the Everwood it did not stir, for wolf-senses had lost the power to perceive its presence there. Through coldtimes and drytimes it waited, while the stars scribed their long, slow stories across the skies. . . .

Goodtree let herself sink into softness, watching the bright leaves that still clung to their branches above her flutter in the wind. In the slanting sunlight they glowed as bright a gold as her own hair, escaping now from its chieftain's knot, as for this brief moment she had escaped from her responsibilities to the Wolfriders. It was so glorious to simply lie here in the drifted leaves, relaxing into the lazy warmth of the afternoon.

The summer had been a good one, with long hot days relieved by soaking rains. On the plains, the grass had ripened to a rich gold that fattened the branch-horns —and the elves. When the approach of the great cold sent the herds southward, the Wolfriders had retreated to the shelter of the Everwood, discovering that the year had left its bounty in the forest as well, stored up in nut and root and berry—especially the dreamberries.

Goodtree giggled softly and reached up to pluck another from the branch above her, opened her mouth, and dropped it in, savoring the tartness of the skin, the cool firm flesh, and the rush of sweet juices as her strong teeth crushed it. The coldtime might be coming, but today was as peaceful and warm as summer. If she could only be still enough, she thought she could touch the silence that waited, just beyond the limits of her perception, like some great beast drowsing in the autumn sun.

Invisibly, the thick darkness of the hollow was stirred, rippling like the still waters of a deep forest pool when an idle hand throws in a stone. Power sensed power, roused from its long sleep and moved in mindless attraction toward the essence that had touched it. . . .

Good year for dreamberries . . . Lionleaper sent, his thoughts feeling as warm and contented as Goodtree's own. She shifted her head against his thigh, as if to reassure herself of his reality—the scars where the trapped branch-horn had gored him were still pink on his belly, and there had been long hours when she and Acorn Songshaper had fought for his life as desperately as the two male elves had once fought for hers.

But that was past now, the memory already merging into the eternal present of the wolfsong. She and Lionleaper lay curled like cublings in the thicket deep in the Everwood with Acorn, who had found the berry bush and graciously consented to share it with them.

Because he knows what we'd have done to him if he hadn't! Goodtree grinned. This was one berry bush that

278

Freshet could not claim, but that was no reason for Acorn to be greedy. She turned just enough to glimpse the third elf's head, pillowed on her thigh as hers was on Lionleaper's.

Beyond him, the ground fell away into cool darkness, then lifted abruptly in an overhanging bank. The edge was clothed so thickly with goldenleaf that no one would ever have suspected the existence of the treasure in this tiny dell if Acorn, walking as usual with his mind more on the song in his head than on the path before his feet, had not fallen into it.

Goodtree shifted a little so that she was directly under the fruit-laden branch, lazily imagining it dipping down to her, offering its fruit to her lips like a she-wolf bringing her dugs to the eager mouths of her cubs. The juice of the dreamberries she had already eaten was beginning to haze her senses. Rainbow colors shimmered through her awareness. For a moment it seemed to her that the branch had dipped, for another cool globule was in her mouth, and she could not remember having reached up to pluck it. Her ears were buzzing pleasantly.

Enough for now, she thought fuzzily. *I have never encountered such potent dreamberries before. . . .*

Nor have I—a *very* good year!

Goodtree lifted her head to look at Acorn, for she had *not* been sending— He blinked at her like an upside-down owl, brown hair ruffled, green eyes gleaming, then turned to plant a quick kiss on the smooth skin of her thigh.

Goodtree shook her head, trying to clear it. Acorn and Lionleaper together had followed her when she ran away to find her soul name, and together they had saved her. Even before that happened, she had been unable to choose between them as lovemates, but she had always tried to keep from hurting either one by not making it too obvious when she was sharing herself with the other.

Since then, she had not wanted to risk their new friendship by loving either one at all.

She realized now just how long it had been. With her control dissolved by the dreamberries, she was only too conscious of her body's demands. Awareness of Acorn's and Lionleaper's feelings throbbed through her, magnifying her own—or perhaps it was the purple intoxication of the berries. She could smell the males' desire, breathed in the heavy odor of her own, and the rich scent of leafenriched soil and the dreamberries' overwhelming perfume. Hands and lips caressed, bodies twined, and after the first astonished moments, none of them knew or cared whose touch was whose.

Joy pulsed outward from the three linked bodies. . . . Magic came to meet it, drawn from the hollow as a plant seeks the heat of the sun, and burst upward in a spiraling wave of energy. Faster and faster it whirled. Now it was a sphere, glowing faintly, if any had had eyes to see. One elf might have attracted it, the passion of two might have stirred it, but three—these three—joined with an energy that could awaken a world.

The ball of light floated above the lovers, waiting for them to notice it, and nascent awareness formed a wordless question—

Even in the midst of her pleasure, Goodtree knew that loveplay had never been like this before. A warm wind seemed to be swirling around her, spinning her upward in dizzying spirals like the leaves. Someone tickled her, and she heard herself laughing, joyous peals of pure merriment that chimed sweet harmony with the deeper laughter of her partners. And the air around them repeated that merriment, not like an echo, but with the half-uncomprehending wonder of an awakening child.

Afterward, they lay still tangled, not yet quite withdrawn into their separate selves, though their bodies' urgency was for the moment appeased.

Do you suppose the high ones knew about this?
Fools if they didn't—
Not fools . . . Longreach, who has taught me as much as he can remember of the old tales, says the high ones were not fools, but not like us, either—they made things not with their hands, but with their minds—
Bodies are more fun!

Someone giggled, then they all were laughing. The spell of the dreamberries still bubbled in their blood, though the first frenzy was past.

"Don't you wish you had the high ones' powers?" said Acorn aloud.

"I don't know—would they help us to hunt?" Lionleaper turned over and Goodtree brushed leaves off of his back.

"Hunting! Is that all you ever think of? Wouldn't it be fun to make something new?"

"Something funny!" Lionleaper reached out for another dreamberry. "With four paws, and arms, too, and big eyes that can see in the dark as well as the day—"

"And colored fur?" Goodtree was laughing almost too hard to speak.

"Like a rainbow!" Lionleaper gestured expansively, then collapsed back across her, giggling.

Color rippled through the faint glow of the sphere. The motion became more violent, and the roundness bulged abruptly, lengthening, changing, extruding six limbs, a round-eyed head, a sweep of shimmering fur. . . . For a moment it held that shape, and then, as Lionleaper's attention faded, shifted back into a glimmering sphere.

Acorn had drawn his knees up and was sitting with his arms clasped around them.

"Not much use just to be funny—it should *do* something. . . ."

"But what?" Goodtree turned on her side, resting her head on one hand. Perhaps it was the dreamberries, but in her mind's eye she saw the creature Lionleaper had described hovering above them, its gaze going from one to another with a comic anxiety.

"Oh, I don't know—maybe be a friend, like our wolves are—like they should be! A friend who would never be off hunting with his brothers when you needed him!"

Goodtree grinned. All the wolves who could run had gone off about pack affairs, as they did from time to time. But Acorn had intended to go up to the bluff that overlooked the forest that morning—a short journey for four legs, but a tiring one for two. Apparently Twitch-ear's desertion still rankled.

"So you would make a creature that would never let you be lonely?"

"Yes, and I'd call it a *Shadowshifter*! Because it would take all my troubles away!"

The being drifted closer to Acorn, curving over him protectively, though he did not see it. "Shadowshifter . . . "it savored the name. "I am the Shadowshifter!"

"If it's so friendly, why not get some use out of it?" said Goodtree. "I'd have a creature that would be helpful . . . keeping cublings out of trouble, lighting fires, and turning bedding—that sort of thing!"

Acorn and Lionleaper looked at her, then back at each other, shaking their heads.

"She wants it to be *useful*! Do you suppose it's because she's the chieftess?"

"Or because she's a female?"

Goodtree's hand shot out, but Lionleaper grabbed her wrist before she could hit him. For a moment they grappled, then Acorn landed on her other side. Knowing from hard experience that the two males together would be too strong for her, she gave way suddenly, then hugged them as they all fell back into the leaves.

The Shadowshifter drifted lower, peering anxiously into the tangle, but the three beings that had brought it to life did not seem to be in pain. After a time their laughter faltered and they lay quiet, still clasped in each other's arms. Their invisible guardian remained in position, trying to understand how they could be there and yet not there, while the daystar's gold faded from the Everwood and the autumn air began to chill. . . .

Goodtree woke shivering in the odd, indeterminate time between night and day. Her head was a little muzzy, and muscles complained at the odd position in which she had let them stiffen, but somewhere a wolf was calling, and wolf-senses sharpened in response. She blinked, and her vision adjusted to show her Acorn and Lionleaper just beginning to stir, and above them an odd glimmer that was probably the last flicker of the daystar.

"That's Fang!" exclaimed the hunter. "The pack has brought home game!"

Abruptly Goodtree became conscious of her hunger. The thought of tearing into a piece of rich, salt-sweet flesh drove all other ideas from her awareness and she leaped to her feet. Lionleaper was tugging on his leggings. Goodtree caught first one boot, then the other, as Acorn found them among the leaves and tossed them her way.

Her short tunic was dangling from a branch of the berry bush and she pulled it on. The branch still bore one bright berry, and for a moment she considered plucking it. The branch quivered invitingly. Goodtree stared at it, then laughed. She had had enough dreamberries for one day.

Acorn brushed off the last of the leaves and finished lacing up his vest. For a moment the elves looked at each other, smiling at memories that were already becoming unclear. Whatever had happened had left an ease among the three of them that had been the only thing lacking in their relationship, and that was what mattered, after all.

Then her own wolf-friend, Leafchaser, called, very close, and the she-wolf's howl was echoed by Twitch-ear and Fang.

"They've tracked us here!" cried Lionleaper. "Come on!" He scrambled back up the bank and the others followed him.

By the time they reached the hurst they remembered only that they had found a remarkably fine bush of dreamberries and there had been some lovemaking. Of the other thing that they had done they had no knowledge at all. . . .

The Shadowshifter waited above the pressed and tumbled leaves, wondering when one of its creators would summon it. But there was only silence, and time, that had passed unnoticed before, now brought a painful loneliness. Loneliness was bad—the brown male-thing had said so. Gently as a drift of pollen on a breeze, the Shadowshifter began to move, following the faint disturbance the elves' life energies had left in the network that was the Everwood as the wolves had tracked their scent not so long ago.

The oak tree was sniffling.

No—not the tree, but someone within it—Goodtree peered inside the hollow trunk and two startled, tearbright eyes met hers.

"What's the matter, cubling?" she asked softly. "It's too lovely a dawning for you to hide. Come out now, and greet the day!"

"Won't!"

"But why not?" She caught the scent of Snowfall's daughter Silvertwig, but what was she doing in there when the laughter of the other children came sweet and shrill from the stream?

"My mother said I moved it and I *didn't*!"

I'm her chieftess too, thought Goodtree, hunkering

down beside the opening. In the hurst, autumn was a busy time, as the Wolfriders prepared meat that had been rough-dried during the summer hunt for storage, pounding it to fragments and mixing it with berries to be stored in skin packets for winter trail-food. Fresh meat was their preference, always and forever, but when the pale hunter called Hunger stalked the land, even wolves would eat whatever they could find.

But for the moment, all of Goodtree's work was done. She had the time to listen to a cub.

"Do you want to tell me?"

Another sniff answered her, and then a very small voice began a tale of misplaced puckernuts that would have been funny but for the grief of the cub.

"And my mother says I must be lying because no one but us two knew that the nuts were there, but I wasn't, and I didn't, and I'm not coming out of my tree!"

Goodtree suppressed a smile. A few words to Snowfall would probably take care of the reconciliation —Goodtree had seen her talking to Joygleam just a few minutes before. She probably had no idea how seriously her scolding was being taken by her child. Goodtree remembered how insolvable problems appeared to the young—not that she herself was old as the elves viewed age, but at least she was past her cub days.

As she moved back toward the clearing, a cold wind seemed to brush her neck. She looked back over her shoulder, but there was nothing to see but a sparkle of sunlight. Goodtree realized abruptly that looking behind her had become a habit lately. . . . She felt as she had in the forest once when the bristle boar she thought she was hunting turned out to be hunting *her*.

But the trees knew nothing of any danger. There was no one there!

The air shimmered where Goodtree had been looking, as if the sunlight had heaved a sigh.

"She said to help. Shadowshifter helped—why is the

285

young-thing sad?" The light seemed to darken. For a moment then it was almost visible. "Shadowshifter does what they said, but no one cares!" Sadness chilled the air. "Got to do more. . . ."

Lionleaper followed the trail at a steady wolf-trot, his light feet hardly rustling the leaves. The spoor he was following was fresh—three dapple deer had passed this way not long ago. He moved steadily, letting his eyes find the trail for him while subtler senses quested for the slight disturbances that would tell him he was near his prey.

Riding Fang might have been quicker, but dapple deer were the wariest of prey. One whiff of wolf-scent would put them to frantic flight. Even more than one elf together had little chance of getting within spear-cast unobserved. On the other hand, a full-grown buck was still small enough for one hunter to carry home. Most of the larger game had already migrated southward anyway.

Lionleaper was happy enough to be away from the hurst, and by himself, whatever the reason. The camp had been strange lately. There had been quarrels, accidents, the Wolfriders were acting as if they had all been snowbound in their dens for weeks instead of still waiting for winter's first storms.

Ahead of him, the trees were thinning. He moved more cautiously now, slipping from trunk to trunk like a moving shadow. Sunlight filtered through an interlace of branches, dappling the fallen leaves. The hunter stood still, amber eyes narrowing as he scanned the confusion of light and darkness. Were those the slim trunks of new growth or slender legs and branching horns? Was that moving shimmer of sunlight the play of light on leaf or a spotted hide?

After a long moment, Lionleaper released the breath he had been holding in a soundless sigh. There was nothing in the clearing, but the wind was blowing toward him. His nostrils flared. Faintly on that breeze came the scent he was seeking. Ever more carefully, he crept forward.

At the edge of the trees he stopped, biting his lip in exasperation.

His tracking skills had not failed him. The dapple deer were there, sure enough, a dozen of them, feeding peacefully on the dry grass of the meadow—on the *far* side! With this wind, any attempt to get closer would betray him. But they were so close! There had to be some way. . . .

Come closer! he thought desperately. *Come on, my pretty ones—this way. PLEASE come here!*

A breath of cold air pebbled his skin, but Lionleaper scarcely noticed. The deer were moving! First one delicate head lifted, then another. He could see the tremors ripple through the shining spotted hides. They were uneasy, but not because of him—something unseen in the wood beyond them had brought them alert, ears even more sensitive than those of an elf swiveling as they sought to identify the danger.

That's it, oh, yes! Now come to me! Lionleaper settled into a crouch, arm drawn back, spear balanced, ready to cast.

And abruptly the deer were in motion—*all* of those that he had seen—and more! They were leaping into the meadow from all sides, exploding forward over him! A glancing forefoot knocked him over as all the dapple deer in the Everwood stampeded over him in a rush of tossing antlers and flashing hooves. His spear flew free and arced up as Lionleaper somersaulted backward. Then the spear stabbed down to sink quivering into the leafmold two feet away as the last of the dapple deer flashed by.

For a long time Lionleaper lay still, waiting for his breath to come back to him and his heart to stop thundering in his chest. Then he stood up, wrenched his spear from the ground, and began to swear.

He was too angry to notice the rainbow glimmer that pulsed in the air above him, or to see it follow him back to the hurst as evening began to fall.

"He wanted deer! He said he wanted deer and I drove them to him! Why is he so angry?"

The Shadowshifter tasted that anger and drew from it a new emotion, less violent but more lasting. Loneliness it knew already, and frustration was becoming familiar, but this was different—a slow bitterness that grew. They must recognize their helper! Even if none of the other elf-things could tell it was there, the three who had made the Shadowshifter had to see!

Goodtree laughed when she saw Lionleaper's face. He did not often return from the hunt empty-handed. But his snarl wiped the smile from her lips. She looked after him, frowning, as he pushed past her toward his den.

The next night Joygleam and Oakarrow almost came to blows over a haunch of forest pig that had been dropped into the smothered fire over which it was supposed to be smoking.

"But why would I do a thing like that?" exclaimed the senior huntress. "I remember when Tanner first thought of smoking meat to preserve it! I don't need to be told how it's done by a half-fledged woodsrunner with the blood of his first kill still wet on his spear!"

At least Oakarrow hadn't accused Joygleam of trying to spoil his meat on purpose, thought Goodtree. The epidemic of suspicion that was spreading among them had not yet driven anyone to accuse another Wolfrider of purposefully destroying the food the tribe needed to survive. But how long, she wondered, until someone did? She was chieftess, why couldn't she think of something to do?

That sense of unease still haunted her. Goodtree knew that the hearing of the wolves went beyond the range of her own, but sometimes she could sense the sounds they heard. This feeling was like that, as if there was something just beyond the reach of her senses that she ought to be able to hear, or see.

Almost—for a moment the Shadowshifter thought that the female had noticed its waiting presence! But now she was turning away, going back to her den where her body would lie still and her mind would be there–not-there in that puzzling way that left the Shadowshifter even more alone. But if there was no reaching her or the hunter, there was one more to try, and there was a strangeness in that one that offered interesting possibilities. . . .

Acorn Songshaper stopped short. There it was again —that sound! He had thought at first that it must be some new bird. But at this time of year the songbirds were leaving, and he had memorized all of their songs before he could even form words anyway. He shook his head, hard, and the music faded.

Perhaps it was his ears, then—he twitched them experimentally, but felt nothing, shrugged, and continued down the path. Goodtree had asked him to make a new song for the Wolfriders—a song that would turn their troubles into something they could laugh at.

He understood. Singly, the accidents that had been happening would have bothered no one long, but the cumulative effect could be deadly. He knew what the chieftess feared—an outbreak of madness that would scatter the elves through the Everwood to face the winter alone, distrusting each other as much as they did humans.

Or which, worse still, would make them as violent as men.

Elves must not kill elves. . . .

That was the Way. But how could Acorn find the saving grace of humor if he was as gloomy as the others? That was why he had left the hurst. He couldn't concentrate with waves of suspicion pressing in from every side. Yet it did no good to leave if he carried the anxiety with him. He shook himself and began to trot up the hill toward the lookout rock where he did his best composing, determined to wrest refreshment from the beauty of the day.

The wind blew back his hair, not quite chilly, but with the promise of coming cold. Acorn took a deep breath, expanding his lungs to their fullest, letting air rush through him until even his skin tingled. Then he let it out in a great sigh. If only he could breathe in the earth itself as he did the rich scent of leaves that were turning into soil! If he could breathe the cool blessing of the water whose damp breath misted up from the ravine beside the path! If only he could make everything he saw and felt a part of him and sing it out again—if he could breathe in the sunlight as he did the wind!

He opened his arms to embrace the wide world, head thrown back, green eyes slitting in ecstasy as he faced the dazzle of light above the path. Such brightness! Sun and rainbow whirled in a wonderful shimmer that somehow translated itself in Acorn's awareness into a ripple of pure *sound*.

He laughed and breathed in, and the radiance rolled over him, around him, through him . . .

Acorn gasped, drowning in light as if he stood under a waterfall. The pressure increased—now he struggled for breath as if his body had grown too tight for him—his senses gave up the struggle to understand what was happening, and left him, and he fell.

* * *

The Shadowshifter stirred, as stunned as the elf was by what had just occurred. It was dark here, and . . . small . . . . There was a dim sense of activity somewhere nearby, but it was hidden, and the Shadowshifter did not know the way.

A push did nothing. Where was the light, the air? Thought and movement were one, weren't they? But no clarity of intention, no force of will moved the Shadowshifter now. It was a trap! Conversations overheard among the elves provided the word, and the feeling of panic at being contained—

"Out, let me out, let me go!"

All of the Shadowshifter's awareness focused in the single demand.

Acorn woke screaming.

He was cold, and stiff, as if winter had come already and he had frozen where he fell. He blinked and groaned, and as sensation returned, nearly passed out again as a passionate tide of relief washed through him. Shivering, he tried to sort out his perceptions.

The dampness beneath him was fallen leaves, soggy where the weight of his body had pressed them into the mud. Acorn plunged his hands into the clammy mass, squeezing until cold leaf-pulp squirted between his agile fingers. And gasped again at the intensity of his response. He shook his hands, sending leaf-stuff spattering. It was not even a particularly pleasant sensation—why was he reacting this way?

He tried to take a steadying breath, froze as he half remembered how he had tried to breathe in the sunlight just before he fell, then let his lungs fill the rest of the way, but carefully. He could not stop breathing just because—just because what? This wasn't making sense at all.

Abandoning the struggle to understand, Acorn eased

back into the comfort of wolf-senses, let body-instinct get him to his feet and start him back toward the safety of his den.

Light and darkness, shape and texture, sound and motion—none of them were what the Shadowshifter was used to, but at least they were there! There were emotions also, but awareness of them now was fading. Was that a threat? Perhaps, but it was not necessary just now to understand it. The important thing was that the world had been restored. The Shadowshifter relaxed and began to enjoy the sensation of movement from the inside.

Music was playing inside Acorn's head, and it was the prettiest tune that he had ever heard. If only it would let him sleep . . .

Afternoon had faded to dusk and dusk to darkness. The music had played the Mother Moon into the sky and brought her cub close after, and serenaded the approach of another dawn, and another day and night again. It was the third evening now. Eyes that had been slitted half-open in mingled exhaustion and ecstasy began to close once more, and once more terror lashed the Songshaper's thin frame.

"No—" he whispered. "Oh no—oh *please* let me be!" Shaking his head, he tried to sing the music he heard, as if that would still it.

There was a time when inner and outer music were the same. Then he became aware that someone was holding him.

"Acorn, what is it? Are you hurting? Are you sick?"

The words were a babble, but the strong hands were something he knew. He forced himself to focus on Goodtree's face.

"Acorn—you're crying!"

A gentle finger wiped the wetness away. His lips would

not function, but some part of his mind was still his own.

The music . . . won't leave me alone . . . He quivered like that of a deer that has run too long, but Lionleaper's arms were holding him now. **Must sleep . . .** He collapsed against Goodtree's soft breast.

Sleep then, my dear one. We will guard you!

The fear welled up to oppose his sweet slide into oblivion, but Goodtree's sending fought it, gave him a measure of peace.

"I can calm him for a little, but he needs sleep most of all—" Goodtree's voice came from somewhere far away. "Ask Snowfall to make up some of her drowsy drink—we'll see what that can do. . . ."

And a time later he felt the rim of a gourd cup against his lips, and his throat worked instinctively as something hot and tart went down. There was a brief struggle as the stuff took hold, but Goodtree's firm command held the fear at bay until blessed darkness made the world go away.

"If I were a human," said Lionleaper reflectively, "I would say that the forest demons were haunting us. . . ."

"But *we're* the forest demons—" Goodtree began, then shook her head and laughed. "I'm beginning to understand why the humans went away! My father used to talk about a tree big enough to shelter the whole tribe. If I knew where it grew I would take us there. . . ." Acorn stirred a little in his sleep, and she reached out to soothe him to stillness as if he had been the cub she did not yet have. Would she ever?

"But I have a feeling that whatever is troubling us would only go with us." She shrugged the distracting thought away. "If I could find something solid to stick a spear into I would kill it! But there's nothing there!"

"Oh, there's something—" Lionleaper objected. "We just can't see it. Something stampeded the dapple deer. Something has been playing tricks around the hurst."

"At least it has stopped playing games . . ." Goodtree bit her lip in sudden realization, and stared down at the elf who slept in her arms. "Yes—of course it has! Now it's got Acorn!"

"What do you mean?"

"I'm not sure I know! Can a Wolfrider go crazy? I don't mean the kind of fighting madness that takes the wolves sometimes, the kind that made Swift-Spear go away. But has one of us ever lost touch with the world?" They stared at each other.

To separate mind from body, to fall out of the wolfsong? She did not know how to even imagine it. And yet, thought Goodtree, if any of the Wolfriders could do such a thing, it was Acorn, who found his songs in a place none of the rest of them could go. She tightened her hold on the thin body she held in her arms.

"Lionleaper, you have to help me get him back again!"

Lionleaper looked at her with a crooked grin.

"I will, of course—I'll do whatever I can. But if I had any sense I would refuse!" he added with sudden vigor.

"What do you mean?"

"Everytime Acorn touches you I wait for the moment when you will say his soulname, and he, yours. . . ." He was not looking at her now.

"You mean Recognition?" Goodtree asked softly, hiding a smile.

"Of course. And then where will I be?"

"Where you have always been, silly. . . ." She frowned at him. "I suppose Acorn worries the same way about you! It would serve you both right if I Recognized somebody entirely different—Longreach, maybe, or Oakarrow!"

"You wouldn't—" Then he saw her laughing and relaxed.

"I wouldn't have a choice. But you would still be my lovemate—both of you. . . ."

Lionleaper shook his head. "Lifemates—"

"Can three do that?"

"Do we have a choice?" he echoed her. "If we get this mad singer of ours well again I think we are going to learn!"

The Shadowshifter waited in the warm darkness of Acorn Songshaper's mind. It was not so frightening this time. The struggle just ended had taught it a great deal. Sensing a creature's needs and emotions from the inside was much more efficient. No wonder the elves had not understood what it was trying to do. The state they called "sleep" was still a mystery, but the beings that succumbed to it always seemed to awaken again. It was not dangerous, then, but dreadfully confining. And boring as well. . . .

The Shadowshifter began to learn patience, waiting for the Wolfrider it rode to let in the world once more. . . .

Acorn floated from sleep to waking on a golden tide. In that strange state which is neither the one nor the other, he was aware of the rosy light coaxing him to open his eyelids as he was aware of a murmur of conversation around him, and another presence, even nearer, who whispered to his inner ear. . . .

"Songshaper, wake up—"

Acorn turned his head against the soft sleeping furs like a cub nestling against its mother's belly.

"Songshaper, listen, and I will give you music you have never heard before. . . ."

Acorn's eyes flew open and he blinked. It was dawn and he was in Goodtree's den, wrapped in her silky sleeping furs. He could see her through the opening, nursing the contents of an earthen pot over a tiny fire. Lionleaper lay wrapped in his own skins on the grass nearby, snoring. But if the hunter was asleep, and Goodtree was busy making tea, then who was sending him thoughts about music?

As if that had been a reply, a ripple of sounds cascaded through his awareness. It sounded as if his bone-flute and his whistle and the bow-harp were all playing at once. A voice sang with them, sweeter than the sound of water falling or the wind in the trees. Involuntarily he shut his eyes. The music sounded louder.

What is it?

There had been music, he remembered, in the night-mare before he slept, but this was different. Now there were words.

Who spoke to me?

"I did. . . ."

Who are you?

"Your friend. . . ."

There had been just a touch of uncertainty in the answer.

Not Lionleaper or Goodtree? He did not really think so. Acorn knew the touch of their minds too well. This contact was strange. *I have friends . . .* he answered the voice within.

"Not like me. I give what you want. Even sleep, if you need it. I want to help you!"

Acorn was remembering more about the days that had just passed. If this invisible "friend" had caused that torment, the elf might be better off with an enemy. Still, the voice had promised music . . . and if Acorn did not agree, an enemy was just what it might be.

Show me. . . .

The music in his head burst forth again, a tune of his own that he had never been able to finish quite the right way. But it was resolving now, gloriously. Acorn sighed in delight—

—and opened his eyes abruptly as Goodtree shook him.

"The music!" he said aloud. "You made the music go away!" Her eyes widened.

"Acorn Songshaper, you drink this tea right now!" She had gotten one arm around him and was setting the cup expertly to his lips. He sputtered, coughed, and then swallowed in spite of himself.

"No. Don't try to talk. Just get well!" Goodtree's tone was brusque, but her eyes glittered with tears.

Goodtree sat cross-legged with Leafchaser's warm belly for a backrest, watching Acorn wander across the clearing. Conversations would stop as he passed, to resume again, more quietly, when he had gone by. Slanted eyes followed him. Acorn did not seem to notice. He was humming under his breath, as he had been doing for the past three days whenever he was awake, except when he whistled instead. When he ate, it was as if he had never tasted food before, but if they did not bring meat to him. Acorn did not seek it—he did not seem to remember the need. At least he was sleeping, though each time he seemed to wake deeper into his dream.

Or perhaps each time he slept the thing that was riding him increased its control. By itself Goodtree had not been able to see it, but she saw it now, revealed through the elf it inhabited as rock shows sometimes the impress of creatures whose forms vanished long ago. But this thing was very much alive, and getting stronger, while Acorn weakened.

Food—sleep—love—the wolves understood them, and so did the Wolfriders, their kin. But the high ones had not always accepted the body's limitations or its joys. . . . Goodtree remembered how she and Acorn and Lionleaper had laughed about that as they lay together in the wood.

In the wood where they had found the dreamberries. . . .

Goodtree's eyes narrowed and she looked at Acorn again. They had eaten the dreamberries and then all these troubles had started. She was never going to touch dreamberries again!

But that didn't make sense. Elves had been eating the berries since they came to the world of two moons, and nothing like this had ever happened before. But the dreamberries certainly had something to do with it! She got to her feet in a single easy motion and started off to find Freshet, who was the Wolfriders' expert on such things, Leafchaser padding at her heels.

The crisp tang of autumn air, the savor of fresh meat, the easy flexing of muscle and sinew as a body moved . . . the Shadowshifter was beginning to enjoy wearing flesh and bone. It still regretted lost freedom, but this body experienced such a wealth of sensations! Each moment brought new discoveries, replacing the previous ones until they were encountered again.

The Shadowshifter was becoming more skilled at controlling the creature it rode. If Acorn tried to resist its commands, it only needed to amplify and elaborate the music that lived in his soul to resume control. The other elves were more difficult, for together their strength was greater. If the Shadowshifter had the body to itself it would be free.

The hurst was a wonder, and the woods around it a treasury of new things. But there were undiscovered vistas beyond them. What lay there? Soon it would direct this body to go see. . . .

* * *

For an eight-of-days every elf and cub in the hurst had combed the Everwood for dreamberries. Freshet said it was too late in the season, but Goodtree knew that if Acorn had found a bush the older elf had missed; there must be others. There *had* to be others. And if some of the Wolfriders feared the search would be fruitless, no one dared to tell her so.

Finally, she had remembered her own skills and forced herself to grow still enough to touch the trees, and then, letting her awareness spread from root to root through the forest, she had found out where the Wolfriders must go. . . .

And now the howled harmonies of wolfsong were echoing through the darkness, summoning the tribe to the clearing in the center of the hurst. One by one they took their places in the circle, fur-wrapped shapes of elves indistinguishable from the silhouettes of their wolf-friends in the gloom between sunset and the rising of the moons.

The elves were different tonight.

The Shadowshifter felt the first flicker of anxiety as the circle grew silent. It willed Acorn to edge away from the others, but Leafchaser and Fang barred the way. Twitch-ear slunk in confusion behind them, taking first a step forward as Acorn's fear-smell demanded protection, then stopping short, shivering, as he sensed the alien mind within. The Shadowshifter began to grow angry, and all three wolves growled.

Acorn's surprise as Lionleaper and Oakarrow grabbed his arms confirmed the Shadowshifter's suspicion that something was wrong. It intensified the elf's panic, but Acorn's struggles were useless against the strength of the two hunters. Still straining, he was carried to the center of the circle.

* * *

"Tie his feet and hands—" Goodtree's voice cracked as she said it, but Twitch-ear's reaction had confirmed her conviction that this was not truly Acorn anymore.

She glanced across the circle at Freshet, who was cradling the big gourd in his arms. The magic of making the effervescent lavender drink that filled it was the old elf's secret. Others had tried to make a liquor from the dreamberries, but only Freshet's dreamjuice never went sour. She hoped there was enough of it. She hoped he had had enough time to make this batch a good one. She had a feeling they were going to need it all.

Eastward a glimmer of silver flickered through bare branches. The child moon, still an infant sliver of light, was taking its first hesitant steps out of its den. Goodtree cleared her throat and took a deep breath. Always before, Acorn had led them in the singing. She had no words, only longing and pain.

From somewhere deep in her chest came a moan, mellowing as it strengthened, bursting from her throat in a long howl. Even as it left her lips, the others joined in, and the sweet singing throbbed through the night. As it continued, one note modulated into another. Its intensity rose and fell as first one voice, then another, took up the song. The infant moon crawled above the treetops, and behind it black branches netted a greater glow as its mother, gaunt from the birth, came after to keep her cub from harm.

Freshet lifted the gourd to the skies in greeting, took a sip of dreamberry liquor, and passed it to Brightlance, who sat next to him.

The singing vibrated through Acorn's bones, stimulating a tide of emotion so unexpectedly powerful that the Shadowshifter resonated involuntarily, amplifying it until the body jerked in its bonds. A strangled sound burst from the elf's throat, releasing the tension, and the

Shadowshifter used that moment to seize control again, fighting the power of the wolfsong.

It was difficult. Everything in this creature's being strove to answer that call. When two of the elves held the gourd to Acorn's lips and made him take a long swallow, the Shadowshifter was grateful for the distraction. . . .

Goodtree let the purple juice slide down her throat, licked her lips, and held out the gourd. All around the circle, elves were beginning to show the effects of the first round. The singing was growing softer, sweeter. Lithe forms began to sway. But the bound figure before her was still struggling, and she tensed every time she looked at him.

Lionleaper took the gourd from her hand and peered at her.

Goodtree—relax. You know this won't work unless you do—

She nodded. **I know. What if we fail?**

He drank, handed her the gourd again, and when she had taken a second sip, took it back to pass to Snowfall. Goodtree took a deep breath, willing her resistance to ease, seeking the dissolution of barriers that the dreamberries could bring.

Her vision blurred. Awareness beat against the limitations that confined her, and suddenly she saw Acorn's body outlined in a faintly lavender glow. She saw them all shining—Brightlance, Freshet, Oakarrow and Joygleam, Snowfall and Longreach and Evenstar, and brightest of all, Lionleaper, glowing with a steady flame. Love for all of them broke through her barriers, and her spirit leaped to join with theirs.

Dancing moons and wolfsong . . . elfsong . . . Acorn tried to sing—

The Shadowshifter gripped tighter, but the body's re-

*sponses were altering. Its wrists and ankles were bleeding,
but it no longer struggled against the bonds. Now the
spirits of the other elves were brightening; each identity
burned ever more clearly as the gourd went round. A
radiance was beginning to flow between them, linking
them in a circle of light.*

The wolves ceased their howling as contact with their
riders misted away. The song the elves were singing now
was one not even wolf ears could hear. They sighed
gustily, great heads lowered, furred bodies sprawled or
curled, noses tucked beneath bushy tails. Dimly they
remembered that this had happened before. They knew
how to wait until elfin spirits returned to Wolfrider
bodies again.

Acorn's spirit flickered and sank and flared again,
seeking that unity.

"Don't sing with them—listen to me. . . ."

I'm a Wolfrider! Acorn's thoughts were momen-
tarily clear.

Acorn! We love you— Goodtree's response came
instantly, backed by the linked strength of the others.

*Music overwhelmed her sending in great cascades of
sound. Music that took the Wolfriders' singing and transformed it into intricate complexities of tone and rhythm
that no living elf had ever heard. . . .*

I remember!

No one knew, or cared, whose sending that had been,
for suddenly all of them were seeing that music shimmering from a mass of crystals played by a being who
was elf, but no Wolfrider. Vision upon vision built as the
sounds continued. Crystal cities floated above land-
scapes painted in colors this world did not know. Shapes
mutated in endless variety.

The part of the tribe that belonged to the forest fell
away as spirits soared into realms of far-memory re-

leased by the dreamberries and the music that the creature formed from remnants of the high ones' magic made.

It was not working—the Shadowshifter tried to stop the music, but now it was the elves whose minds were making the melody, and producing visions which loosed the creature's hold on the flesh it occupied as they left their own bodies behind. . . .

Acorn, is this your music?

This is the music I have dreamed . . .

But where is it coming from?

From you, from me, from— Abruptly Acorn became aware of the Other to whom he had become linked so strangely. And at the same moment all those who were joined in the music saw it too—shadowing Acorn's radiance.

Who are you? The focus of a dozen minds compelled an answer.

"I am the Shadowshifter. . . ."

Three among them recognized that name, and what they knew, the others knew also.

Where did you come from?

"You wakened me . . . let me stay with you. . . ."

There was a sorrow in that response that could not be denied.

Not this way! Goodtree's sending came distinctly. **You will destroy his body. You must set him free!**

"Won't . . . can't . . . don't know how . . ."

It could not be done in violence, or the Shadowshifter's fear would destroy the body in which it lived. It could not be done in hatred, or the elves would be flung back into their own bodies and it would be all to do again. . . .

"Please help me. . . ."

Pity, unexpected and overwhelming, blazed through Goodtree's spirit, sparked an answering flame from the others, swirled around the circle in a vortex that sucked the shadow free from Acorn's spirit and spun it into a column of rainbow light.

"I only wanted to help you. . . ." The panic had gone, but the wistfulness remained.

Dimly, Goodtree remembered the accidents, the misunderstandings. They could not live on dreamberries. . . .

We are too different—

"But what can I do?"

Bless the Everwood. . . . Goodtree reached out to touch the life in bush and tree. The amplitude of life in the forest could absorb even the high ones' magic. She sent her vision of the connecting network of living things that was the wood, and her love for it poured toward the Shadowshifter.

Panic . . . diminished as the concentration of magic that together had been the Shadowshifter was surrounded by love. Gently it lifted, almost imperceptibly it dissipated, as starlight is lost in the radiance of the moon.

The effects of the dreamberries were dissipating too. With double awareness Goodtree felt the ground cold and hard beneath her and heard a last shimmer of music. Then there was only a memory of melody, and a haze of light that floated above the trees.

Acorn stirred and groaned. Mastering stiff limbs with an effort, Goodtree crawled forward and broke his bonds. The moons ran down the sky toward the west. All around the circle, Wolfriders were staggering off to their dens or curling up with their wolves where they lay.

Will Acorn ever forgive me? she wondered then. What if she had been wrong. The songshaper had possessed a piece of the high ones' magic, and she had torn it away. . . .

We're Wolfriders— Lionleaper's thought denied

304

uncertainty. **If the magic of the high ones was any use they would still be here! You did the right thing.**

Goodtree didn't know if that was true, but the hunter's faith was comforting. Then Acorn opened his eyes. She bent over him, heart pounding.

"Did you eat all the dreamberries?" he said muzzily.

Goodtree began to laugh.

In the trees that circled the clearing, bare branches sparkled with an unseasonal flowering of stars.

Epilog

The stars wheeled overhead as the stories were told. After a time the darkness began to give way to pearly light in the direction of sun-goes-up, and the daystar rose. Longreach continued to spin his webs of words and Skywise listened, rapt, well into the new day. At last, as the daystar began to settle itself to the horizon, sleep claimed them both.

Longreach woke first, sometime during the night. At first he was unsure of where he was, then saw the sleeping Skywise curled up next to him and smiled. He could not remember the last time he'd told so many stories! But the youth's face seemed at ease, his body relaxed as he slept. Longreach grunted, barely audible, "Good."

Far off in the distance, the storyteller could just hear the sounds of the holt. They're probably wondering where I've gotten off to, he thought to himself, though he knew no one was truly worried. If that had been the case, the tribe would have found him with ease, privacy or no. He wondered with a chuckle if Foxfur was still looking for her lost "love"—that was a bit of unfinished business he'd have to attend to. But first . . .

As gently as a dream, for he did not want the sleeping elf to awaken, Longreach sent to Skywise. **You're not the only one to hear the song of the stars, the elfsong of the high ones. Perhaps it seems that you must listen to only one, to that or to the wolfsong that sings in all of us from the world beneath our feet. But you're not alone, and never have been. There have been others who felt faced with the same choice. Perhaps you, my young Skywise, will choose neither—or both.**

In the distance a wolf howled, and the pack took up the chorus. Longreach looked up. Hmp, he thought, they *are* the same as last night. Then he rose, stretched hugely, and began the long walk back to the holt.